Praise for *Bloodletter*
by Warren Newton Beath

"Hollywood has been rarely been so gothic. Warren Newton Beath comes on like a James Ellroy with a cape and fangs, transforming Tinsel Town into a Bloodsucker's Babylon. Drink deeply."
> —David J. Skal, author of
> *Hollywood Gothic* and *The Monster Show*

"Wow. Warren Beath is my kind of writer. He's hip, sophisticated, and he gets right to the point. He's surreal and he's clever, and his book was great, scary fun—a kind of *The Dark Half* meets *Vampire Junction*. I'm definitely looking forward to his next one."
> —Nancy Holder,
> Winner of the Bram Stoker Award,
> co-author of *Making Love*

"Just when I thought I'd read every possible twist on the vampire legend, along comes BLOODLETTER. It's unpredictable, brutal, shocking, sensual—and, above all, *realistic*. I haven't been so convinced to believe the unbelievable since *Salem's Lot*."
> —Mark A. Clements,
> Bram Stoker Nominee,
> author of *Children of the End*

"Dealing with Hollywood, fame, and the vampire—and writer—as cult idol, Beath takes dead-on aim at the tackiness behind the glamor . . . This is prime social satire, with an extra element of chills."
> —*Locus*

"The premise is clever, the prose energetic and Beath's love of the genre apparent."
> —*Publishers Weekly*

TOR BOOKS BY WARREN NEWTON BEATH

Bloodletter
Who Killed James Dean?

BLOODLETTER

WARREN NEWTON BEATH

A TOM DOHERTY ASSOCIATES BOOK
NEW YORK

BLOODLETTER

Cover art by Joe DeVito

A Tor Book
Published by Tom Doherty Associates, Inc.
175 Fifth Avenue
New York, N.Y. 10010

Tor Books on the World Wide Web:
http://www.tor.com

Tor® is a registered trademark of Tom Doherty Associates, Inc.

ISBN: 0-812-53393-3

First edition: August 1994
First mass market edition: June 1996

Printed in the United States of America

0 9 8 7 6 5 4 3 2 1

This book is dedicated to
Jane Jordan Browne
and
Matthew Rettenmund
of Jane Jordan Browne's Multimedia Product Development,
who shaped it.
Thanks also to Greg Cox of Tor for
his invaluable, incisive editorial assistance.

The Vampyre does not walk with the souls of men or look down upon the earth with human eyes. His passions make him a stranger. The Vampyre may wear the form, but he has no sympathy with breathing flesh. His joy is the solitude of the iced mountain, to follow through the night the sinking moon and catch the dazzling lightnings.

He dives in his lone wanderings to the Caves of Death, and draws forbidden conclusions from withered bones and heaped dust, passing nights of years in sciences untaught save in the Old Time.

The Vampyre has made his eyes familiar with eternity . . .

Stephen Albright's
BLOODLETTER
BOOK ONE: I, VAMPYRE

1

Extra Tissue

DIVER DAN GENTLY STROKED THE TATTOOED HUM-mingbird on the breast of the female body in the trunk of the DeathMobile 88. Her pillow there in the wheel well was a fat paperback.

Stephen Albright's
BLOODLETTER
Book One: I, Vampyre.

She gave him a sense of security: the vampire Bloodletter could not say Dan wasn't on the job.

He had tested the HumDinger out on her, a six-foot electrical cord with a plug at one end for 220 socket, the other end stripped and attached with an alligator clip to a six-inch embalmer's trocar. Designed for pumping formaldehyde into cadavers, it was the wickedest needle you could mail-order. He had hung her up on a hook in the bathroom ceiling, a hook attached to a pulley and come-along, hoisting her up. Then he'd stuck the trocar in her ass and plugged it in, waiting for the juice. He had hoped the body would jerk and dance spastically, knees and arms jerking and dancing like a crazed marionette, he would have been delighted— Only, nothing happened. The flesh had started to burn around the needle, smoking. The experiment was a flop.

Now, in the parking lot of Tiny Naylor's off Hollywood Boulevard, Dan was furtively kneading her breast and thinking how he hated that rubbery feeling. Not his own skin's, but somebody else's. It was due to alkalis and acids. He knew that from his subscription to *Professional Embalmer*. "Rigor mortis," it said, "*is just another timeless pattern in the scheme of man's existence.*"

Easy for them to say. They never fucked a corpse.

When death first interrupts the oxygen cycle, the muscle cells react by developing an alkaline condition. The head can be turned with ease and the arms and legs moved to any position without the slightest resistance—

That was prime time. That two-to-six hours before the alkaline condition began to convert into acid and a gradual creeping rigidity that flowed through the muscles of the face, trunk, arms, and legs. That was the honeymoon corridor, the love zone. "*Love Zone,*" he said. He liked the way it sounded, the palatal buzz of it. *The Loner with a Boner*.

Dan had always been lonely, even in the hospitals. He had felt invisible and had always hated that feeling. His mother had made him feel that way. The only way he could render himself substantial was to do something extraordinary, like hanging that batch of kittens on the fence by fishing line threaded through their scruffy necks.

Ah, life had not been easy for Dan: as soon as he had reached puberty he had begun to turn into a girl. Congenital dysfunction of the endocrine system; the additional X chromosome in his genes produced too much estrogen. Klinefelter's syndrome, the doctors had called it. He'd had a secret fantasy of being a doctor since the age of twelve, when he had an operation to remove six pounds of extra tissue from his breasts. He still suffered premenstrual cycles—and a recurrent nightmare from his time as a child in that first hospital: a nurse shaving his body hair, when suddenly he gets a hard-on. The nurse makes a face of distaste and taps it clinically and professionally with a toothbrush. It shrinks obediently.

He still woke up screaming.

He'd been in a lot of hospitals in his lifetime. That was where he had met the vampire: at Eisenhower. That was where the many voices that had always spoken to him, confused and incoherent and wicked, had congealed into a single voice that was very clear as it whispered in the dark.

The vampire wore one face for the world. He fooled them all because he looked charming and harmless. But he had shown Dan his true face and spoken to him in his true voice and that had made an impression. Dan had always felt helpless and afraid, and here was power incarnate. Since his release from the institution, his life had never been the same.

I am the Bloodletter. And you are Caligula in whom I am well pleased.

"A necessary evil," The Bloodletter called him in the paperbacks. Necessary to destroy Thanata when she was identified, because she alone the vampire could not lay his hand upon.

The Bloodletter had even coached him on how to handle the social worker during her monthly visit. Told him how to act and what he should say. He felt anointed, smeared with the unguent of distinction and selection. Strangely beatified with all his senses so much sharper in the clarity of purpose and mission. He had started to read the books, and it gave him a better understanding. *"We inseparable three have lived forever, you and I and Cesare the*

Magico, who invoked my soul upon this earthly plane. But there is one who would separate us. We must beware the woman. She must be destroyed before she destroys us. I cannot touch her, but you——"

How will I know her? Dan had asked.

"She will bear the stigma on her body."

Diver Dan had already killed her four times and secretly wished the vampire would make up his mind. And what was in it for Dan, besides self-esteem? Once he had dispensed with Thanata, he'd be allowed to join the vampire ranks.

He closed the trunk at the approach of two men in white tennis shorts. They passed, holding hands obliviously. Dan drove off, still cursing them. Faggots, like that little fruit Stephen Albright. A six-month-old clipping from *Celebrity* was affixed to his rearview mirror and he glanced at it, now.

ALBRIGHT, RISING STAR OF CONTROVERSIAL HORROR FICTION, NEARLY SUCCUMBS TO PRIVATE DEMONS

Eccentric writer attempts suicide on the eve of his greatest project . . . In Lugosi's last apartment, a paperback writer comes to the end of his rope—

Pulling the battered 1967 Chevy Impala to the curb at 1219 North Vine, he fished in the crevices of the torn upholstery. His pants had slid down to reveal the split of his buttocks to anyone looking through the windshield. He found lint, a nickel, a Chiclet, and a stale Fig Newton. He ate the Fig Newton. With the nickel, he had correct change for a newspaper. He bought the *Los Angeles Times* and counted how many times his name was mentioned.

Only six. He'd do better when they discovered the abandoned thing now ripening in the DeathMobile's trunk. He'd do it on her face and they'd find it hanging like an

icicle from her lash. He'd spread her legs revealing the
Cave of Death so they'd understand.

Waiting for the UA Cinema to open, he walked Las Palmas and took a seat at the open fajita stand on the corner.
The meat turning on the spit looked like a cat. No: a
woman. He saw her thighs and breasts in the orange flame.
Then it was alive with maggots, but that passed.

Dan paid his admission and walked into the dark theater
early, the very first patron. There was an old black man in
the lobby: grizzled white whiskers and horn-rimmed
glasses. Black men had big dicks. Bloodletter had a big
dick, too. The black man looked uneasy, a little frightened,
averted his face behind his paper.

Diver Dan sat in the front row, the red stub of the ticket
in his hand. In his other hand was a box of Goobers, and
the Jujubes were in his lap. He held a Jujube up to the light
to see what color it was. Red, a good sign. He was reminded
of the Thorazine they had dosed him with at the hospital,
the little water chaser in a tiny paper cup. He popped it in
his mouth.

He stared intently at the blank screen. The pictures in
his head were much more entertaining.

Oily women danced glistening nude in the light of unseen flames, twisting, sinuous full-breasted serpents. In the
background two giant pillars rose out of the desert floor
like legs of Golem. They were the legs of the vast H of the
HOLLYWOOD sign. The dancers were performing before a
crowd of mesmerized dead, their cataracted eyes the color
of egg white. A noise was rising on the wind. It filled the
desert like a vast pipe organ, but an organ on fire, the silver
throats melting and collapsing in screams that tore Dan's
brain. The desert was alive with maggots writhing in the
dust.

Through the flames of sound he saw a legion of agonized dead that howled and yapped, throwing dirt on

themselves while contorted human trunks, armless and legless, twisted and wallowed in pain as they struggled out of the sand.

In the middle of it was The Bloodletter, his shiny head suffusing and bursting as his ruddy and straining face contorted. Then his head opened in a volcanic coming, but instead of semen it was blood flooding and spurting rhythmically. The jubilant upturned faces of the refreshed dead and the dancers, their arms upraised to receive the shower of blood that spattered the ground and made their skin shiny . . .

The movie in Dan's mind dissolved to buzzing static. Dan didn't need a Thematic Apperception Test to know the significance of his dream. It was The End of Days when the sky would rain blood and the vampires would rule the earth.

The souls of his victims were suddenly speaking to him. That one in the trunk—even now he felt her soul fluttering behind his pupils with those others, all of them beating against his eyes like hummingbirds screaming to get out. Diver Dan felt his skin suffusing. The headache. He needed relief fast and had to leave the theater.

He went to his seedy room at the Hawaiian Gardens and arranged all thirteen of the Bloodletter paperbacks on the floor —*Diabolus, The Cult, Anima, Death-Dream, Rood Awakening*—and spread out the newspaper stories about Diver Dan. He spread out his high school notebooks with lists of over one hundred of the hometown girls along with their waist and bust measurements.

Now, he stripped off his clothing and donned a pair of women's panties and a deep-cupped brassiere in which there were two balls of sponge rubber. He connected an extension cord to an outlet of the 110-volt house current, stripped the ends of insulation and with Band-aids secured a bare wire to the nipple of each breast. He arranged the nylon cord from the pull-switch on the outlet and tied it to his big toe while he worked the noose around his neck. The rope hung from the pulley he had installed in a cross-beam of the ceiling.

He pulled the kitchen chair closer, stood upon it. He held the other end of the noose in his hand.

At the same moment he cast off and jerked the cord to the current.

It was devastating. His body whipped and arched deliciously, shivering with the voltage. He saw the souls of all those he had loved. He blacked out then, in seizure, releasing the rope, plummeting to the floor. The Korean man in the room next door pounded on the wall with a broom handle in protest, but Dan did not hear it.

2

Psychiatrist Lady

"OH BEAUTIFUL LADY DOCTOR, LET ME SING YOU A song of—*the Vampire.*"

Phil DeMarco had been giving a bravura performance since he entered the dark restaurant where even the shadows were plush. Eva had not had the heart to tell him he was trailing a small piece of toilet paper from the left heel of his Italian shoe. "For the vampire *must* be sung . . . at least, *Stephen's* Vampire. Baron Bloodletter the Undead has been kept alive for centuries by anonymous scribes in penny dreadfuls, traveling mimes and wandering balladeers singing around medieval campfires of the vampire and his Thanata . . ."

Eva LaPorte regarded the literary agent across from her while waitresses in black décolleté gowns, summoned by his snow-blinding smile, swarmed him. Phil DeMarco was a magnetic pest-strip of a man. He was striking in his early fifties, outfitted beautifully in a white double-breasted suit and looking incongruous among the living dead who were the habitués of trendy Necrofils, a "theme" eatery on

Canon Drive. The white hair was styled in a massive tsunami back from his broad forehead. To the Bedford Drive psychiatrist in her charcoal wool suit, his slightly blunted features made him look like a fish market owner who had won a lottery and now dressed like a television evangelist. White, grinning incisors gnawed at the bitten plastic tip of an empty cigarette holder. He had crowed all the way to their table about his recent and astonishing victory in a libel suit against the tabloid that had called him the *Crème de la Crap* of Hollywood agents.

Eva wondered whether it was the man making her tense, or her cramps. Or the restaurant. The bread sticks were arrayed in small caskets; napkins were bloodred and the menu bordered in mortuary black. The pervasive fish smell had a sexual edge.

"Join me in an Evian? Good. Try this—*bouillabaisse des brains*... No? That's sick, huh? Anything but the snapper; it's got so much mercury you can read a magazine by it. Jesus. Listen: Stephen's Bloodletter is an ancient vampire summoned from hell in Medieval Europe by the young magician Cesare, who sort of got carried away. He's well intentioned, but a dumb bastard. He trades his soul to the demon for power and worldly success. He's even got this special amulet he always wears so the vampire can't bite him. How's that for a concept?"

Her admission that she hadn't read any of Albright's epic series had provoked this summary.

"It's Faustian," she said.

"*Huh?*"

In the moment's insecurity, Eva saw the real DeMarco. His vocabulary and phenomenal memory had been acquired at Saturday success seminars in hotel banquet rooms. She felt badly that she had broken his train of thought, then realized that she was witnessing more of a memorized performance, a modified sales pitch, than anything else. She knew he wasn't as crude as he made out.

". . . But The Bloodletter turns on his restorer, and extorts his continued cooperation by playing on all Cesare's weaknesses. Makes him a slave to his own sensual appetites. This vampire wants nothing less than to take over the world. Cesare's only hope is Thanata." He wet his lips and his eyes squinched like, Eva's father would have said dryly, a hunting dog's asshole.

"Thanata?"

"She's our heroine, see? She's Cesare's only salvation, and the vampire's nemesis. A recurring figure of purity, and the vampire's enemy since time immemorial. She's going to keep being reincarnated to pursue the undying Bloodletter. See? These three characters keep coming back through the centuries on a karmic merry-go-round. So there's this dramatic tension because wherever Cesare and Bloodletter appear in history, they're always looking over their shoulders for . . . *Thanata.*"

She knew that DeMarco was more of a personal manager than agent to his star client, Stephen Albright, the ostensible subject of this dinner appointment, which had been arranged through DeMarco's secretary. Her back ached and she had wanted to go straight home and unwind in a warm bath; that was the carrot she'd held out to herself all day. Yet she had changed her plans in a hot second. Why? It was the glamour quotient of Albright's name. It had a definite cachet; the man was a sex symbol due to the potency of his imagination, the dark fantasy and unspeakably pornographic configuration of mind that cracked and spilled into his novels. Her eagerness made the Beverly Hills psychiatrist feel more Beverly Hills than psychiatrist.

But if DeMarco would not get to the point about Albright, she would continue to study the agent himself. Gold jewelry glittered from his open shirt and at his hairy wrists. He was unusual: the strength and bulk of his shoulders were in bizarre contrast to the delicacy of his head. He had that artificial hothouse muscularity of men who take up weightlifting during midlife crisis, the manic ballooning augmented by protein powders.

He looks, she thought, like a guy who would use nose hair tweezers. Or jerk off in front of a mirror.

"Am I *boring* you, O Lady Psychiatric Person?" His red eyes were hurt and a little resentful.

"Not at all. I'm with you."

He threw his head back again and she was sure they could hear his laughter across the room—a gruff barking from the thick throat with its corded muscles; it was disconcerting and a little embarrassing. She reviewed what she knew of him while he ordered a domestic sauterne, which he declined to sample; when he popped a Gelucil, she believed she knew the reason. The stomach was the Achilles heel of most of these overdriven types. He had recently diversified and invested in a chain of slim and fitness salons with the abrasive name Venus DeMarco's.

Eva had seen a cover article on both agent and client in the entertainment section of a recent Sunday *Examiner*. DeMarco's father had been an alcoholic hack, a second unit director bounced from studio to studio in a checkered career that had seen him helm a few Gower Gulch cheapies. Yes, including the last atrocious films of Bela Lugosi, one of Stephen Albright's heroes. His eccentric client was reclusive; DeMarco was anything but. In the competition to sign Albright he had exercised brilliant oneupmanship in leasing and restoring Lugosi's old mansion in the Hollywood hills. If that was an irresistible attraction, his client was definitely infantile.

"Thanata," the agent resumed, "is the *key*. It's she alone who can destroy The Bloodletter."

"How?"

"Hmmm?"

"How can she alone destroy him? A stake through the chest?"

"Yeah, but Stephen knows that's a cliché, so he made his vampire too slick for that. This story has a lot of heart. It's a people story—and a super love story. Bloodletter is dependent on Cesare's art for his continued existence. The vampire's gotta enslave and protect him at the same time. Cesare's hot for Thanata, and that's the threat. She appeals to his good side— See, she's the one who can put some spine in him. Give him his balls back so he tells the vampire to go to hell. Quits working that ol' black magic that sustains Bloodletter, send him back to limbo—"

"How?"

DeMarco's mouth had fallen open. She'd distracted him and he'd lost his place.

"Where—? Yeah. So Bloodletter must get to her, first. He'd love to make her a vampire, but there's a complication: any vampire that bites her will die, and he can't find one dumb enough. It's one rare vampire that'll do that. That's why—*Caligula*. He's sort of a troll with snotty eyes."

That would be the misshapen and sadistic hunchback who helped the vampire secure his victims and who guarded his casket during daylight hours; Eva knew only because it had been a sufficient coup to be touted in the trades when teen heartthrob Joey Tipp had been cast against type and signed to play Caligula in the film. Along with the rest of the world, Tipp was reportedly a tremendous fan of Albright's Bloodletter.

"Ms. LaPorte. I know your time is valuable. You know my time is valuable. I am just trying to impress upon you that we are talking *megabucks*. Stephen is bigger than Anne Rice—and he's gonna get *bigger*. Look around you, perspicacious female Ph.D. person. Vampires, everywhere." She did so, and he provided the voice-over for the tour. "The faces of these young women: cold and amoral. Their brows are shaved to the skull or painted waspishly. Their enameled nails are black. Their eyes tinted with contacts of blues and purples, or hidden from the daylight by back-swept designer sunglasses. Skin tones inclining toward the embalmed. And this is *Canon Drive*, for Chrissakes. The look: *You, too, can be a vampire.* And as Beverly Hills goes, so goes the world. And all because of one man. Stephen Albright!''

She realized with shock and amazement that the words were not DeMarco's own; he was quoting to her verbatim the article that had appeared in the *Times*.

But she got the point. Albright was a commodity, an industry unto himself who had signed a contract for a million dollars on the delivery of his next book. Albright's vampire, Bloodletter, had caught the popular imagination, and a minor cult had in the last two years boiled over into the general consciousness. His saga could be read as pure escapism, not only from banal day-to-day existence, but also from the bonds of conscience and morality.

''The Bloodletter series is a cook's tour through a staggering variety of depravity and experimentation. The vampire's sexual palate has become jaded through eons of indulgence, so he gets his kicks in increasingly kinky sensualism. Hell, in the first forty pages of *Diabolus* alone, you got rape, sodomy, necrophilia, bondage, and blood ritual. *Kirkus* said Stephen's female fans find the books 'a deliciously diabolic Kama Sutra.' ''

Yeah, Eva thought to herself: rape and sodomy and necrophilia—what more could any girl want?

A man dining alone at an adjacent table was eating oysters. The knot in Eva's stomach cinched tighter.

''And the vampire's coat of arms? Get this—*The World Is Not Enough.*''

''Neither, I guess, is the missionary position.''

His face looked shocked as if she had committed apostasy; then he decided to roll with it. "You're a funny lady. A brilliant, but funny, lady."

"Mr. DeMarco, if you're trying to tell me that your client is a very important and significant person, I understand. I'm impressed. Everyone's heard of him."

Everyone knew the controversial Stephen Albright's name, which had become synonymous with terror, though few knew much about him. His past was a mystery, and he was fond of saying, "Between books, there is no Stephen Albright."

He was the Prince of Paperback Horror. His releases were consistently runaway bestsellers, and he wrote two a year. Wrote compulsively, millions of words, diarrheic novels of excessive supernatural gore; she'd long suspected he must be hypomanic. It was unusual for depressives to have such high energy levels.

And he was certainly depressive: his last suicide attempt was by pistol, six months ago. No mere dilettante, he'd used a .357 Magnum. On the other hand, there was a part of him that wanted to live, otherwise he would have put the bullet in his head. He was obviously conflicted. She had written a professional paper on the methodology of suicide, finding in the chosen method indicia of personality types. She'd remarked to herself at the time that, ironically, the author probably owed his life to his choice of instrument. The high-velocity bullet whizzed right through. A slower projectile, like a standard .45, would perhaps have tumbled and been more like a two-by-four driven through his ribs. The bullet had nicked his ventricle and lung before blowing half of a rib through his back.

"But you said you never read the books. You never read any of the Bloodletter series."

"They don't sound like something I would read, but that doesn't mean . . ."

"Oh, I understand. Brilliant psychiatric woman writer

doctor person. Contempt prior to investigation. Do you think they're beneath you just because you can buy them at a supermarket counter and the women on the cover are naked? Not like the books you've done, huh?" He'd saved his ace for last. "Unless we forget, uh . . . what was it called? The one about dreams."

She lit a menthol, inhaled deeply.

"*Myth-Analysis.*" Congratulations, Mr. DeMarco. You struck the nerve.

Ishtar, her first book, had been a feminist interpretation of mythology in which she had examined the concept that primitive social organizations were matriarchal and that patriarchal society was a comparatively recent development. It was also a guide to the development of a woman into a whole person. This, at only twenty-nine years old. The next had been *Only Women Bleed: Menstruation in Mythology and History.* It hadn't sold well, but had enhanced her reputation. That was followed by *Virgins and Demons,* a study of the depiction of women in fairy tale and fable.

Then, *Myth-Analysis: "Who are you in your innermost dreams? Virgin? Demon? Seductress or fishwife? What can you expect in your love life? Do you have trouble telling his fantasies from your own? Maybe it's time for . . . Myth-analysis, a tour through your personal pantheon of image and fantasy, an adventure in self-discovery which may just unlock the Sleeping Beauty in you."*

Oh, Jesus. She regarded the severe reflection of her own charcoal-gray wool suit in the wall mirror, surprised the other diners had reflections. "I sounded like a snob. I guess it's been a long day. I'm all ears. Tell me about your client." The admission relaxed her.

DeMarco smiled and savored the moment. He leaned across the table. "I like a person who can admit she might be wrong. She might not know everything. That's the type of person I like to work with, Eva. Call me *Phil.*"

* * *

"He's been in Eisenhower Psychiatric Hospital since he recovered from surgery. He was supposed to keep going back on an outpatient basis, but he won't do it."

"Does Mr. Albright think he would benefit from continued therapy?"

DeMarco faltered and his eyes were incredulous. She sensed her affront.

"I think he would benefit."

"That's not always the point—"

"Stephen is no longer the best judge of what he needs."

"Is he on medication?"

"They've prescribed antidepressants to stabilize him, but I suspect he's not taking them."

"Any psychotic episodes?"

DeMarco's voice was edged.

"Psychotic? Are you the only one in Hollywood doesn't know he's crazy? But I believe that in his tax bracket the expression is still 'eccentric.' "

She knew the agent needed a little ego massage. She said, "The contractual world of Hollywood can be such a pressure cooker, deep-frying the brains of the most resilient. Right?"

"Hollywood. Contracts. Sweet Jesus, Eva. *I* need the shrink. I cut my own heart out with what I've done for that man. Don't talk to me about Hollywood."

He began to talk to her about Hollywood.

Looking over DeMarco's shoulder and out the dark window to the open-air tables, Eva watched as a hummingbird dipped its stiletto beak in a hibiscus. A bored waitress fondled a third-century sculpture of Siva and Purvati, hermaphroditically joined.

Hollywood had been interested in the series from the beginning. For months the paperbacks had boasted SOON

TO BE A MAJOR MOTION PICTURE. But the author had always complicated the negotiations with his extraordinary demands.

"I got such a contract for that man . . . got him casting approval. *Casting approval* for a *writer!* And what's he do to me in return?"

The trade papers were already writing about a curse. The Polish starlet cast as—*Thanata?*—had died suddenly during the first quarter of filming with several major scenes yet to be shot. No one had even known she was ill; she had got past the insurers because she had that necrophilic look down so well. Leukemia.

"You can *bet* Stephen *loved* her. Probably knew she was dying. Just his type—wasted. Skin like wax. Hell, she looked twelve years old. I think they had a *thing.* Chaos. The director has a breakdown and Stephen insists on replacing him with Fassolini from Europe . . . a guy, by the way, who makes our boy look like a centerfold for *Christian Science Monitor.* The search for a new female lead commences. Stephen could give a shit, he just wants to see tests. Tests tests tests. A simple matter, but they don't know Albright. And they're leaning on me, like it's my fault. *'I want to protect the artistic integrity of my vision.'* I don't think he's about to accept the Virgin Mary at this point. Accountants raise the red flag. Christ, sets have been built, players contracted. It gets worse: millions of dollars of elaborate special effects have been designed and shot because Stephen's obsessed with them like a kid with a toy. Fassolini could give a shit, because his agent's a bigger shyster even than I am, and he gets his money whether this masterpiece gets shot or not. Fassolini's probably going down on a Cuban busboy in his bungalow at the Chateau Marmont right now, laughing at me."

It must have been with relief that the front offices learned that the writer had attempted suicide; a clean denouement to cost overrun was foiled by his unexpected survival. Attorneys grappled during his hospitalization, seeking relief in a judgment of incompetence.

"He says he'll never write another vampire book. He's said that before, but the immediate problem is he's changed his mind and doesn't want the picture to be made. He's throwing up legal obstacles. All kinds of threats and injunctions."

"For instance?"

"For instance—he's even exercised a script approval option by rejecting his own screen treatment. He's dragging his feet, and delay is the same as death in this town— financially. The studio's getting cold feet. And I feel helpless, I gotta go along with him."

It was an almost irresistibly perverse impulse that Eva repressed to say something like "So, do I hear you saying things are not going well?" Too cruel: a line of sweat had appeared along the thick white forest of his scalp line.

"I understand," she said instead. "After investment of millions and the shooting of miles of film, *Bloodletter—The Movie* exists like an elaborate cinematic frame without a portrait under the glass, an epic disaster."

His eyes were impressed. "You have a grasp of it. You do. You're a beautiful person. A spiritual person, and very attractive. You have kind eyes."

"Phil, there's been an upside to all these setbacks, hasn't there?"

His eyes glittered a compliment: Eva, you're sharp. You know this town. I can't kid you. "Yeah. There's an offset. The tremendous publicity. Why do you think DeMarco's still alive? I've convinced 'em we can turn all this to our advantage. I'm even working on the mayor to declare a special Bloodletter Day. *Maximize* on the publicity."

Cash in, Eva translated. Exploit. All the vampires in Hollywood were not in Albright's novels.

"It's not too late to save the day. *If* Stephen will cooperate and get his head together." He leaned away from her coq au vin as if it were garlic. "Of course, I'm concerned about his well-being on a purely personal level, too."

"Of course."

"But they aren't two different things, his writing and his life. Unless he works through his problems with the one, I'm afraid. Eva: there's not only big bucks at stake, but a human life."

His eyes were sincere. Across the room a couple got up from their table; on their abandoned plates were the split husks of crab shells. The black eyes on stalks watched her as DeMarco spoke.

"Now for the nitty-gritty. There's a spin on this thing that I been living with all by myself. Eva, no one knows what I'm now going to tell you—not yet. Now, Eva: are we talking confidentiality? Talking privileged information?"

"Albright's not even my patient, yet. But I do consider any discussion about any potential patient privileged."

"Eva, I knew you were ethical. A classy lady. And a beautiful one. Beautiful classical ethical lady . . . Stephen's going to like you. He's read your books, you know. He *likes* them. You'll be good for him, he's so wrapped up in himself. He never gets out, gets around. I'm remodeling this mansion for him, but he still lives in this crib on Harold Way. You know why? I'll tell you: because Bela Lugosi died there. Jesus. He's had no real relationships with women . . ."

"The Polish starlet you mentioned . . . ?"

"Who can pronounce her name?" He gave a dismissive wave of his hand encrusted with rings. "She doesn't count, she was terminal. I'm talking about real relationships."

"Phil, make one thing perfectly clear for me: you're not arranging a date. If you think you are, if you think the sex of the therapist should or could be a component in a patient's recovery, you're not only mistaken, you're possibly doing your client significant harm.''

The deep red of the fresh strawberries he'd selected as dessert were stark against the undefaced glacier of ice cream that had melted down into the bottom of his dish. His eyes were suddenly rheumy and in need of Visine. He spoke softly.

"Eva, I'm sorry if I offended you. I'm sorry if I'm indelicate. I admit my deficiencies. My background, Eva, was in personal management. I started with pugs, punch-drunk fighters. What do I know about geniuses? That's why I need your help. I'm talking about a man who not only writes about a vampire, but who believes in the vampire. One of my favorite quotes from *Hamlet,* Eva: 'That is the question.' Are you following me, Eva?''

She wanted to refocus him. "Stephen Albright believes in vampires.''

He grimaced, blew a small burp into his closed fist as he leaned over the tablecloth toward her. "Sometimes Stephen believes he *is* the vampire. He *is* Bloodletter. It started out as his method, he had to sort of get into character to write. But now——''

"He has delusions? Or did they diagnose him as multiple personality?''

"They only made a tentative diagnosis of 'borderline personality,' whatever the hell that is. Like I say, he wouldn't stay at Eisenhower. He's smart, Eva. He outsmarted those doctors. He's no better now than when he went in.''

When he wet his dry lips, she knew he was coming to the hard part.

"Eva. I'm sure you're aware of 'Diver Dan'?''

Sure, she was.

* * *

As recently as yesterday she had read in the paper the latest exploit of the psychopath anonymously strewing the jogging trails of Griffith Park with his own grisly signature. Like Albright, he, too, had caught the popular imagination. Southern California went through things, she thought, faddish temblors and pop-cult earthquakes that threatened to trip it into insanity.

She did not know the nature of the mutilations of the victims. It was only rumored that Dan delved into his victims in a peculiar way, just as it was rumored that each of the victims had been abducted and kept alive by their murderer for an indeterminate period of time. Details would certainly be withheld pending his capture, when they would aid in his identification by weeding out the compulsive confessors. There was only the cryptic and quickly officially censured comment by an ambulance attendant regarding one body that there was "more of her outside than inside." Eva pictured viscera slung over shoulders like garnish. The serial murderer had been nicknamed Diver Dan by the police, and the papers had quickly adopted it. She thought of the old obscene high school association. *Muff dives.*

"This putz has been writing letters to Stephen. I turned 'em over to the police. The contents haven't been disclosed publicly yet, they're keeping a lid on it. But I can tell you he considers himself Bloodletter's number-one fan. He thinks Stephen *is* Bloodletter. Says he's killing the girls for him."

"You're worried about publicity if that becomes general knowledge? It's a sad commentary on this real world we live in, but it would only enhance Stephen's image with the kind of people who read his books. After all, he's a horror writer. He's not supposed to be Beatrix Potter."

"Huh?" DeMarco's expression was stupefied. "Did she

do all those 'Hollywood Wives' miniseries things? Couple seasons back?''

Eva was tactfully oblivious.

"Eva. What if Stephen himself was writing those letters?''

The back of her neck felt a chill; the candles seemed to flickered on the table. "To himself? You think he might be Diver Dan?''

He hushed her with an agitated finger to his lips. "Don't even *breathe* that. Of course not. But Stephen has this guilt thing. Like he's involved or responsible. The cops terrify him but he's like got a compulsion to draw their attention to himself. I feel like he wants to bring his whole world down. He's very self-destructive.''

No shit, Eva thought.

She said, "He seems a very gifted, but very troubled man. Even ten years ago, depression was regarded as a defect of character. A moral problem. We know better today, and most people respond to a combination of psychotherapy and drug therapy. I agree it would be a good idea if Mr. Albright continued to receive professional help. The first step would be to make an appointment. He could look me over, check me out, and decide for himself whether he feels I'm someone he might trust.''

"Exactly. That's it exactly. We're on the same wavelength and I'm sure there's no impediment to that which we can't resolve.''

"Impediment?''

His face was pained and reluctant; his voice almost a whine when he got the words out. "He's real paranoid about authority figures—like doctors and cops. They're the ones who locked him up. And he doesn't go out in daylight.''

"Oh? He sleeps in a coffin?''

When did the tension come back? It's making me glib.

Irritably: "No no no no no . . . He doesn't drive, either. He's real uptight about going someplace where people might stare at him. Lookee here, this is the kind of letter he gets all the time." He took the folded paper from his pocket and spread it next to her plate.

. . . Even if you are crazy, I'm glad. I get so absorbed in the erotic situations you create in your novels. It's opened up a whole new awareness of life and love. Even the sensuous way you describe death. It sounds so wonderful. The ultimate. May I go there with you? And the lovemaking is so vivid, so involving and imaginative. I insist that my lovers read you. As I read, I feel your arms around me . . .

Eva got the picture.

"Christ, you know what happened after he shot himself? There were kids out on the sidewalk dipping hankies in his blood while the ambulance pulled away. For souvenirs! He never gives interviews, and last time his picture was taken he was on a gurney with an oxygen mask over his face. So he doesn't want this to be a media event. He'd like to meet you on his own turf, so to speak. Check you out, like you said—but someplace where he's among his own. Where he's comfortable."

"I don't make house calls."

"I know that. I figured that. But what about a little intimate meeting, like we're having? You're not uncomfortable now, are you? Not with old Phil DeMarco. And Stephen's a great guy. A fascinating guy. Eva: you'll dig him."

3

Vulval Burning

EVA LEFT THE RESTAURANT WITH A TREMENDOUS headache, which told her she was conflicted. Freshening her lipstick, she was confronted by an orange-bearded lunatic who had apparently been hiding behind the potted sago and mistaken her for the Whore of Babylon. "It is The End of Days," he raged at her with trembling fist. "California will sink into the sea, and the sea is the spawn of Satan—" She flickered a grateful smile at the two security men with black capes who had materialized under both his arms.

"Born-again jerk," one of them mumbled to her apologetically, and then they were whisking him antiseptically away, oblivious to the placard bearing a citation from Revelations with which he was desperately assaulting them.

She stepped to the curb, avoiding a charred paperback book John the Baptist had apparently drenched in lighter fluid and then attempted to ignite.

Waiting for the valet to pull her car up, she admitted that she had had venal motives for wanting a client with the glamour of a Stephen Albright. There were no secrets in Hollywood. If she were to pull him out of his depression and get the troubled film project back on the road, it would be a signal victory over the best efforts of Eisenhower and enhance her stature in the professional community. She'd be the hero of the hour. It would lure more wealthy clientele in the arts. Plus, she would enjoy an inside track on an ongoing movietown soap opera.

This was not the way my mind worked when I got out of graduate school. I wanted to heal and do good and help the world. The severe twinge of cramps was only partial penitence.

At forty years old, her body had been going through so many changes this year. It was difficult to sleep for the hot flashes. It had sometimes been hard to control her emotions. Control was very important to her. She felt irrational often, knew she was not herself, that something was happening to her. Tears might start up for no reason. She had always experienced pain during sex due to scar tissue from the incident at Brown when she had been a student. Perhaps the laparoscopy, scheduled for next week, would finally identify a physiological basis for some of the mood swings.

Mid-life. It had taken new meaning. Her gynecologist had advised that it was perhaps time either to have a baby or get a hysterectomy. She had a prescription of estrogen. The depressions were not so deep, just dull malaise. She was in flux, a physical rite of passage. Her periods were erratic. Her bleeding had become profuse.

She tried to blot her physical self from her mind. She told herself she should take a year off and produce another book. Even that thought was a source of pain.

Ishtar, Only Women Bleed and *Virgins and Demons* she had been proud of.

Then there was a line, in her mind. She felt she had sold out with the next, the dumbed-down best-selling *Myth-*

Analysis, a manual for waging and winning the battle of the sexes through dream interpretation. It wasn't astrology, she told herself, and there were some practical things in it for the woman alone, the needy woman who felt she needed a man to validate her. It had also given her a minor celebrity, and she had moved her office from mid–Wilshire Boulevard to Bedford Drive. *Why am I still frustrated?*

But there was an imaginative part of her that had never been satisfied. All of her books had been written to formula with an editor and later, various graduate students working as researchers. Always, there had been her then-husband, Tony, also a psychiatrist, looking over her shoulder and guiding her. She numbered many actors and artists among her clientele. *What would I tell them if they were similarly confused? What* have *I told them?*

If I take a year off, why does it have to be to write a book? Why can't I just have time to myself? Why can't I take even a weekend without working on a paper? Why must lunches be meetings and trips out of town workshops and seminars? Why do I feel guilty when I relax?

Because the practice is faltering? I need more and wealthier clients, the kind that call you on weekends because the poodle has parvo. Because relocation to Beverly Hills and remodeling of the office last year put me in the red—

Because you don't deserve it, Eva. That was the dark secret she hid inside herself while she waited for the valet to drive her car around. *Eva, you feel basically worthless and each day is a litigation with existence. How can you counsel others when you haven't resolved your own core issues? Have you confronted the failure of your marriage? Do you feel unfulfilled because you are not a mother?*

But consider the available breeding stock, she thought wryly. She had just ended a relationship. Scotty had flown helicopters over Saudi oil fields and wore one of those thick black skin-diving watches reversed so that the dial was on his under-wrist. She had suspected him of sensitivity when he cried while talking about his wife who had died three years earlier of cancer. She felt she had tried him on like a coat, tired of men who wore knit ties and had tassels on their shoes. The sex? A shot, a lurch, the cracking of his whiplike spine and the long exhalation of air like a deflating tire. "That was first-rate," he would say to her when he returned from washing his privates in the bathroom . . .

The parking valet had brought her BMW screeching to a halt at her feet. He handed her the keys and she fumbled in her purse for his tip. The young man held the door open for her and she noticed he had a large angry pustule on his neck.

Eva's reverie resumed as she drove to work the next morning.

Take Tisha, her receptionist: she was twenty years old and had already been divorced. She had the daytime polish that made her an adequate receptionist who dressed sensibly and conservatively during business hours, but at night she donned leather, splayed her hair with mousse, and sang in a punk rock band called Skee Zoyd. She had a six-month-old mulatto son named Kareem and a bass player boyfriend who had an earring in his nipple and bought her edible underwear on her birthday with her own money. She worked through an agency and would be at Eva's practice only until Maggie returned from maternity leave. Eva had seen a passion bite on her left breast when she stooped to retrieve a file from the bottom desk drawer. Stupid? Yes. Is her life bleak? Yes. Is she happy? Yes. Eva knew that Tisha, with her half year of junior college, was also aware of her employer's basic insecurity.

"There were three messages on the recorder this morning from that Paula girl," Tisha reported adenoidally when Eva entered the deco, modern front office of her practice.

"She said it's an emergency but you have to call her after eleven now because she's taken three Valium and that's when she expects to wake up. Doesn't she get on your nerves? Doesn't she sound whiny?"

Tisha, because she never worked very long in one office and liked it that way, was immune to sympathy for clients. "That's fine." Yes, Tisha. Paula gets on my nerves. But she's a special case.

To Eva, Paula was a sort of doppelgänger of herself, the ghost of her girlhood past. Paula, who tended to overweight, had said she felt there was a skinny person in her trying to get out; Eva felt within herself always the presence of the pudgy teenager she had been. Bulimia had remedied that in her twenties, until she had herself entered therapy. Perfectionist. Overachiever. Eva noticed the fat paperback with its title painted in blood spatters bulging from Tisha's purse.

"I want to take a look at this, okay?" she said, removing the book and spilling three Virginia Slim cigarettes from the pack crammed next to it.

She recalled seeing her young receptionist engrossed in the novels while she ate her vegetarian lunch during break. "What do you think of this Stephen Albright?"

"Him? Oh, he reminds me of Axl Rose."

The answer had startled Eva. "Why do you say that?"

She fairly gushed. "Because everyone knows he's a bastard, but he's *so damn cute*. He's got this sort of lightning bolt of silver through his black hair."

Later, Eva had a fallow moment, one of those empty unjustified times when an appointment had unavoidably canceled; she utilized it by bringing Tisha back into her office with the door open so that she could monitor the lights on the phone. "All this time, I've had a resident authority on vampires here and hardly known it."

"Just Stephen's vampire—just The Bloodletter. He's

cool. You can only see his real face if he wants you to, because he's got this charisma which affects women and men. It's like a spell that makes him irresistible. He's suave and real polished. But then, he's had centuries to get his rap together."

"What does he look like?"

"Oh . . . you know, tall, dark and handsome. Whatever you think's sexy—that's him."

Eva examined the lurid cover of *I, Vampyre:* eyes set in commanding shadows that seemed to shift with potent sensuality from the subtly raised image. She could feel the eyes with her finger. A smile that was gentle and disarming except for the serpentine tongue caressing the young woman's proffered and erotically pulsing carotid artery. *"His whisper shapes fear into desire, the cold icicle of terror in the heart into a scalding vulval burning . . ."*

Vulval burning. Hmmm.

". . . manipulative and seductive, entering the mind of a woman through the window of her unique weaknesses, assuming the pleasing shape of her personal symbolism and unfulfilled desire."

She had heard the agent's version of Albright's vision. Eva wanted to see if Tisha shared that interpretation. "Who is Thanata?"

"She's the one who has the power to destroy him. She follows him through the ages and all these exotic locales. She haunts him."

"Why?"

"The books don't really say, just that during her first earthly life, he committed the Unspeakable with her."

"What exactly is that?"

"My guess? The Big Nasty, but worse."

"Say again?"

"The Wild Thang, Eva. No one knows, it's up to the reader. Don't spoil it. But her soul's going to wander the earth in different reincarnations until she gets even.''

"*. . . His life is a deathless dream. He seeks her reappearance in every woman he meets.*"

"How do you recognize Thanata? I mean Cesare or the vampire, how can they tell?''

"She may not even know who she is, that's what's neat. But she has a mark— These are weird questions, from you, Eva. Why are you so pumped about vampires? It doesn't seem like your thing.''

The Wild Thang.

"I had dinner last night with Stephen Albright's agent.''

"You *did*? What's he really like?''

Eva knew Tisha's "he" didn't refer to DeMarco, but couldn't resist teasing her. "His agent? Between us girls, he's a hypertense Type-A. In this case, the A is for asshole.''

"Seriously. I know you can't talk about clients and things. But do you think you're going to meet him? In the future?''

"Possibly.'' For the first time, she saw admiration in her receptionist's eyes. For the first time, she approached having something that this twenty-year-old divorcee, who had a baby and a crummy apartment in El Segundo and who drove a doddering primered Volkswagen, wanted. She liked the feeling; the girl's excitement was infectious.

"Read this . . .'' Tish was saying, thumbing through the book. "This part here.''

. . . The Bloodletter took her hand and led her from the pool of blood. Her breasts glistened crimson in the rays of the sun which set over the purple mountain of ice. Thanata saw her own shadow stretched across the desolate plain, but the shape was now strange, transforming.

The vampire stood naked before her. He enfolded her in his arms and when he released her his engorged organ was bright with blood. He began to move, his joints eerily pliant, the movements of his neck fluid as a cobra's.

The vampire dance was beautiful.

Thunder cracked and the earth was washed in red as across the plain the blood droplets spattered. He entered her, then, and she felt his energy gathering like a boiling storm cloud to erupt and flush red seed up her intimate channels. He thrust to her heart, splitting it and spilling the soul as both their floods collided and churned.

They became one being . . .

"Eva. Take it. Read it. My old man loves them—he says they've really loosened me up, sexually. You need a little vacation from yourself. Do yourself a favor."

Her eyes solicitous: do yourself a favor.

4

Zombie Zoo

TISHA'S EFFERVESCENCE AT PERSONALLY RELAYING
the message from DeMarco regarding a tentative meeting
that evening with his client Stephen Albright had been
tempered only by her dismay at the address. "I know the
place. Are you going there at night? Alone?"

Still, it had been difficult to restrain Tisha from her sis-
terly suggestions for a makeover that would let her employer better fit into the ambience of the Zombie Zoo, a
club off Hollywood Boulevard.

Eva would not go unarmed; she prepped herself on vampires for the meeting with help from an unlikely source.
She had received one of those irritating and impulsive
phone calls from Tony, who said he would be leaving soon
to the East Coast for six months on a consulting contract,
and would she have dinner with him? She had been unable
to resist spiking her refusal by citing her appointment to
meet Stephen Albright. Tony had been predictably impressed, and even sent over to her office an envelope of
Xeroxes that he thought might be useful.

They were copies of his notes of an outline and syllabus for a proposed graduate course he anticipated teaching in the fall: The Vampire as Icon in Contemporary Culture. Tony had always been one to pontificate on the current craze. It was important to him to appear young and hip— to be a "happening" guy.

All right, Eva thought. *You're such a smartass, Tony. You tell me. What exactly is a vampire?*

Her ex-husband's introduction was hardly dazzling. The word "vampire" was Magyar in origin, and Tony quoted an eighteenth-century English dictionary: *"The bodies of deceased persons, animated by evil spirits, which come out of the graves in the night-time, suck the blood of many of the living, and thereby destroy them."*

Tony wrote that the vampire had its ancient origins in the human psyche, a sort of erotic dream produced by sexual conflict. When normal aspects of sexuality are repressed, the conflict takes an extreme form, where hate and guilt dominate and oral sadism is manifested. The idea had taken shape in old times through anecdotes of maniacs with an unnatural craving for blood, stories of premature burial, and common religious motifs of restless souls. There had always been perversions that paralleled the acts of the vampire—eating dead bodies, mutilation of corpses to induce sexual excitement, and sexual intercourse with a corpse . . .

This is pleasant reading, Eva thought.

The vampire. There were two views of his nature: one, that he was a demon who entered a dead body; and the second, more common, that he was the spirit of the dead person who himself inhabited his own body. According to various legends, likely to become vampires were those who had led a wicked and debauched life, or been excommunicated by a bishop; those who had died under any kind of curse or malediction, those buried without proper rites;

suicides; and the stillborn illegitimate children of parents also illegitimate.

Church fathers had taught that a vampire was an angel who fell because of lust for women. The demonologist Sinistrari had believed that the devil shaped for himself a body to have coitus with man or woman. Thomas Aquinas wrote in *Summa Theologica* that "sometimes children are born from intercourse with demons . . ."

Eva saw that Tony had really warmed to his work. She had come to "Sexual Aspects: Vampire as Erotic Cultural Hero."

Saint André said, "The vampire has no more basis than a dream, a perverted imagining, and very often the dream of a woman . . . "

Tony *would* love that idea, Eva thought. She noticed he had collected with relish many early accounts emphasizing the intense pleasure of diabolic intercourse.

> *A girl of Biarritz aged fifteen years affirmed that it seemed the member of this vampire for its full length was of two parts— half of iron, half of flesh. She had heard many women who had slept with the vampire say that he made them cry out like women in travail with child . . . A "wench of intelligent appearance" burned in Paris in 1616 confessed, "The vampire had known her once before and his member was like that of a horse, and on insertion it was as cold as ice and ejected ice-cold semen, and on his withdrawing it burned her as if it had been on fire."*

Tony's enthusiasm for vampire penis lore was transparent:

> *. . . some accounts describe it as generally sinuous, pointed, and snakelike, and commonly forked like a serpent's tongue . . . said to be able to perform both coitus and sodomy at once, while a third prong reached to his lover's mouth (!!!). A*

vampire cum membro bifurcate *was mentioned as early as 1520 . . .*

Pure Tony. He would get off on describing a bifurcated penis to nubile coeds; Eva shook her head. The rest of his notes were fairly pedestrian. Vampirism and epidemic ravaged southeastern Europe—Chios in 1708 . . . Belgrade in 1725 and 1732 . . . Serbia in 1825. Calmet the Benedictine had written "Nor can men deliver themselves from these horrid attacks, unless they dig the corpses up from the graves, drive a sharp stake through these bodies, cut off the heads, tear out the hearts; or else they burn the bodies to ashes." Five of Albright's works were included on the syllabus.

Tisha read the material and said the penis business was news to her, but it sounded "hot." She seemed more preoccupied with Eva's choice of earrings for that night's rendezvous.

The Zombie Zoo was a small cinder-block box huddled stolid and nearly invisible in the shadow of the Hollywood Freeway overpass. The single unbroken streetlight glinted on the crushed glass of the gritty macadam. Eva almost skewered a discarded condom with her heel. She wrinkled her nose. Raucous music seeped through the walls. Porsches and Ferraris were incongruous next to chopped and porcine Harley-Davidsons.

And one Rolls-Royce Silver Cloud limousine with tinted windows. Was Albright already here? The black female chauffeur lounged uneasily against the car, the material of her uniform flowing liquidly over the soft curves of her body. She was engrossed in a book. Her eyes caught Eva's, eyes a striking green. The young woman reached up and took a comb from her hair and shook out rows of tightly oiled braids. Suddenly hers was a panther's face peering through dripping equatorial vines. She smiled and said musically,

> *"My lips are moist, I know the science*
> *Of losing in a bed's depths my defiance—"*

Eva nodded awkwardly and walked on, startled and embarrassed.

She felt nervous when she stepped through the door, waiting for her eyes to adjust to the flashing of a strobe light. The dancing people inside jerked and flickered like phantoms. When it stopped, she felt dizzy.

There was hardly room to move. The ceiling was oppressively low. The atmosphere was a thick miasma of cigarettes, marijuana, alcohol, and sweat. Eva, in her cobalt-blue suit, felt as though she were being pressed into an armpit. The red lipstick of the women bled onto the filters of their cigarettes beneath embalmed eyes. A pencil line of blood etched in the corner of the mouth. An occasional autopsy incision with stitches tattooed cleverly down the cleavage. Slam dancers smashed into one another and sprayed coronas of sweat into the hot blue strobe.

Just last evening there had been a segment on "Entertainment Tonight" on the wave of merchandising. "Vampire-Mania." There were vampire board games; elementary school kids with black T-shirts on which was scrawled BLOODLETTER in red spatters. Special-issue magazines. Television spinoffs. Lookalike contests. Fan clubs. A line of lipstick and a new line of lingerie. Souvenirs and posters. A toothpaste. The paperback racks were glutted not only with Albright, but his imitators.

Eva was dazzled for only a second; then, a young hostess appeared at her elbow, a livid black smile revealing shiny braces. A delicate hummingbird was tattooed on one breast, and her bangs were short, the back of her neck freshly shaven. Her head ticked with unnatural alertness while she escorted the psychiatrist quickly through the massed buttocks and shoulders to a secluded table at which sat a lonely figure in tinted glasses.

He stood until she'd taken her seat. She knew him to be thirty-nine years old, but he looked hardly thirty. The sport coat and slacks were black. His long hair was slick with gel and carefully styled so that he looked sleek and polished. In the back it hung over the collar of his dark red shirt with its loose black tie. The striking feature was a single thick streak of gray that ran like a racing stripe from his temple to his crown.

He was not drinking, but ordered a coffee for Eva from the hostess, who seemed protective of him. Eva noted that the girl took the opportunity to rub her left breast against the writer's arm as she whispered in his ear; the girl's nipple hardened like a thimble.

I don't blame her. He's an appealing man.

"Would you mind taking off the dark glasses?" she asked. "I'd like to see your eyes."

He complied, and for a moment her words rang in her ears. It was not only that they were captivating—clear blue and clear—but his soul seemed to spill out of them so that his face underwent a startling transformation that made her breath catch. She could only approach her sudden emotions obliquely: *No doubt some women find him irresistible.*

She had always been fond of saying that intelligence and creativity were to her the ultimate aphrodisiacs. She was also fond of saying that some women found power and wealth sexually stimulating. The sayings now seemed just a pose as superficial as kid gloves, and now she felt as though the gloves had been peeled off and snapped in her face. She felt weak and transparent—and strangely *teased*. In some mysterious way, he had removed his glasses and revealed *her*. As if throughout her life, by trial and error and process of elimination, she had fondly and unknowingly been developing the composite drawing of a certain man, an evolving collage of qualities and features. Its image had been a secret even from herself, and now—

Now she had to catch her breath. His proffered slender hand was veined and artistic like a classical guitarist's. The soft tentative handshake was that of someone unused to touching people. The blue lighting made his boyish face stark and dramatic even in its indifference. Or maybe that was an element of his magnetism. His skin glowed with eerie opalescence that never saw the sun, only electric lighting.

He had to shout for a moment against the blizzard of decibels until her ears became adjusted to the din of the music:

"I said, I told her to watch for someone who looked out of place and very uncomfortable. Would you believe that in the thirties this was a swank Hungarian eatery? Called *Mai Szinlap*—'Today's Playbill.' European film expatriates gathered for boiled vegetables, people like Korda and Curtiz. Bela Lugosi had his own table, until he drank himself under it."

Then he just looked at her. He seemed aware of her surprise and amused by the disparity between the public perception of him and his reality. Though he might be reclusive, he was not immune to enjoyment of the effect he created; but in a self-deprecating way. He was smiling now. "I know. You were expecting a vampire."

Under a sexual spell, she was not sure she had not found one. The light was suddenly filtered red, washing them in splashed blood. Drinks sloshed on the vibrating tables. Eva was aware of other envious eyes burning like coals. Aware next that the author had caught her staring at the unusual charm on a gold chain around his neck: a cunning little silver hummingbird with a ringlet at the end of its sharp beak. She had focused on it to regain her composure, but he held it closer for her, dangling it self-consciously.

"A jeweler on Olympia duplicated this for me from the first novel—it's like the talisman Cesare wears. His protection. Wards off vampires. If you're already infected, it slows down the process." He slipped it inside his shirt and she knew he was trying to relax.

Was that also the significance of the hostess's tattoo? To slow infec—

Eva's coffee had arrived, and Albright seemed to enjoy watching her first sips. His skin now burned in the lights with that phosphorescence of Van Gogh's self-portraits. She had never seen a picture of him, to her knowledge, and the words eccentric and recluse had conjured someone else. The only thing that fit her preconceived image was that he was dressed in black and red—an Andy Warhol sort of thing.

Or Vidal, my flouncing hairdresser. The one all the female customers want to turn into a heterosexual . . .

She asked about his health to make preliminary general conversation, realized before the words were out that she was prematurely broaching the subject of the suicide attempt; he didn't blink, just told her unselfconsciously he had almost completely recovered from the surgery to repair the damaged heart. The doctors considered him a medical miracle. He thought it ironic that were it not for his celebrity and value as a fiction industry, perhaps the renowned cardiac surgeon would not have curtailed his Vermont vacation and responded to the emergency call from the hospital chief of staff. He discussed his injuries, the reconstructed ribs, the patched lung, with detachment. "They tell me I probably shortened my life by fifteen years."

She had to lean across the table to hear him, at first. She noted that his hands tended to flutter; he would catch him-

self and restrain them, lower his voice, which had a tend-
ency to rise in pitch. Only once did he make a face of disapproval, when she started to light a cigarette. Perversion,
apparently, was fine, but carbon monoxide was another
matter. She snubbed it out.

*He flickers between handsome and almost . . . beautiful. Those
long lashes. Charming. Intriguing.*

She was feeling a growing and intense curiosity about his
sexual orientation. There *was* something androgynous
about him. What was that joke that had been making
the rounds about the bachelor writer at the time of his
attempted suicide? *Bloodletter sucks blood. Albright sucks
cock . . .*

Then he would laugh and be distinctly masculine and
dispel the insinuation; it went back and forth that way.
Since he seemed relaxed and candid, and since she did not
want it to be from the outset the social relationship
DeMarco had seemed to be promoting in his ignorance,
she was frontal. Would he be embarrassed? Withdraw?

"Why did you do it? Shoot yourself."

"Eva," he said with mock shock, "are you the only one
in Hollywood who doesn't know I'm crazy?" From that
point, he seemed quite willing to carry the conversational
ball downcourt. "What did you think of Phillip?"

"He said I would 'dig you.' And you do seem like a nice
person."

"Person? Not 'man'?"

"I didn't mean anything—"

"Thank you for your consideration in meeting me here,
which I'm sure is out of your normal Beverly Hills orbit.
And the hour must be inconvenient."

"It's really pretty interesting. Unusual, but interesting."
Actually, all the weird energy was exciting.

"The inconvenient hour. My apologies to your husband.
You're married?"

Now *he* was being frontal. *But I'm flattered.*

Her lips tightened in a professional line; for some reason it brought to her mind her student years when she had felt herself ugly and dressed in shapeless sweaters under uncombed hair to project defiantly her poor self-image to the world. If he was playing the same game as DeMarco, for whatever reason, he was more deft. She took a chance.

"You know that I'm divorced. Mr. DeMarco told me it was no accident I was the therapist he approached. And he was very concerned about confidentiality; I imagine he investigated me thoroughly before he had his secretary call, and I imagine he shared with you as much as he could discover."

"And what he couldn't discover?"

"The atmosphere here may be informal. The hour may be unusual. I may be deprived of my office and desk and even my onyx pencil sharpener. But . . . me therapist, Stephen. You . . ."

"Therapee?" He laughed.

Press to the point. "Your agent feels you're in a crisis of sorts. That you are suffering a serious conflict that is affecting your career and happiness."

Leaning closer, he had eyes that could peel the skin off your face.

"No conflict. Success is an addiction I'm trying to break. I don't want to do the vampire anymore. And I don't want the film to be made. I will take every legal recourse and drag my feet to see that I accomplish this, even if I sink a studio. I'm not writing any more vampire books."

At a nearby table, Eva noticed a dark girl squeezing her full breasts together until it must have hurt. She was laughing. Incense was burning in the ashtray. She was alone.

"Would you mind telling me the reason? I'd like to understand."

"I have my own reasons."

"Any therapist who indulges your evasions for very long is not a therapist who will do you much good in the long run."

"The long run? Let's just make this . . . a short sprint."

"I was told you were very elusive," she said amiably.

He looked around as if afraid of being heard; then forced a smile to relieve the impression of paranoia. "Perhaps if I told anyone the true reason, they would not believe it. Perhaps they would think I was insane, which is very distressing for someone who only recently was released from confinement."

Eva noticed with a start that the strange lighting made her hand on the table look shriveled and blue. "Try me."

She caught the glint of a small diamond in his left ear. He seemed amused and challenged.

"You try this: When I was sixteen I saw a few fragments of F. W. Murnau's aborted silent vampire masterpiece, *Der Vampyre Magnus*. He had already made *Nosferatu* in Germany in 1922, and had been brought to Hollywood still fascinated by the vampire theme. What I was privileged to see were rare remnants spliced together and exhibited during a retrospective in this little pit of an art cinema. Shortly afterwards, even those bits disappeared from circulation entirely. But what I'd seen changed my life in that spellbound darkness. My series is a retelling of the legends of the vampire Magnus, 'The Bloodletter.' Interested?"

She noticed for the first time that the nail of the pinky finger on his left hand was painted black.

"Murnau was an incredible eccentric. He makes me look like a centerfold for . . . what is it, Phil says? *Christian Science Monitor*? But Murnau was a genius. Films like *Sunrise* and *Nosferatu*. Do you know how Murnau died? His Filipino houseboy was fellating him while the master tooled along in his Stutz Bearcat. When his leg tightened in orgasm, he depressed the accelerator and shot over a cliff. His neck was caught between the boy's knees and the steering column. It snapped—'' Albright snapped his fingers in her face.

The shocking and irrelevant story was both denial and approach-avoidance, she knew, but her own laughter caught her by surprise; she wondered if she had been too nervous.

The writer seemed to enjoy her genuine display, warming slightly.

"Only eleven people came to his funeral—but one of them was Marlene Dietrich. Well, Murnau had grown up with these obscure European legends of an actual vampire, Magnus. In medieval times, it was thought that Satan accepted promising young scholars as apprentices—but claimed every tenth scholar for himself as his due. The devil chose young Magnus and seduced him with a question. 'One of these shall be yours: earthly riches and anonymity, or fame and immortality. Which do you choose?'

"Magnus, who hankered after celebrity, and was well aware of the duplicitous nature of his sponsor and the tortures he was fond of inflicting on the avaricious, opted for immortality. He said, 'I would prefer no world at all, to one in which none knows my name.'

"His wish was instantly granted. Satan condemned him to the vampire existence, with a twist. He would be granted entrée to this world to slake his thirst only on condition that he keep his name before his public. The rest of the time, he had to suffer in limbo, waiting for someone to celebrate him and invoke his spirit."

There was a growing tension to his smile.

" 'The Vampire must be sung!' That's the first line in *I, Vampyre*, the first in the *Bloodletter* series. The Bloodletter lives not just in legend, but *only as long as there are legends*

about him. He is the black muse of the luckless artists or
magicians who dare to call on him. It was a magico, Cesare,
who first called him back.''

"You think his involvement with the vampire story destroyed him?''

She was getting definite signals from the writer's body
language. His shoe was tapping nervously. "Let's say I want
to profit from his example. This vampire must die. I won't
deliver him anymore and I won't let anyone else, either.''

"And by killing yourself you destroy the vampire? Do
you sometimes feel that's the only way? That you owe it to
the world in some sense?''

His smile was making her uncomfortable. "Would you
like to save me, Eva? You have no idea what you're getting
into. No one does.''

"No one? Are you referring to the 'Diver Dan' business?''

Something subtly crossed his eyes. It was a fear. Eva was
feeling sudden control, and it was odd. She was not sure
she had wanted this reversal. He shrugged, looked away.
She'd seen abused kids do that same thing when you got
too close.

"Dan? I'm almost enchanted by his sensitivity to the iconography of Hollywood. Did you know the nude bodies
have all been found within sight of the HOLLYWOOD sign in
the hills? Did you know that in 1932 Peg Entwistle committed suicide by jumping fifty feet from the top of the H to
the prickly pear below? She was halfway through the shooting of *Angel of Death* with Bela Lugosi . . .''

His defenses had kicked in. She said nothing. Her polite
but unflinching gaze told him that she was not to be di-
verted. Eva thought she saw new respect in his eyes. His
speech was pressured and his eyes intense. He was going to
dispense with this subject quickly.

"Look. I know I've pandered. I've been a whore. *'An industry of blood for a sick society.'* That's what somebody wrote about me. Dan, he's only the inevitable and logical extension. I've been trapped by my public. I can sympathize with Dan. He's got a whole city in thrall now, and he's loving it. He'd probably like to quit, but his public won't let him. He's thrilled and terrified at the same time. He's gotta be asking himself 'What can I do next that's bigger, better?' I know the feeling. And The Bloodletter is a part of that cycle. And Albright."

The writer was pointedly ignoring a tall young man in tight leather pants who was eyeing him over the shoulder of an attractive older man with a neatly trimmed beard. Albright replaced his dark glasses, leaning closer to the psychiatrist.

"There's a whole cult out there and I renounce it. There's even this band of female thugs called 'Bike Bitches from the Grave' who want to be my personal bodyguards."

The donning of the glasses had signaled his withdrawal. With the same stroke, Eva felt it was in some way her punishment. She backed off and waited.

Several black men, painted as voodoo priests, had risen and were slowly taking up their instruments. Switches clicked with long spatulate fingers, and speakers buzzed. A bottleneck whined eerily up metal strings. A girl with a gangrenous green forehead took her place behind some congas. The music was subdued, the rhythm relaxing.

The dancers were suddenly languid. The couples were transforming into single figures, new creatures, as they pressed hips together sexually in a hypnotic undulating. Necks moved sinuously. Eva felt she was in a den of rutting snakes. Yes, she thought. The vampire dance was strangely beautiful.

He was studying her reactions with apparent enjoyment.

He seemed to have relaxed. A good sign—he had lowered his sunglasses, halfway at least, and was peering at her mischievously over the frames.

"But if I have to have a therapist to stay out of Eisenhower, I couldn't have one more charming. This is a portentous meeting. A vampire's life is at stake—Eva? May I call you that?"

"It's your life I'm concerned about, Stephen. Sure. Eva's fine."

His smile was devastating in its appeal and her lower stomach responded. She realized that she did not want this man as a patient. Any other man, not this one. They had come into one another's lives with an ethical shield between them that for all of Eva's professional life had been a more effective contraceptive than fear of AIDS. Perhaps he considered that a challenge. She wished fervently that she had met him under any other circumstances, and she felt like an aggressive shit because she'd used probing questions to keep at bay the threat to her emotions that he represented.

Eva was feeling exhausted. She felt Albright's eyes on her and they seemed to give her a headache. In the shadows his face seemed suddenly reduced to the sharp equation of a skull.

Driving the next morning down Rodeo in the urine-colored smog, her ears pricked when she heard "The Bloodletter" mentioned on the radio. She raised the volume and the indifferent chatter congealed to the morning call-in talk show hosted by KZNZ's madcap morning tag-team of Pete and the equally obnoxious Re-Pete.

"... so, yeah," the dazed young female voice on the line was saying in accents of Valley-ese, "it's like, why live with one hand tied behind your back?"

"Now *wait a minute,* little sister," Pete interjected in his burbling DJ baritone. "You mean to tell us you and your teenybopper friends drink blood? Miss—?"

"We wanna hear you play more heavy metal music. It's your new format that sucks, not us. Springsteen blows chunks."

"What do you call yourselves—?"

Re-Pete in the Morning butted in.

"The Big Kahuna's gotta pick a *bone* with this ghoul. You mean to tell me that when I tool home at night in my five-point-O and scope the chicks out front of Licorice Pizza, they could be little vampires?"

Pete was not to be outdone. "I used to work for a vampire, I won't mention the station. Honey, how many would you say there are, conservatively?"

"A lot of kids are infected. But people are only interested in the real dead ones—that's the last stage. They don't care about all the hurt you have to go through to get to that stage."

"I see," said one of the jocks, their voices now indistinguishable. "There's a lotta drugstore Bloodletters, little wanna-be vampires."

"Look," the girl said wearily, "I gotta split. I gotta get to class. We just want to hear more heavy metal."

"Don't get me wrong. We're always glad to hear from you kids, living or dead."

"Sorry I called," the girl said. "Someday I'll see your head on a stick. You two jerks really bite it."

The line went dead. Re-Pete segued effortlessly into a fast-food commercial.

Tisha's first question as Eva entered the office was pretty bald.

"Well. How was he?" Her eyes were bright as she waited expectantly. Eva surprised herself when she felt the slyly knowing smile on her own face. She quickly recovered from the impulse to tell her receptionist everything.

"He was very charming. He was very polite and is certainly very intelligent. And nice-looking. I suppose it's easy to see how those qualities, along with his reclusiveness, have made him appear enigmatic and a sort of sex symbol."

Eva knew Tisha did not know what "enigmatic" meant; she was sure all Tisha had heard was "sex," and that was sufficient to communicate the essence of her impression at a subliminal level. Eva knew it was wisest to now disinvolve her titillated receptionist from what her instincts were telling her would be a potential case file; but she permitted herself one last question.

"Tisha, you've read all the books. I have a practical question. How does a potential female victim resist being seduced by a vampire?"

The girl did not disappoint her.

"Eva," she said with awe. "Wow."

5

Obscene Throbbing

EVA SIPPED THE COLD DREGS OF RICH COLOMBIAN coffee and crossed her legs to relieve the stiffness in her lower back as she opened the paperback. Tish had recommended she start with the first book, *I, Vampyre*. The Cinemascope strip of sky above the offices outside her window had faded to a ghostly blue by the time she had loosened her collar and picked up the book.

Cover: Two fangs and trapped between them a man and a woman. The man's eyes darted to things moving in the shadows and the woman cowered at his side, breasts spilling, in what seemed to Eva stereotypical fear and subservience to the stronger male. The title in the signature blood flecks and a tantalizing quotation in italics: *"There are myriad ways to make love . . . There are infinite forms of possession . . ."*

Inside, reactions from sources as various as *Publishers Weekly* and *The Atlanta Constitution*. *"The symbolism is complex but consistent. Albright has a unique voice . . ." ". . . A sensuality to his handling of the most excessive grotesquery that makes it di-*

*gestible, even attractive." "The undead epic is an allegory, a soul's
journey through varieties of sensual experience almost religious in
intensity . . ."*

The scheme was Manichaean, an elemental struggle between emissaries of light and darkness fought on two
planes—the physical and the eternal. The vampire was
astride both planes. His opposite number on the eternal
plane was The White Witch. She represented white magic
in opposition to the black arts of The Bloodletter. She
waged war against the vampire on the material plane by
invoking the different incarnations of Thanata at crucial
points in history when the monster's new emergence
threatened the stability of creation.

The Bloodletter wanted nothing less than to dominate
the world. An antichrist figure, his social agenda was to in-
augurate The End of Days, when vampires would rule the
earth. And who said he shouldn't enjoy the task?

In the first paragraphs the vampire was quickly seducing
a contessa in a purple episode abounding with such oral
imagery as chewing, biting, and tearing. It was a masculine
fantasy, and one thwarted at the pregenital level. Woman
was something to be cracked and split to finally permit escape back into the womb. It accommodated a theory Eva
had long nurtured that the American woman is raised and
societally molded to confuse love with abuse.

*His penis hung heavily between his legs like dark, full fruit.
She felt The Bloodletter's touch before his mouth brushed her
skin. The vampire felt her quiver under his soft breath, his lips
poised just above the nearly invisible transparent hairs of her
throat. She knew she was herself one of those tiny trembling fila-
ments. She was begging when finally his groping mouth pulled
absently at her pale nipple. He raised her chin and she saw him
as a black shadow eclipsing her whiteness. Their navels nearly
touched, her frail blond triangle softly opposing his stiff-clubbed*

*and heavy-veined organ bobbing perceptibly with the pulse of
his heart.*

Yeah, Eva thought: she's really going to enjoy it, this girl.

*She had never made a study. Perhaps furtive glances at them
spent and flaccid, withered dumb, vulnerable as a pulpy crab's
body caught outside its shell. This was different. It was a skull
on a prehistoric neck, rapacious lines of unfathomable prowess.
It had life that fairly surged beneath a personality and expression impudent and insistent.*

Now, the inevitable tribute to his power:

*She felt divorced from her name, her identity, but perfectly in
touch with her own flesh. She was soaring in the airless region
high above the city, a gliding and fantastical creature. She
struggled through her own arousal. She felt herself being pursued and finally possessed in a dark sightless region of existence
she had never imagined. She felt him opening his eyes inside
her.*

*He made her drink . . . Her lips were glossy with a patina of
his blood. Sweat glistened on her neck and damp hair streaked
her face. Her breasts trembled, all her nerve endings wires pared
of insulation.*

*The Bloodletter could see inside her. Her heart had changed
and was suddenly a red vulval thing, throbbing obscenely and
opening to swallow him in numerous leering labial mouths that
sucked and quivered . . .*

. . . ending with an image of infantile male revulsion and
sexual fear. The castrating bitches deserve what they get,
right? My, my, Stephen. Then there was Thanata, whom he
feared and yet had placed on a pedestal.

*Thanata is the door. She wears the mask of eternity. In an
intolerable world, we live within roles from which we must break
forth, to live out of the dream part of the imagination. She is the
guide.*

Women were either whores or saints. If The Bloodletter
was a sort of conjured spirit, what was Thanata? Both
Cesare and the vampire were fixated on her, looking for
her reappearance in every woman they encountered.

Eva recognized a correspondence to the sixteenth-
century Spanish Saint Taniada, a semi-historical regional
heroine whose marble image she had seen in Toledo ca-
thedrals. Her symbol—wasn't it the hummingbird? She
thought of Albright's talisman. Early church documents
had Taniada sacrificing herself to appease Satan, who was
afflicting the land with plague. Eva had conjectured in one
of her books that the Satanic figure was the bubonic
plague bacterium personified. Substitute vampirism for
plague, and the archetypal antecedent for the Thanata
motif was obvious.

Eva was more interested in the portrayal of the hapless
Cesare, whom the author called a "magico." He was a sensitive artist dabbling in black sciences who awakened the
spirit of Bloodletter, an ancient vampire who promised
him fame and wealth in return for his sustaining alchemi-
cal protection. Predictably, Cesare became disenchanted
with hollow riches and wanted to recover his soul. Too late.
Thanata, in her redemptive aspect, was his only hope of
salvation. Cesare desperately consulted a white witch who
invoked the saintly lady's incarnation in a local girl.

The whole business was never really resolved by the end
of *I, Vampyre.* The intimation was that the three tormented
souls would continue to reenact their triangle in different
incarnations down through tempestuous centuries.

She opened the small article from a glossy entertainment magazine that DeMarco had apparently clipped and inserted as a bookmark. It described the plans for the massive movie and was obviously written before the debacle. There was a summary of the intended plot. After an establishing scene, a black-and-white prologue that would portray the three main characters in medieval times, the action would be whisked forward into the twentieth century—in fact, present-day Hollywood. Cesare was incarnated as a talented and sensitive director who made artistically acclaimed horror films. His mistake was making one about the Bloodletter legend. As a result, the ancient spirit was conjured as a parasitic producer and now held Cesare's soul in fealty, insisting he make a second epic in which the vampire inaugurates The End of Days.

The plot seemed to hinge on their joint search for a leading lady for the epic. The director, of course, was looking for Thanata so she could free him. Bloodletter wanted to identify her so she could be destroyed. Same old themes, modern dress.

Eva wondered how much of it, if any, the author took seriously. What was serious and disturbing was that unprepossessing and personable Stephen Albright had a very violent mind. The refinement of the sadism and perversion implied a lifetime of the most unwholesome sort of masturbatory contemplation. The basic perversion was hematodipsia. The fetishist fixated on one particular thing—the flowing of blood. What coitus is to the lover, the bite and the sucking of blood is to the hemotodipsiac. The tooth replaces the penis. Eva wondered what trauma the writer might have suffered or witnessed in his infancy that had imprinted such obsessive fantasies on his mind.

There were definitely two Stephen Albrights and she had seen only one. She tossed the book on her desk and checked her appointment schedule, wondering whether any woman had ever met the other.

6

Vampire Dance

HE WOULDN'T HAVE BEEN SURPRISED TO SEE A YELlow parking ticket under the windshield, because he had dozens in the glove box. But to have his car towed away—that shook him up. He had to walk five blocks to the impound garage located at the West Hollywood police substation. He smiled to the cop at the desk after stating his business.

"And your name, my man?"

"Strachan. George Strachan. My man."

The cop was looking through the yellow tags on the wall and talking over his shoulder. "How 'bout those Raiders?"

"They took Kansas City?"

"Ten-six."

Strachan whistled through his teeth. "It's tough to stop the Chiefs on the ground. Birden's a deep threat. I think he got a hundred eighty-eight yards the last game."

"Ah! Here we go . . ." the cop was saying.

It took some smooth talking and most of the three hundred dollars to recover the car. The tires squealed as Strachan drove up the concrete ramp, sucking fervently on cough drops. He heard the body roll and bump in the trunk. It had been close.

She was number five. He had stalked her three days and then moved on her at Griffith Park. He had locked in on her with laserlike infallibility as if he were a great dark bird. There was a single beat of wings and a rush of air as he hit her. She had regained partial consciousness in the trunk. Once in the apartment, she had responded to witch hazel held under her nose. Dan forced sedatives into her and amused her by swallowing pins, while they both awaited the summons to an audience with The Bloodletter.

That summons arrived with the night, and Dan had further tranquilized his prize with an injection of Demerol before obediently taking her on a strange twisting road for what seemed like hours to a place where he had never before been, but which seemed awfully far away. Then Dan had found himself leading the girl—his nubile zombie—by her hand through strange shapes in a brown fog to the edge of a cliff. Dan was afraid of heights.

The Bloodletter had appeared from nowhere and beckoned them between two ancient urns in the thick pyracantha. He wore a shiny sharkskin suit—on him it looked good—and was showing them a door Dan had not seen, a door into a small hideaway where Dan had never been. Dan understood somehow that it was not the abode of the vampire, but a sort of refuge. Within were shadows, and a bubbling Jacuzzi or hot tub with candles arranged all around it. The water boiled and the flames danced the vampire dance.

"Bloodletter," Dan asked, "am I real?"

The vampire smiled. "Isn't your name in the papers?"

There was nothing else in the room but some drawings. They were of a naked woman splayed atop the large H of the HOLLYWOOD sign.

Dan mustered the termerity to ask a second question. "How can you tell if she's the one?"

"When I meet her, I will know her."

Then things had become hazy. The Bloodletter could do that . . . could show you what he wanted you to see and make you forget if he chose. Could make you think you were seeing things or it was all a dream. He could round the edges of what happened so it was like a dream, and you doubted yourself. Dan always felt exhausted and headachy after being with the vampire. It was a sort of sexual intoxication—that must have been what it was, because then the scene became silly.

This stupefied girl was smiling as she obligingly unbuttoned her blouse to accommodate the vampire's fingers as he inspected the hummingbird on her breast.

The Bloodletter had said, "So you think Birden's a deep threat?"

Dan had found it difficult to talk and his own voice had suddenly become drowned and strange. "They took Kansas City . . ."

The girl had not been Thanata. The Bloodletter had apparently been unfed—he watched his weight—because he took care of this one himself. He bit the girl viciously, and not only the throat. That was where the books were wrong. The bloodletting was frenzied. The girl's face was goggle-eyed like a fish being filleted on the pier. She hated what was happening to her. Dan had to look away once, where he sat cross-legged on the floor, beating off.

The Bloodletter had harvested her soul and sent Dan off packing with the husk. Griffith Park was becoming so hot with surveillance—he'd have to wait until the weekend, when it would relax. He was pulling back up to his apartment at the Hawaiian Gardens when his sixth sense told him to keep going. He felt intense paranoia. Dan was becoming terrorized by the shrinkage of his world. He parked the DeathMobile on a side street behind the Chateau Marmont and walked to the Kitty Kat Adult Theater where he sat through *Second Coming* four times. He came out blinking in the sunlight, still seeing starlets Eeka and Loy Bang under his eyelids, only to discover his car had been towed. He had recovered the car, but where to go?

Dan was anxious and wondering whether he could get himself admitted to emergency somewhere and maybe have an appendectomy, or something. Most of his expendable organs were already gone through just such games. Since his youthful surgical experiences, he'd been obsessed during times of stress with piqueur acts—jabbing sharp implements into himself or others for sexual gratification. But for the last few years he had been unable to get past Admission—the scars on his body were a road map of his addiction to unnecessary surgery. He felt like crying.

Where to rest? He yearned for the peace of the dead. So he drove to Hollywood's Memorial Park Cemetery to be near the dead. He had his own box in a decrepit maintenance shed disguised to resemble a crypt and fit in with the mortuary decor. It was his home away from home. He sat in the car for a long time reading an Albright paperback until he was sure no one was looking. Then he opened the trunk and carried the dead body to the maintenance building. He closed the door behind them and put a rake through the ancient handles to bolt it. He arranged the girl sitting up against the gray plaster wall with her chin on her breast. The descending light through the high transom signaled the approach of nightfall. The smell of mold and the sound of creaking wood lulled him to sleep.

Dan was doing the Bad Thing in his dream. *That thang.* It was bad because the woman was alive. It was opening with wounds and Dan could see the pink flesh underneath as the skin was turned inside out. She was curling and trans-

forming into a swollen gynecological mess, all oozing red
smiles—

Dan stirred awake and realized his loins were wet. He felt
the hard little pellets of mouse droppings under his shoulders. He was lying on his back in the box. The box was
dark. It reminded him of when his mother would lock him
in a closet after discovering him masturbating.

He crept out of the box and saw that it was night. He
stretched and surveyed the walls of this shed with its rakes
and interesting implements. That weed-eater had real possibilities. Might it be modified with piano wire to slice
flesh? He was nude and his belly jiggled. On the wrists of
his meaty arms were vertical scars with deep cross-stitches
up the veins, denoting his history of serious suicide attempts. Strange crescent moons of pink tissue smiled beneath each breast.

Something was giving him what his mother had called
the *"all overs"* . . . that quivery feeling of someone staring at
you.

He saw the still girl in the shadows. The fingers of one
little hand uncurled out to him in a plaintive gesture. She
was stripped and her legs were open. Her mouth was open
and her eyes wide open. Much of her was turned inside
out. That part of the dream had been quite real.

He thought, *What a relief. I was afraid I'd been losing my
mind!*

He had been a total of three days with this one, counting
dead time, and found himself becoming fond. She relieved
his loneliness. Were the light better, he might do her nails.
He would miss her once he had dumped her at Griffith
Park early Sunday morning.

Dan stealthily opened the door of the gardener's shack
and stood revealed by the full moon. He had always been
able to feel the full moon, even in isolation wards. He
would feel it through the walls and would pace like a ferret,

blowing chuffing breaths in and out while he rubbed his
hands together, warmed them on flames that hung in the
air and that only he could see. It made him crazy. It made
him mad. His hands throbbed on his wrists and he could
feel the hair curling tighter on his knuckles. Time had
slowed. Hearing was acute and even his teeth were sensitive. The world was washed in the magical.

He was in a Disneyland of the dead. Hundreds of bone-
white pilings jutted from the ground like stark ribs of
beached whales revealed at low tide. Even as a kid he had
been fascinated by tombstones. They were like people because they came in all different shapes and sizes—short
and fat and tall and thin. He felt so safe looking at the rows
of graves and knowing at least half of them were women.
He was envisioning all the supine forms of invitation and
seduction. Quiet. Yielding. No squawking. In his mind he
rested his hand on the still bosoms and arranged their brittle fingers in his hair.

His mind. Let the doctors say what they would, he pre-
ferred it his way. He was not playin' vampires—he was
living it. He had been months without antipsychotic medication and he was receiving the signals of higher bands of
existence much more clearly. On cue, there came a noise
like the faint laughter of children on a distant radio, and
his heart sped up.

They were out. The Children of the Night had come out
to play all around him. They were creatures of unearthly
beauty with white shining skin. A doctor would call it hallucination, but all Dan's senses testified to their reality.
These were the spawn of The Bloodletter. Some he
drained dry as week-old toads, and others he infected. It
was a grass roots plague of the Undead. He started always
with the street people and domestics, and worked his way
up.

He had shimmering impressions of ghostly girls playing

and he ran to where they had appeared. *Oh, so it's going to be hide-and-seek. I'll bite.* He was out of breath and thought he'd lost them for good when he saw them again—huddled in a bevy around the iron doors at the top of the vast steps to the great mausoleum. The Bloodletter no doubt had given them a key. It seemed to Dan that they had seen him and were giggling at him, the bitches.

There was a hollow clank and sibilant gasps. The covey parted and their voices trailed off hollowly as they disappeared into the black mouth of the open door. He saw one more face white as china, and then she too was gone. Dan stumbled up the steps after them.

Quiet. Still.

The air was the cold noiseless whispering of marble. Weak moonlight filtered through the large stained glass transoms sickly and bent, vaguely flared with color before settling like dust on the floor. The smell was a moribund blend of toilet water and snuff and his own dead grandma.

Stone apostles stood stricken in paralyzed silence. A red choker was around the neck of St. Peter, and Matthew's wrist sported a black garter. Hazy motes of dust stirred by Dan's own feet swam within their fuzzy coronas. He recalled the words of Christ: *"He who eats my flesh and drinks my blood abides in me, and I in him."* Jesus knew the score. Dan suddenly wanted to be deliciously crucified.

Down an aisle to his left stretched a receding infinity of vaults like marble dead-letter drops. There was a fleeting glimpse of ankle. Voices trailed off up another aisle, haunted laughter that echoed and faded. Dan chased it for a while with no luck. Breathless, he leaned against a glass case of large urns burnished like yachting trophies. They were full of ashes. One contained Peter Lorre's.

He walked slowly, and the dark was cool on his nakedness. He touched his penis experimentally—he had been nine before his testicles had descended. A light drew him to a niche on his right. The Bloodletter had been known occasionally to sleep here. There was a dry breath like a sigh through the empty aisles and it made dust roll through the air. The shiny nameplate:

STEPHEN ALBRIGHT
"The Prince of Paperback Horror"
1951–

The nameplate was on the floor at his feet. The dark vault was open and vacant. The dark of it seemed to breathe and bulge outward.

Suddenly the silence was richly symphonic with awe. Dan's erection died and he saw himself as if from the high, arched Gothic ceiling, a small naked figure in a shaft of moonlight. He trembled and felt himself shrink against the marmoreal vastness. A chill blew up his arms though the tired brittle flowers in the copper receptacles did not stir, and the smell of his own fear was going up like a flag, and swirling things began to roughly shape themselves from the darkness. His balls were sucked up into his body.

The Bloodletter was out.

Dan heard close laughter and whirled. There was the distant impression of white figures skipping out the door. He followed, praying to Jesus and feeling a horrible fear at his back. When he stepped back out into the night it was like being born again.

Where were they?

There were more of them now, cavorting distantly across the narrow bridge over the artificial moat encircling the little island with its private crypts. The girls assumed poses or lounged like marble angels atop the vaults. Some held hands and danced in a circle like a carousel. It was eerily beautiful. Some danced out of their clothes and dropped them into the water, where the gowns inflated and floated like lilies. Their skins seemed to gleam wetly and their laughter was clear and hollow now over the water. He thought he saw faces from his childhood among them. He thought he could see Eeka and Loy Bang doing the Funky Chicken.

Dan shook his head and blinked. He longed to follow, but knew he could not. If this was a dream, he did not want to wake himself up. They would disappear and he did not want that. He knew well that some would say his mind was going—but then, some would say there was no such thing as vampires.

Suddenly, there was The Bloodletter. He was naked and had jumped onto a crypt like a wolf as all watched. His face was afire with the rage of his appetites. He mounted a shivering girl on her hands and knees. Her face burned and her braces gleamed brightly. She clasped the marble vault white-knuckled with her face back-flung.

Dan knew the scene would haunt his sleep, and he rippled with a spasm of sexual excitement. When he opened his eyes they were gone. A gnat swarm traced dots of light in the darkness before his eyes, dancing the vampire dance.

7

Gower and Santa Monica

THE NIGHT MANAGER AT THE THE VILLA DEL MONICA
Apartments had been roused by female screams from
room 214 in the early morning hours. When the police
had arrived and battered down the door, they found a
balding ascetic man of middle age with disoriented eyes
kneeling on the breasts of a nude and terrified young
woman whom he had apparently sodomized with a magnum of champagne. In his hands were the knotted ends of
the girl's mesh hosiery, which he was tightening around
her severely bruised neck.

The year was 1926. The girl was a young German production assistant who spoke no English, and her attacker
was silent film director F. W. Murnau.

Eva had done some furtive research and discovered
there was a whole vampire culture rampant at that period
in Hollywood. At the UCLA library she had dug up Albright's out-of-print first book, the dense and scholarly *A
Soul on Film*, a biography of Murnau. She reviewed the story
as she drove down Hollywood Boulevard toward her sec-

ond meeting with Stephen Albright. What had a dazed
Murnau claimed as a defense when interrogated?

The girl had betrayed him to the vampire. She *was* a
vampire. He accused her of being a servant of Magnus,
who was using her to control him, destroy his life. The vampire was always using women to enslave him . . .

The episode had landed the broken director in a rubber
room at an Encino sanitarium for six months, and the
young production assistant had fled to Germany. It
seemed the history of Magnus—The Bloodletter—was
steeped in neurotics. Albright, too, exhibited schizophrenic tendencies and paranoid ideation, Eva thought as she
turned the car onto Gower.

The meeting place that DeMarco's secretary, an "inso-
lent bitch" according to Tisha, had arranged two weeks
after the Zombie Zoo was equally atmospheric and bizarre:
Hollywood Memorial Park Cemetery at the corner of
Gower and Santa Monica, a vast park overgrown with rank
weeds and hedges around dark ponds in which giant lily
pads floated. It was sometime after nine P.M. Amazingly,
Albright had his own key to the Gothic iron gates, which he
had left unlocked for her. The black sky was swept with
shoals of deeper blue and the Hollywood Hills were dark
tumors above the freeway.

In the foreword to the Murnau book, Albright had described the indelible impression a single fragment of
Murnau's lost vampire epic had made on him during his
teenage years—the climactic End of Days when the undead finally outnumbered the living and erupted from the
ground as the sky convulsed overhead in a rain of blood.
Great drops of blood spattering in the dust like bullets
while the vampires raised their shiny red arms nightward
in profane jubilation, the blood burning rivulets in the
earth and drowning the living.

A breeze blew up, and she saw something fish-belly-white float sluggishly to the surface of the rank pond. In her uncertainty, she thought she recognized the bloated corpseface of Albright's engorged vampire. It slowly receded before her unbelieving eyes with a winnowing motion that identified it as only a ragged and ancient carp.

A fear scampered across her exposed shoulders, and she wished she'd worn another dress. She was walking past Baby Land; the white cherubs with silent lips seemed alive. Then she heard the laughter of dead children, dry and cold and harrowing as the tinkling of glass. The white gravel crunched under her feet. Shadows reached out their long clawed fingers to clutch at her ankles, and she hurried her steps.

Poor Albright was under many pressures. The morning's paper had covered a session of the board of supervisors in which a parents' group had demanded the boycotting of southern Los Angeles music outlets that promoted CDs by the heavy-metal band The Bloodletters. At issue was their new release *Infected!* with its controversial and indecipherable lyrics, which a matron-spokesperson had obligingly interpreted.

> *They gotta eat that thang 'cause they're INFECTED!*
> *The kids are all right—just INFECTED!*
> *Gotta feed that thang*
> *That wormy thang, that thang that thang that thang*
> *By the grave rejected,*
> *By the night protected*
> *So damn dejected—*
> *When you're INFECTED!*

The father of one of Diver Dan's early victims had testified about the youth culture and the sickos who bred violence and exploitation. Eva found herself unconsciously humming the catchy synthesized hook. "That thang that thang that thang that—"

Following Albright's explicit directions, she experienced what at first seemed another optical illusion, a great stone mosque looming up above the praying heads of giant palms in which rats scampered dryly through the fronds. It was the Cathedral Mausoleum.

There he was. Albright wore a baggy black sweater and was slouched against one of the two stolid Corinthian pillars atop the steps. He smiled and Eva felt a sudden sexual dizziness that took her by surprise. He straightened and walked toward her, and there was an aura about him that became stronger as he came nearer.

What the hell was it? It wasn't strength or indomitable will or a masculine authority. It was more subtle and insidious in a way. It was a sort of charm that seemed to play on her private fantasies. It was also a casual indifference. He was sipping a diet drink and had considerately brought an extra can. There was the refinement of a plastic straw, which he adjusted for her. Her stomach found it damned romantic. Damn.

Something inside her resented her own responses and wanted to take it out on him—wanted to disconcert him and disturb his casual poise. But she smiled when he offered to give her a brief tour of the mausoleum. Even as he showed her the crypt that he'd already reserved for himself so that he could lie among silent film stars like Valentino and Theda Bara, she heard herself making despised noises of girlish appreciation. She felt like they were two children who had gone through the enchanted door, dwarfed by the silence and the marble walls. She was glad to get back outside.

He told her that this cemetery was one of his favorite

places, and that Lugosi had almost been buried there, but an ex-wife had prevailed and he'd wound up at Calvary where his eventual bunkmate was Der Bingle, Bing Crosby; a shame. A shame, she repeated.

Everything that should have disturbed her was having a different effect. A suicidal man showing you his reserved crypt after insisting he meet you at a cemetery—and she was finding it exciting. Conflict was draining her, and her weakness made her vulnerable. Stephen was some sort of psychic vampire, at least. Could any man be as oblivious of her female responses as this one acted?

Yes, she'd be glad to sit down. There was a convenient marble bench on the bank of a concrete lagoon. Out on the water was an island on which a private marble vault shone. Albright pointed out to her that the bench on which they rested was actually a tombstone—Tyrone Power's. He inquired about her day and caseload, which gave her time to get a grip. She would concentrate on the illness and not the man. No more moonlight and gravestones.

Normally, she would have a new patient recently released from institutionalized psychiatric care sign a waiver so she could access the records of his treatment history; but she had to handle this one with kid gloves. Or did she really want him as something other than a patient? But the question was already out.

"My diagnosis at Eisenhower? I have tremendous highs and lows. They were unanimous that I suffer from bipolar mood disorder—manic depression. Also, I have a schizoid personality with paranoid delusional features. I can also boast anxiety disorder and obsessive-compulsive behavior. My pharmaceutical résumé would probably interest you— I've been prescribed lithium to regulate mood swings. In the hospital they fed me Thorazine and Stelazine at different times—those were delightful. Haldol and antipsychotics to stabilize me and reduce the fantasizing. What am I leaving out?"

"But you feel the fantasizing is essential to your work."

"They said drug therapy would help ground me in reality, but I'm not sure reality's not overrated."

"Have you had major dissociative reactions? Psychotic episodes?"

"A breakdown when I was twenty-three, as I was finishing the first book—I've done some of my best work in hospitals. My emergency admissions to the clinics were under the diagnosis of psychosis, suicidal."

"What about blackouts? Do you suffer discontinuities in the passage of time?"

His reply was a little arch. "Those are the symptoms of multiple personality. Forget any subtle traps—I learned a lesson at Eisenhower: as long as I told the truth I was kept locked up. As soon as I denied it, I was enjoying my first Twinkie in a month."

She was noticing for the first time that he had a hollow sweet tooth. He kept taking candies from his pockets and popping them in his mouth; she wondered whether he was hypoglycemic. She spoke cautiously. "Stephen, I work with many imaginative people. Many artists never go into therapy, no matter how miserable they are, for fear that their creative processes might be affected by too much rational scrutiny . . ."

"Insecure artists. People unsure of their talent."

"Stephen, I'm not arguing. What I was leading up to was that, if you were to tell me you've had to believe something absolutely to write about it, I'd tell you I've heard that before. Often. And that if sometimes you've doubted yourself, wondered if you weren't becoming overwhelmed by the characters that populate your imagination . . . it's not the same as being unbalanced."

For a moment she felt swallowed by the writer's personal reality: she heard the dead whispering in the grass. When his eyes glazed distractedly toward some point over her shoulder, she was afraid to turn her head.

"But in my case, I've already shot myself in the chest. There were two overdoses before that, and one attempted hanging. They all took place in the bathroom. Eva, does that mean anything, the bathroom business? Anything serious I should worry about?" His eyes were humorous. He was feeling playful.

My first mistake was making an exception for him, Eva thought. *I should have been strong and insisted we meet at my office. I need my stuff, my professional psychiatrist stuff. I need some wall between us.*

She said, "You've survived all that. It wasn't yourself you wanted to kill, but a dark part of yourself you'd like to renounce—call it the vampire, if you want. Something inside you wants desperately to live. Something keeps bringing you back."

"It's DeMarco and his flunkies. I seal the windows and turn on the gas and they're at the door with a respirator."

She imagined the agent as vampire with fangs and cape hovering over his client with an armload of contracts. "Perhaps he cares about you. Are there any other people in your life who care about you? Or whom you care about?"

Suddenly everything was all wrong: it was a question she had asked often in therapy sessions, so it had come easily from her lips. But she was not in a therapy session; she was sitting on a marble tombstone in the middle of a cemetery. There were stars overhead and stars underneath; water rippled blackly near their feet. Electric blue light from the street translated all into the chiaroscuro of silent film. A breeze blew and palm fronds whispered.

And she was afraid to hear the answer.

* * *

She felt that he was more comfortable, too, as they walked up the gravel drive to her car and into the brightness of Santa Monica Boulevard. Eva was trying to do a rigorous inventory of herself. She had fallen victim to her own poor self-image and was bolstering it with Stephen Albright. She had met him twice outside of the office, and this acute discomfort was where it had taken her. Now, she was taking him home, neither of them speaking. This would be the end. He would either be her patient, or he wouldn't; DeMarco had tried to sell him to her and she had been trying to win him to her, vying for him. She was angry at herself. She would drop him off on Harold Way and that would be the—

But instead he was leading her on an impromptu driving tour of Hollywood. The evening seemed to be turning into a date, albeit the most unusual she'd ever been on.

He showed her the parking lot where Sal Mineo had been stabbed to death, and guided her to the old Alto Nido apartments where the Black Dahlia had lived before her bisected corpse was found in the tall yellow grass of a vacant lot. They cruised Afton Place, where Marie Prevost, a Mack Sennett bathing beauty, had been found dead in 1937. "Her pet schnauzer," Albright commented with relish, "unfed for days, had eaten most of her legs by the time neighbors, alerted by the smell issuing from her room, discovered her. And who says Hollywood is a generalized attempt to disguise the inauthenticity of modern civilization? I love it." Beachwood Drive, and he pointed out the house where Peg Entwistle had lived that day in 1932 when she had walked up the hillside and climbed to the top of the H in the HOLLYWOOD sign.

And then they were on Melrose, and he saw the little art movie house, which was showing *White Zombie*, a 1932 feature starring Bela Lugosi. He was beside himself with excitement and insisted not only that she pull the car over, but that she accompany him inside. He was nonplussed that she had to pay; he apparently never carried a wallet and money was, anyway, insignificant. Then it was hamburgers at the outside patio of a Carl's Junior, and he was still raving about the film. "Lugosi turned down the part of Frankenstein. It made Karloff a star and Lugosi had created his own greatest rival. You know the unkindest cut? Years later when he was down and out, he *had* to play the monster in *Frankenstein Meets the Wolfman.* It was during World War Two. No lines, just grunts. He was, like, sixty years old—"

She was amazed as he chattered boyishly on and on with an air of urgent confidence as if he was sharing his most precious treasured secrets. He was obviously more comfortable with old films and dead actors than real people. Over his shoulder she could see the glowing letters of the HOLLYWOOD sign on the distant hills.

"Why did she do it?" Eva interrupted. "Why did Peg Entwistle jump off the H?"

He sucked on another candy nervously while he spoke. "One story had her pregnant and unsure who the father was. A variation circulated that she was in a depression after a bungled abortion."

Eva felt her face redden. She felt a twinge in her uterus, and he reacted with his eyes. *He doesn't miss anything,* she thought. He paused as if startled and now studied her cautiously. "But . . . I've heard that Lugosi believed to the end of his days that it wasn't really a suicide. That she was pushed."

He leaned closer. "You went to Brown?" he asked.

She nodded and was aware that her fingers were trembling. He couldn't know. *Not exactly.* But his sensitivity was uncanny. If he didn't like people, he had certainly made a study of them. Now he was acting absently distracted, but his hand had crept across the table and for an instant warmly covered her own. Then it was gone.

"What was your growing up like?" she asked quickly.

Suddenly it was his turn to be defensive. "You tell me."

She hesitated. *Here's what I see, Stephen Albright: a lonely boy who stayed up all night watching movies, the light flickering on his face. He was in love with untouchable women and saw himself in the inaccessible heroes; he purged his own frustrations and revenge fantasies in the havoc-wreaking monsters. A dream-starved child. And afraid of the dark.*

But she modified her thoughts before she bit.

"As a child? You were precocious and tended to be withdrawn. You were sensitive, and easily hurt. You found solace in horror films and escapist reading. You felt powerless and tended to want to identify with the monsters."

"It's called 'conversion,' huh?"

"But I lose it, there."

"Okay. I went to college back east. A year in Europe for graduate studies. Probably the best year in my life." She noted that he used a lot of ketchup and removed the tomatoes from the burger.

"Why?"

"I was a real scholar, a serious student pursuing something that was fascinating to me. I was trying to track down in its entirety Murnau's lost masterpiece, *Der Vampyre Magnus.*"

He had always been intrigued by the work of F. W. Murnau, the German surrealist film pioneer transplanted to Hollywood in 1923. His master's thesis on Murnau turned into the biography, *A Soul on Film.* More importantly, his introduction to the legend on which Murnau purportedly based his film resulted in the first novel of what eventually became the Bloodletter series.

"I had a sort of nervous breakdown near the end of my work on it, and the final chapters were completed in a hospital. Ideal working conditions because no one had any expectations of me. An auspicious launch by a large publishing house and extravagant popular success despite lukewarm reviews resulted in another Bloodletter novel, then another.''

"And the rest is publishing history. But you're bored with yourself."

"I am."

She was trying to think of an answer when she noticed the Rolls from the Zombie Zoo parking lot easing heavily to the curb. She realized suddenly that Albright's limo had been discreetly following them all evening awaiting his pleasure. The black girl with the green eyes had tucked her braids under her cap and her mouth was almost brutal. Eva felt a strange pang.

"She's very striking," Eva said to Stephen.

"She's a graduate student at UCLA—I'm helping her through film school. She grew up in Watts. She was sixteen and pregnant when police made a raid on a crack house while she was inside. A bullet went through her stomach and killed the fetus."

He smiled, and she realized she disliked the part of him that enjoyed shocking people. She knew it was approach-avoidance. She was thinking of the paranoiac Murnau and his delusional fear of the opposite sex. She fixed him with her eyes.

"Do you trust me, Stephen?"

"I really do, except for the clinical part of you that doesn't believe in Evil. I think I trust you as much as I trust anyone."

"You want to test me, Stephen?"

"Yes." He paused between bites and a smile flickered on his lips. "Eva, you know what real trust is, to me? Could you ever care about someone enough to shoot him in the head?"

Eva felt something ebbing inside her. It was strength or willpower. A large raindrop from an unseasonal thundercloud plopped wetly on the table and pulsed redly in the reflected streetlight until the writer wiped it self-consciously away with a napkin.

8

Quantico

"HOW GOES IT WITH OUR BOY?" FOR SOME REASON, DeMarco's voice was like ground glass over the phone. Eva felt her ears burning slightly; moving the receiver to her other shoulder did not help. She did not want to put the call on the speaker phone, either.

"I'm really not comfortable discussing the substance of my contacts with Stephen."

"Stephen? Good, I'm glad to hear you're on a first-name basis."

DeMarco did not seem at all bothered by the headline of that morning's paper:

DIVER DAN CLAIMS NUMBER FIVE

"He's still not my patient." Nevertheless, she had reluctantly started a chart on him with meager clinical notations. It was significant of her ambiguity that she kept it guiltily in the bottom drawer of her desk rather than the filing cabinet outside her office.

"Oh, I know. That's a formality. I think he's coming around, Eva. I think he's gonna start writing again."

"Why so?"

"I hear him getting into character. Stopped by to see him and he's, uh, talking to himself. And answering himself. Complete conversations, and he answers in another voice. Bloodletter's voice."

Her intestines tightened like a slipknot. "That doesn't sound like a good sign at all."

"Oh, hell, he snapped right out of it. That's the difference. He's got a handle on it. Before he went in the hospital, sometimes I'd have to pretend he was Bloodletter or he wouldn't speak to me. Go on for days, it was that bad."

Her ears stung. "Why didn't you tell me that? Did you think it would scare me off?"

"I'm sorry. It's a trust issue—Stephen's just real touchy about some details. I been his window to the world, he trusts me. I always gotta walk a tightrope with him."

"Why are you telling me now? Is there anything else you haven't told me?"

"Like I say, I see the light at the end of the tunnel. He even let me fill his prescription—the lithium. And he mentioned getting a driver's license. He's still got this rusted-out old Impala he had in high school. I think it's stored on the grounds here. He can't get rid of anything. If you could see his apartment—"

"Why haven't I heard from him?"

"Wondering that, huh? The last three days he's been closeted with these two J. Edgars from the FBI's unit at Quantico."

"Why?"

"Don't worry. He came out like a champ. He was *helping* them. This guy who's been paranoid of cops. See what I mean? They were some kind of scientists trying to come up with a psychological profile—"

"Behavioral. Of Stephen?"

"No! Not Stephen! Diver Dan. They thought he might have insights how the guy's mind works. You're a psychiatrist, what sort of a deranged person do you think would do that shit?"

"I don't know." She didn't feel like sharing her opinion, but it was there. *Caucasian unmarried male in his twenties. No more than high school educated. Isolated, withdrawn, unprepossessing in his disposition. Reads cheap pocket books and has spent a lot of time in movie houses specializing in sadomasochistic and occult eroticism. His communications display characteristic signs of magical thinking, narcissistic infantilism typical of the schizophrenic—*

"You have no idea?"

"No." *He's a borderline psychotic; pseudoreactive schizophrenia; his bizarre behavior is a cover-up for underlying and more hidden psychosis. A sexual sadist. When apprehended, he'll reveal a history of swings of emotion from intense euphoria to deepest depression. If he doesn't commit suicide first. The omnipotent figure of evil who holds a city in terror usually turns out to be some wretch with a sexual dysfunction in search of a cure. Enacting the symbolism of his private ritual and mythology in which alone he finds arousal.*

"Eva. I've got a call on another line. Keep me up on the hot poop." He hung up in her ear.

Stephen, why do I have to hear all this from your agent? "It's a trust issue," DeMarco had said. She calmed her center and realized she was feeling embarrassment, frustration. And something else.

It was a Thursday evening and Eva was waiting in her office for the last appointment of her day: Rashmikant Dabaloo was the teenage son of a wealthy Saudi who had a controlling interest in a major studio. The boy had recently been convicted of several Beverly Hills burglaries during which he had stolen lingerie from dowagers' bedrooms and crapped on the bed sheets. She smiled bitterly at the destiny that had charged her with making Bel Air safe from the fecal scourge.

It was a quarter to eight. She was reviewing not her case files but her financial statements; they were spread across her desk.

She was worried despite her accountant's reassurances: not only had there been cost overruns on the remodeling, there had been problems with the original contractor and until resolution of that suit there was a cash flow problem. Solomon, her CPA, had projected anticipated revenues and saw a squeaker, but no problem. Eva did not like such a thin margin for error: she did not like uncertainty. What if there was a malpractice suit, or if waves assaulted the Malibu beach house again this year? What if her gynecologist recommended corrective surgery when the results—

Eva groaned inwardly as she heard the receptionist's padded approach up the hall on the deep woven carpet that had cost her an arm and a leg per foot. She pictured herself armless, legless. Tisha was probably on her way to announce, with customary smirk of distaste, the Saudi's son's arrival. What did she call him? *The Scat Burglar.* Eva realized she had come to rely on Tisha's expressing the attitudes she herself could not voice. It would be such a wrench to talk to a rich teenager whose rebellion was shitting on the bedspreads of bejeweled matrons, when she could be enjoying the familiar and adrenalizing fear the ledgers always inspired.

But Tisha was breathless when she came to the door. "It's *him.* Stephen Albright!"

Her financial insecurity suddenly seemed blunted, and she realized why she had found it consoling: it staved off the sharper anxiety that had gnawed her like rat's teeth for the past two weeks. That was how long it had been since she had heard from Albright. She had been unaccountably upset for three days after DeMarco's phone call, even wished she was still seeing an analyst herself; but there just wasn't time in her schedule.

So she played her own doctor and counseled herself about poor self-esteem; rejection; even conflicting fear and desire regarding a romantic involvement. She had clarified the ethical issues and determined a course of organized action that involved a tighter schedule and more work. She clarified and dissected endlessly, and it was a week before she realized what she really was: obsessed.

She felt awkward when she saw him, especially because he was not alone. The black girl who drove his Rolls was at his elbow and lighting a cigarette, then looking around resentfully for an ashtray. Albright himself seemed tense and uncomfortable. The smart collar of Eva's wool suit felt suddenly abrasive around her neck. "I wish I'd known you were coming. I have an appointment in a few minutes. Unless you want to wait?" She did not like surprises; good or bad, she tried to insulate herself from them.

"That would be fine. May we wait here?"

"Certainly. Would either of you like coffee? A soft drink? You can catch the late news on television, if you like."

She realized for the first time that she was self-conscious about her office; it suddenly seemed not imaginative and classy, but superficial and imitative. The corny Monet she never noticed anymore, the color combinations that were soothing but so bland. It was yuppie hell. Laughable. The office of a phony. She regretted the choice of prints, the design of the light blue wallpaper, and especially the over-size of the plush chair the decorator had insisted was her; her own smile seemed vapid and mindless from the ski-ing trip pictures which she had arrayed so that people—

especially Solomon, her CPA—could see that she did, too, know how to relax. It had been years since her hair was like that.

Tisha: damn her, she saw it all. Her eyes were delighted. She knows I'm beside myself like a little girl. Tisha—

But it was the receptionist's lips that were moving: "Ramkwat, or whatever . . . he's here." She excused herself. Albright seemed to be avoiding both their eyes, but appeared distinctly uncomfortable with Tisha.

The session was interminable but only an hour like every other; she knew it was close to nine when she heard Tisha's Volkswagen cranking up in the alley through a wall that was supposed to have been specially insulated acoustically to screen out just such intrusions.

She quickly drew the session to a close. The boy's bovine eyes were runny and his shoulders slumped. He had the complexion of brown pumice, and his teeth were bad. His mother had disavowed drugs as his problem, though he had failed a screening during a psychiatric evaluation, blaming instead the fast crowd he had fallen in with since arriving in decadent Southern California. Especially distressing was his penchant for hiding large and bloody cuts of meat in bizarre places, including the zippered cushions of sofas. Mom had even brought to that first session an underground tabloid that claimed to expose cult activity in the central basin—charges of occultism and grave desecration bolstered only by arcane interpretations of downtown graffiti. The boy had seemed terrified, but lately had responded to the Mellaril she'd prescribed. She knew she was now giving him the polished psychiatric equivalent of the bum's rush, but was not deterred. *Take this, sin no more and I'll see you same time next week same charge—*

When she returned it was to find the author absorbed in something on the television; her face flushed. She had forgotten about the cassette in the VCR. It was a videotaped therapy session, and confidential. She was stunned at her own gaffe at leaving it in.

Her own voice, off-camera. *"Paula, how did you come to be estranged from your sister?"*

"We'd always been sort of rivals. She drew all the beauty from the gene pool, while I got the dentin. So I have no cavities while she always had a mouthful. It was all I was proud of. Until she married our dentist.

"That last visit . . . They have this beautiful home in the Palisades. Ruthy steps out the front door onto the manicured walk while I park in the drive. A three-year-old on one hip and an eighteen-month-old on the other. Spandex tights, she looked ridiculous. It was great to see her, but a shock, too. She'd spread out. Childbirth. Like her pelvis had been disassembled like a python's jaws when it swallows a deer. A man did that to you, I thought, flattening and distorting you. 'You look wonderful,' I told her. She said they were opening a Venus DeMarco Slim-Ways at Del Amo and she was going to enroll. But we hugged and cried. I was glad Borzoo wasn't home—that's her husband. He's Persian.

"I guess I set myself up, fantasizing about how we'd spend the whole night catching up, drinking coffee and talking, talking, talking. Then Borzoo comes through the door, he's still got on this white dentist's smock which offsets all this ugly black hair at his wrists and neck. How could she have ever found him handsome? He even has hair on his back. Who could stand those fingers in their mouth?

"I never liked the way he stared at me. It's only six o'clock but he changes into a black bathrobe, sulking around the house the rest of the evening until he angrily calls Ruthy to bed. What was his problem? Ruthy was embarrassed. Men are babies, but Persian men are worse. I been there hardly six hours, and he has Ruthy all the time."

Albright's hoarse voice. "Please. Don't turn it. She's fascinating."

Eva hesitated. Of course it's fascinating, but it's not supposed to be entertainment. He was so engrossed that all she could do was stand there.

> *"I had to sleep in the kids' room. And I was laying there thinking . . . Is it 'lying' there? . . . No, I was remembering this time at the lake. It was right after they were married. I was twenty-one and Ruthy was still nineteen. When we were all still friends. I was standing with Borzoo at the outdoor shower, washing sand off. Where was Ruthy? I don't remember. But Borzoo had this wet bathing suit, some filmy material which stuck to him. And I felt his hands on my breasts, these hairy hands, and the warm breath from his nose on my back."*

She was crying.

> *"What gets me, is, it was like I couldn't move. I just continued looking out to the lake, not moving. Ruthy never knew . . ."*

Eva's conscience snapped her out of it.

"I really have to turn it off, these sessions are confidential."

"I'm sorry."

"Don't be, it was my fault for leaving it in. It was thoughtless."

"Paula is your patient."

"I'd rather not say anything about this tape." The asperity in her tone surprised her; it surprised Albright. Poor Paula. She wasn't exactly a pro bono case. Paula's father had been a friend of Eva's family, and when he had approached her for help with his daughter, she had accepted as a sort of penance for her not living up to her own collegiate idealism. Paula's father wasn't poor—they lived in Palos Verdes Estates—but he had suffered a coronary and they were distressed, in a Palos Verdes Estates sort of way. Eva realized she was a little jealous: *she's fascinating*. The writer obviously did not get out much.

"Syreeta," he said to the restive black girl when he noticed Eva's discomfort, "that's all. I feel like walking tonight, you go ahead and work on your term paper." The girl shrugged warily as she snubbed out her smoke, apparently loath to let the writer out of her sight. Paula wondered whether she took orders from Stephen or his agent.

Albright surprised Eva with his sensitivity about the video; he was apologetic. "You know, I always had difficulty portraying women in the novels; it was a constant criticism. They always came out one-dimensional."

"Why do you think that is?"

"I don't really know any." *You must have had a mother,* Eva was thinking. But maybe that's one more thing you don't trust me with.

"I'd built up the expectation of this Thanata thing to such a height that whenever I had to introduce her it was paralyzing. She had to be so *special*. I never really found her."

Eva bit her lip and spoke. "I encountered the legend of Thanata, or Taniada, when I was doing my book on myths and feminism."

"I never claimed she was original. One regional variant of the European fable has her with child after violation by Satan. She killed herself rather than bring into the world the devil's spawn. The Antichrist."

"Can a suicide be a saint?"

"That version is a local aberration, but I adopted it. It appealed to me."

"You put her through an awful lot. You seem to have mixed feelings about her."

"But she's not alone—I love her too much to put her out there all by herself against the monster. I gave her a powerful friend—the White Witch is Thanata's holy guardian angel, or spiritual protector."

I love her too much. Thanata did have a lot to live up to. How had he described her?

> . . . *The paragon of all paragons of beauty, the reply to all desire and the goal of every romantic quest. She is mother, sister, mistress, bride. She is whatever in the world has lured and promised joy—in the deep of sleep, if not in the reality of the world. She is the soul's assurance that the bliss known prior to existence will be known again.*

Albright proceeded to startle her by reciting: " '. . . The Virgin goddess has been with us from time immemorial. She was Artemis and Diana. To the Hebrews she was Wisdom. Her enigmatic smile is the Madonna's, and it is she who looks serenely out at us as the High Priestess of the Tarot. To the mythic mind she is the moon. The moon is spirit, the cosmic uterus around which the worlds rotate. Her belt is the zodiac.' "

"You're quoting my book. That's very flattering." *Virgin and Demon.*

"You understand what it's all about, Eva. I think that's why you've come into my life. You were able to write that because it's an aspect of yourself." There was an inflection in his voice and timid smile.

She had been feeling so defensive that it had blind-sided her. Eva. Thanata.

She sat across from him. "Dammit, Stephen. DeMarco called me and it sounded like you were going through a rough time. He didn't say that, but that's the feeling I got. I'm sorry you didn't feel comfortable enough to call me."

She was more hurt than sorry, but she was still treading the line between friend and therapist.

"So, I'm a shit. It wasn't intentional. I feel I have to be so together when I see you. I guess there's a part of me that's still afraid that if you really knew everything about me, you'd get me locked up. For my own good, of course. I can't go back there."

The window had grown dark and the indirect lighting was more shadow than light; the fine music station played softly and for the first time that day Eva could hear it. She felt he was struggling to be honest. Suddenly that thing was in the room again, that thing she felt whenever she was alone with him. There was not enough air in the room.

She said carefully, "That must be scary for you. Sometimes you feel hopeless. Sometimes you feel like suicide is your only escape."

He smiled awkwardly and she was moved. "Sure. That, or finding my Thanata."

He was looking in her eyes, and what she saw in them would not go away. She was falling into them. She knew her body would not give her much time to think, so the bizarre rationalizations were coming furiously. He was not her patient. What were the elements of a contract? A meeting of the minds and consideration—but there was even less time than she'd thought. Already, her impulsive hand was touching his leg. A weak, unguarded moment.

His own hand was on her leg, then up her skirt. Raising her skirt.

"What's this?" he asked a little breathlessly.

"You're not my patient," she said desperately. She felt his fingers on her inner thigh and lowered her eyes. Had he heard her? He was tracing the brown stain she'd had since birth. It had always embarrassed her and she was glad it wasn't on her neck.

"I've always had it. Do you understand what I said?"

"It's beautiful."

She didn't want to talk about birthmarks. His absorption was unnerving. She had to ask, "What do you see?"

"A bird. There are the wings. There, the . . ."

She felt she was wearing a Rorschach on her flesh. She supposed it was significant. Birds were sexual symbols. Hitchcock, among others, had been fascinated by them. She did not know if his lips parted in surprise or if he was waiting for the kiss she felt already on her own mouth.

His breath was warm and his face was soft. When his arms were around her she could feel him trembling. She was afraid to think, afraid to open her eyes. *We're loosening our clothes*, she thought, *but I'm doing too much of the loosening.* She wanted him to sweep her away and relieve her of the responsibility. *The puckered scimitar of a scar under his nipple.* She felt it with her fingers.

I know his appeal, to me. Not money. Not power. It's his sensitivity. He's gentle and doesn't threaten me and when I'm with him I'm not afraid to feel. That's why— It woke up something inside her she could hardly control.

She tried to guide him carefully, arousing him with her mouth on his soft penis; it shook her up that his eyes were almost horrified; but as he knelt suddenly beside her, his kiss was encouraging. Then they were on the floor because it seemed he could hardly stand. His fragile arousal was spent and withered in an instant and then he was shivering breathless underneath her, holding her tightly.

But she was just getting started. She hadn't realized until that moment how much of her sexual self had waited for the man and the moment when she could finally be out of control. She felt herself grinding against him in arousal. *I can't stop.* Incredibly, she climaxed for the first time in years. She was shaken, and it had all happened so fast.

He couldn't look at her. "I'm humiliated," he said through clenched teeth.

"It's all right."

"I'm so ashamed—"

"It'll be fine. It was fine, for me."

There was this revelation: she had known power. For the moment she had been the woman on the cover of his books with her lips passionate at the violation of a demon lover. Except that it all got reversed with his timidity or inexperience, and she was the demon lover.

She suddenly saw them as two parts of a whole. She saw them answering the needs of one another. She saw herself coming home to him and attending premieres together. She saw herself writing on the lanai while he toiled inside their mansion. She even saw them writing a book together, both fabulously successful and vindicated. She suddenly felt the possibility of fulfillment and completion.

"Stephen, I want you to live. I want you to keep creating."

She bit her lip; she had always wanted to inspire someone and shape their life for the better but she had lost that impulse, and now he had given it back to her. She closed her eyes at the beauty of it. "For me," she whispered.

She held Albright in the dark and he didn't speak but still shivered, the little talisman around his neck. The wetness between her legs was turning cold as she caressed the purple scar ridges of the hole in his back. Confused.

"You've been real good for our boy," DeMarco said three days later in a surprise phone call. "I suppose you saw the news coverage?"

Who hadn't? Just the day before the studio had announced that all legal impasse to the resumption of shooting of *Bloodletter—The Movie* had been resolved. Albright had signed appropriate releases and dropped suits on the troubled screenplay.

"He's got a reason to live," DeMarco crowed. "He's got some color now, and he's writing like a bastard. How's this for a promo hook? *The Reign of Blood.*

"We even got the end of the film worked out, and get this: Bloodletter dies, but not before he gets Thanata knocked up. He rapes her. She's been sleeping with Cesare too, of course. So, the end of the film is we don't know if she's carrying a little Bloodletter or not—right? All our options wide open for the sequel. We're in business again. I knew you'd be good for him, Eva—"

Like a rich daddy who'd got a hooker for his son on his sixteenth birthday to get him bloodied. What hurt was that it was DeMarco calling instead of Stephen. She'd heard nothing from him since the night in her office.

"Another reason I buzzed you," DeMarco had said, "I'm throwing a housewarming thing at Stephen's new place off Laurel Canyon on Friday the thirteenth. About two weeks away—an End of Days bash, I'm calling it. From Stephen's books, you know."

An orgiastic vampire revel was the seventh sign of the apocalypse. The main entertainment was a captive Thanata paraded in humiliation before the assembled ghouls. The Agony of Thanata. It was her Passion that marked the beginning of the end before the Ripening of Days in which the earth would spit up the dead, who would turn on the living. A bit he pinched from Murnau, she thought vengefully. *Stephen may be living, but I feel dead . . .*

"It'll be wild. Wacky thing, all kinds of people there— people who count. Little Richard maybe, I'm working on it. Coupla songs. Costume thing. Eva, there's only gonna be one Thanata there—that's on the RSVP. DeMarco picks her."

He'd cleared his throat. "And DeMarco would be delighted if Eva LaPorte would be his date and his Thanata for the night. Walk in on my arm—give the whole thing an intellectual sort of polish. I'd send a car for you, whole shooting match. Queen for a day, belle of the ball. I take care of my friends. A lot of potential clients'll be there for you, Eva." He lowered his voice to an urgent whisper.

"One guy's head of a studio and he only gets off when his daughter does it with the Rottweiler—go figure. I could tell you stories, but my phone's looking like a Christmas tree. Put it on your calendar—"

"I don't really know," she'd stammered.

"—think it's Little Richard. Good Golly, Miss Molly. I'm gonna be in Atlanta for a few days, but maybe lunch or something next week, huh? My girl'll be in touch—"

And he was off. Eva was steamed, then confused. Thanata. Captive. Humiliated. Could he be that dense? Albright's agent was treating her like a hood ornament. Maybe she'd get a rep as an industry "fixer," the shrink to call in a clutch. All Albright had needed was to get laid, right? And he could barely do that . . .

He was like two people, one considerate and even courtly, and the other—

Eva experienced a chilling confluence of thoughts. Albright. Sexual dysfunction.

Diver Dan. Some wretch with a sexual dysfunction in search of a cure. Isolated, withdrawn. Sadomasochism and occult eroticism. Magical thinking, narcissistic infantilism. History of swings of emotion from intense euphoria to deepest depression. Suicidal . . .

Snug fit. But that was ridiculous. How many millionaire serial killers were there? How many psychotics wrote bestsellers?

Tisha had it right, damn her. Albright was a beautiful man, but merely a bastard. She tried to generate some defensive anger. But all she really felt was confusion and hurt.

9

The Basalt Shore

DADDY, SINCE THE CORONARY, WANDERED WANLY
around the house like a ghost, terrified even to make love.
Paula Kightlinger had heard Mother speaking to Doctor
on the phone. Daddy's eyes were haunted. He had actually
been clinically dead for a few minutes. *What did you see,
Daddy?* He would not talk about it. Always a lover of des-
serts, he had been placed on a diet so strict it made Paula
guilty to eat her favorite foods in front of him.

Why was it so impossible for him to understand she was
being smothered? Twenty-three years old, a sexually active
woman, and still living with her parents.

I am not a strong person, she thought. I just have a
strong personality. The illusion of emotional self-suffi-
ciency was the cross the lonely but vivacious had to bear.
"You have to cut the umbilical sometime," Eva had said.
"You're twenty-three years old."

She had been six full months at the little sixty-bed hospital in the desert, which Daddy's insurance had refused to
cover because it was not exactly a breakdown. *What do you*

have to do? Actually kill yourself? Sometimes it did not pay to hold yourself together. Blue Cross would not pay to have her teeth capped, either.

She blamed herself for his heart attack. She wondered if any other man would ever have that depth of feeling for her. The half-hearted suicide attempt had been a selfish thing to do. She wondered if they had kept the note, but was ashamed to ask. All that fucking Sylvia Plath poetry. She knew how worried he had always been for her, his Sensitive One. Not to mention the money. Mother had started going to mass every morning.

You, too, are Ishtar, daughter of the Moon Goddess.

Eva had helped her out of her agoraphobia, the morbid fear of leaving the house. "I'm afraid I'm losing my mind," she had told Eva, who had explained to her the difference between a neurotic and a psychotic. *The neurotic dreams of a castle. The psychotic lives in it.*

She should have been the one to get on *their* nerves— eating, smoking, pacing, dieting. But she found herself yelling at *them*. Paula felt badly when her mother would come home from a day at the phone company to find her on the Floto-Lounger in the pool where she had lain all day, slowly rotating herself behind sunglasses and greased with solar screen thick as aspic. Well, it didn't hurt to look healthy on job interviews. She was working, in a way, with pencil in hand and yellow legal tablet on her oily stomach for once pleasantly concave as she lay supine. But the book that would make her famous just couldn't quite get started.

Poor Daddy got on her nerves the worst, shambling aimlessly with a frightened face, his eyes beseeching. It seemed they were always running into one another, she looking for a quiet place to write alone or eat undiscovered, and he on his endless haunting circuit of the familiar rooms where he had spent the best years of his life. Nowadays he was always wanting to talk about his dead mother and his childhood.

With all the anxiety, Paula eventually put back on the weight she had lost.

In her lowest moments she wished she had been careless. Wished she'd gotten pregnant. Not so that Larry would know and feel guilty or want her back. But so that she would have something inside her, something of Larry.

She had to get away, at least for a couple of weeks and she patiently explained it. It couldn't actually happen until it came to head in a crisis. *There has to be a scene.* Mother was hysterical: *the family is coming apart.* Daddy was dazed and hapless, pressing his Mastercard through the Toyota's window while fretting about the air pressure in her tires. She rolled up the windows and screamed as she pulled out of the drive in the dented silver aspirin can.

Where am I going? Paula had never felt so horrible in her life. What would she do? She knew she had turned the wrong way on Artesia when she ran smack into the Pacific, the waves crashing in a convulsive vomiting of foam on the pale beach. She saw the boys and the girls in bathing suits playing volleyball and skateboarding on the promenade. She wrenched the wheel and headed back the way she had come, squeezing out of the crowded commuter lanes and into the 405 onramp like a dollop of toothpaste. She cringed at the vision of her return home if she were to turn around. She realized, as the highway signs slashed past, what she really wanted.

Larry. Not Larry van Heusen the way he had been when she left his apartment the last time, precipitating her latest crisis; but the way he had treated her when they first went out. That Larry. He had become so cold. Why, when she told him that, was he flattered? Part of her heart started to defend him. He was a wonderful person, but an emotional coward. He was afraid to care. Maybe he was just immature. Maybe there was nothing wrong with her at all. She ran down the grisly catalog of her physical defects. Maybe she

was unattractive—too heavy. It made her sick to see the
emaciated vampire women on the vast disembodied planes
of advertising overhead.

Not only can I not control my life, she thought, *I can't control
my car.* The traffic jostled and swept her from one rushing
lane to another as if she were an embolism coursing
through an artery. She was trapped. She had an impulse,
just for a moment but almost irresistible, to release the
wheel and allow the Toyota to drift off the highway and
into the embanked ice plant. She threw herself into those
future seconds, saw it tumbling end over end imploding on
itself, the waxy vines grabbing at her like green fingers as
clots of damp earth were rooted high in the air. She saw
herself, red hair tousled, but beautiful with an impeccable
pencil-line of blood trickling from her mouth, unconscious behind the bent steering wheel as young men from
passing vehicles rushed across the highway to her.

What would the nuns at Sacred Heart School think of
that? Suicide was probably no worse than using a diaphragm.

The beauty of it was almost orgasmic. Reality was so taw-
dry. Reality was that she refused to be trundled into an ambulance by winsome paramedics while wearing underwear
in which the elastic was stretched out. She summoned up
the single thought to which she had clung so often: I won't
die until I've lost twenty pounds.

But she was succumbing to the nitrous oxide of total depression in which her will seemed to evaporate until even
the most familiar things, her hands on the steering wheel,
her eyes in the mirror, looked alien.

The Toyota was being herded past LAX. The jumbo jets
hung like mobiles suspended in the sky and then were
slowly lowered like so many fat bathtub toys, their reflections corrugated in the vast mirrors of the aquamarine
Herbalife building. *Unreal.* Everything was giving way to

something else. *This is how it starts.* She had to get herself together. But she was almost to the San Fernando Valley. Once on the freeway out of the Los Angeles basin, there would be no turning back.

An exit—SUNSET BOULEVARD.

Paula had turned off at the last instant. The name drew her. It was the title of one of her all-time favorite movies.

She had taken action, made a decision. She felt a calm almost immediately. The boulevard broadened and curved past the UCLA campus. Beverly Hills and the security gate to exclusive Bel Air beyond those vast clipped lawns and fountains of mosaic tiles hot with the orange flames of bird of paradise. The boulevard took her past redolent arbors of splashed roses, and pipestem palm trees swayed bravely in the wind against the pink towers of the Beverly Hills Hotel. Gradually the lawns and tennis courts died away, an emerald wave receding from the basalt shore. A sign told her she was in West Hollywood.

Hollywood.

Amazingly, it was Paula's first time. Daddy had always given her explicit routes so she could avoid it on the drives to her therapy sessions. It was so thrilling to recognize the tall gilded Oriental spires and green leering dragons of Mann's Chinese Theater. Her mind swarmed with movie house memories. *A Star Is Born.* Her little-girl game of being an actress as she practiced tears in the bathroom mirrors. She had pretended there was a camera behind every tree. *Suicide scene. My big scene.*

She saw looming over the city the copper domes of an observatory like three greenish bald heads. Nearby was the HOLLYWOOD sign, the huge white fluoride smile gaping crookedly with death's-head teeth. The Mountain of the Skull. A billboard featured the menacing silhouette of the vampire atop that same sign.

STEPHEN ALBRIGHT'S
BLOODLETTER—THE MOVIE!
Is Coming Soon.
See you in Hell.

She had seen on *Hollywood Insider* that the production had at one point been halted while they searched for a leading lady. *Little Paula . . . a star at last.* A sense of unrightness overwhelmed her. She pushed it back, both hands on the wheel as if she were asserting control of reality. The hot scent of open-air food stands was sexual in its pungency, like the warm smell of her sheets the morning after Larry had made love to her. Then she was smothered by exhaust fumes as a bus pulled alongside.

Suddenly the red temperature light on the dashboard flickered. *What do I do?*

There was no place to turn out. She wandered onto Santa Monica. Her heart began to pound. She cut straight across oncoming traffic at the intersection and directly up the inclined drive of the scuzzy Villa del Monica Motel.

Maybe the engine would be all right if she just let it cool. She was so tired, too tired even to cry. It was a symptom of her depression. Unless she found a bed, she was going to fall asleep standing up. She had to find someplace to unplug her overloaded synapses. The old mission-style motel was a sleazy pit, but its little courtyard was like a sanctuary.

The Indian woman who was desk had been watching soaps in an anteroom when the door summoned her. A nursing towel was over her shoulder and there was a damp spot over one of her breasts as she regarded Paula sullenly. The baby wailed in the background. The crying stung Paula and touched something deep inside her.

"I'll wait," Paula said. "Go back to your baby. I'll wait until you're through."

"She fine," the woman said irritably in a thick accent. Through the open door came the soap opera music and the child's cry. Paula was seeing spots before her eyes.

"Go back to your baby," she said.

The woman's eyes darkened threateningly, and the brown lips beneath her faint mustache opened to speak—then stopped.

The crying had called something up from Paula that was steely and implacable. She felt the momentary ability to make her eyes a cold blue that bent the woman's will like psychic bending forks with sheer mentality. "She needs you," Paula said.

The woman took a step back, then hesitantly returned to her child. Paula closed her eyes at the baby's warm contented puling sounds from around the mother's nipple.

In a few moments she got a room with twin beds on Daddy's Mastercard and carried her things upstairs in one trip, afraid someone might break into her car. The blinds were open and room 210 seemed to cringe in the brutal light. At least, the telephone worked. She knew the number by memory. Eva was unavailable, so Paula left the motel number along with the desperate message.

She closed the blinds and walked to the bathroom with her eyes half shut, her lashes gauzing and softening the dingy walls and the brown ring around the base of the toilet. If there were any hairs on the sheet when she turned down the covers, she did not want to know. She tried to turn up the air conditioner, but its thermostat was stuck. She dozed on and off in the oppressive afternoon heat.

10

Perverse Impulse

FOR EVA, THERE HAD BEEN DAYS AND DAYS OF WAITing for his phone call, some word. She riffled once more through the memos Tisha had left on her desk. *Paula is at the Villa del Monica in Hollywood. She has to—*

Every call but the one she wanted. Eva felt like her life had become all false starts and dashed hopes.

She wondered whether the large and negative article that had appeared in the *Times* had sent him into withdrawal and hiding; the feminist reviewer was pretty fed up with the whole brouhaha over the Bloodletter film; she equated Albright's books with topless bars and pornography in contributing to the sick moral climate that spawned sexual abuse and other crimes of violence like the current serial killings.

> . . . *The Bloodletter is the projection of an abnormal, sexually stunted personality. Unaware that aggression is a normal part of sexual feelings, the aggressive feelings, now present in love emotions, turn into hate. Murder and sadism are an uncon-*

scious attempt to enhance self-esteem by achieving power over women. The imagination grows monstrous in proportion to the impotence of the flesh.

The last part of the article was a sort of open letter to the author:

> . . . *Mr. Albright, I'm going to take exception. The words might be beautiful, but the treatment of women is grotesque. Rape, murder, and sadomasochism. There is an underlying misogyny that poisons love. If I were a psychologist, I would wonder about the mind that produced this. Fear of sexual deficiency? Homophobia—?*

Eva was always irritated by the ridiculous psychological presumptions of journalists, and her blood was boiling now. Despite the disclaimer at the beginning of the piece, the *Times* was apparently pretty confident that the author's pathological aversion to publicity would preclude him responding with a lawsuit. His isolation was his protection.

Eva thought, *He's protected himself from me pretty well:* she didn't have his phone number or address. She'd entered the kick-yourself-in-the-ass phase, her eyes wandering to the guilty ghosts of their lovemaking in the soft woof of the office carpet. It was approach-avoidance. She had gotten too close to him.

Now two weeks later—unannounced and unexpected—Stephen Albright had come to her office on this Monday night, tapping at the glass door like a UPS man after hours. He must have waited in the shadow of the mimosa until Tisha had driven away. A millionaire skulking in her alley. Writing like a madman, his agent had implied. He looked it: he hadn't shaved in days and she doubted if he'd changed clothes. His silk tie was loosely knotted and askew on his white shirt.

"Eva? Have you missed me?" His smile made her uncomfortable: what had been vulnerability now alternated between Bad Little Boy and uncomfortable Stud. "Well, here I am."

Something was definitely wrong; he looked almost disoriented. She could not smell alcohol, and his pupils seemed okay. But he could hardly meet her eyes. He was disturbed and he was coming apart. *What happened?*

When she asked him how long it had been since he'd slept, he didn't answer. They had to get in her car. There was the sound of a siren from the direction of Gower, and Albright cringed reflexively. Paranoid? *Of authority figures,* DeMarco had said, *especially doctors and cops.*

Then they were on Sunset and the street felt all wrong to Eva, just like the night. "Left, here," he would brusquely direct as she drove, and then turn to peer out the rear window of her BMW.

"Is someone following you?" she asked with mounting irritation.

He smiled crookedly. "You could say that. You could say I'm trying to lose somebody."

"Are you angry with me for any reason?"

He averted his face to the window and what she could see of his smile was sardonic. He was staring at the invisible scaffolding of the sign high atop THE HOTEL KNICKERBOCKER. She followed his gaze and thought she saw two eyes underneath the white neon, eyes winking redly. Her mind conjured a shadow for the eyes, a wind-torn figure against the Hollywood moon that hung plump and pendulous as a breast in the August night. It was clutching the scaffolding with claws and watching them intently.

She shook her head. The menacing silhouette of The Bloodletter was everywhere. One more illusion in a city of illusions, one more example of the power of suggestion of

the novels, not to mention the infectious quality of paranoia in a car seat next to you.

"And the Vampire Still Pursued Him . . ."

That was what Albright had titled the section of his Murnau book that dealt with the last months of the director's
life. He had suffered a breakdown and believed that The
Bloodletter was always following him. He would fire a re-
volver through walls and doors in his conviction of what
was lurking just outside. He saw the vampire everywhere,
saw him slithering lizardlike up walls, saw him in narcot-
ized dreams. Always haunting him and exhorting him to
revive the failed project that had promised to elevate him
once more to public consciousness. The vampire would
not be denied. The pathetic picture of the once-great director of the classic *Nosferatu* found by a neighbor huddled
emaciated and shivering in a dark and tiny clothes closet in
his own sprawling mansion. What had he said in his thick
German accent after hushing his discoverer to con-
spiratorial silence?

"I am trying to lose somebody."

Reading it, she had recognized that the vampire was the
conflicted director's projection onto the outside world of
his own sexual fears; the bogeyman was his own homosexu-
ality, which he had tried most of his life to evade and to
which he'd never been reconciled. Of course, Stephen's
books were also rife with images of sexual rage and frustration. She turned on the car stereo in an attempt to lighten
the mood.

—*That thang that thang that thang*—

A mistake, and she quickly turned it off. Tonight would
be the night she would insist Stephen talk about his
mother and father, his family configuration.

They had been going in circles, she finally realized when
they got to their destination. *His* destination: the run-down

motel on La Cienega. *The Villa del Monica?*

"They used to be apartments in the twenties. I began the first book in one of these rooms. This is where it all started," he said. He hesitated, and her mind furnished the words — *and where it will end.* Suicide? She felt the goose bumps mottle her cool forearms, but it was fortunate he was not alone. He'd already reserved a room. She was shocked, then hurt. The way he was looking at her again. *He's pretty confident about me. Sorry, Stephen, but don't assume anything.*

Then she was angry. *We'll talk. If this is the only place where you'll feel comfortable, I'll meet you that far. Don't just assume I've been eating my heart out so bad I'll jump right into bed. Don't think your eyes scare me so much I'll do whatever you want. It's not that I'm curious or excited or that I want you under any circumstances. If we are to be lovers or even just friends we have to arrive at an understanding—*

He seemed unable to breathe until the motel room door was locked behind them. Through the wall there was the rasping buzz of manic television laughter and tinkling of ice in glasses. She looked out the window down upon the intersection at Santa Monica where the headlights formed radiant crucifixes on the street and she felt him glaring at her back just because she had parted the curtains.

The men in my life, she thought. *I've worked through that part of myself I didn't like which lived in them. I don't have to find my personal definition in my reflection in a man's eyes. I've faltered with him, but he's going to understand. He can't take me for granted. I was rash and stupid. We're both paying for it: he's coming apart whether he'll admit it or not. If he'll admit it that will be a start.*

She saw herself then in the mirror: a wobbly and panicked woman. He was taking off his coat; there was a big stain of perspiration down the back of his shirt. He sat heavily on the small bed and released the breath from his upper chest. He ran his slender fingers through his long hair.

"Eva . . ." he stammered. "I'm so goddamn scared."

Then she was beside him and holding him and his own arms were around her. His lashes flickered against her cheek.

"That last time we were together—I felt great for days. Then it began to prey at me. I made such a crummy show-ing . . ."

She felt herself melting and his shivering was familiar against her chest and his tears on her neck were warm. No part of her could despise his weakness; she knew he was hating himself.

Wouldn't it be wonderful if I could make it right, fix him. Help him.

"I don't know who I am anymore. Whenever I get a little ahead or feeling some woman might love me for who I am, he gets threatened and he has to remind me . . ."

That clown DeMarco? she wondered.

"Are you feeling jealousy? Does this have anything to do with that silly party?"

His reply startled her with its dripping condescension.

"I'm talking about The Bloodletter."

It wasn't what she wanted to hear; she closed her eyes and tried to get hold of herself. "Well, do you feel safe now?"

He withdrew from her suddenly, and she opened her eyes to see him peering furtively out the curtains as if the vampire might be pacing the parking lot outside. It would have been comical if it wasn't so sad. She could almost see his imagination working, see into his mind where the cha-otic swarm of words danced into images that swirled them-selves away up an invisible funnel to assume other shapes. He was not looking at her as he spoke.

"He always gets to me through women."

Then he stood in front of her. She put her arms around him, instinctively rested her head vulnerably against his chest so that he could be the man. Then his breath started to get desperate and she felt his fingers run down her thin arms, cleaning them of all the chains and bracelets. *Not now. It's not going to make things better. This isn't a good idea. Stephen, we don't have to. It's not a test, it's not the most important thing.*

He was feverishly unbuttoning her pewter-gray blouse and pulling it down her thin shoulders. She whispered calmly in his ear, "This isn't the answer, is it? You don't really want to do this now, do you? You think you have to. You think you have to for me. It's not what either of us wants right now. You put too much pressure on both of us."

But when she tried to firmly restrain his fingers he threw her hand off and she felt his whole body tense. Then her blouse was off and she felt his fingers start to trace the bones of her high ribcage, distinct under her skin as piano keys. The little singing whine of her zipper was the only sound in the room; the skirt around her ankles in the dark. His own shirt was off, the little hummingbird on its delicate chain was hanging askew on his narrow breastbone. His slacks.

Stephen, I want you, too. You don't know how badly. You can't know because you can't love me when you don't even like yourself. You're setting yourself up, you want to humiliate yourself. I'm not going to help you. You want it to be a disaster so you won't have to see me anymore, so you won't have to . . .

She was aware of her own fear when she saw her face over his shoulder in the dirty mirror: a fear she was disappointing him. She saw a thin woman whose skin had begun to sink around her collarbone. *Aerobics has kept my stomach flat, but my ass has begun to fall.* She breathed deeply. *Find your center, baby.* His lips were trembling against her mouth.

She tried to recall a passage from one of his novels that had struck her with particular force.

> *She had risked, revealed. She felt herself reborn in him. Whatever else he was, he alone could see inside her. It was wonderful, the way he saw her essence. She felt they were reintroducing themselves on another plane more intimate than anything she had imagined . . .*

She wondered if she could get into it; he was too rough. *The aggression of the male patient toward the female therapist? No, we're man and woman. That's all.* She wanted to stop and talk but feared her sudden withdrawal would make him angrier; she could hear the blood pounding in his chest, almost see it ticking in his temple and his limp penis. She tried to blank her mind and be responsive. *Don't try so hard, Stephen. Give yourself a chance. I don't feel like it either, you don't have to prove—*

She had thought she would sense his frustration before it turned to rage. She hoped he would dissolve in tears before it came to that and they would have a long talk. She thought she might be able to make him believe she had understood the conflicts that were tearing him up. *Your childhood was probably abusive, that's why it's painful to discuss. Tremendous pressures for years. It's gotta be a burden to have this public perception of you as a literary sexual symbol while you feel so unworthy. When you doubt yourself. It can't be easy to be the focus of a cult which seems to want to drain you of your—*

What she wasn't prepared for was that he would throw her suddenly and almost viciously on the bed with surprising strength. He had flopped her naked onto her stomach and she lay there for a second stunned, the only image in her mind that of a pursed rosebud. *No previous symptoms of anal-sadism. Hallucination division deep neurosis depression but not— But how the hell would you know, Eva—you've never seen the file from Eisenhower . . .*

Stephen, that's it. I want out. Now.

She tried to turn her head, and he grabbed her hips and turned her over roughly. The face she saw frightened her so that she did not move but waited to see what he was doing. He began kissing her navel wetly. She closed her eyes, chafed and red as an exposed nerve while her mind rang disbelievingly. *What do you do now, Eva? You're alone in a cheap motel room with a very disturbed man who is in some kind of episode.*

Her voice firm: "Stephen, stop it. I'm not enjoying this. It's not even giving you pleasure."

When he raised his head a thread of spittle from his lips to her stomach snapped and fell. His eyes were wild but his face was disconcertingly quizzical even while his hands held her wrists against the mattress.

"Because pleasure is the point, isn't it? What lives for the flesh, Eva? The vampire. *Eva the vampire.* Were you ever real? Were you always hollow and useless?"

Then his lips were tight around his teeth and for the first time she noticed he had an overbite and the bottom teeth were uneven and too small. His voice was mocking. "You betrayed me. You brought me back to life for one reason, so I'd keep writing. So I'd keep him alive. Did it for him."

He buried his face in her breasts and his teeth bit her nipples; then he seemed to collapse and fall against her, but his hands still held her own and his knees were on her thighs. She stared at the ceiling trying to compose herself because she knew that whatever happened she would have to be calm. Her heart was hammering until she could hardly hear what he was mumbling. He was lowering her hands to hold them firmly at her sides.

"Wasn't that the whole point? To humiliate me, make me weak? To show me I'm really nothing and he's everything? That I'm nothing without Bloodletter? He wants to control me through you."

She closed her eyes again and her voice was tremulous. "I know you're feeling terrible about what you're doing. I know you'll feel worse if you hurt me any more. I know it's yourself you're hurting and you're in a lot of pain——"

When he lowered his head between her legs suddenly she felt his probing tongue and arched her back uncontrollably against a raw, almost after-sex sensitivity in which each movement and contraction was crucifying. "That's hurting me, Stephen." She thought of trying to break free and striking his face with her hands; pictured him suddenly infuriated. *You're in a lot of trouble, Eva. Do whatever you have to to get out of this room alive.* A sentence from his book floated up to torment her.

"She feels the burning in her stomach, the heat of her sex turning up to consume him . . ."

How could she stall? For a second she was a radio station that had gone off the air. She needed to think, so hard to think. Some way to bring him back to earth.

"Stephen, I am your friend. You're not to blame——"

Suddenly she was staring into his distorted face and terrified eyes, the muscles in his throat rigid as if he were strangling to cry. "What do y'do now, Eva? When it's so informal, I mean, you don't have your desk or your pencil sharpener? When I'm between your legs how do you bring me under control? Isn't that what it's all about?"

She did not know what to say; she knew from his eyes that he would not be able to hear her. Sweat glistened on her neck and damp hair streaked her face. Even her breasts trembled. It was ironic, but she'd never been alive as she was at that moment, in that terror.

"I mean, I'm the one who's disappointed, Eva. I really wanted you to be what I thought you were. I wanted you to be anything but what you are."

She was devastated.

When he pressed his mouth brutally to hers, his face mashing hers, she fought his invasive tongue. He tore his lips away to breathe and seemed to collapse on top of her, his ragged breath in her ear. But his hands still held her wrists.

"Stephen, I want what's good for you. I want you to write if that's good for you and if it's not, I don't want you to hurt yourself. I'm on your side, Stephen, no one else's . . ."

It was as though what she'd said had scalded him. His face was in her own, eyes wild and cheeks drained. He tried to smile and she saw that his dry cracked lips were bleeding from her own resisting teeth and the blood was smeared on his chin.

"How's it taste, Eva? How'd you like to be my vampire?" *Who the fuck do you think you are? Who do you think I am?*

The silk tie must have fallen on the bed when he had undressed her, because now it was in his teeth. He jerked her hands over her head and was deftly wrapping the tie three times around her wrists; the other end he tied to the bedpost. "*Publishers Weekly* said I could make even the most perverse grotesquerie somehow attractive, Eva. Let's find out."

Her arms outstretched helplessly above her, and then he was tying something around her neck. *My hose. Maybe now he'll be able to do it. Maybe he'll expend himself and it'll be over. Maybe that'll be enough.*

His eyes disabused her: they were chilling in their intent. "The carotid artery. Really, a neglected erogenous zone." *He is going to kill me.*

Then he was holding a leg of the sheer hosiery experimentally in each hand, testing it. She felt the constriction bite into her throat. He was pulling it tighter. She knew she would soon pass out. In the awful awareness was a resignation and a physical and emotional letdown. She was even aware of pity for him.

The perverse eruption. From where?

She was swept by revulsion and a nasty ripple. *Don't, Eva. Don't do that.* But there had been a defiance to it. It was her rebellion, the only one she could make in her last moments, against the submissive role he'd assigned her in the sexual fantasy he was enacting on her. *Who the fuck's business is it how I die?* She quit struggling against the purely physical arousal from asphyxiation. *Damn it. Damn me. The screaming of a thousand pipe organs.* Her orgasms had always been violent and almost epileptic, her body jerking as if with electric current.

There was the darkening impression of his eyes stricken in helpless panic. She thought, *You hadn't expected this, huh? Not what you'd planned . . . ?*

"Stop that," he said desperately. "Don't look at me."

Then the other hose was in his hand and he was tying it roughly around her eyes. There was silence for a moment in which she was aware of his suffocating weight and sudden stillness. She felt his physical alertness; a tense hypervigilance. He held his breath. When he mumbled it was not even as if he was speaking to her. *"He's here. He's just outside. I know him."*

Who? She hoped it was someone at the door, but really she felt more fatalistic. It was more like Albright was absorbed in some conflicted dialogue with himself.

"He's coming through the window."

His psychosis is intensifying, she thought: visual and auditory hallucinations. Then there was a demonstration of her own terrorized suggestibility as she strained to see through the gauze of the stocking. There was Albright's vague shadow before the window, and the panicked impression of the shadow splitting and doubling so that there were two of him.

But you already knew that. You even wondered if any woman had ever met the other one.

There was a change in the room; the temperature seemed to have dropped. Her breath was a razor blade in her chest. She could not be sure if there were two voices in the room, one sobbing and guttural, the other a deep whisper, or if they were both only two poles of his schizophrenia expressing themselves. What was real was that the side of Albright that was her only chance of escape had finally vanished.

Something had taken his place on top of her. Its breath was hot and dark and it moved with confidence and when it loomed over her she felt the coldness of shadow. His psychosis was apparently complete. Literal or metaphorical, she knew it wouldn't make a difference as far as she was concerned. *The vampire is in, doctor.*

Breath on her face that traveled down her cheek to her throat, and then the dark inward sigh as something closed on the swollen carotid above the crude garrote of her hosiery. Her vein, she knew, was plumped and prepped and swollen as if by a phlebotomist.

The sting was like an injection of succinylcholine, an icy numbness around the punctures at first, and then a chill that progressed upwards with the evacuation of her blood. She'd had no idea one human being could actually do that to another. Her legs were frozen and then her fingers. The tingling was crawling up her arms toward her chest. It was like standing in a blizzard with the snow rising up ankles, then knees, then thighs, finally icing her heart. She lay supine, but the dizziness of exsanguination made her feel as if she were hanging upside down.

I'll be damned.

Hysterical laughter tried to well in her throat before everything went to exploding darts of purple and yellow against the fabric of black to which her consciousness was contracting. Her dying mind emptied except for a single image: a shiny silver thing fluttering towards the surface of a pool through redly diffused sunlight. It was a hummingbird on a silver chain.

11

Stiletto Beak

THE SMILING, CORPSELIKE MAN WITH LIVER-SPOTTED
forehead and hollow cheeks was in a wheelchair. The lips
were bloodless but the smile congenial. "I hope you're enjoying tonight's Chiller Theater on this Monday night. I'm
your host, Algernon W. Sherwood. Our feature, *The Devil
Bat*, starring Bela Lugosi, is brought to you by Venus
DeMarco Slim and Fitness Salons."

Two skeletal young women in aerobic suits appeared on
the screen, SLIMWAYS across their plumlike breasts. It was
happening to Paula again: the television was talking to her.
She had fallen asleep in the motel bed watching it. All her
life she had depended on TV for white noise and friendly
images. What had waked her now at some indeterminate
hour past midnight was the raucous ear-graffiti of the
drunks and hookers vomited out onto Santa Monica from
the winked-out clubs on Sunset. It was a werewolf city, menace oozing from the grates of the curb drains.

"*Are you getting all you should out of life? Has romance become
just another word in the dictionary, somewhere between 'bored' and*

'too tired'? There is a way to change the way you look—and the way you live!"

The room had been nothing to start with but now on the nightstand there were crumbs and crusts from the pepperoni pizza she had ordered, invitations to the roaches she was certain swarmed inside the walls. The ashtray was crammed with butts of her menthol cigarettes. How had she messed it so fast? It was just like her room at home. Eva had said it: "There's no escaping yourself, Paula."

The girls began to squeeze her head with their eyes. Eva, again: "You're not crazy. You're just lonely." She slipped out from under the covers to switch the channel but got no further than her reflection in the motel mirror: she was trying again to see herself with Larry's eyes, to decide whether her body was sexy or awful. She sat back down.

One foot dangled off the bed: a small foot. The open bathrobe revealed a plump but nicely shaped thigh. *Isn't everyone obsessed with herself?* Sometimes she would look at a particular feature so long and closely that it would detach from the rest of her and linger disembodied.

She extended her legs; she wished they weren't so short. Her long red hair was tangled across her broad face with its nose—bobbed? pug? pert? elfin?—she couldn't tell. She blew a wisp from her eye so she could see better. She had been told her face was Irish, but what the hell did that mean? She had so many questions about herself. If she could just know one thing for sure, it hardly mattered what. She was helpless against waves of inferiority and waves of superiority; worse, she never knew which wave was coming when.

Physically—the word was painful to her—she thought of herself as an economy car, compacted and not especially attractive, but with some first-class appointments and extras. Her skin was reddish, but the perpetual pillow burns on her cheeks were nice, like the light brown freckles sprinkled under her eyes.

She lifted a cigarette to her lips. Larry had said her hands were artistic. Large and strong, but graceful, with tapered nails blood red. She had painted them for him. She believed that, of all the ways she'd tried to excite him, he was most aroused by her hands with the red nails on him. They weren't the hands a coroner would have matched to her body after, say, an airliner crash; they seemed as if they should belong to someone else. *Unworthy*.

Her breasts. They had terrorized her the most. She opened the robe. On the left was the small emerald tattoo of a hummingbird—the stigmata of the mysterious Thanata in *Bloodletter*. Larry had suggested it, and she had complied to please him. How had she let Larry talk her into it? He had coaxed and wheedled by insisting the ornament would make her breasts prettier, somehow delicate.

Sometimes it seemed they had determined her life, those breasts. They had always attracted attention, introducing her early to men she would have been scared to talk to. Unconfined, they hung far down her ribcage; supported by her industrial brassieres they seemed nuclear and overpowering. She felt sexually overblown and precocious when she entered a room or even passed a man in the hall. More than one had taken her cleavage as an invitation. As she stared at the collapsed nipples they took on the wizened faces of Taoist monks.

I am a cake that has fallen. I want to reassemble myself, squeeze my teeth closer together, stretch my legs and neck and deflate my breasts two sizes so I won't be round-shouldered. And lose twenty pounds. Her mouth tasted terrible as she lit the cigarette, exhaling the smoke through her nose as she tested the shadows, her good side changing to bad and then back again in confusion. Eva: "Two sicks don't make a well. You don't need a man to make you all right."

She felt suddenly insecure and got up to check the dead-bolt; she tried to change the station, but Sherwood was on every channel. No, there was only one station. She turned it off and the screen shrank to a tiny pinpoint of light that was consumed in a somber green cathode sea. On her way back to the warm mattress she checked the motel bureau.

Predictably, she found a matchbook, a Bible, a *Guide to Dining Out* and a paperback novel. *Stephen Albright's* BLOOD-LETTER. *Book Three: Incubo.*

There was a photo of the author on the back. His face was sensitive and pale and his eyes a haunted gray. She read the meager biography: born on Christmas Day, 1951. The quote *"There is a monster in each of us. The Bloodletter is mine."* There was a resemblance; the vampire on the cover was almost a brutalized and sexualized version of the writer on the back. She wondered if it was an insider's joke. Larry was hooked on these Albrights but she'd refused to read them.

Ruthy, too: in her bathroom at her house Paula had discovered a fat Albright paperback — *Book Four: Blood-sucker* — and asked her about it. "They're neat," her sister had said. "They're almost bedroom manuals." *Yeah, written by the Marquis de Sade.*

She had wanted to tell her sister about breaking up with Larry. The tears had hardly started when her sister had said, "Good. I'm glad to hear it. He was just using you and you let him." Ruthy had seen the shock on her face, the betrayal. "I know," Ruthy had said as she lit one of Paula's cigarettes. She had quit during her second pregnancy. The dark children staring at Paula dumbly with Borzoo's eyes and syrup on their faces. "You think I don't understand. You think it's easy for me to tell you because I have a home and a husband."

Paula felt she had been slapped. But it was true. How

could Ruthy remember what it was like, if she had never
known? Ruthy had been the popular one in high school,
and right after graduation she had married. What did she
know about a woman alone? The things that happened to
them?

"Not all women are like you," she told Ruthy evenly.
They both knew what she meant. Paula wanted more from
life than squalling babies and scouring the brown ring
from toilet bowls for an ingrate husband who wasn't even
American.

"What did you ever see in him?" Paula asked. "He's
such a slug." It was a term from high school. "He's so shallow. And he walks all over you."

Should I tell her, Paula's mind darted, *about the shower at the
lake—*

But she knew that at some level Ruthy already knew. She
couldn't even claim that secret from her sister.

"What you're doing to Mom and Dad," Ruthy was sputtering, "it makes me *barf.* Holding that over their heads,
and him so sick. Both terrified of you that they'll do something wrong and you'll get depressed and go crazy and
swallow all your pills again, only not so many that you'll be
sure and do the job—"

She had raised her eyebrows tartly. *True?*

They were both screaming so that the babies started to
cry. Then Ruthy and Paula were crying, too. "It's not working out," Ruthy had said. She told Paula she could not
sleep under her roof, eat her food, and talk about her husband that way. "He's a good man. He really cares about me
and the children. Paula, you'll have to go back to Mom and
Dad."

"Cares." The word burned through Paula like atomic
acid.

Maybe the book would distract her, and it would certainly make her less hungry than the *Guide to Dining Out.*

CHAPTER ONE: THE CRYPT.

"I don't think of myself as vampire. I regard myself as 'incubo.' That is the old Latin for 'nightmare.' Literally, 'to lie upon.'"

Her eyes had dilated with interest and his voice was dusk. "Imagine a cathedral of experience . . . screams, breath and consciousness . . . all flying upward on wings of terror to the arched vault of awareness, the music of a thousand silver tongues flooding the mind and ears . . ."

She felt like a novitiate under his tutelage.

"What I introduce into the womb is not any ordinary semen in normal quantity, but abundant, very thick, very warm. Rich in spirits and free from serosity. I copulate with women of like constitution, taking care by any means that both shall enjoy a more than normal orgasm. For the greater the venereal excitement the more abundant is the semen—"

She felt something hot stirring drowsily in the pit of her stomach but resisted the temptation to pursue it.

"Here is my invitation: Become at once the natural object of sexual desire and the object of a desire hopelessly perverted by fantasies. Embody the fatal power of all illusions, inflaming and degrading desire without ever satisfying it."

She was starting to feel creepy and spooked from the night behind the window curtains and that shipwrecked crew on the sidewalk outside.

On her way to her purse for fifty milligrams of Valium she let the book fall between the bed and the wall where Bloodletter's yellow eyes, clouded with dust bunnies, wouldn't follow her around the room. Her lids got heavy; when she fell asleep near dawn, she had a bad dream.

She was at a lake and was wearing not her yellow one-piece, but a bikini that was far too small. Some boys who looked like foreign-exchange students were laughing and making fun of her, jabbering in a language she did not understand. Her breasts were too large. They were spilling out of her suit like Jell-O overflowing a mold, but she could not cover herself with her hands. She could have died.

12

Ice Cubes; Bruised Nipples

EVA AWAKENED WHEN SHE SWALLOWED THE FLY.
There had been a tickling on her lips, the faint prop
wash of iridescent wings. She could not move to brush it
away. She felt it exploring her slumberous mouth. It
crossed thick pink nodules of her tongue and she saw it in
her mind, gigantically bloated and obscene. There was a
symphonic buzz that filled her head in stereo as it took
flight in her mouth, collided with the pinkly arched vault
of her pallet. Then the involuntary insuck of air as it fluttered against her adenoids, sucked frenziedly to the back
of her throat, stuck on the alveolar folds as if in a Venus's-
flytrap. She swallowed thickly, felt it struggling, followed its
reflexive progress by involuntary contraction down her
neck.

The smell of mesquite in her nose. She was in Sedona,
Arizona. Six months at the drying-out clinic. The memory
was idyllic; there had been a Beatle and his wife under-
going detoxification. He winked when she passed him in

the hall whistling "Lucy in the Sky With Diamonds." After the divorce she had got stuck in the fast lane. *Coke. The cure. Purple sunsets and sweet smelling sage. Notes for a novel.* Her system steam-cleaned, she felt as if she had really got in touch with herself and met some real people. She had even admitted halfway through the therapy, *I am one of the phonies.*

No, I'm not in Sedona.

Her head rang.

She was naked. She slowly unfolded to life. The sun was burning hot on her reddening shoulders. She was hardly able to groan. Her eyes split through their crust. There was the dart of a thistle in her breast and it hurt to move. She raised herself to her knees and fell heavily onto her back. Overhead loomed the giant letters HOLLYWOOD in foreshortened perspective, triangulated up into the clear birdless sky. Peg Entwistle and all that. She was covered with leaves and debris as if a dog had tried to bury her. She felt as if she had been through a collegiate hazing.

Below her the freeway coursed noiselessly. A billboard.

THIS SUMMER: STEPHEN ALBRIGHT'S
BLOODLETTER

"Summer" had been crossed out. *Like my last three years. What day is this? It's got to be Tuesday.*

Something moved in the brush, a prairie dog scuttering into a dusty hole. Suddenly the terror was completely awake, too. She scrabbled backward, cradled her arms, shivering, around her knees.

The dump site.

She shuddered. These hillsides were where the bodies had been found. She remembered something Stephen had said. "I'm almost enchanted by this maniac's sensitivity to the iconography of Hollywood. Did you know the nude bodies have all been found within sight of the HOLLY-WOOD sign in the hills?''

She crawled sobbing down the embankment along an animal trail, then followed the jogging path to the first houses on Observatory Drive. Her feet were bleeding, and when the pickup stopped she kept walking. He spoke to her in Spanish. He looked young, maybe sixteen. The old truck was full of rakes and lawnmowers. He put the greasy sweatshirt over her trembling shoulders. Mercifully, it was a long fit. She nodded insensibly, her hair in her face as he zipped it. He had driven her a few blocks toward the Hollywood police substation when she stopped him at the suddenly familiar corner of Rogerton and Edgerwood.

She got out. He looked at her as if she were crazy. The truck disappeared, clattering up the street. *You can't go to the police.* That was what the wry eyes of the boy in the truck had been saying to her. *I don't know who you are, lady. But you fucked up Big Time. Had a date not quite like you bargained for, huh? What'd you do? Tease the wrong guy? Your age you ought to know better. A psychologist? They're always the most fucked-up people. A patient? I didn't think you were s'posed to do that. What were you doing in a motel room? Albright? The wacko writer dude? Get a clue, lady . . .*

Breathing rapidly, she followed the familiar sidewalk, leaving red footprints on the concrete from the blood that squished between her toes. She saw them and ran on the grass up the cul-de-sac and through the pool entrance of the gate. The lock had never worked. She stood on the patio of Tony's secluded condo. *Our condo.*

Catch my breath. It had changed. In her absence he had finally imposed his taste for shadows and occluding shrubbery. She knew he was gone, just as she knew she would find the two keys where they were hidden in a niche in the mortar between two bricks of the wall shielding the lanai.

The first unlocked the security system, the second, the sliding door.

It was comfortably dark. She did not feel like a trespasser. *He would have invited me in.* On the surface, the divorce had all been an adult arrangement and not at all acrimonious. She had received financial equity while he had kept the condo.

She entered the bedroom off the patio. That was as far as she got. She slid, shattered, to the floor and finally started to tremble uncontrollably. She was getting a new take on the night before.

How could I be so stupid? I'm a doctor. I should have recognized his instability. Christ, he's only tried to kill himself. He probably thinks he's killed me. She saw herself before a review board. *This could be very high-profile. There goes the license. This could be very ugly. What did they call therapists who had sex with their patients? "Cripple rapists"? What've I done to him?*

She tried to cry but the tears would not come. She put her head between her knees and inhaled deeply. She looked around. She had not been to the home in a year—and not to this, the bedroom, in four years—since the divorce. The emperor-sized water bed brought recollections, like the Miles Davis Tony liked to have playing softly over his sound system during what he called their sexual "bouts." She noted that all traces of her own existence in his life had been succinctly eradicated. The bedroom was gloomy and still smelled of his aftershave.

There had been little emotion to Tony from the beginning, but she had been young and overwhelmed by his charm and his own high opinion of himself. He had admitted at the end that he'd never expected it to last more than seven years, when it would be time for a change for both of them. She hadn't known, either, that he'd never intended to have children.

Something small brushed her ankles, startling her. The

Siamese. She had remembered it as a kitten. It purred warmly, the aristocratic eyes only slightly irritated at her return. It must have come inside through the pet port. Her heart began to quicken. Who was feeding her? Then she recalled Tony's dictum. The cat must fend for itself on the sparrows and the rodents that lived in the dense ivy. He couldn't stand dogs, but admired the independence of cats, especially the aloof disdain of the Siamese. He had not wanted to interfere with its natural predatory instincts. In fact, he'd cultivated the cat's prowess, always patiently admiring the splayed feathers and shattered wings she deposited for his approval on the rough straw mat by the manicured potted bonsai near the door, waiting for the gentle chin strokes that were the invariable reward.

There it was. The telephone. A princess, strangely effeminate in Tony's decor, which was calculated to project a ruggedly masculine image to the female graduate students. In the mirror she saw the passion bites on her breasts. Her office was probably in chaos right now. She had no clothes; she did not want to call Tisha so much as she wished she *could*. But Eva felt off-balance and unsafe. Because suddenly she was not sure who she really was and she was afraid to move until she knew. What had happened to her had recast her whole reality.

She knew that if she tried to stand, she'd be dizzy. Say she made the telephone call. What would be her story? She could see the story. *Vampire Writer Bites "Psychiatrist to the Stars" on Neck. Love Bites Tell Story of Motel Tryst Gone Awry.* Or this one: *Reclusive Author Commits Suicide on Eve of Testimony in "Love Bite" Case.*

She braced herself but her haggard face was still ghastly in the bathroom mirror. What she had not expected was so much dried blood on her neck. It was as if her throat had been cut and there were the smeared impressions of his mouth. *Oh my God.* She watched goose bumps crawl up the reflection of her naked stomach. She had to sit down on the toilet seat. She was still trembling.

Get a grip. Think, Eva.

The first thing was damage control. Stephen Albright: he'd had a psychotic episode. He was not a bad man, just a very sick one. *And today he probably thinks he's committed a murder.* What if he didn't remember anything? What if he was a multiple personality? How terrifying it must be to wake up with blood on your hands and not know where it came from. The episode had been as traumatic for him as for her. *Wherever he is, he's probably feeling remorse and disgust. Depression. He could easily kill himself. His world's come apart, too.*

Suicide Note Tells Tale of Motel Blood Orgy with Sexy Sex Therapist. Investigation Continues . . .

She would have to locate Albright and talk to him before he put a gun to his heart again. She had no idea where he might be, and there was no one she could trust to help her with any of this. There was no getting around talking to DeMarco. His client should be committed, voluntarily or involuntarily, immediately. The next twenty-four hours would be critical. He needed to be under suicide watch.

And even then, the intake counselors would try to extract the story from him. Maybe DeMarco had clout, pull. Juice. To keep it quiet. The agent would go to extraordinary—

She paused.

Perhaps it was DeMarco who had dumped her body on the hillside in imitation of the Diver Dan victims, just to avoid a scandal involving his author. DeMarco. The fixer. A panicked call from his psycho client. Leaves me for dead in Griffith Park to get his wonder boy out of a jam.

Or maybe it's no imitation. Maybe Stephen is Diver Dan.

Brace yourself: you know what has to be done. You're going to unplug your feelings and put on your rational head. You wish you could get yourself together, but time is an element. Albright needs to know he's not a murderer before he grabs a gun and it all spins out of control. *DeMarco. With any luck, in the next few minutes I'll be talking to a man who's just dragged me out of the trunk of his Cadillac and into a shallow grave, probably raking leaves over it with the toe of his Italian loafer . . .*

She dialed the agency. "Do interrupt him. Just tell him it's Eva—tell him she wants to talk to him about Diver Dan."

It was enough to get magical results. Suddenly the agent was on the phone, in only the time it took to lock his office door. He was wary and took some time confirming she was who she said, all of which confirmed her suspicions. Like the relief in his voice.

"Eva, darling. Where the hell are you? I tried to call your office— What the *fuck* have we done, you naughty girl?"

His words were still a shock; she was angry at herself because she was not nearly as steeled as she thought. She knew her voice was hurt and frightened and she despised herself; she wanted it to be all rage and indignation.

"I'll bet you tried to call. What have *I* done?"

"Yeah. Congratulations. If you intentionally set out to destroy that young man, you couldn't have done a better job. You know what kinda shape he was in. He's not a worldly guy. There's nothing casual about him. He's a regular Humpty Dumpty and I don't know if all the king's men can put him back together, this time. You've really done it."

She controlled her voice. "I see. What is *your* version of the events of last night?"

"Nothing happened, that's my version."

The suggestion stunned her. The agent wasn't about to admit to anything. She seethed.

He snorted with disgust. "To think you'd take him to

some cheap motel. He's like a little kid, real impressionable. I thought he was safe with you.''

She felt her face burning but took the offensive.

"Stephen Albright is Diver Dan and you've been protecting him. You've been helping him. And then you drove over to clean things up. You thought I wasn't breathing and you took me out of that place and dumped me off a riding trail . . .''

"Bullshit. What the fuck? You know you're talking to an attorney, lady? Yeah, I passed the bar in Montana. He's got airtight alibis for all those Dan deals.''

"May I guess who?''

"So what? Try me. I did nothin'—if we decide *anything* happened last night.''

It did seem farfetched and bizarre that the agent would be a participant in a *folie à deux*. His interest was all about keeping his client out of trouble. Maybe she could appeal to his aversion to scandal. She tried to say it reasonably.

"He is seriously mentally ill and last night he had a full-blown psychotic episode. I've got to talk to him because he's got to know I'm alive.''

"Oh, don't worry, I'll tell him. But talk to him? You? More therapy? Congratulations, like I say. You're one more in that long line who can boast they've fucked over Phil DeMarco. And I'm always the bad guy. I don't believe it. But you know, Eva. They only do it to me once, and I cut 'em off. That's it.''

"Let me speak to him. You don't know what you're doing.''

DeMarco was sarcastic. "Sure, I'm the crazy one. I got a crazy writer. I got him a crazy doctor. Now I'm going crazy. Don't get tough with me, ballsy lady. Don't pull de-macho on DeMarco, I been bluffed by real experts and you're outclassed. This is a fucking joke and the laugh's on me and Stephen. But we can take it from here.''

"Stephen—"

His voice infuriating as he became soothing, trying to calm a hysterical female.

"Eva, I know this hasn't been easy for you. I'm really glad you're okay. Why don't you write yourself a prescription and take some time off? We'll all chalk this one up to experience. We all got careers and if this gets out of hand nobody's gonna smell like a rose. That's the question, Eva."

"He's in a lot of danger. He needs immediate professional attention."

"Did I say he wasn't going to get it? Not your kind, maybe. Don't think I don't know what this guy needs. We been here before, that's what you can't understand—"

"You're admitting this has happened before?"

He suddenly seemed beaten down. "Uh . . . just in certain situations. Just with women in certain situations. But never anything like this. I'm telling you the truth."

"And you didn't *tell* me? I suppose that was something else he was 'touchy' about?" Her voice was incredulous.

"DeMarco doesn't lead with the chin. You were the fucking psychiatrist, the egghead professional. You were supposed to tell me, you were supposed to make him bet— Where the hell are you calling from? These phones aren't—"

"My ex-husband's condo near Rogerton and Edgerwood. Will you bring Stephen here?"

"Your ex-husband knows about this? Is he upset?"

"He's out of the country. No one would have to know."

He was lowering his voice, probably not wanting his words to be heard through the door. "There's nothing you can do for him that I'm not doing. I got him under watch twenty-four hours a day. He's in seclusion. Nothing happened. That's my story, and if there's a brain in that head of yours, it'll be *your* story."

He continued trying to mollify her.

"Eva, no one's gladder than me that you're still breathing. But you and I've got nothing to talk about. This conversation ain't happening. You and me never heard of each other. That's the bottom line. Okay? You let me down, Eva. Let Stephen down. Just send me the invoice."

The phone went dead in her hand.

Eva did feel some relief. Albright's agent was containing it; he probably did have things under control. And it was doubtful Stephen was Diver Dan. After all, he hadn't actually killed her. Nor had she been seriously mutilated. And it was not incredible that because of all the pressure he'd been under, and his fixation with the maniac, that his delusional psychosis would find an imitative expression. She was after all a psychiatrist, and DeMarco's protestations had the ring of truth.

The hardest thing to admit was that he was probably right when he advised her to chalk it up to experience.

Eva lay curled up under a blanket on the rolling water bed in the dark bedroom. The weakness resulting from the evacuation of her blood had left her with a strange, warm vulnerability—almost a cuddlesomeness. For the first time in the last few hours, she could afford to give some attention to the inner Eva and what had happened to her.

Everything was unreal. Yesterday had been another life. She realized that she felt closer to Albright—they were linked by the trauma they had shared. Her drowsing mind finally landed on what she'd been evading and repressing: her own disturbing reaction to the violence of the night before. Maybe that was why she was stuck in this paralyzing inertia.

For some reason she thought of Scotty and his inability to have relations with her during her period. Then she recognized the association: the blood business in the motel room. What she hadn't recognized about Albright, among so many other things, was that there was apparently a well-developed subsystem to his personality. He called it The Bloodletter; certain emotional detonators would set it off and he would act out. It was a dissociative reaction, a protective mechanism, which at crucial times of stress could apparently overwhelm him.

My blood is inside him, she thought. There had been a scene in one of his novels, a female vampire inside a confessional, recounting to the horrified but sexually aroused young priest on the other side of the curtain her sensual addiction to The Bloodletter.

"I have drunk his blood," she said.

It was strange, out loud. An unspeakable admission. The most profound intimacy.

"Father, forgive me, for I have sinned. I believe he drank my blood. My blood inside him. More intimate than . . ."

She mixed a Bloody Mary and drank it languorously. She fished out an ice cube and rubbed it on her bruised nipples beneath the open bathrobe. It brought her back reluctantly to the erotic edge she'd experienced the night before, and she didn't feel strong enough to deal with it. She felt unclean and went into the bathroom.

The shower was good; she was one throbbing bruise. *Degraded? Debased?* All that, but something else she couldn't avoid: she was strangely in touch with her body for the first time in years. Last night had flushed away the inhibiting corrosion that had crusted over her terminals of sensation. She had worn her rational head for so long she'd become unable to find her emotions when she wanted them. Now she was reminded she was an organism, too. There was an animal part to her and Albright had awakened it.

She couldn't deny that her brain was now definitely connected to a body. She pinched her breast and the pain banished the physical flatness of devastated nerves. In the sanctuary of the shower stall she found herself trying to recall the taste of fear and its livid colors. A little disappointed that already piquancy was wearing off like the effects of a not altogether unpleasant drug. All other experience was now inferior.

Stephen. What have you done to me?

13

Eager Beaver

IT HAD BEEN A ROUGH LAST TWENTY-FOUR HOURS for Number Six. Something about a party at a mansion in the Hills. Something about a part in a picture, and something about a hot tub. Something about passing out, and something about waking up in the trunk of a car.

And something about Stephen Albright. Ah, yes. And now she was naked in a a salon-style cosmetician's chair, her hands bound behind her back with a tight nylon cord. She was in squalid room redolent of vampires. Spread across the floor were dozens of Albright paperbacks with their spines broken and passages scored with yellow Hi-Liter.

"You're a fan?" she said in an attempt to start a conversation. It was difficult to sound casual when you were trussed up. She had come to hours ago to find her captor drawing a happy face on her nude body. Her nipples were the goggle eyes and her navel the nose. Her healed caesarean seam was darkened to a smile.

He had not answered, but lowered the adjustable chair.

He commenced to shampoo and condition her hair with tender fingers. Conditioner was then applied. That her scalp felt fresh and tingly was not much consolation. She was nineteen years old and had been in a lot of situations in her short life, but she knew this was the most serious. She had figured out in whose clutches she had fallen.

She knew she was in a small apartment but had no idea where it was. The small television was tuned to the home shopping channel, and the most frightening thing about the room was what sat in the rocker before that TV.

Number Six thought of it immediately as "The Wire Mother." This was on account of something she had read long ago about a behavioral experiment in which monkeys were taken from their mothers and deprived of nurturing. Instead, they were supplied with a thing made of wire. Number Six could not recall the effect it had on the young monkeys—but arranged in the rocker in an old dress with floral print was a thing shaped with black twisted wire. A blond wig was atop the head, and two blue artificial eyes were mounted beneath them. All seemed arranged around the open, yellow dentures that were locked in a gape at the shopping channel.

Sometimes the man would brush against the chair on his way to and from other rooms, and the figure would rock in an eerie semblance of relaxation.

She knew she was to be Number Six because he had written it across her upper chest when he had taken the "before" photos—written it right above the emerald tattoo of a hummingbird. Then he had raised the chair, done her hair and dried it with a blower. She had been blinded momentarily by the drops and wondered whether they were acid—

But it was Visine. To get rid of that redness, apparently. Because what had followed was two hours of glamour shots. She had been posed with a feather boa, which effectively hid the binding which cut into her wrists behind her back. He painstakingly posed her in a variety of boas and hats; she wondered whether they had once belonged to his mother. There was an agonizing choice of necklace. Then followed the bizarre ordeal of the glamour shots. At least the elaborate operations had given her time to think and to study him.

The figure might have been comic had she not been so absolutely in his control.

"What happens now?"

He did not answer.

She was determined not to be like the others. She was smarter and would prove it—not educated smart, but street smart. She read *Real Detective*. She knew about serial killers and what you should do to stay alive with one. Don't make him angry and try to keep him talking. Tell him your name and show him wallet photos. He will try to depersonalize you—try and let him know you're not an object, but a *human being*.

She wondered whether that was why he had not spoken to her. She had begun to wonder whether he *could* speak.

Dan was in a special mode as he bustled about—the *Interactive* Dan. The *people* person. He winced at the recently applied Deep Heat that burned his rectum as he put away the photographic equipment.

"Do you like Disneyland?" she asked. She had noticed he had a minor collection of Disneyana—watches and ties and piggy banks.

"What are you?" she asked in frustration. "Why do you do this? You must be very lonely."

Dan knew she believed she was touching something deep in his core—the emotional equivalent of a paprika enema.

Dan knew that this relationship was coming to an end. Each encounter had its own poignance like a ballet. Bits of theater. They were vignettes of life compressed and accelerated. You received all the satisfactions of a normal relationship in the course of a few hours, consummated by the intimacy of the Death Moment. He was becoming bored with her, and irritated as any old husband who had been married fifty years.

"Dan?" she said hoarsely. "Should I call you 'Dan'? Do you like that? Why do you do this, Dan?"

Dan's face clouded. Then he began to gesticulate dramatically.

"What are you trying to tell me?"

He held up a finger apologetically, he retreated momentarily into what she assumed was the bathroom. He returned in an outfit of tight, black spandex shiny as snakeskin. He was pulling on white gloves. Apparently the outfit gave him more range of movement. He began to mime the cradling of a—

"A baby?" she guessed. "A baby!"

He smiled delightedly and pressed one of the white-gloved fingers to a nostril. *On the nose.*

"Something happened to you when you were a child?" she asked.

He nodded energetically.

"Something terrible must have happened to you, that you have to do this to people," she said thoughtfully and, she hoped, compassionately.

He shrugged doubtfully.

Then he was on all fours, protruding his front teeth as he groveled on the floor.

"An animal," she breathed. "You're some kind of animal?"

She ran through a litany that lasted a quarter hour. He rutted and chewed on the table leg—this animal was involved in some activity. Finally he came closer to tentatively nuzzle her pubic area.

He saw the revulsion in her eyes and shook his head significantly. *No, it's not a pussy.*

"A beaver," she said disgustedly as she averted her eyes. From the corner of her eye she could see him nodding happily in the affirmative.

He had produced an electric razor, which he held up for her inspection.

The Sterling Eager Beaver.

He began to shave all the stubble from her legs; it seemed to offend him especially.

He was trying desperately to indicate another animal. He even put on hand puppets and began an elaborate allegory—

"I can't play anymore," she said wearily.

His face was crestfallen as he philosophically discarded the hand puppets.

He held up a fair-sized box for her inspection. It seemed to contain some sort of gardening implement.

The Lawn Weasel.

With his gloved hand he indicated the features as if he was a game-show host.

Electric Blower Vac
Motor 9 amps 120 volts AC
150 mph air velocity

One feature seemed especially significant to him:

Mulches As It Vacuums!

Dan knew the technological aspects were beyond her. Like the two High Impact Blower Tubes and 30 degree Concentration Nozzle. The whole thing weighed just under nine pounds.

He removed the wicked-looking thing from the box and

turned it near her ear; it sounded like an airliner taking off as it pulled at her hair. She squeezed her eyes shut. She felt its hot frantic breath moving down her body, pausing here and there to suck at her skin like a ravenous mouth. When she opened her eyes, she was covered by red and round sucker marks, as if she had been in the grasp of a giant octopus. It seemed to have some significance to her captor that she could not fathom.

In his own mind, Dan was in the Octopus Garden. He was in a vast marine cemetery of coral bones. There had been a time in his growing up when he had loved to spend hours stationed beneath an escalator at the nearby shopping mall, enjoying the vantage as he looked up women's dresses. More than once he had to be escorted from women's clothing stores where he had stationed himself near the curtained dressing room with a handful of packages as if waiting for his mom to finish trying something on. Since his release from the hospital, he had discovered SlimWays. SlimWays was the best. He identified it with vampires—perhaps because of the commercials on his favorite, *Chiller Theater*. That was where he had been introduced to Number Six.

He had been stationed on the sidewalk near dusk looking into the Venus DeMarco's Slim Ways window; anonymous humanity flowed indifferently past him. Dan felt eyes upon his back and tried to brush them off—actually took the small whisk broom from his pocket and brushed them off. He was entranced by the female figures working out on the shiny chrome exercise machines, which seemed so resonant of pain and exertion. They were beautiful specimens, flawed only by the circumstance that they were still alive. These women were works of art awaiting a master's hand to achieve perfection.

The hand on Dan's shoulder startled him, and he turned. Turned to face the vampire. Dan looked up and up, into that dark face in which the eyes burned electrically. In the hypnotic shadows of those eyes he could see the willowing of the drowned women in the octopuses' garden. He felt weak.

"Care to go inside?" The Bloodletter asked. "Take a look up close?"

Dan nodded.

"Then let's go," the vampire said as he held the door open for Dan. "DeMarco is a clown, but he *could* have his uses—"

And then the vampire had unfolded a plan for the Dawn of the Undead. A chain of figure salons through the state—*the fuckin' country!* A proliferating string of gyms, and each a nest of vampires. *You could even advertise. Have membership drives. All those creatures dissatisfied with their bodies, searching for that skeletal look. Wanting to be objects of desire. How to keep that fat off? A liquid diet. Strictly high protein. You'll have more energy. You'll become a new person—share it with your friends!*

Dan looked into the dozens of mirrors and realized with a start that it was not only The Bloodletter who cast no reflection. He could not see himself. *Yet that's happened different times all your life.* But there was more. Half the women working at the gleaming, pumping machines cast no reflections.

"That's right," The Bloodletter said. "Many of these are already in *The Life.*"

"I'll be goddamn."

Number Six was an instructor, a pert and enthusiastic girl with no body fat and oh so vivacious and bouncy in that aerobics outfit, which displayed to advantage the tattoo above her left breast. Dan could hear the beat of its wings as if his ear was to that breast. The Bloodletter explained that fat-trimmer at a gym was not her goal in life; she was a Hollywood hopeful. In fact she had tested for *The Movie.*

"Here's her test," the vampire said as he handed Dan the cassette tape. "Give it a spin at home—see what you think."

"You'll get back to me?" Dan asked.

The vampire smiled and his mouth was full of white razors. "Don't I always?"

Then The Bloodletter disappeared, and Dan found himself suddenly visible. He was escorted roughly out by two well-muscled ruffians in DeMarco sweatshirts. More than insensitive, they were *un-Christlike*, they were—

"Would you like to look at some photos in my wallet?" Number Six interrupted.

Dan smiled at a better idea—he took a cassette from atop the television and put it in the VCR, situating the wire mother in the rocking chair so she could have a closer look. Number Six gasped. It was her screen test for the movie. There she was in living color as Thanata, trying to look virginal and frightened at the same time. It was the asphyxiation sequence, and she was tied to a post atop the HOLLYWOOD sign. The blades of the wind machine tossed her hair, and The Bloodletter kissed her neck preparatory to wrapping his cloak around her half-naked body.

Then Stephen Albright himself interrupted the action to show the vampire actor how to tie a proper knot so a woman would be at your mercy.

Not bad, huh? Number Six's eyes asked Dan with enthusiasm.

He made a so-so gesture with his free hand while he fast-forwarded the cassette.

The next segment took place in an office environment—an odd screen test.

"That last visit . . . They have this beautiful home in the Palisades. Ruthy steps out the front door onto the manicured walk while I park in the drive. A three-year-old on one hip and an eighteen-month-old on the other—"

But Dan was entranced. *Big tits. Perched upon one of them, a hummingbird. Billows of red hair.* He had watched it again and again, watched her ass as she stood and paced nervously. It seemed she had looked right at him in recognition through the TV, and it was all he could do not to make a bleating noise. Then she was looking through him as if he was invisible. That pissed him off. He was suddenly having a mood swing.

"Who's she?" Number Six asked irritably.

He indicated with his fingers.

"Seven?" she asked. "Number Seven?"

He took the cassette from the VCR and turned his mother to the wall. Something malignant crossed his face. Number Six knew she was in trouble.

"We never did get to look at those wallet photos," she said weakly.

Dan was applying epoxy glue between her fingers. He used an egg timer to clock the time it took to set.

"What are you doing?" she asked.

He loosened the bindings, but her hope was short-lived. He was handcuffing her hands in front of her. He retied her to the chair with the nylon cord around her waist. He raised the chair a few more degrees so she was sitting absolutely straight.

"You must be very lonely, living like this," she said. "I'd like to be your friend. Would you like me for a friend?"

He had walked quickly into the bathroom; through the open door she could see him scrubbing up with Phisohex, then snapping on rubber surgical gloves.

"You self-centered sonofabitch," she said to him.

Dan lowered a screen on the wall behind her, then took his place behind an object on a pushcart. He snapped a switch and she was blinded by the light from an overhead opaque projector.

Number Six twisted her head to protect her eyes. When

she squinted painfully, his face was only a dark shadow in a corona next to the light. She looked down at her body and saw superimposed on her breasts and the rolls of her heaving stomach some sort of anatomical diagram or schematic. It was as if heart and lungs and kidneys were stitched in her flesh by the hot, harsh light.

He approached with a felt pen, hushing her to stillness with a finger before his lips. With the ticklish tip of the pen he began to make dotted lines along the superimposed images on her flesh.

"I don't deserve this," she said with mixed rage and terror. "I'm a human being."

"No you're not," he said sharply.

Dan approached her. He had a scalpel in his surgically gloved hand.

"You're a pomegranate."

Her expression was quizzical.

"That's right," he said. "A pomegranate. Or a banana."

An occasionally heart-wrenching, but presently unwieldy, envelope of blood and viscera.

"You're an unbruised fruit which has to be peeled to be enjoyed. And then"—he indicated the Lawn Weasel—"an adventure in primitive liposuction. We'll 'chew the fat,' as it were, with an Electric Blower Vac."

Her tears had started up; the relationship had come full circle. "I don't deserve this," she gasped.

He paused. "I'm sure that you're a beautiful person — *inside.*"

The scalpel glinted in the light from the opaque projector. "The problem is to *get there.*"

14

Ghoul Girl

HOW DO YOU KNOW WHETHER YOU'RE TURNING INTO A vampire? That's a question I never thought I'd ask myself, Eva thought.

Wednesday afternoon, and for the last twenty-four hours Eva had watched herself do strange things. She lay down on the couch, lighting and smoking relaxedly one of Tony's Turkish cigarettes. She unwrapped one of the imported toffees in the coffee table dish with one hand. She sucked hungrily at the candy. It was infantilism, regression to the oral stage, the need to be chewing, to bite and suck. She did feel like a baby.

It was now Wednesday, and she was still waiting for the anxiety to kick in—except it didn't come. She was feeling safely hidden in the dark condo. For the first time in years no one had any expectations of her. She knew she ought to call the practice and tell Tisha she was all right. The girl had already no doubt dialed her at home and probably called the police. Oh, Jesus. *And the bruises on my neck? The monkey bites?*

She said to herself: Eva LaPorte is on a little vacation. She's on emergency leave from herself. Want a practical reason? She's waiting for her bruises to go away. Eva always has to have her shit tight together to greet the faces that she meets, and right now she's a little unstrung. She's crashed and burned and it didn't happen in one night; it's been coming on for years but she couldn't see it. She needs her space right now, she deserves it. She's got to take a little personality inventory before she restocks her emotional shelf.

Eva: you're obsessive-compulsive. It's helped you accomplish things and set goals and see them through. But there was chaos inside you. You've been an unfulfilled woman for years. When you were seeing Beverly in Santa Barbara, she told you, "You're not Superwoman. Take some time for Eva. Do something nice for the little girl in you." Then you stopped seeing her because the drive was too far and you were so busy.

These weren't new insights, but she'd never actually stopped and internalized her awareness because life was such a blur. Eva LaPorte had been the moving target, afraid to stand still because she might catch up with herself and feel the fear and fall into depression and grief. *Baby, now you're here. You've got to feel it and go through it.*

The denial and protective mechanisms made the next admission a hard one.

Eva: you fell in love with Stephen Albright. You met someone who was sensitive and original and was bored with himself and interested in you. It doesn't mean you were stupid. Yes, he's troubled and unstable. But the other faces you saw were real, too. He's a driven personality who's pushed himself too hard too long and now can't get back. But you understand that, don't you? You're two peas in a pod and you instinctively knew that. Two unhappy people who saw something in each other. Interlocking neuroses.

She wished the world would go away, all the pressures

and stresses that had come between them and distorted who they really were. Were there conditions to her love? Was it love if there were conditions?

She closed her eyes and felt herself doing a little unconscious myth-analysis on herself. She was glad no one could know it was the first time she'd ever really tried it. The spontaneous imagery that arose involved two Stephen Albrights. One was the one she knew and the other was a vampire. They were locked in struggle, not only over his soul, but over her.

How do you know if you're turning into a vampire?

According to Albright's novels, there were phases. First was a glow phase, which began as a prolonged fantasy. The newly infected often lingered intoxicated in this condition. They were the unambitious morgue rats, the street children who came out at night and lurked in alleys—the lowest form of vampire. They fed on carrion and leavings and were stuck in the loo until they marshaled the courage to graduate to the next stage. What was that?

All passions require victims, Albright taught. The prospects must prove their worth by taking a life. The voice of their infector in their blood would guide them—sponsor them, so to speak.

Once an object of desire is selected, time seems to slow down. Sounds and colors become more vivid, odors more intense, the flesh sensitive to the slightest pressure. Everything is bathed in strange sensation. One enters a portal between two realities. On the one side is the everyday world, and on the other the vampire's.

The last step? Killing. It was a rite of passage, a translation into a different mode of being. A quasar of experience. Then you'd really earned your stripes. There was the brief discomfort of wasting away and then physical death, but it was only a prelude to glorious awakening as an immortal.

Baloney, Eva thought, as she tossed the paperback onto the floor from where she lolled on her ex-husband's waterbed in his dark condo.

But her face was beginning to look unfamiliar in Tony's mirror. The skin seemed stretched tighter so that her eyes were larger and the teeth behind her lips more prominent. The wounds on her neck had not healed; if anything, they were more angry and swollen. She felt listless all day, and when she parted the curtains to look outside the sunlight almost made her nauseated. *Or is it just the prospect of resuming my life?* The thought was a sour glaze on her tongue.

The condo suddenly seemed so large; she was aware of the dark halls and the moaning mouths of doors. The clock in the far bedroom chimed and the haunting notes hung suspended in the air.

You've got to eat, girl, she had told herself. Half a canned ham sandwich and her throat and nose were flooded with revulsion. It was as if *everything* inside her was suddenly expelled. She was surprised at how natural the violence in her body seemed, and she coolly relaxed her throat so the retching would not tear it. The goddamn bulimia was returning. *I hope. Because I think the office medical plan excludes vampirism.* Her laugh was unnatural.

She felt she was splitting in half. One part was concerned about responsibilities—caseload and accounts receivable—the other side tantalized with infinite possibilities. *You've come to live too earthbound, shackled by inhibition and, yes, materialism. You've become one of the hollow women. To show up at the office tomorrow would be such a treason to your feelings. Your life is strangling you and you haven't even known it. Until now.*

For the first time she turned on the television, to decompress herself for reentry into the world of reality. *Top of the hour,* the pert Japanese news girl called it, her mouth a red jellyfish swimming in an immobile face, opening and contracting around brittle white teeth. Eva's own face looked back at her insipidly from the screen. Eva heard the report that her own office had been broken into and trashed. *Why?* It hit her: *DeMarco wants any files and notes I have on Stephen. Covering his tracks.* Small wonder he had seemed so confident on the phone.

Then there was footage of her BMW with the trunk open as cops rummaged through it. No longer psychiatrist, but *missing psychiatrist.*

So many people were missing in Hollywood. It was the mecca of the dispossessed. Runaway children from Nebraska and all points north and east streamed here. What black hole did they disappear into? Drugs. Prostitution. Pornography. Weepy mothers and distraught fathers made inquiries to police, tacked up posters on walls and phone poles. REWARD. They made tearful inquiries at teen crisis centers where born-again counselors consoled them with donuts and Christ and coffee, rifling through Rolodex registries of lost souls who had surfaced briefly before being sucked under.

Diver Dan Claims Sixth. The body had been mutilated beyond recognition. The police chief at a news conference announcing the formation of a task force. It was the news girl who had asked him about the rumor the unidentified body might turn out to be the missing psychiatrist-author. The chief refused to speculate, and the question seemed just to hang in the air. Eva had the uncanny feeling she had just watched her own obituary. The confusion did have its flattering aspect: they had all been so young, the victims. Nineteen or twenty.

She pictured the poor lifeless thing on a chromium slab at the coroner's. *I'm depriving another woman of her identity, even if she is a corpse. I'm taking advantage of her. Her poor parents. I've got to clear this up.* But surely it could be resolved without her. Blood typing. Dental records. Depending on the extent of the mutilations. *Surely the police would not entertain seriously or for very long the idea that it's me.* The victims seemed all to have been little street types. She recognized her own suppressed snobbery.

But it was a bizarre opportunity. She had died, in a sense. That death offered the possibility of reemergence in a new form, release from a life emotionally, artistically and sexually confusing. All she knew was that somehow the world was alive again, full of wonder and terror.

I'm afraid. Afraid and exhilarated. Afraid of going forward. Afraid of going backward.

Darkness breathed cool through the curtain of the open window. Shadows dripped surreally up the walls from the floor. She lay on her side on the couch and hugged a cushion. She drew her legs up but still felt something invasive but invisible between them; her body was having its own memories.

Mentally, she conjured the writer out of those shadows so that he sat across from her as he had in her office. Beside him was a large casket of dull bronze; a pale sinuous hand hung out from the lid. Albright's hand was handcuffed to the vampire's wrist so that he could only worry his long black hair back from his pale forehead with his left hand. His beautiful eyes were tortured as he tried to explain. "Eva, can you forgive me? My fear was just too crucifying. Of a relationship. Of myself. I never got that close before, I didn't have the emotional vocabulary. It was all I could do."

She answered him out loud.

"I understand. Stephen, you're conflicted. That's why the novels, you're telling your own story again and again. There's Cesare, the sensitive feeling artist who doubts himself and his gifts. And The Bloodletter, who is dominating and strong, the hyperpotent male figure . . . what you think a man has to be. It's all your own quest, this imaginative groping. You're seeking a woman commensurate to your vision. The one you can love, the one who can understand and transform your lonely life. I believe in you . . ."

The temperature had dropped a few degrees and Eva's arms felt cold; the back of her neck was brushed by the lips of her own imaginings, and she shivered. Tisha was suddenly in the room with her adenoidal voice like a fly buzzing against a pane.

"Eva: get a clue. How far are you willing to go for this guy? Are you willing to go crazy? He thinks he *is* a vampire. I mean, how many guys take you out and then strangle you and drink your blood? Sometimes you gotta meet a guy halfway, but in this case? I mean, a few minutes ago you were seriously asking yourself if you were becoming a vampire."

She shook her head to banish all the voices and visions. She was alone in the room again. It was night and she was coming alive. There was a quickening in her blood and even a voice. She wanted to think it was the writer calling to her, telling her to come to him.

But where are you, Stephen?

The night was suddenly a shimmering song calling to her.

The cash she had found in Tony's jewelry box with the car keys—over a thousand dollars. She would pay him back, later. The sweatsuit she had found gift-wrapped in a closet. Undoubtedly a present for a lady friend. *He likes them young.* She dabbed rouge on her neck wounds. An experiment.

She went into the garage. The electric door yawned darkly, noiselessly. The Cadillac growled obediently and crept down the street, headlights extinguished for a cautious distance. The rain had stopped, but the sidewalks glistened with moisture.

Las Palmas. Hollywood and Vine. The neon of X-rated theater marquees cold and dark. She was taking a detour, as if the car were turning of its own volition. Subtle snobbery had enforced avoidance of Hollywood Boulevard the last few years. Large murals of Gable and Monroe. First stop: Ghoul Girl, which happened to be all that was open. An all-night sidewalk sale on Hollywood Boulevard. She walked unseen through the tattooed bikers and leather-punks who massed at the glass counters displaying the silver death's-head earrings and drug paraphernalia.

Black skirt, so short. Heels. The heavy cable-knit black sweater. Disguise was what she was after and she regarded the unfamiliar clothes in the dressing room. They weren't her, but surprisingly flattering. Knocked a few years off. Five? Ten? She looked at her legs, the scooped neck of the skimpy blouse. Black purse, belt chain, the choker to cover the throat. Bought several other outfits and accessories as if she were on a binge. She applied the red enamel nails she'd bought at the drugstore and liked the effect. *Tisha wouldn't recognize me. My mother wouldn't recognize me.*

It was not Eva LaPorte who walked the sidewalk in the night after depositing her packages in the car. That Eva had been discarded like a snakeskin with the sweats in the dressing room.

There was a rush of feeling to her new emergence, and all her perceptions seemed sexualized. The long thighs of the prostitutes whispered above clicking icepick heels. The ozone was foul with aerosols and exhaust. She breathed the spermicide, the sloughing sweat, from the black shadows between the whores' legs. Bus stop cigarettes glared hotly with night eyes, arced and traced like fireflies.

No, it's my eyes that are incandescent. My lips are moist. There

*are the Hollywood nights, like nowhere else. The moon itself is
bleeding. Drawing the dream-starved like threads of ants. Everyone
needs someone to be.*

All the forms walking the street were redefined as objects of desire. Life was all turned inside out. Diver Dan
and Albright had revitalized Hollywood with excitement,
disrupted all the old patterns. *The goddamn city is tingling.
This is the edge.* Eva saw it all in a new glimmering. Life. Passion. The senses. *I feel infused, like a withered plant with dry
roots suddenly refreshed. The roots of my hair tingle. Associations
are tumbling. Like he's impregnated me. Our blood mingling, his
and mine . . .*

A small Hispanic girl of perhaps eight years old clutched
her mother's protective hand at the bus stop. Eva paused at
the child's fascinated brown eyes and smiled. She recalled
something, a memory she had buried. Now it erupted in all
its repressed force.

It was the thrill she had felt once before when as a teenager she had watched her older sister's baby for an evening. Her boyfriend had come over—she had forgotten
his name. The baby would not stop crying, and she had
stood over the crib, appalled at the helplessness of the in-
fant, its mute, contorted and angry face. Something had
come over her and it was all she could do to stop herself
from pinching it, knowing it would never tell, that she
would never be caught.

No. You did pinch it. And there was a decided sexual edge—

The voice had come from within her, but it had not been
hers.

The blood. Like in the novels, the voice in the blood.

The bus pulled up, the doors hissed. The mother was
looking at Eva suspiciously. The bus swallowed the little
girl, and Eva felt a keen sense of loss.

Goddamn, girl. Get a grip.

In the window of the boutique across the street was a

mannequin in a white bridal gown with arms outstretched. It looked like a vision or an angel—the White Witch from Stephen's books, protectress of Thanata, and the vampire's nemesis. It seemed to glare at Eva even as the arms beckoned her across the street. The hairs went erect on the back of Eva's neck. She walked quickly on the sidewalk.

She suddenly felt paranoid. She felt stalked and followed and spied upon. Her heels clicked as she tried to sort her thoughts. The lighted stores thinned out. She felt simultaneously consoled and threatened by the gathering shadows. She was not thinking of Stephen now, but The Bloodletter. In her mind she saw him crawling out from beneath the cover of a hardback book as if it were a coffin.

She paused momentarily to check her reflection in a dark store window. She could not find her reflection in the murky glass—which frightened her. Yes—there it was. Only her skin looked transparent. She was fading away. Then as she watched her face began to shine with that same strange opalescence as Albright's.

She realized she had wandered from the comparative safety of the lighted shops. She was not even in screaming distance of the nearest human being, just alone with her misty reflection.

She turned quickly to escape—

And there they were.

Her heart tripped and there was the beating of wings of fear in her ears. She was surrounded. Six black-clad boys and girls on soundless feet. Something was fantastical about them. *Why did I not see their reflections behind me in the glass?* Two lounged insolently atop a car at the curb, while another hung onto the pole of the broken streetlight.

Where did they come from? The alley? Are they wisps from the storm drain?

She tried to still her pulse, told herself these were hardly more than children in their black leather and boots. *Chil-*

dren of the Night. But there was silent menace in their pale wasted faces. The eyes were soulless—eyes focused on her.

They seemed to have a leader, and he motioned for the two lounging on the car to come down. The six threatening shapes came hungrily closer in an eerie ballet. Leather squeaked like bats. There was the glint of the silver spikes that studded their belts and wristbands. Death's-heads smiled from the earrings of the three blond girls.

"What do you want?" she choked.

The shiny faces chilled her; at the same time she felt the irony. These were his children, the spawn of Stephen Albright and his paperback horrors. Their brutal faces were haunted.

"Leave me alone," she gasped. The answer was a clicking sound like a switchblade opening. But no, they were making the noise with their teeth—restless jaws working in unison. She could not stop her imagination from filling their piranha mouths with white razors, sharp canines and incisors.

"Get away from me," she demanded as she retreated a step—and her back was against the window.

The nearest figure had held up a hand, and the others paused. It was a boy. He took a plug from his ear, and she heard a snatch of the song from the transistorized radio hung on his belt. *"Infected—!"* He stepped closer. She recognized him.

Rashmikant. My fecal client.

There was momentary shock on his face; then something like wonder as he looked her up and down. The expression in his subtle eyes was more than recognition. It was *acknowledgment.* His lips slowly curled in the wry smile she knew from his therapy sessions.

She made a sudden motion toward him before speaking his name—

And the figures started, suddenly fluttering and frightened. Rashmikant's hand was still upraised, and he motioned them all warily back.

They're afraid, she realized.

The boy's smile flickered but never left his lips, as the dark shapes withdrew subtly back into the shadows from which they had materialized.

I feel my power.

Her nipples were suddenly so hard they hurt.

15

Frederick's of Hollywood

THE MORNING OF THAT SAME WEDNESDAY HAD started about nine o'clock for Paula. Check-out time at the motel was eleven. She had already spent *two days* holed up in the room. Two hours, and she would have to make another decision. She couldn't bear to think of it. To think, even. She dressed quickly. The white cotton tank dress. *I bought it for him.* Keep moving, as if she could stay one step ahead of her own mind. She hated to walk anywhere, especially in the heat. A gray Rapid Transit Bus pulled up at the corner and when the door hissed to her fiercely she couldn't refuse. The seat near the back was still warm. On the floor at her feet, that morning's *Times* smeared with a snail-track glaze of Danish.

Southern California was a sick, lurid paperback world. *Massive Collision San Diego Freeway. Death by Fire. Plane Crash.* In Verdugo Hills a flash flood had caused a hillside cemetery to fall away like a slice of head cheese, the mudslide sweeping dead bodies into the streets. DIVER DAN. *No Clues to Sixth Victim.* There had been a kid in school with that nickname. He was famous for his mustache rides.

A picture caught her eye. *Psychiatrist Missing.* Paula felt shock.

Inquiries had been made when she had not shown up at her practice Tuesday; that afternoon her abandoned car had been discovered. Paula's eyes raced along the print. Mention of only one of her books, *Myth-Analysis,* "a self-help handbook for waging and winning the battle of the sexes through fantasy interpretation." Numbness swept her.

My doctor. My friend. Now, I'm really alone.

Twinges of guilt, too, because she'd been pissed off at her therapist for a week. Sometimes Eva's detachment had been infuriating. Paula had been really stung that Eva had told her to quit *"fucking in your head."* She'd asked the psychiatrist for her birthdate and even the hour, then gone home and done a complete astrological workup on her. She'd been excited to discover they both had Venus in Scorpio, plus the conjunction of several significant houses, but Eva cut her off when she produced it during a session; she didn't want to hear that. She'd made it clear: *"We're not pals. I'm your therapist. You want to talk about everything but your core issues."*

A related article speculated that the body of a sixth murder victim, which had been discovered near the freeway, might be the missing psychiatrist's. *Wow. What if Diver Dan got her?* A silly emotion surged in her throat: envy. She had always wanted to be Eva, she was her ideal. Mature, brilliant, accomplished. *Size three.* Now, Missing. *Take me with you, Eva.* She suddenly wanted to see their faces: Ruthy, Larry, and her parents as they got the news after days of worry that she had died horribly and all alone.

Eva. Now you've abandoned me, too.

She was sitting directly over the motor. It purred and rumbled up through her seat, a not unpleasant sensation.

Then the harsh gray fumes came up to her face through the window. She grimaced and put on her large sunglasses to hide her reddening eyes, looking past the dull bronze plaques that studded the Walk of Fame like pennies pancaked on a railroad track. Frederick's of Hollywood was a nauseous purple.

Diver Dan. He could be any one of those unfriendly faces passing—

The bus shuddered, growled and began to move. The sticky sweet roll-on deodorant was like candle wax in her armpits, and the sweaty slick inside of her knees sucked at the upholstery of the seat. She hated to perspire. It was so hot already. The Santa Ana winds out of the mountains were the dry, racking cough of an asthmatic down the concrete canyon of the boulevard.

She rode around for a long time, lost with Larry on one side of her and Eva on the other. When the bus stopped at a light, she was startled at the street signs crucifixed by her foreshortened perspective of the intersection: Hollywood and Vine. The heart of Hollywood, but nothing. *Like everything in my life, a swindle.*

The loneliness was becoming unbearable. She jumped out at the next stop, impulsively, as if diving into a water trough because her hair was swarming with flies.

She felt eyes all over her, a physical sensation like cracker crumbs inside her clothes. So many thoughts in the air. The unfeeling people passing her had the coldly brutal faces of vampires drawn along their self-absorbed ways by their appetites. The other minds pulled at her own, sucked her down alleys where she did not want to go. *Eva said I would be most vulnerable when I'm depressed or insecure.* Everything was becoming animate, ready to leap. She saw deep strange things in the whorls of her fingertips. The soggy configurations of trash in the gutter were portentous as tea leaves in the bottom of the cup of her mind.

She began to walk. Her brain was so dusky, her world shrunk and contracted to the halo of sidewalk at her feet. *I know I'm self-obsessed, that I'm eating myself alive, but that's not like being able to do anything about it.* She felt herself losing even that much clarity. *This is how they had picked me up when I ran away to Fresno, wandering in a daze. They took me to a hospital, then. A caseworker held me in his arms and I wasn't able to stop crying . . .*

Stephen Albright's BLOODLETTER
Book Thirteen: The Violator

The window at Dalton's Booksellers was piled high with the paperbacks. A young girl floating in space on the cover, her hair and gown trailing to the stars. Two bloodshot eyes watched from the blackness. *I feel eyes on me, too.*

I'm getting paranoid.

There were whispers and mocking; footsteps behind her tried to step on her heels. There had been a boy in high school who was obsessed with her, and he had driven a beat-up Chevy Impala just like the one slowing beside her to take a closer look. She saw the Hollywood sign in the distance and thought of walking up that hill, climbing the sign and throwing herself off.

Instead, she ducked into Frederick's, where she bought the red nightie she had seen from the bus, then pushed back out onto the street. A crowd had gathered at a bus stop and she could see between their figures an old man in a wheelchair. Both his legs were missing below the knee. The indifferent faces managed to watch him curiously and ignore him at the same time, as he made frantic, guttural noises. He looked around beseechingly and made plaintive gestures with gnarled hands that trembled with palsy. She saw the reason he was inarticulate: his upper plate had fallen out and the teeth were resting on the wine-stained shawl over his legs. No one wanted to pick them up and replace them in his purple gums.

"Here you go," Paula said softly as she reinserted the dentures into his mouth. His eyes reddened emotionally as he looked up at her, arthritic hooks of fingers reaching out to touch her hem.

She did not notice. There was the Chevy Impala again, now parked at the curb with its door significantly open. *Try not to think.* Her mind emptied as she walked on. She was losing the boundaries of her self and melting anonymously into the people on the sidewalk. Then she became one with the sidewalk, the sun glaring up into her face from the pavement and the heat entering her eyes and burning away all caring.

She checked for messages at the desk. There was none from Eva. *There will never be one from Eva. Who is going to write my prescriptions?*

She bought a bottle of vodka at the corner. The policemen swarming the motel were a comfort. She wondered whether they could be investigating Eva's disappearance — then smiled at the thought. *She'd never be caught dead in such a dump.*

She went back up to her room, where she pulled the blinds and slipped under the covers. She washed the Valium down with the alcohol and arranged her hair on the pillow. Her stomach began to feel like an aquarium of Siamese fighting fish. She wished they could all see her now, waiting for the warm dark to swallow her. It was a sick world.

She woke up once in the dark, and the eleven o'clock news was on. She made a single phone call and was aware of her voice slurring. Larry van Heusen repeated her name a few times and she dropped the phone. She suddenly had a better idea, which involved her going to the bathroom. Halfway there she changed her mind as the overwhelming dizziness washed over her in a cloud of spots. She fell across the bed in the dark and did not move.

The frantic electronic voice coming out of the dangling telephone receiver was not so much concerned as annoyed. Typical of the whole relationship, she would have thought, had she not been busy dying.

16

Whisper of Parting Flesh: Sexual Edge

EVA WAS HEADING TOWARD BEVERLY HILLS WITH hands that trembled on the Cadillac's wheel. She was still flushed with the intoxicating spell of the power she had felt during her encounter with the night children. She was once more trying to get a grip.

Look at you, she thought. You know what's going on. You've met a man and now you're cashing in everything you've built for some escapist fantasy. A disturbed man, Eva. You're a forty-year-old woman dressed like a hooker cruising at night on your way to——

. . . *Gliding through Hollywood, evoking ancient patters of encounter and seduction. Beautiful and coldly crystalline. Drunk on your own potential as a new creature. Amoral and living a deathless series of sensual adventures, flushed with the exultation of power and muscles and instinct. Why live with one hand tied behind your back?*

There is a monster in each of us and the vampire awakens it. Asleep inside me. Within the nailed coffin that has been my life. *Your account of experience has been bankrupt. Eva, you haven't lived.*

She had hoped she would feel something besides regression—unpleasant immersion in her old identity—when she parked in the reassuringly familiar alley behind her house on Calla Vista Drive. She went around front and noted that the gardener, though she had been gone only three days, had ceased to assiduously cut the bamboo whose subterranean suckings below the fence from her neighbor's lawn terminated in spear-like thrustings knee-high through her own grass. The small house itself was murky and silent beneath the bright Spanish tiles of the roof. The key was on a small hook near the empty bird feeder. She stumbled on a package before the door. They were paperbacks; DeMarco must have sent them over as a courtesy in that other life before the shit hit the fan. Now she unwrapped them and looked at the women on the covers. Red-haired and voluptuous; yet indistinct, quivering and shimmering at her center.

She unlocked the door and it squealed open. She stood there breathing the close exhalation of a pent-up house.

Why am I sneaking? Why do I feel guilty, an impostor? I am haunting my own house. She saw the familiar objects, the chairs and the table, yet now they were at an incredible remove from her. To think of touching them made her nauseated. The house was strange. *Or am I now a stranger to the house?* Her own reflection in the mirror startled her and she paused as if encountering someone who should not have been there.

The cramps were excruciating, and she got the medicine from the bathroom. She would have to ration the pills. It would be too risky to refill the prescription, with her face on the news and her picture in the papers. Tisha was out of the question, and she'd realized she had no other female

friends to help her. They had all dropped out of her life.
For years, she'd lived in a man's world. She had even felt
superior to most women, until now.

While she was here, she might as well check her phone
messages. She was on her way across the room when—

Headlights flared across the wall. A car was parking at
the curb out front. There was the click of heels up the walk,
but no knock on the door. Eva had crouched next to the
couch, but could see through the window darkly as a face
was pressed against it. *I'll be damned: it's Paula Kightlinger.*

What would her crazy client not do to find her? Then
the dark figure was moving around out front, peering into
other windows. Eva felt threatened and afraid. *Anger.*

Which made sense. She'd felt that surprising stab of jealousy when Albright had expressed interest in her that evening in her office. There were other associations: Paula was
identified with her own repressed shadow self, the girl she
was afraid she was inside, from whom she'd always wanted
to escape. She always had to be on guard around Paula because the girl sensed this unspoken kinship. In fact, Eva
was sure Paula had a crush on her. Oh, she couldn't recognize it and wouldn't see it in those terms. But Eva had to be
cautious and aware of the dependency.

A hesitant knock on the door—

Eva's heart stopped and she found herself vividly imagining Paula's murder. She was straddling her, her hands
tight on the ends of a scarf around the soft throat. Then
her fingernails were like razors. Whispering down the soft
breast, the flesh seeming to part of itself, like the peeling of
a fruit. The heart, jumping there, like an excited fly en-
meshed in a web of arteries and pulsing vesicles.

*Of course: Paula represents the part of myself that I want to
die—*

The phone on the coffee table next to her suddenly rang
and Eva snatched the receiver, huddling with it below the

breakfast bar. She thought of hanging it up, but it might ring again. She listened to the receiver and heard his voice. It made her shiver.

His whisper was fierce. "Eva, you've got to help me."

Suddenly she was in the real world. Thank God he was sounding rational and lucid. Even calm. She wondered if he was tranquilized. The connection was weak, distant, scratchy with static.

"Where have you been? You've got to help me out of this. I can't go anywhere, I can't see anyone. They don't know I'm using the phone."

The female figure who had been at the window was clicking back toward the car at the curb, getting inside. But the car was not moving. Eva collected her voice, realizing it was hoarse from disuse as she whispered.

"At my ex-husband's condo. Stephen, where are you—"

"I'm at the house in the Hills. But they would never let you in. I'm surrounded by vampires. They could be listening to me now."

She felt sick to her stomach and she could actually see the numbness creeping up her arm with the goose bumps that made her flesh resemble the skin of a freshly plucked quail. She peeked out the window. *She's still sitting in the car. Why isn't she leaving?*

Albright said, "Do you still want to help me?"

"Of course, Stephen. I want—"

There was a hoarse moan from the phone and it tore her heart.

"I'm so ashamed . . ."

"Stephen, try to talk to me. You're not going to hurt yourself, are you? Are you having those kinds of thoughts? Is there someone to take care—"

"I don't know what's happening to me. I was sure Phil was using you to control me, to keep the vampire alive.

And now it's too late for you. You're one of them and it's my fault."

He began sobbing and Eva felt a sickening dizziness.

"Stephen, you're saying you believe I'm a vampire, too?"

Somehow she knew he was nodding his head like a guilty child at the other end of the phone, tears spilling out of his eyes. "Yes," he croaked finally in a small voice.

"Stephen, I am hearing everything you're saying. I want to ask you some important questions about where exactly you are and what's hap—"

He sighed heavily.

"He came in the window. He'd been watching us and waiting. It was horrible what he did to you—"

The writer's voice broke and she heard him sniffling, composing himself.

"He just looked at you, and then he looked up at me and he said with his eyes, 'You little fruit, you don't even know what to do with a woman. You better stick to the writing.' Then his hands were on your breasts and his mouth was at your throat. I couldn't move. I couldn't look, I covered my ears but I could still hear the sound of his lips at your throat. I didn't do anything. I let it happen. And he would have got me, too. But I have the magic charm. I wear it around my neck, it's right—"

"Stephen, I want you to listen to me—"

"And he wants you to listen to him. He's inside you, now. He wants you to think I'm psychotic. He wants me to think you're a castrating bitch. Eva . . . ."

"Stephen, are there doctors where you are? Has any—"

"Eva?" he interrupted fearfully. "I've been caught. Now he wants to talk to you. Do you want to talk to him?"

He giggled inappropriately.

Suddenly DeMarco was on the phone. "Well, Eva. I'll be

damned. Know what? I thought he was talking to himself. Yeah. Just like he's been talking to himself all day. What do you know, you were really there."

"I've been in seclusion, too."

"Oh, I figured that. I figured you were maybe taking a little break or something. How long you gonna stay in hiding? Forget I asked, I don't wanna know. What do you think of him now? Stephen, you satisfied? Eva, you happy, too?"

"Put him back on, DeMarco. I've got to talk to him."

"Sorry, Eva. Stephen's on his way to bed. It's past little Stephen's bedtime. Stephen's all doped up. Because of Eva. They got him doped up so he won't break out the fucking windows. You're gonna bring down some goddamn heat on yourself. Do you think it's a joke when police are looking for you? They're gonna be mad. That's the question you oughta be asking Eva about now."

"He wants to talk to me. It will help him . . ."

"What? Oh, Stephen has a message for Eva: he says DeMarco is a vampire. Last week Eva was a vampire, and sometimes Stephen is a vampire. Now it's DeMarco's turn. Yes, Stephen, I'll let her know. Eva, Stephen says everybody's a vampire. Good night, Stephen . . ."

Eva said, "He desperately needs medication, he'll be in psychosis until—"

"How about Mellaril, Ativan and Haldol?" DeMarco chirped. "When the results of the blood test come in tomorrow morning, he starts lithium. He's gonna need a lazy susan for the bottles. You want doctors? You know Bergman? How about Belknap and the Jew—" DeMarco was suddenly worried; she sensed it.

"Eva. You don't sound so good. You gotta hold up. You're not gonna do anything stupid, are you? You gotta keep your shit together. What are you up to? Eva?"

"Did you find the file? Hardly worth it, was it?" she asked him sarcastically. "Did you tear everything apart just to make it look like a burglary?"

DeMarco seemed bewildered. "What files? Not your patient notes—"

"Don't act stupid. I saw the news."

"It was on the *news*? Tell me I'm not hearin' what I think I am. Are you telling me you *lost* your files on Stephen?"

She hesitated. He did sound genuinely fearful. Or he was a consummate actor. She decided to exploit his apparent confusion.

"Let me talk to Stephen. Now."

"The *news*? Eva. We've got to talk. Eva? Are you there ...?" His voice seemed to fade as if someone had picked up another line.

What are you wearing?

She was startled. She fingered the choker she had put on to cover the wounds on her neck. The phone was cold in her hand.

"Stephen, how did you know? Stephen, your voice, it's so ..."

The blood. So no one can hear us. I miss you, Eva.

"Stephen. I'm scared. Something's happening to me. I'm changing."

You're searching for something. You're leaving one condition for another. Exciting. Do you feel equal to it?

I want you to release me, she thought.

"I want to be different," she said.

Your only hope is to explore every new awareness, submit to the vampire experience. You must shed the logical and rational to let the imagination live out its forms. I'll guide you. There are steps and you must do what I say.

Your blood is in mine. We are always together, now ...

What? The movement of the second hand on the wall clock suddenly seemed hypnotic.

"Eva—" DeMarco was shouting. "What's wrong? Can you hear—"

Her own nodding head had startled her awake. *What happened to me?* She heard DeMarco slam down the receiver. She stood there for a while with her own phone dead in her hand.

A breeze rippled the curtains. Once more the door of the car out front was opening; the click of approaching heels.

You can do her, Eva said to herself. *Right here right now, and nobody'll know. You're missing, presumed dead, remember?*

Words from the novels were coming to her. The books were the only road map she had to Albright's mind.

> *She felt the true meaning of the vampire thirst. To be truly parched, physically and spiritually. Sensually. To have a soul caught in a wasteland, craving relief. To be drawn to the fountains of the heart, the red bubbling brook . . .*

Once more a face pressed against the window with hand shielding the eyes to penetrate the shadows. Eva started as she peered out of her own darkness where she cowered next to the sofa. Scales had been lifted from her eyes. It wasn't Paula at all. It was Tisha.

Worried. Looking for me. She liked me, we were friends. She suddenly felt a wave of guilt for the murder fantasy.

Eva held her breath until her secretary returned reluctantly to the car parked at the curb and drove away. Only then did she breathe a long sigh.

Stephen, which is it? What do you want me to be? Woman as savior, or woman as destroyer? Thanata or the vampire? Or am I supposed to be the one to live the two opposites into some kind of unity for you? Or can there even be an answer before you decide who Stephen Albright really is?

17

Labial Mouths

"LIEUTENANT SMOTHERS," THE COP HAD INTRO-
duced himself to the female clerk at the Villa del Monica
late Wednesday evening. He flashed a badge, but did not
give her time to look at it. "I'd like a key to room two-ten,
please."

The clerk looked Syrian. She held a baby who spit up
suddenly onto the diaper draped on its mother's shoulder.
She said in a chopped accent, "You don't look like no
cop."

"Undercover. I'm part of the Dan Task Force looking
into that missing psychiatrist, and you've got an attitude,
lady."

The clerk rocked the child irritably. "You guys been
here all day. People scared to come stay here, now. You
don't care when it's just those kids dying. Now it's that psychiatrist lady, it's a big deal." The woman's eyes were suspicious.

He shook his head in exasperation. "Don't break my
balls, honey. Just hand over the key."

She shook her head. "You show me your badge again. It looks like dime-store badge. You're no cop."

"Look," he said. "The woman in two-ten went into her room four hours ago. She hasn't come out."

"Maybe she's sleeping."

"I'm worried about her—I knocked and she didn't answer. What if something's happened to her?"

"You wanna arrest her, or something?"

"I'd like to take her into protective custody—just a precaution. I have reason to believe someone's been stalking her all day."

"Get lost," she said. "I get creeps like you in here all day. You see some woman on the street and then you follow her because you want to meet her. A woman stayin' in a motel gets you all hot. You get out of here."

"Be that way," the man said disgustedly. "I'll be back and it won't be alone. There'll be building inspectors and sanitation officials. I got a feeling everything ain't up to code around here. Got that?"

"Sure," she said insolently. "You do that."

He turned but paused at the door. "One more thing: can I hold the baby for a minute?"

She looked at him as if he were crazy.

"Please? Let me hold the baby?" He took a step toward her but she retreated back into the living quarters off the office area.

Diver Dan shrugged philosophically as he walked out of the office, checking the copies of *The Watchtower* in his jacket pocket. It had been that kind of a Wednesday. He had followed the girl along the crowded Hollywood streets. Now he was back where he had started—the motel. He had known where she was staying from the note in the psychiatrist's office. *Eva: Paula is at the Villa del Monica in Hollywood. She has to see you and it can't wait. Please contact.*

The woman in the office had been right about one

thing: the cops had been around all day. Hollywood thick with cops. That was why he had been unable to snatch her from the busy streets.

It had been anxiety that had driven him to the motel office to try the cop ruse. He usually loved the stakeout part, the waiting game and the choosing of the moment. But now each job was fraught with more problems than the last. Nerves were getting the better of him. The Villa del Monica was hotter than a two-dollar pistol since the psychiatrist's BMW had been discovered up the street at the Zombie Zoo. Even now he could see an unmarked police car in the handicapped space at the Winchell's on the corner of Santa Monica and La Cienega.

He had a splitting headache from the pulsing alarms of instinct going off at cruisers and plainclothesmen. He knew he was in jeopardy, knew he was taking extraordinary chances. Like walking up to her room now. He took out the Jehovah's Witness pamphlets.

The Villa del Monica, Dan thought. It had ambience. It was a great place to sky up. The whole motel just nominated a female guest GIRL MOST LIKELY TO BE FOUND DEAD ON A HILLSIDE.

The Villa del Monica was sanctified with memory. Not your average Hollywood hotbed. More interesting than the hanky-panky was the hinky-kinky associated with this one. A favorite for decades of epicures and cultists who fancied private digs to indulge fantasies from autoerotic suffocation to necrophagia. There'd been some damn good eatin' gone down behind those nondescript doors.

Murnau had stayed there when he'd come to Hollywood in the twenties. Lugosi and Peg Entwistle had their assignations there in the thirties. The sixties? Jim Morrison, the Lizard King, had his own room where he sodomized nubile groupies after his early gigs at the Whiskey A Go-Go up the street.

And the eighties. It was here that a young and impoverished Stephen Albright had taken a weekly room when he'd started the first book.

This Paula bothered him. He did a passable imitation of her voice from the tape. *"He even has hair on his back. Who could stand those fingers in their mouth?"*

Dan's heart pounded as he walked up the steps. He was driven by a vision, a smile on his purple lips. He held Thanata's head by the ears, mouth open in terror and eyes bulging; he moved it back and forth fellating him. The head wasn't attached to her body. The head was dead. Dead head. He'd woke up just as the plainclothes dicks were changing shifts. Remembering that job he'd got fired from in high school, only job he'd ever had, fired for playing with the women at work. He had been a night attendant at a Fresno funeral home.

He paused before her door and imagined her naked on his bathroom floor. He could lean her here upside down, upper torso against the wall over the toilet, when she was fresh. Legs open at the cave of death. That way all the blood would be drawn down from her heart and fill up those big breasts. He imagined it, making slits with a razor just below the big nipples, lapping it up as it oozed out in a syrupy dripping.

Now, the thrill of the hunt made his nipples harden. He knocked on her door and got his rap ready.

"The Kingdom of God is within you. The blood is the life. Do you know Jesus? Would you like to—?"

But there was no answer. The blinds were drawn so he could not see into the room. He pounded more loudly. "Gas leak," he shouted to the door. "We're evacuating this motel—"

No response; he was beginning to wonder whether she was all right. He felt the eyes of other tenants as they passed him en route to the ice machine.

No problem, he tried to tell himself as he walked back to his car: if this one could not get abducted at the Villa, he knew she would seek out some place where it was more dangerous. That was the way with these victim types: you just sat back and they'd do the hard parts for you. This girl probably didn't know herself why she'd picked it. She didn't know it but she'd been drawn there like an iron filing to a murderous magnet.

He ensconced himself in the torn upholstery of the DeathMobile and picked up the article he had neatly clipped from that week's *Variety*, which he'd found in the public library.

BLOODLETTER — THE MOVIE
Third Time Is Not a Charm

It rehashed the history of a little-known Hollywood hoodoo. Two earlier attempts to bring The Bloodletter to the screen had also met with disaster.

1923. F. W. Murnau and his original screen treatment *Der Vampyre Magnus*. Insistence on retaining the Germanic spelling of the script he'd written was the least of his infuriating eccentricities. He'd hauled cast and crew to a location in the California desert where elaborate sets had been built. He'd battled sand fleas, temperatures of 120 degrees, and a mutinous crew for almost a year before the studio heads pulled the plug on their cuckoo Teutonic *Wunderkind* and confiscated his thousands of feet of incomprehensible footage. Murnau begged for a second chance. Paragon Studio was unwilling to throw good money after bad and suggested he bark at the moon instead. Five years of litigation ensued only to be settled unexpectedly and spectacularly when a suspicious fire at the studio warehouse destroyed the master negative. The old nitrate stock went up like napalm in the inferno. Murnau suffered a broken heart and, eventually, a broken neck underneath the steering column of a Stutz Bearcat.

The studio collected insurance. Fragments and outtakes were said to exist in private collections, the eclectic mish-mash reputedly spliced together and exhibited at de-praved parties in European capitals, Beverly Hills and Sherman Oaks. An orgy sequence and the "Waltz of the Vampires" were rumored to be especially prized by afi-cionados and cultists. In the sixties stories abounded about a dedicated archivist who had restored close to a half-hour of film, which hinted at the ambition of Murnau's vision. It reportedly toured select art houses briefly before its myste-rious withdrawal from circulation, never to be seen again.

Enter Bela Lugosi, born Bela Blasko. Enamored of the possibilities of the Bloodletter legend, he envisioned an in-dependent production that would be the horror film to beat all horror films, and would restore the laurels he'd inherited from Lon Chaney, then lost to Karloff. When his real-life mistress and reel-life Thanata, Peg Entwistle, killed herself ungraciously with only half her scenes in the can, the production was sunk and the old Dracula was relegated to poverty row cheapies and serials that looked as if they had been shot in someone's garage. The fifties found him a morphine addict and alcoholic, appearing in a few cameos, which were the guilty industry's equivalent of mercy-fucks for the lonely man who'd saved Universal in the thirties.

This time, Dan knew, the picture had to fly. It *was* going to reach the screen. And the premiere would signal The End of Days when the undead would rise and rule the earth.

And Dan wanted to be there, by God. And then . . . Dan looked forward to the day when he could be an actual vam-pire and sleep in a casket.

He reached into the glove box and tore from the pack

two LR6/AA/1.5v Maxell alkaline batteries and popped them into the Sony Walkman. The sound bolted to life, up the cassette player and through the wires to his earphones. It was a song from *Abbey Road,* one song retaped and looped again and again for ninety minutes. He had made the tape from the record, slowing the turntable from 33 rpm to 16 so that the sound was stretched like taffy to a hellish groan.

It was all about being in an octopus's garden. Ringo was singing about a shady place beneath the waves where the octopuses writhed and waved their feelers.

The rumble of noise slowed his heart, retarding the metronome of his nervous system. Calming. Dreaming of the garden in the shade under the sea, with octopussies, count 'em, eight quivering labial mouths, quivering and sucking from mustaches of anemone, the dead women mired in silt at their ankles, their hair swaying up over their heads like seaweed. And he was sitting in the middle of them in the shade of the garden. There would be Oh What Joy when you were in the garden of the octopus. What Joy in that shade.

Dan popped a cross-top white and waited for the amphetamine blaze across his brain. *The Man of the Hour has a Great Power.*

The octo-pussies' garden in that dark maternal shade . . . Quivering mouths and sucking mustaches—

Darkness fell but Dan did not abandon his post. Wednesday crept slowly into Thursday, but it was all the same to the dark outside and the shady dark inside him. The motel and the street quieted as dawn approached. Dan became more alert. A desperate plan had formed: if the quiet maintained he would rush up her steps, break down the door, and carry her down to the car slung over his shoulder like a sack of—

But someone beat him to the punch. A Buick had pulled

into a parking stall and a muscular young man was running up the steps to pound on the door. When he got no reply, Dan saw him furtively remove a credit card from his wallet and use it to deftly unlock the door. Dan watched him slip inside the room.

Damn.

18

Paula

RAIN SPATTERED PAULA'S FACE — NO. SHE WAS IN A shower, her bloodless cheek pressed against the cold stall. It was early Thursday morning and she was not alone. It wasn't a dream. Larry was there. She felt a groggy, wonderful joy. He was turning the nozzle to cold needles. She began to hyperventilate. *He had come.* Now he was taking care of her, oblivious of the water soaking his shirt. She closed her eyes, felt his arm around her nakedness, holding her up. She let herself go limp. He held her face in the freezing spray.

And all it had taken was a post-midnight phone call informing him where she was and that she was overdosing on vodka and Valium.

She had met him at a party in Burbank where he lived. He was a go-for, a minor assistant in the production of the television show "Code Red." It was a weekly docudrama about paramedics. He wasn't happy there. Larry van Heusen did not want to answer phones. He wanted to write for the movies.

He had turned off the shower and was chafing her thighs briskly with a green towel as she leaned groggily against the wall.

He was handsome. At just under six feet he was two heads taller than Paula. He had a slender, muscular physique unusual for men in the production end of television, mostly flaccid types with a perpetual Styrofoam coffee cup in one hand and a glazed donut in the other. He worked out with weights. There was something compulsive and flagellant in the intensity of his exercising. He was so dissatisfied with himself, never passing a mirror without pausing to study his looks, the chestnut hair that curled to his collar.

They had been an on-again off-again thing for eighteen months. But he had come, now. She felt wonderfully weak and so grateful he was there. Incredibly, he was taking care of her. Walking her. Forcing black coffee into her. Her head was clearing. She had thrown up all over the bed.

"Probably what saved your life," he said grouchily. She loved his hair. His hands shook as he lit a cigarette. He saw her watching him bring his fingers under control. "I'm not hung over. I haven't slept and I'm whippy."

"You were worried about me," she said. *Say it. Say it.*

He was turning away. "Paula, you're a nice person and I really like you. But you make people feel guilty. That's your game, I guess." He blew smoke. "You were right about one thing: you need real help."

He sat on the bed, closed his eyes as he leaned back.

"You didn't have to come," she said.

He was rubbing his eyes. "Like, what could I really do? A phone call like that."

"You don't care what happens to me, do you, Larry? You were afraid I might leave a note to embarrass you."

The day was passed largely in the dark motel room as Paula alternately convalesced and argued. She did get up to join him for lunch, afraid he would not come back if he went to Taco Bell by himself.

Surprisingly, it wasn't hard to get him to stay the night with her. He'd apparently been fired and then kicked out of his apartment. They sat in the dark motel room and ate potato chips all day. Larry drank beer. She thought he was alcoholic. He was getting that bloat and his features were starting to blur. They were both troubled people, couldn't he see how much they had in common? *You're such a sad person. I so desperately want to understand you. Why won't you let me in?*

Darkness fell, and with it a strong expectancy. Really, Paula thought. *Are we going to share the same room and not sleep together?*

But do you really want that?

It was nearly eleven o'clock. She showered and rubbed herself hard with the towel until her skin was red. She combed her long hair out and daubed perfume on her neck and between her breasts. Enchanté, the scent she had worn on their first date. She raised her arms over her head and slipped into the red negligee as if emerging from a pool.

She saw herself transform in the mirror. She shut off the light, giving her face to the shadows. Exhaustion, vomiting, the hangover—all the concomitants of even casually attempted suicide—had drawn her face and deepened her eyes. *I bet I've lost five pounds.* The sheer material hung on thin spaghetti straps from her shoulders and down to dull points at her nipples. She shook her head to tangle her hair and liked the effect. The tops of her breasts were white and round. She turned to the side, stepped on the balls of her feet. Her legs ended in teasing half moons at the panties. It was only by straining that she could see stretch marks or dimples of cellulite. She would lower the lights in the bedroom, too.

She had a strange feeling. Dizziness. Fear. *A hunger.* Her knees trembled. She went into the other room. Larry was snoring, passed out on the other bed, a Stephen Albright paperback with broken spine opened on his stomach. The TV was on.

"Well—it's official. The mayor, ignoring strident protest from local interest groups, announced today that this Friday—the thirteenth, naturally—the city of Los Angeles will celebrate 'Bloodletter Day.' The declaration coincides with resumption of shooting on the beleaguered Bloodletter—The Movie. *Insiders say the mayor has buckled to pressure from industry execs for support of a troubled project which threatens to capsize a studio—"*

His Honor was shown with the board of supervisors as he read the declaration, a little defensively. *"With millions of books in print, Southern LA has embraced Albright's characters. Millions more will be entertained—"*

She turned off the set.

Vampires. She was thinking of them as she cried into her pillow and then dozed. She had put on her terry cloth robe for warmth and it was comforting. She dreamed her eyes were open and she was gazing up at the crucifix at St. Anthony's. Where was Father Kennedy?

She turned her head, saw the plush pink satin, and just above eye level the tips of the pink baby rosebuds. The flickering of candles.

She was in a beautiful white casket, the lid open. Quilted pink softness embraced her. She sat up. A chaplet of orange blossoms was in her hair. *That dress. My First Communion.* The drip of tallow, puddles of soft wax in votary glasses. She clambered out to find herself alone. No one had come to her funeral, and that made her emotional. The church was empty and her steps echoed hollowly. Instead of pews there were walls with vaults.

A mausoleum. *But I have never been in a mausoleum.*

A nameplate on a crypt.

POOR PAULA.

The candles were blown out by the wind, an extinguishing insuck of breath.

Dark. The vaulted ceiling was suddenly hung and haunted with shadows. The crypt began to bulge as if it were pregnant. The marble slab behind the plate had begun to move, to grate dryly one way, then another. It fell to the floor shattering in fragments. Dust rolled up heavily from her feet.

The hole. She stepped closer.

It seemed to lurch, to pour out upthrust, a dark thing that quivered. Then it appeared to gather itself, to stand upright. A smile in the center of the dark face.

The Bloodletter's face, the smile from the cover of the books. He was dressed in Father Kennedy's clerical robe, the one he wore when he heard confessions. He loomed above her and his breath was in her hair. He was charismatic and dominating, confidently peeling away the confirmation dress, deftly unsnapping the bra, her shoulders sagging suddenly under the released weight of her breasts.

His kiss was like nothing she could describe. His tongue went in and out quickly, probing and possessing her mouth, then caressing her throat.

He enfolded her in his arms, arching her back, his lips on her neck. The sting of his teeth. Sucking noises, her dizziness. He had lifted his robe, she could not see but felt him entering her, filling her and evacuating her at the same time. She felt his indomitable masculinity growing impossibly inside her until her stomach swelled, engorged as his organ continued to coil and release, flooding and filling.

Then the Virgin was beside her; but in black, her smile beatific beneath her designer sunglasses. *Eva.*

The Bloodletter released her, detached himself, and Eva

led Paula to the altar, where she nestled her serenely back in the white casket and closed her eyes with soft maternal fingers.

Paula woke with a start. Her thighs tingled, her sexual parts vibrant and sensitized.

The moon was hugely fluorescent in the window. She had pulled the covers up to her neck. The television was off and Larry was under his own sheets, his back to her. Suddenly her eyes were wide awake. She tested her mouthwash with a cupped hand. She heard the bedsprings squeak and it was her own body moving. She went to the bathroom and painted her lips a plush red.

Her diaphragm. She splayed her legs for an instant, reached in, plucked it out. Looked at it in her palm, then placed it on the case with the squeezed and nearly depleted tube of spermicidal ointment.

The terry cloth robe slipped to the floor. She felt nearly crazy with tension and fear and night and love. She sat on Larry and saw his open eyes bright and frightened. She knew he liked it when her nipples filled and pinkened with blood before his eyes.

His confused hands were awkward on her soft hips. She kissed his mouth. The lips were dry from cigarettes, coffee, and sleeplessness. She smelled the booze. Her teeth brushed his cheek and her hands were in his hair, mashing her face into his own as she sucked his warm breath. His tongue was timid, hiding in his mouth. She had never been on top before.

She sensed his discomfort. He was used to choreographing their sex. She pressed between his teeth as he closed his eyes against her own direct blue gaze so close to his face, and she found his tongue at the same moment, drawing it out and into her own throat. Startled, he tried to break away. Her strong hand whipped back the sheet to reveal him. He opened his eyes, desperately, then closed them again and did not open them.

He submitted, and she felt the slight arch of his back. Her searching hand found him, worked at his softness, fitting him roughly into her as she drowned in the kiss, near to passing out, lost in the hollows of her collapsed cheeks as she devoured him. When their lips broke, starved for air, she was a blazing wire ripped from a fuse box. She fell across his chest, frazzled and breathing raggedly. Her head was on his nipple and she felt the pounding of his heart.

She straightened, shook her hair out. He was going to show her. She felt his mounting excitement inside her. He always chose his moment to dissolve breathless in her eyes. Control. She felt enraged. She would not slow, but ground against him and worked his febrile excitement relentlessly. She felt him shiver, and she took all of his excitement into her as he tried to stop himself, to assert his sex. But it was too late, and his face contorted in pain as she continued to pull him, contracting herself around his sensitivity, now excited herself, open and sliding furiously around his slick colloidal coming.

Already, though, he was withering, collapsing, curling out of her. Then he was gone. *That fast.* His face was red, his hair damp. He smiled a little sheepishly. His single glance was angry.

She felt defeat. He fell asleep almost instantly, his back to her. Paula stroked his hair, trying to enter his dreams. The color of her lips was smeared across his face. It would be on the pillow in the morning. That gave her pleasure.

19

Rings of Mystery;
Voice in the Blood

EVA ALSO SAW THE NEWS THURSDAY NIGHT. *"WITH millions of books in print, Southern LA has embraced Albright's characters. Millions more will be entertained—"* No new news on her own missing self. She turned off the set and tried to breathe.

She had been terrified since her drive back to Tony's condo early that morning, the world strangely ovoid through the curved windshield as stars disappeared smokily in the tinted glass at the top. *Racing against the dawn?* Her life was flashing in front of her. *Explore every new awareness. Submit.*

The first man who had ever used that expression with her had been Todd. He had been a student, too, and her first lover. They had started out as good friends, in that time when she had still believed a man and a woman could be just friends without the sexual beast intruding its head. The perfect companion for the student tour of Europe. Her roommate had warned her, "If a man and a woman are alone seven times, they'll screw." His gentle entreaties in the van after the romantic campfire in the wine country. "Let's make a baby." He was silly and high on marijuana. Such an odd invitation, endearing and irresistible. He had underestimated her naïveté. Venice was ruined when she missed her period. Caught, my first time out. His stricken face. Then, "Don't worry. We can unmake a baby."

She locked herself inside the condo, shaking her head to disperse that memory. She had gone to bed but been unable to sleep. *It's got to be that way, huh, Stephen? The vampire experience?*

She eventually ambled out to the kitchen and sat at the table. She looked up to see the Siamese on the patio. It frightened her, the electric glow of eyes on her. She looked more closely and saw the cat had a dead gopher in its teeth. The cat dropped it and slowly lapped at the gopher's blood. She felt they were sisters, that the eyes watched her with impassive feline understanding.

Now even the cat was talking to her.

You have a conflict, Eva: you are in flight from yourself and your life. The lost child within you has always been in a lot of pain and you've never let that child have it. You've never done any grief work, yourself. You've even been uncomfortable when your patients expressed real pain; you had to frame their emotions for them and put them in rational perspective. Feelings themselves were inappropriate, weren't they?

She drew the blinds hastily.

She looked at her hand. It was scalded red across the knuckles and there were angry water blisters. And all she'd done was try to draw open the curtains the morning preliminary to driving to her office and turning herself in. But as a blade of blinding sunlight had fallen across her fingers, she had felt a scalding pain and withdrawn her hand from the window as if from boiling water. The vampire's allergy to daylight? Eva, you just want an excuse not to have to go outside and get in that car. That there was sufficient psychic energy to inflict a psychosomatic symptom on your hand is an indication of the depth of your own psychopathology. *You need treatment, girl.*

Why don't you talk to someone rational? You're lying here squirreled up in Albright's books just like that sick chick who wrote the fan letter. "When I read you I feel your arms around me . . ."

And where has it taken you? You're scared of sunlight. You sleep all day and come alive at night. You feel like you're coming out of your skin. Daytime noises hurt your ears. You're losing weight, you're lost in fantasy. It's the power of suggestion: you're projecting all the symptoms that contessa suffered after The Bloodletter seduced her. She had to commit suicide to escape it. How far are you going to have to go?

Why are you afraid to snap out of it? Because then you'd have to smell the coffee? That you've convinced yourself you're in love with an inaccessible sicko who's incapable of loving anyone, even himself? You wanted to be Mother Teresa, to rescue him. But if that doesn't work, you're willing to jump into schizophrenia with him. Maybe you could have adjoining rooms at Eisenhower and hold hands during arts and crafts—

At least you're not sucking on raw hamburger. Not yet . . .

She lay on the couch with *Book Five: The Vampire's Consort* in her hands folded across her breast. She closed her eyes and waited for the spontaneous imagery she had promised would come, promised to the readers of her book.

Let's see: she imagined herself dead, then coming awake. Eyes open.

She saw herself riddled and leaking on a mortuary slab. The room dark with other cadavers still under white sheets; the shark's fins of noses and toes through the white sheets. She quietly stirred, detached the tubes and quickly removed the surgical instruments that lay on her chest, opening the forceps and pincers that clutched her flesh. She sideslipped off the gleaming drained slab of the autopsy room and took her clothes from the evidence bag—

Eva's eyes snapped open. So much for myth-analysis.

Her stomach curled and growled, only she wasn't really hungry. Not for cereal. She had an urge to pee, walked quickly to the bathroom, snuggling her feet in the rug as she settled herself on the toilet and read a little more in the book.

> *Through the window she saw the night differently. To come from the box was to be born. We all live in boxes. And the great Outside was a frightening place full of assaultive images and loud noises. True peace was to walk in the dark, to creep furtively, fugitive, to kneel at the pools and sip secretly.*

Numbly she flushed the toilet.

> *"I am The Bloodletter, a ghost doomed to haunt the world, rejected by the earth, something expelled and spewed even from the mouth of death . . ."*

She remembered the Andes plane crash survivors and their sloughing off of the mental accouterments of civilization when they were revealed as useless and inimical to the stark new world into which they had been thrust. Resorting to cannibalism with nausea, at first, and then with epicurean fastidiousness and progressive refinement as certain parts of the body became more palatable, even delectable.

> *Morality is a luxury. There is something liberating about the lone figure, pitted against society and morality. True loneliness is to have one foot in both worlds.*

Like me, Eva thought, looking up. I already am dead. My life is a death.

Thanata had gone through that conflict. She was in love with the sensitive but powerless Cesare on one hand, and

attracted to the insensitive but brutally charismatic Bloodletter on the other. That contessa's rambling internal med-
itation on suicide:

> . . . *It is intimacy. It is sick. But that sickness is our exclusive
> precinct more intense than any bedroom.*

Tisha's practical voice: "Eva, Crazy Stephen wants you to
play crazy, too. He wants to suck you in. He's got two personalities and now only Vampire Stephen wants to talk, but
only with Vampire Eva. He's never grown up, he's not in
the real world. It's a game and no man is worth—"

That's right, she said to herself: *Get that eyeliner off your
face, Eva. Take a shower and trash the Happy Hooker hardware
and get a good night's sleep. Shake hands with yourself tomorrow
morning. Cut your losses, live and learn, pick up where you left
off* . . .

It was a relief when night fell once more. She went to
take a shower, but the chromium faucet came off in her
hand, so she had to take a bath instead. Tony had never
been much for home repairs. She tried to replace it without success, finally gave up and shoved it back onto the
pipe. Life was so mean, so small sometimes. She felt almost
a nausea at the thought of all the crap, the minutiae that
consumed life, the thousand little irritations, the plumb-
ing and bills and the people who didn't count because they
weren't movers and shakers and just wasted your time.

Eva sat in the tub, shaving her legs in the dark. Relaxing.
Then a voice in the darkness.

Eva. Experiment. To relax your inhibitions. A dare, if you like.

She drew in her breath.

Be washed in blood.

Her stomach was queasy. I'm not listening. I'm going to
resume my life and not walk around with a stomach full of
Siamese fighting fish. Go away.

Close those tired eyes. Release your imagination. What do you have to lose?

Her skin seemed to warm. A deliciousness stole over her. Then, firmly to herself: *I'm not playing. I'm through fucking in my head. This is bullshit—*

She turned on the small light on the sink and jerked back in shock. The tub was filled with red. *My period?* No. Her recalcitrant cycle still refused to come. It was the razor. She must have cut herself shaving and not even felt it. She shuddered involuntarily, and the water rippled around her in concentric rings of mystery emanating from her body.

She stood in revulsion, ripped the stopper out so the water would swirl away. She draped herself in the towel and trotted trembling to the kitchen, where she began to clean herself off with a damp dishrag. Then she felt the dream of his blood and closed her eyes.

Eva. I need you.

A single sound slowly came into the audible. It was a hollow plunking, faintly resonant, water falling from a vast rafter height onto a concrete floor. His voice inside her sounded so distant.

Do you feel capable of following your feelings and passions and ego down to their roots, to face without fear the unconscious well of desire on which they feed? Do you have the courage? The awful daring of a moment's surrender?

May I suggest a step? An exercise?

Kill the cat.

20

El Presidente

"ONE THING ABOUT THE VAMPIRE'S APPEAL WHICH no one has really put his finger on is his emotional control. We in the mundane world know pain and envy and jealousy and sadness. Only the vampire can shut off and shut down so that he feels nothing. His sleep is untroubled by dreams—a consummation devoutly to be wished."

The speaker on the dais this early Friday afternoon was Algernon W. Sherwood. A man in the second row was snuffling and his eyes overflowed. This encouraged Sherwood, who offered to take questions from the sea of youthful hands in the UCLA audience packing the auditorium. The rapt attendees had been drawn to a special retrospective, *The Vampire in Cinema.*

A plump bespectacled coed was asking him about Bela Lugosi. Sherwood shifted in his wheelchair, and an attentive member of the English department adjusted the old man's microphone. "A very interesting fellow," Sherwood said. "He liked to have the bottoms of his feet rubbed with the bowl of a pipe."

The man in the second row let out a small cry; he was attracting some stares.

"You know," Sherwood continued, "I met Lugosi once. His life was nearly over and I went to see him at the county hospital where he'd checked himself in for drug addiction. He was a charity case. He came shuffling out in the lobby wearing this frayed bathrobe—I was speechless. The great man was in front of me. When it was time for him to go back to his room, he said, 'Got bless you for comink to see me.' He disappeared on down the hall in his slippers. He was a sweet old guy."

There was applause and the auditorium lights were going up. The man in the second row had a tear-streaked face. A prematurely balding kid with acne scars seated next to him was solicitous. "Are you all right? You must be quite a buff."

The other man nodded wordlessly as he bit his lip.

The cueball head was sniffing the air. "Do you smell something burning? I think it's your shirt."

A small black spot had appeared over the other man's considerable stomach; gray smoke curled up and there was the faint sweet smell of burning flesh.

"You're on fire," the balding youth said. "I'm a premed student—"

"It's nothing," the other man said, intercepting the kid's hand by shaking it. "Thanks for your concern. Strachan. George Strachan." He was already out of his seat and clambering to lose himself in the crowd. He breathed more freely, once in the parking lot.

Inside the DeathMobile, Dan stripped off the white shirt on which an orange flame had started to widen. He stamped the fire out on the floorboard. Revealed on his stomach, and held in position by electrician's tape, were two small wires with no insulation. A cord led to a modified transistorized radio with battery pack clipped to his belt.

He called it the Silent Partner. It administered a mild but continuous electrical shock, allowing one to mortify the flesh throughout the day as the wearer participated in other activities. It still had bugs to be worked out.

His eyes were pleasantly distracted by the two female dolls on the backseat. He had made them himself, anatomically correctly. He called the lifelike process Plexi-Flesh. They had been made from human female flesh; their hair was real. One was slender and dark, the other plump and reddish.

He took the dark one's hand and placed it in the hand of the light one. He spoke in a little girl's petulant voice.

"Kiss her, Eva."

The dark Eva kissed the plump one with red hair. He made the dark one touch the plump one's large breasts.

"Make love to her, Eva," Dan said in a Donald Duck sort of voice.

He mashed their faces together and made their small feet dance on the car seat. Then Dan was sobbing with rejection, and coming apart. His yells in the killing jar of his car had attracted the stare of a little girl, who was peering in his window while her mom tried to tug her away. Dan quickly put the dolls aside and started the car.

"Do da Funky Chicken," he said like a mantra to calm himself. "Do da Funky Chicken." He opened the small Coleman ice chest on the seat beside him to check the object preserved inside. The object was a memento of Number Six. ". . . Da Funky Chicken."

"Do da Funky Chicken!" Dan said. He had arrived at his destination. Unlocking the door, he went straight to the small kitchen and opened the refrigerator. The cooler was in his hand. He opened it and placed the object in the vegetable crisper, then walked back the way he had come with barely disguised contempt. The place had been a hovel, a mess. Now, take the abode of The Bloodletter—

* * *

. . . Dan had toured it that very morning after The Bloodletter had recalled him with new marching orders. The thick red carpet felt sexy beneath his feet, in the tower where everything was so richly red. In the center was a huge black bed underneath a great mirror in the ceiling. There was a mural in hypnotic colors. There was a door that slid open to reveal a sparkling panoply of instruments of pain. All to die for . . . and on a velvety sable was the *ne plus ultra*—a large black phallus with its own key light.

Dan had fallen to his knees and worshiped there, contemplating He who would sexualize the world. When Dan had first seen the face of the vampire, it was as if that image had always been inside him and had issued forth from Dan's own deepest dream. Dan had felt both love and arousal, and he felt them still.

When Dan had risen from his devotion, he had been drawn as if in a spell down circular stairs and into a vast dark place lighted by flames in Gothic holders. Dark images of The Bloodletter looked down upon him from the rough walls. They were the icons of this holy place. And in the center of the room—

The casket was breathtaking. It was the bronze El Presidente—a Duraseal metal unit with London Mist Polished Finish. The interior was richly lined in 900 Aero Supreme Cheney velvet, magnificently quilted and shirred. There was matching jumbo bolster and coverlet. There was the Beauty-rama Adjustable Soft-Foam Bed. The Geneva Sculptured Hardware decorative handles and hinges completed the regal effect . . .

A pearly mist issued from the lid, and Dan was awestruck like Moses before the burning bush, as it darkened and took form. The vampire stood before him in majesty, still redolent of the plush velvet upholstery of the casket. Dan loved that smell. The Bloodletter loomed over Dan and riveted him with deep hypnotic eyes. The figure reached out and when he touched Dan, there was a distinct electrical shock. Then Dan realized with disappointment that he was standing on nylon carpet.

The vampire spoke in a chilling, resonant voice. Dan had darkness inside himself, but it was nothing like the well of night reverberating from the vampire's chest. Those resonances echoed down through centuries. That voice came from dark caves and hollow crypts.

"Pulled off the case?" the crestfallen Dan had the temerity to protest.

"Only temporarily," the vampire said. The Bloodletter remarked on a recent decline in the quality of Dan's work. "I have someone who will follow up on her."

Dan was feeling agonies of insecurity. "Who?"

The vampire explained, then said in consolation, "I have another job for you, now."

Each time, The Bloodletter had appeared to him and sent him on a nocturnal mission with the words, "We are inseparable, we eternal three—The Bloodletter, Caligula, Stephen. Who is the weak link?"

"Stephen," Dan said aloud. He knew the catechism by heart.

"Yes, Stephen is a weak link. Another woman. Another interruption. She is chaos. She is destruction. Another one you must bring to me."

Was it Dan's fault none of these women had been the right one? Each had hummingbirds, and each had smiled at Albright and aroused in him . . . How had the vampire put it?

"Albright wants her for the Bad Thing. The Big Nasty. The Wild Thang. The Funky Chicken."

Uh-oh. The sluts.

Stephen Albright, Dan would think, *I'd like to fix his fruity ass for good.*

But the vampire would enjoin Dan angrily, "Keep your hand from him. Him alone you cannot touch. If he should die, then I would fall back into uncreation."

Dan had concerns. "What about DeMarc—"

"All are clowns. DeMarco is a clown. I will dispense with him at the appropriate time. Until that hour . . ."

Driving now in the DeathMobile, Dan found his voice husky as he began to scream for no good reason at the top of his lungs. *"Da Funky Chicken!"*

21

Morgue Rat

IT HAD STARTED LATE FRIDAY AFTERNOON AFTER surreal hours spent pacing back and forth. Eva had thought she would be incapable of doing it, but there was something about night that was releasing. As if the faucet of reality were turned off. It was a dream. That was how she had wound up on her hands and knees as dusk fell in the condo.

Here you are holed up alone. You're talking to no one and denying yourself any reality checks. You are hearing a voice in your blood, but it is not the vampire. It is the voice of your suppressed self, which wants to feel and live and be heard. You are building a fantasy and building a man out of your repressed dreams.

Where was the damned cat? She looked beneath the couch and clattered among the chairs beneath the kitchen table. She looked behind doors and in closets—

Your enslaving defensive mechanisms are so ingrained that the fantasy must be violent and cataclysmic. You don't feel yourself capable of merely modifying your obsessive-compulsive personality.

You feel you have to become a completely new creature. That's the allure of the vampire escape.

Her knees throbbed with carpet burn, but she hardly noticed. She had taken the broom and was sweeping beneath the sofa with the handle. "Here Kitty Kitty—"

And it comes complete with a man, doesn't it? You want to believe that Albright is inside of you and compelling you. Speaking to you and seducing you in the little bubble of psychopathology you two share. And it's dangerous, the mind and suggestion can be a powerful thing.

The cat.

On an inspiration she went into the kitchen and rattled the Siamese's food dish, which usually brought the cat racing. No luck. Smart kitty. Eva walked stiffly up the hall, trying to think like a cat.

You've been rigid and a slave to order and ritual. Achievement has been your compensatory strategy for feelings of failure and worthlessness. You've felt like a fraud and phony because you demanded you be in control all the time and wore yourself out with pretense. Because you knew you weren't—

It was in Tony's closet that she found the Siamese asleep at her feet, purring hoarsely with its belly full. She was out of breath with exertion and fear as she cooed to it soothingly, carrying it into the kitchen, where she sat it on the floor by the food dish and it finally began to eat, if warily. She wanted linoleum beneath.

She had looked inside herself for a long time until she found it. The rage. The rage at Tony. She thought of herself handcuffed at his pleasure in his cold rage, rendering herself to his fantasies. "Sophisticate," he called himself when he had inaugurated her into his brand of marital love. The rubbery flapping of his flaccid thighs against her buttocks from behind. His contempt for women, his patronizing of her dreams, his squelching of her individuality. She had only to release memory for rage to well up in a rush, and in that instant she knew what a man must feel at the release of hot seed.

And it was happening, then, the fury possessing her hands as she imagined Tony under the knife, pressing the wooden handle, driving the blade between the cat's ribs. It squalled once, like a baby, head snapped upright, hair standing on end. It twisted violently, scrabbling across the floor for only a few inches on the linoleum, dragging its hind legs as if they were useless, broken. The look of shocked hatred in its yellow eyes.

She watched horrified at the thrashings.

She rose dizzily, staggered to the sink to vomit. It filled her nose and mouth.

And what was the revelation? She sagged against the sink, afraid to look at the floor. Nothing. *No. I don't want to know.*

That she could kill a cat if she pretended it was a human. It was easier to take a human life than a cat's.

The feline corpse was motionless. The stillness, the quiet, was beautiful.

It's horrible.

She washed her hands of the blood, nauseated again, but fascinated by the red crescents around her cuticles, in the life lines of her palms. Albright was like a nightmarish tree of knowledge, and each bite she took of its fruit imprisoned and liberated at once. She felt as if the lobes of her brain were splitting apart with confusion.

She could not drink the blood. But she felt The Bloodletter's blood singing inside her. *If only it was human blood?*

You have crossed a line in the dust. It's unleashed a wealth of associations and experiences. Myriad sensations and satisfactions. And it was only a cat.

She did not know whether she was immoral, or merely

moving beyond morality. *You have murdered. Get real. It wasn't only the abortion. With your inhibition, your fear, your materialism, you've already smothered Eva.*

I have murdered myself. The rest should be easy, the dead are so free . . .

Rationalize. *That was why I sent the dream. Symbolically, the young woman in the dream was yourself. You must murder yourself to be reborn and reshaped. The imaginative part of yourself is transforming. Emergence is painful.*

But was that all?

Her body seemed in flux, too. The cramps had mysteriously eased, though her period had not come. It was as if all her internal lines were simplified, cleaner. She felt a new strength, capable of any vision.

Her eyes rested on the dark spreading pool of cat's blood on the patio. A small movement, something tiny and dark, coming to life at the lapping edge of the stain, buzzing suddenly to hover facing her at eye level behind the glass, the buzzing wings shimmering, iridescent.

The hummingbird, the black pin of a beak red with blood. The tongue darted, once, and the bird disappeared. A sign.

You must help me. Eva, you must obey my call. Who am I? When you find Bloodletter, you will find me. And yourself.

Even as she walked to the closet she told herself she was having a dissociative reaction. She told herself that her conflict and confusion were becoming so acute that she was turning the reins over to a subsystem that had developed in her own personality the last few days in anticipation of this moment. And she couldn't stop it. She was numb but there was relief, too, in the compulsion she was obeying.

She laid out her clothes on the bed. The black suit. Choker. Purse. The stiletto heels. She tried on the sunglasses as she painted her lips.

No. The suit is wrong. She changed into the black dress. *Draped bodice, cinched waist. Spaghetti straps, good. Tapered legs with shirring at the ankles.* Her body was caressed by smooth flowing polyester knit. *Not bad.* The jacket had padded shoulders and dolman sleeves. *Be ready, Eva. The moment is coming when we will be together once more. I will arrange everything. When man and woman dream the same dream, it becomes real.*

She jumped when the phone rang. It was just too much. But it wasn't Albright.

"It's Phil," he said. *Phil.* His voice sounded different. Gruff, but plaintive, conciliatory. "I got your number through your husband's service. Eva, we've got a problem." *We've?*

Why are you calling me now?

"Turn on your set. Turn it on KCOP."

There was the silhouette of a young woman, her face obscured by computerization. Her voice was a drugged monotone.

"I know what I am. I'm a Morgue Rat. The others give us things to eat. To make it happen faster. Things I been ashamed of. The Bike Bitches was a good club, until they got into the blood thing—"

Eva started to interrupt, but DeMarco was snappish. "Just listen."

"I don't want to live this life . . ." the girl was moaning. *"I want to get straight, get clean. I gone to the clinics and I'm gonna beat this. I'm going public at this time because of what the mayor is doing. The keys to the city? That's just what they want. People gotta be warned. Everybody's afraid to say his name, but I'm not. Stephen Albright has gotta be stopped. Someone is killing all the Thanatas—"*

The interview was abruptly terminated as a newscaster resumed a summary of the ceremony that afternoon on Hollywood Boulevard. Eva recognized a puffed and glow-

ing DeMarco accepting the oversize key on behalf of his
shy client.

"This cult shit," the agent was saying, "is breaking my
balls. It's getting everyone all excited. I got it on the inside
that they're gonna form a cult task force. There might be a
grand jury, and me and Stephen would get subpoenaed.
Eva, I don't need this. Nobody can see Stephen like he is,
now."

She said nothing.

"I know you have genuine concern about Stephen. As I
do. Believe that. I've tried to represent what I felt were his
best interests personally and professionally from the word
go, and perhaps I've made some mistakes—"

"Is that all? You've got attorneys. They could plead
incompetence to testify. Your doctors could present affida-
vits. No court would argue with that in his current condition."

There was a pause, and she tried to imagine the expression on the man's face from his voice. It was uncomfortable and evasive.

"This time they may get onto something. Not the cult
deal but—

"Do you still consider, uh, that you're bound by confidentiality? Remember, I know what happened between
you two. I hope you realize you bear an ethical responsibility for his current—"

Her cheeks were burning. "Yes. I'm aware of my 'responsibility.' "

There was the tightening in her chest, successive waves
of guilt and fear. "Has he tried it again?"

"Well, uh, that depends on what you mean—"

"Cut the attorney bullshit!"

He was taken aback, then plunged on; she imagined his
fingers drumming on a desktop, or doodling dollar signs

with negating slashes through them, hunched over one of those damn conference phones.

"Sure. I understand your pique. I apologize. It's like this—" He hesitated. "I think our boy has deeper problems than I realized at first. I was unaware of some things. Truly. I'm not just covering my ass."

He was quiet, uncomfortable, and she let him hang in the silence.

"Are you familiar with M'Naghten?"

The M'Naghten rule, she knew, was the litmus test applied in a court of law to determine whether an accused who was pleading insanity to evade the gas chamber had been capable of differentiating between right and wrong at the time of a murder.

She answered, "I've testified at dozens of trials. Why? Do you think he has a legal problem?" Her heart was racing; she felt the moistness in her palms, the chill condensation of fear inside her brain, lips dry—

"Well, you know artists, and Stephen— But perhaps it's all gone a little further than I suspected. It's come to my attention . . . What I'm afraid of is that Stephen may have found an impressionable, uh, partner in his fantasies, for want of a better—"

Her tone was acidic. "What do you mean 'partner in fantasy'?"

DeMarco lowered his voice, trying to sound casual. "The Bloodletter has this slave called Caligula. He uses him to kill the Thanatas."

He coughed deep in his throat as if he could hardly get the words out. "There was someone Stephen met at Eisenhower. A real psycho name of George Strachan. He was a sex pervert with a wealthy mama who wanted the shrinks to straighten him out. He knew Stephen, and he was cut loose before Stephen was. He evidently came out thinking he was Caligula. Now the cops have singled him out. The task force thinks he's it. The Diver Dan guy."

"Mr. DeMarco—Phil. Do you believe that Stephen may be involved with him some way? That he exerts some sort of control—"

The man was flustered. "I didn't say that. They haven't put two and two together. But I think we need to gird ourselves, be prepared for any eventuality."

She felt her brain freezing. The voice in her blood surging up, a mouth inside her crying in agony. *Don't listen to it, Eva, hang up the phone now—*

"What exactly do you know?"

"It's the business of the tattoos. All the victims had 'em. Hummingbird, the Thanata thing. The cops have been holding that back from the papers. In each case the tattoo was cut out of the skin."

"Is that all?" Her breath had relaxed.

"Uh, no. I'm concerned . . . I've seen certain things in Stephen's apartment which indicate he may have a legal problem if Strachan is responsible for any criminal activity—"

"Like what things?"

"Things that might link him to the murders as far as complicity. Things I've gotta remove. If Strachan's caught, he may claim that Stephen brainwashed him in the hospital. I won't discuss this on the phone, we have to meet and come to some kind of agreement about the eventualities and our position—"

"Have you talked to the police? You've got to—"

"The hell I do. I mean, not until I have a handle on this thing. Do it the right way, you know. Maybe there's nothing to—"

Nothing to any of this?

"Then you wouldn't be calling me." Her voice was flat, determined. "I must see Stephen."

He seemed relieved. "I'm glad to hear you say that, because he hasn't got better. He's become sort of . . . *unmanageable*. He won't talk with Bergman and Epstein. He says he'll only talk to you. And he wants to meet with you. You helped him before when no one else could."

"Where is he?"

"I'll bring him to you. Don't come here."

"You'll bring him *here*?"

"He'd never do that, wouldn't feel safe. Have you ever been to his Hollywood apartment? Harold Way? It's a wastebasket with walls. I think he'll cooperate—to make sure, I'll up his dope so he's feeling no pain. You'll talk to him there. I'll work it out and you be there."

"He's there now?"

"Hell, no. He's on the grounds of the house in the Hills, but he's not going anywhere, that's a goddamn guarantee, until we solidify our posture vis-à-vis . . . I've had to restrain him. The man's tried to kill himself twice—"

"When? What time should I be there?"

"Now, this is going to sound callous, but I've scheduled that damned party this evening—it's the thirteenth."

Ah, yes. The End of Days bash he'd invited her to a world ago. Who would be Thanata on his arm tonight, if not she?

"Why does shit come at the worst possible time? Answer me. I can't get out of it. Some important people—Fassolini included—and I don't want to do anything to arouse—"

"Stephen's going to the party?"

"Hell, no. He never shows up at things like that, so we're okay. But I gotta put in my appearance, business as usual. This is a time to be cool-headed, because we have to avoid even the appearance of anything unusual. There's so much at stake here, more than you can appreciate. I've made commitments, there're investors and obligations and all these people are already skittish. I'm gonna have a drink and calm down. We gotta get our ducks in a row. There's so—''

"What time?"

"I'll try to cut it short. Say, one o'clock? That's only four hours. I suppose I don't have to tell you to come alone? Remember, I'm the one who impressed you with the urgency—''

He sensed her disgust, that none of it was washing with her.

"Forty-two sixteen Harold Way, Number B. There's some things that you need to see. Wait in your car for us."

"I'll be there."

"I'd appreciate it. Stephen will thank you, too. Not now, maybe. But later. And Eva . . .''

"Yes."

"You know, besides me, you're the only one who's seen the other side to him. You got to help me. You got to help him. And you got your own ass to cover in this thing, too— don't forget that."

"I won't forget that."

22

Lugosi's Mansion

PAULA FOLLOWED LARRY ACROSS THE ZOMBIE ZOO parking lot. She had got all dressed up in a low-cut red lambsuede dress with thin satin straps, which fit her like a second skin. V-front, satin piping. But instead of some nice place, Larry had helped her make a cash withdrawal on Daddy's Mastercard and then dragged her resisting to a party at a squalid punk club where the sweating slam dancers were dressed as vampires. The noise and smoke gave her an instant headache and Larry ignored her for an hour for some black bimbo he claimed was an old friend from Narcotics Anonymous who had landed a bit part in *Bloodletter—The Movie.*

The club hushed near eleven o'clock when the wide-screen TV over the taps flared to life. The volume was turned up for the still-ringing ears, and all fevered eyes were on the film coverage of that afternoon's ceremony on Hollywood Boulevard. An older man in a three-piece suit, plump and stuffed like a game hen, was proudly accepting the golden key to the city for Stephen Albright in absentia before a crowd estimated at two thousand. A cheer went up in the bar, obliterating the man's acceptance speech. Then, a booing as the image switched abruptly to the computer-obscured profile of an anonymous young woman ominously intoning, *"Yeah, I was a Morgue Rat. I'm not proud, I just wanna warn the city of LA—"*

The set went dark all at once. The lights in the club flickered twice and there was a mysterious exodus for the door.

Larry had drunk too much, and now he staggered against his white Buick Regal and vomited. His face was blanched. She held his forehead as his stomach convulsed. The sullen black girl stood before them, popping her gum and then rolling the collapsed bubble into her face with a red serpentine tongue. Paula suspected that those striking green eyes were contacts.

"Coming?" she asked Larry, who nodded between pukes.

Paula looked at him in confusion. "There's going to be an End of Days gig at Phil DeMarco's," he said. "Toney Carboni's supposed to be there to shoot a video. I told them we'd follow."

Larry had to tell Paula that Toney Carboni was the drummer for The Bloodletters.

Larry's face was queasy green in the lights of the dash as the car slid roughly onto Hollywood Boulevard then up Laurel Canyon. Paula drove. The smoke had made her contacts greasy and she squinted to see the black Jaguar that glided easily through the red intersection lights toward the sea. The sports car turned sharply up Benedict Canyon without signaling. She saw other sleek machines ahead and behind her in a cortege.

"Why are we going?" she asked with hostility.

She knew the answer. *We might never get a chance again.* The road climbed steeply. The Buick faltered and the Porsche behind them honked. Paula felt the engine under her foot straining to keep pace with the muscular transmissions of the sports cars up Laurel Canyon. His stomach must have settled. He popped a Rolaids and she knew from his voice that he was excited. Hollywood was falling rapidly away, obliterated by dark hills. *He has no idea what I'm feeling.*

She tried to comb her hair in the mirror. "Paula, watch where you're going!" The Buick's engine relaxed as the road flattened on the crest of the hills. Out the windshield she saw once again the far-flung lights of Hollywood. It was breathtaking. The headlamps were vanishing up ahead as if swallowed by a giant lizard. They braked in the thick dust, red eyes flaring angrily. She found herself on a circular drive over which loomed the silhouette of a great house before it was swallowed in the flamelike shadows of the sixty-foot cypresses that pierced the sky. They passed beneath an ancient wooden arch with the weathered superscription:

DENN DIE TODTEN REITEN SCHNELL.

" 'For the dead travel fast,' " Larry enthused. "Heavy. This is Lugosi's old house." He leaned forward to see through the windshield. "It's been vacant for about ten years. Albright'd always had his eye on it. Trippy. Excellent." His eyes were shiny. "Albright's a super freak. What a head that guy's got. I wonder if he's gonna be here. That's one dude I'd like to rap with." He was checking himself in the mirror as he talked.

The pocked drive followed the curving terraced stone works of a mansion of odd, almost Moorish, architecture. Sagging pomegranate with burst and rotted fruit alongside dusky olive trees bordered overgrown hedges and rank unweeded gardens of dark flowers. Fractured statuary and primitive steles. The party crew disgorged from the sports cars was walking quickly up the steps to the house past a black bubbling fountain in which pale shapes glided to the surface and then faded.

A hollow clank of the oaken door opening. The party crowd and their laughter were sucked into the black mouth.

Paula felt strangely weak as soon as they entered, as if she were in the airless hull of a submarine. The mind-numbing strobe light was filtered red, washing all in splashed blood. Cigarettes smoldered untended in ashtrays, and cubes of ice melted and slipped silently down glasses. Some of the furniture was covered by protective sheets like big condoms, and dust was thick on the mantel and the floor. Despite the dirt and must, a few young costumed revelers from the club, eye sockets painted deep purple and cheeks hollowed with dark grease and all their makeup running from dance-floor exertion, lounged comfortably and familiarly on the floor before the large plush sofas and the twin love seats with their twenties-era patterns of ugly purple flowers. But no Toney Carboni and no Bloodletters.

The unfinished walls were hung with full-color blowups of the covers of Albright's paperbacks. The macabre centerpiece was a bronze casket with lining of red velvet on a bier that supported a cardboard promotional poster for the unfinished film. Black candles burned in Gothic candelabra and a detached hand beckoned to visitors from atop a grand piano.

"What are you looking for?" she asked Larry in irritation.

"The holes in the walls where the secret cameras were," he said. "I heard about this house. Lugosi was kind of a voyeur and had hidden cameras and two-way mirrors. That sort of thing."

How nice. Paula felt out of breath. A butch older woman with suet-colored skin had her arm protectively around a

young girl with dead eyes and purple hair. Lots of leather
in the room. Even a hint of violence: some older, more
conservative business-types seemed resentful of the intrud-
ers. The dresses of their wives looked casual, but Paula
knew Rodeo Drive when she saw it. The fact that the booze
had been flowing for a while probably dulled the tension.
Laughing softly, the women moved with languor. Small
groups broke apart and re-formed around faces that
looked familiar to Paula from television. She tried not to
stare. But it seemed too many people were looking at her
suspiciously. Nameless, groundless fear.

"DeeeeMarcooooo," Larry whispered portentously in
her ear. She saw him. It was the stuffed shirt who'd accepted the key to the city on the news. "Albright's agent.
He owns all the SlimWays, too." The cadaverous women
on his arms looked more familiar. Where? Larry recognized them, too. Tall and dark beneath black hair that
flowed down her supple back, the first wore a black satin
acetate sheath out of which poked the thumblike nipples
of her round breasts. The other was a beautiful Asian, who
reminded Paula of a little girl dressed up in mother's
feather boa, eyes wasted in a bony face. "The look." *I'm
surrounded by vampires.* Paula was acutely aware of her own
body. *I'm too alive.* Larry supplied the names.

"That's Eeka, and Loy Bang. Hard to tell with their
clothes on, huh?"

They were the actresses from so many of Larry's pornographic videocassettes, the ones he'd insisted Paula watch
to "loosen her up." The two beauties had starred together
in the classic *Cluster Fuck.*

Eeka was an American Indian, or half-Indian, red and
statuesque, who'd also done some sort of exercise tape.
Loy Bang's small tapered fingers rested lightly on the inside of DeMarco's taut thigh on the couch where he held
court. Paula was fascinated, watching them, recalling

graphically their most intimate body parts and the varieties of sexual experiences they had enacted for her and Larry in the privacy of his dark apartment. A strange nostalgia swept her. *Private Dick. Wet Dreams.*

Paula's attention had gravitated to a mass of flesh that had formed itself around one tortured end of the settee opposite DeMarco. One of the man's coterie of boyish sycophants addressed him as Fassolini. He was young, but must have weighed four hundred pounds. She caught the barest intimations of a weirdly pitched effeminate voice as he spoke, sometimes in Italian. Underneath his fashionable polo shirt his feminine breasts were revealed, fascinating Paula until she found herself unable to look up at his face. Fat had always fascinated her.

Paula, lighting her cigarette, felt eyes on her back. At the same time, Larry was startled by a strong hand on his shoulder. DeMarco was standing in front of them a little uncertainly. His vodka stinger, in which a lime circle swam dully, was about to slosh on the carpet. She saw the gray hair on his knuckles; his hands were huge and meaty, the nails large.

"What are you people doing here? All you people? What's with this? People I invited don't come, and people I don't invite—"

Paula felt Eeka and Loy Bang, smelled them before she saw them, as they came up behind her to flank DeMarco. She avoided their impassive eyes, but felt Larry's tension through his arm. The girls' eyes wandered distractedly and they were trying to calm the older man, pull him away. "No, goddammit. I'm talking to these people. Everybody thinks they can just crash here 'cause DeMarco's a nice guy . . ." Slurring his words.

The porno queens' eyes. *How many men?* Paula wondered. *What must that feel like? How do they see themselves?* And yet she suspected they were more comfortable with their

images on the movie screen than she was with her own reflection in the bathroom mirror in the morning. They had
such wonderful complexions. *Semen facials? It agrees with
them.*

Then they were leading him away and he had changed
faces, and was Mr. Nice Guy blowing smoke up some big-
wig's ass. "Problems? No problems, just opportunities . . .
within a year . . . premiere . . . rough cut . . . few select
locations . . ." His voice receding.

The guests were stirring, rising and ambling through the
outer door after DeMarco as if the room was an hourglass
upended and emptying. With Larry she trickled into a hall
dimly lit by flickering wall lamps. The air was dusty. The
short walk opened into a larger room.

"Albright's private theater," Larry said excitedly.

A movie? *Night of the Living Dead?*

The seats were in curved rows of plush red. Most were in
need of reupholstering and the carpet was worn and
frayed. Musty smell. The curved ceiling, in which artificial
stars of gold mosaic glimmered like dull fireflies, showed
urine-yellow stains of water damage and white patches
where stucco had fallen away. One wall was decorated with
a decayed fresco of Romeo and Juliet. Their faces, though,
were over-painted with skulls. The ancient curtain was parting with an audible swish to reveal the movie screen, stirring a thin haze of dust.

In the first row, old women were clustered near the president of Bela Lugosi's fan club as if she were a bulbous
queen termite. "Jesus," Larry said. "The Lugosi widows.
They used to come into this restaurant I bussed at."

As they found a middle seat, Paula was trying to warm
the dankness by breathing through her nose. She froze.
The tall swarthy figure was half-hidden in shadow. It was
the vampire from the cover of the paperbacks.

"His name's Jurgen Mohler," Larry said. "He's the new

discovery who's going to play The Bloodletter in the film. Big secret. I think he's Fassolini's boyfriend.''

The blood had returned to her heart before her color betrayed her.

She felt cold fingers brush lightly on her neck and turned to see a girl with braces settling into the seat next to her. In her hand was a small mirror on which was piled and reflected a tiny pyramid of cocaine. She cut it deftly into two lines with a razor blade. Paula's heart was beating fast. She smiled uncertainly, but then Larry had taken the mirror from her hands.

"When in Rome . . ." he said with a silly smile. She chilled as she watched him snort a thin line with the little straw, his nostril magnified, gaping and cavernous in the mirror. His eyes teared as he passed the coke on to a young man sitting alone two seats down from him.

She wanted him to see the disapproval on her face, but he wouldn't look. She knew what he was thinking. Maybe he was ashamed of his queasiness at the club. *I never tried to stop you from doing anything.* She prided herself on her sophistication. She even had some curiosity and would not have minded trying the cocaine, but not this way, among all these strangers where she already had so much anxiety. She resented him. Sucking up all his drinks so fast. She knew what he was doing. He was putting her in the position of nursemaid for the night and she did not like it. She looked around the theater at the shadowy faces, alarmed, searching for someone familiar, any point of comfort. Nothing.

A snatch of overheard conversation: ". . . She'd apparently said, 'May I take your stole?' But what I heard was, 'May I harvest your soul . . . ?' "

The electric light faded, the room darkening.

A white beam shot to the screen, which flickered to life at the lower end of the theater. There were clicks of cigarette lighters and yellow flames like distant campfires that were extinguished in halos of gray smoke. Giggles were quickly hushed like the lighters clicking shut.

It was a teaser. A pale and attractive man standing against a dungeon wall. He was tightly confined in a straitjacket. His eyes were demented.

"Good evening," he said, slurring slightly. "I'm Stephen Albright. I'm sorry I couldn't be with you in person, but I'm unavoidably restrained." Here he looked sheepishly down at the straitjacket to appreciative laughter in the theater. "I appreciate your loyalty and support. I would probably even be emotional and moved if I wasn't heavily medicated." There was more laughter as a figure in a lab coat walked into the frame and drew an absurdly long syringe full of clear liquid, spurted it experimentally in the air as the writer continued contemptuously. "You may all be morons, but you're my morons. And the sicker you get, the better stories I'll have for you. That's all." He was gone.

"Vintage Albright," a pipe-smoking geek in a sweater was yukking from a seat behind them, slapping his knee for emphasis.

The next film clip was scratchy.

A group of people lounged around a swimming pool squinting into the sunlight.

"Home movies," she heard a gruff voice say behind her, and she turned her head. It was DeMarco. He had quietly taken a seat in the last row to the left and was leaning forward to whisper in the ear of an older man with a toupee and a fertility symbol around his neck. "Lugosi's. We found a cache of this stuff in the attic, reels and reels. That's this very house in the background—recognize the cupolas?"

The paint on the house looked fresh, the gardens neat and trim. The people were nude, lounging around a pool in the sunlight.

Cut.

Building movie sets in the desert. Bare-chested carpenters with hammers, sweating over fake fronts. DeMarco again, talking into the other man's hearing aid.

"Lugosi tried to finance his own remake of *Der Vampyre* . . . What's his name. He was gonna direct and star in it with Peg Entwistle, but she committed suicide."

Cut.

A night scene. A party.

The men had stripped off their coats and were in white shirtsleeves, drinks in hand. The girls were scantily clad and greased in some kind of oil. A starter pistol was fired noiselessly and they raced across the lawn on their hands and knees, the men rushing after them to grapple at the oily bodies, floundering atop them, or heaving them over their shoulders to carry them into the dark bushes.

The scene changed. Another crude splice.

Whose film was this?

The figures were dim, shadowy as if shot from a hidden camera, or through a mirror in bad light. There was the form of a man approaching a bed on which something stirred among the covers. A head upraised, the hair tousled and smoky against the diffuse light of the window. There was the cantilevered silhouette of her breasts. He turned her tenderly over, her lips moved noiselessly, the mist of smoke as she extinguished a cigarette.

He was on his knees over her, slipping something over her neck. A necklace. No, a cord. Her face relaxed into the pillow, her small round buttocks high in the air, round as moons. He tensed into her, his profile sharply handsome.

He tightened the rope. Her spine became rigid. His legs tensed. Her shoulders twisted, her head drawn up, the lips contorted. They froze into a tableau.

Her body struggled then relaxed, the shadows clouded and obscuring. The muscular hands seemed to relax. The chest heaved with passionate breath. He waited. She stirred. The small fingers of her hand fluttered. There was the insinuation of a smile on her indistinct face.

He began to move on his knees, rocking slowly. She weakly assumed his rhythms. His wrists drew up on the ends of the cord around her neck as if they were reins, and a sigh broke from his lips.

It went on and on, murkily, a strange adventure of movement, a dumb show of suggestion and old shadows. A movement, heads raised. *There are four of them in the bed.*

Music came to life on the soundtrack, deepening, darkening. Paula's scalp prickled. The violins had risen to an eerie whine cold as space.

Paula was aware of a new dynamic suddenly in the theater. There was a tension, and a coldness as though the temperature had dropped. Hands had appeared to crawl over armrests like tarantulas on a load of fruit, entwining the fingers of other hands. Soft cheeks inclined onto shoulders. The couple in front of Paula fell into a passionate kiss. Small sighs and exhalations, cries of joy, drifted through the darkness. The girl with braces sniffled in her seat next to Paula, a tiny trickle of blood running out one nostril and down her lip. She licked it absently and there were tears in her eyes.

The aperture constricted to a hypnotic dot of light.

Paula was holding Larry's inert arm. She noticed his eyes were bright and sharp. Paula felt the hairs on her wrist tickle. She was surrounded by foreheads that were half-illumined in the reflected light of the screen. The white made-up faces of the teenage girls glowed.

An acne-scarred boy from the club, sallow and pouting under arched painted brows, leaned his head on the shoulder of DeMarco, who seemed to have fallen temporarily asleep. With his other hand Albright's agent casually stroked the plump breast of a young girl with smeared lips and violet eyeliner who inhaled deeply on a cigarette as she watched the screen between bites on a candy bar.

The screen and the theater went to black. Paula felt her mind decompressing. There was a pause, and the screen splintered and scarred over a splice. Grainy black and white, the camera trembling.

Dirty walls. Scuffed. Tile floor.

A barren operatory. A girl, frightened, above the sheet her face white, the texture of oleomargarine, sweating and terrified. Below the sheet she was horribly exposed, her bent knees clamped in black iron gynecological stirrups. The camera came closer to her nakedness. Forceps. Opening the cervix. She seemed to strain with arched back to escape the metallic intrusion. Rubber gloved hands. She squirmed desperately. The camera closer. A sponge stick, dilating the cervix. A curette in the gloved fingers.

Paula looked away. She could almost hear, almost feel, the internal scraping of the blade in the uterus. A wave of nausea. Even Larry seemed a little sick to his stomach. "Mondo Weirdo," he whispered. "Looks like a Tijuana abortion, or something. Christ, and they wonder why Peg Entwistle offed herself."

Paula heard the film clattering on a spool in the projection booth behind them. She reached for Larry, but he wasn't there. She stood uncertainly and felt someone pressing her as she groped her way awkwardly to the aisle and into the hall. She found herself feeling the wall among the close bodies, disoriented as if it were a carnival funhouse. Finally, they came into the murky green light of the main room. She could breathe.

Larry?

She saw him in a corner in conversation with Eeka and Loy Bang. All had drinks in their hands. The dark Eeka, a head taller than Larry, was demonstrating something with her tongue. Loy Bang giggled against the curtain, her dimpled knee brushing his leg as he lit her cigarette. *He's making a jerk of himself. They're making fun of him and he doesn't even know it.*

Paula felt her face redden. The nausea returned. She wheeled abruptly on her heel and ran into the muscular flared chest of Phil DeMarco. His red eyes looked startled, too, as if he had been lost and was seeing her for the first time. He looked a little blearily across the room at Larry. His pursed mouth was solicitous. Were his eyes laughing?

"DeMarco, Phil," he said, extending his hand. "Those clips shake you up? Pretty damned tasteless. Why do these kids get off on 'em? Go figure. I'm Albright's agent. You've read his books? Everybody loves his books."

His face was the same color as her father's when he got drunk. He put a heavy paw on her shoulder. "Let's go for a walk, Nice Pissed-Off Young Woman person who crashed my party. I'll take you on a little tour of Stephen's castle."

The man guided her through another door and into a dim hall. He lifted his hand from her shoulder. Had he sensed her discomfort? But he was only activating the indirect lighting, which appeared to have been recently installed. The hard floor was thick with plaster dust fine as talcum powder. "The contractor's been out here all week," he whispered. "It's a vast pain in the ass." The dust rose with each step and covered their shoes.

They had come onto a veranda. The air was crisp. He flicked a switch and buzzing electric beams shot out across the nets and freshly painted courts.

"Tennis?" he asked, but he looked in no condition to play. "Do you know who built this house?"

"Larry told me. He's the guy I'm with."

He shook his head.

"Lugosi owned the house, but it was built by F. W. Murnau in 1924. Lugosi had met Murnau and was fascinated by his work. He had to have this house, just like Stephen had to have it. And I got him for it. I mean, I got it for him."

DeMarco rested a muscular leg on the loose railing, the thick meat of his flexed thigh stretching the thin white material of his trousers. She kept seeing Larry with the two women. She was aware of the strange warmth of DeMarco next to her and his smell, which was sort of like her father's, and it crossed her mind, for an instant . . . But would Larry even care? He might. He would want to hear all about it, and she would have his attention—for a little while.

"Here," he was saying. "Are you any kinda student of films? This is interesting."

There was a glossy photo of Lugosi with a motley line of Indians in the California desert. "He came to know them when he was shooting *Angel of Death* in the summer of '32. They worked cheap." He laughed. "That was his retitle of 'Der Vampyre . . . Magnum,' whatever. Shot at the same desert site Murnau built his sets."

The red Indian children were touching the hem of Lugosi's tweed coat, which he wore despite the heat. His long fingers rested paternally on their shoulders. "Old Bela. 'Suffer little children.' "

She found herself following DeMarco's hard buttocks up a steep Spanish tiled stairwell. They look like bowling balls in his trousers, she thought. There were dozens of steps and through the occasional crescent of window the stars were bright and close. At the landing he unlocked another door. The light was already on inside.

"We're up in the tower," he said, breathing hard. "You prob'ly saw it from the drive." He nodded for her to precede him. "This is what Stephen's room's gonna look like." The drink sloshed in his hand.

She recognized the distinctive window. *From that weird film. The man and woman.* There was a huge black bed in

the center of the plush red carpet. He saw the reflex of her
face, her eyes. He pushed past her into the room.

"This is the heart of the house. Stephen wants to move
in next month. I'm gonna fix up his word processor and
stuff and he'll work, right here."

The future home of Stephen Albright. She was struck by the
mural, a fresco in deep greens and indigos of a plush garden where the red-veined plants seemed to throb and ripple from thick pulsing roots in moist earth. Paula saw her
own reflection in the great faceted crystal mirror set in the
ceiling. The room was oddly shaped. She counted. *Pentag-
onal.*

"We're restoring this wing, first."

She remembered something Eva had said. "The neurotic dreams of a castle, while the psychotic lives in one."

"Maybe this'll be a museum some day. The estate was a
real white elephant. It's been vacant the last ten years. In
bad shape, really run down. But a lot of the original furnishings were still here. Many of Lugosi's personal articles
had been sold at auction after he went broke. Goddamn
IRS. You bet I played hell tracking them down and buying
them from private collectors."

The carpet did feel luxuriant beneath her shoes.

DeMarco winked. "Me and Stephen are tight. We're like
this. Nobody knows him like I do. For instance, he has a
sense of humor. Even had a special effects guy actually
make up phony body parts out of latex, just to pull my leg.
Leave 'em lying around just to see my reaction—"

She started to light a cigarette, but DeMarco shook his
head peremptorily. He whistled low, walking slowly away
from Paula across the room. He sat on the bed, his hands
gripping his knees. He turned to her. "You don't talk
much. You're not a reporter, are you?" He satisfied himself, his mouth relaxing. "Maybe I'm paranoid. I been

going through some rough times recently. A writer tried to get up here last week disguised as an electrician. Anything for a story."

He was watching her face.

"Please, relax," he said. *He just wanted to get me up here. I bet it works, too, on the young Albright groupies.* He stood, and the mattress springs rose slowly to fill the cleft hollow his buttocks had left. He wasn't sober, yet.

"What's in there?" she asked to distract him. He seemed uncomfortable as she moved the sliding door to reveal a concealed closet of pegboard studded with hooks. Ropes. Whips. Handcuffs.

"Stephen's gonna display his collection there. What a pack rat—collects instruments since he was a kid. Anything that's kinda odd or unusual."

There is so much unhappiness in this room, Paula thought. *I'm drowning.*

He closed the door almost on her fingers, distracted. "Check this out," he was saying in a bored but subtle voice, diverting her by nodding to a sculpture on the mantel above an art deco vase of fresh tuberoses and bird of paradise. She stepped closer. On a velvety sable was a large black onyx phallus. DeMarco adjusted the small key light beneath it.

Her mouth was dry. She wondered if this was supposed to be the pièce de résistance in DeMarco's standard seduction. It caught the red light from the lamp and reflected it back at her. He stood close behind her as she read the card.

All men shall try to copy, thro' vain tears, the living magic beauty of his ART.

"Ever see a vampire's dick? It's supposedly a relic of the original Bloodletter. Murnau bought it in Europe. Lugosi acquired it from the estate. Now it's Stephen's.''

She could not look at the man. She did not want to see him, have his eyes search her face, yet she did not like to feel his eyes on her back, her neck. The red carpet, the Chinese red walls, were crawling with pain. The plush of the carpet was suddenly obscene under her feet.

She tried to step away, felt the man pressing against her. His eyes were still studying the black dildo.

"It is, perhaps, uh . . . *artistically enhanced*. It's so big—right?" He winked. "But this *is* the City of Dreams."

She faced him; she had to.

He smiled and a distant filling in a hind molar sparkled silver. He rubbed his thumb nervously inside the elastic waistband of his beltless slacks. His breath was sharp and sweet from the liquor. He smiled more widely and the taut skin above his cheeks drew his ears down perceptibly. She did not like what it did to his face. A red flush had appeared at the edge of his scalp.

She felt herself sweating under her arms, felt a drop slide down her side within the loose dress, suddenly turn cold.

"Where is the ladies' room?" she asked. It was an embarrassing ploy but all she could think of. *I have to pee.* He raised his eyebrows, nodded to a narrow door with a gilt knob. "I'm sure I can find my way back," Paula said assertively, with more confidence than she felt.

He winked with resignation, maybe even relief. "Sure you can."

She closed the door behind her. She was glad for the chance to think and catch her breath. There was a large bathtub with ornate fixtures and an old cast-iron wall heater. A white rug warmed her feet as she kicked off her shoes. It was a habit she'd had since she was a little girl. The toilet seat was softened by white sable.

She lowered herself carefully. She had always been most

comfortable in bathrooms. It had been her sanctuary at home, the inviolable precinct where she hid. It was like time out. You locked the door and the world relinquished all expectations of you. She was opposite a full-length mirror with beveled corners and delicate gold-leaf scrollwork. The etched monogram BL. Larry would love it. *Where is he? Has he even noticed I've been gone? How did I get here?* She felt the tickling of an almost hysterical giggle. The tension. Eva said, "Find your center."

She thought she saw a shadow, and then a flicker and brief arc of light darkly through the glass. It was gone. She retraced the gesture in her mind. A cigarette lighter. The definition of the shadow sharpened again, seemed to lean toward her, then recede. She was suddenly aware of her own naked knees splayed before her. *Two-way mirror?* Larry had been right. Someone was watching her.

Tears rolled. Her vision swam murkily. She daubed at herself numbly with the nauseous green paper and stepped quickly to rearrange her clothing with trembling fingers. She opened the door and held her breath.

She walked stiffly through the bedroom and down the dark stairwell. She paused in the hall, listening for laughter from other rooms. She knew her face was deep red with shame. Something had broken inside her and she felt diminished. She was desperate for a way out to the car but did not want to chance running into DeMarco, into anyone. The keys? Larry had them.

She tried another door and found herself in what appeared to have been a sitting room. Dust was thick on the floor. The light switch did not work. She heard a rustling. There was a whimper, and then a groan. A grunt. She walked quickly through but could not stop her eye from catching the graceful turn of an ankle dangling over the arm of a chaise. A man's scuffed brown boot was on the floor. She froze. The figures were shadowy. A head upraised in vague surprise, the hair tousled. It was a bearded biker with his pants around his ankles. Beneath him, Paula saw two small round female buttocks high in the air, receiving him. She turned quickly and stepped through a veranda door around which green curtains fluttered invitingly.

23

The Prince of Paperback Horror

THE AIR WAS REFRESHING AS A GLASS OF WATER splashed in her face. She began to recover her equilibrium. Larry was probably wondering where she was by now. He could try to find her. *The prick*. Terracotta tiles clicked under her heels as she walked down the terrace toward the vast emerald lawn. She shuddered once across her shoulders at the house behind her.

She walked among the strange shapes of black funeral steles, which erupted from the grass like resurrected dead. Vague laughter and gliding window shapes receded. She stared into the shimmering green of an old swimming pool where deep drowned aquamarine lights burned coolly at the bottom.

Her head snapped at the sound of laughter from the acres of lawn to her back. The bushes, the squirming figures. The girls were scantily clad and their bare flesh glowed in the moonlight as though they were slicked with Vaseline, while naked men chased and then tackled them, grappling and then floundering atop them in the whispering grass. She strained her eyes in fascination for a moment, then walked resolutely on.

She found herself at the edge of a cliff. The lights of Hollywood were poured out on the valley below then swirled back up and scattered as bright stars high overhead. She felt herself being siphoned off into coldly infinite nothingness. In the distance, the vast gap-toothed sign on the hillside, lest anyone forget where they were.

A squat shadow to her right. She thought at first it was a dark cabana almost hidden by thick pyracantha. But it was enclosed, of dark redwood. Strangely sightless. No windows. A converted groundskeeper's cottage; no, it was a newer prefab structure. Something drew her and she stepped closer through the waxy leaves of some rank hedges. Curiosity. It was strangely expectant.

The voice was a fierce whisper through the thick door.

"Who is it? I know you're there." The voice frightened her. "Closer. Come on. *Please!*"

She pressed her ear to the door.

"Who is it?" the voice asked again.

"Paula. Paula Kightlinger." There was an intake of breath and then silence.

"Who are you?" she asked finally. No answer. She turned to leave, suddenly apprehensive. The voice had recovered itself, was urgent.

"Paula." The tone was imperious.

"Who . . . ?" she started to ask, but he was speaking again.

"There are two keys under that urn. A large one and a smaller silver one. They fit the locks."

"I want to know who you are."

"Me? Stephen Albright, the Prince of Paperback Horror."

No shit?

"Why are you locked in?"

"It's sort of a management dispute thing. Where's DeMarco?"

"He's up at the house——"

"Unlock this damn door. Please."

The urn was large and heavy, and she strained her back scooting it five inches on the brickwork. Her fingers searched in the dark through the silty humus that had leaked from the holes in the bottom of the big clay pot. She stood uncertainly, the keys in her hand.

"Got it?" It was a tense demand, startling and confusing her. Her fingers trembled as she fit the keys into the ugly industrial security locks, which seemed to have been recently installed.

The door opened inward. There were damp footprints from the door and across the floor. She saw a word processor with reams of paper, yards and yards of print coiled like a paper snake vomited from the printer. *Writers fascinate me, they're so creative and sensitive. They have whole worlds in their heads.*

"I'm here."

She followed the words. She was embarrassed, realizing she was staring into a sunken hot tub encircled by crystal glasses in which candles flickered in the breeze. The blue water swirled and frothed hotly, glimmering with fragments of fire that churned around a naked body. She recognized him from his portrait on the back of the paperbacks, at the same time realized she was herself silhouetted against the lights of the house.

It *was* the man from the movie at the house. The bony face was handsome but frightening above the odd silver medal that hung from his neck. He was a razor, the features too intense and sharpened as if by starvation. Pared of flesh almost, like a demented galley slave, and his eyes were feverishly expectant. "I was waiting for you."

He must have seen me leave the house. But there are no windows in here.

He slid quickly along the slippery tub to rest his sweating face on his arms. Her heart began to pound. She could see nothing beneath the foaming water. The skin of his chest was incredibly thin, so thin she felt she could see his thoughts rippling the flesh.

No. They're scars. It shocked her. *I remember. He keeps trying to kill himself.* She felt kinship and sympathy.

His smile was disjointed and flickering, and it bothered her that he wasn't talking but just staring at her. She had to look away. She crossed her arms over her chest, felt her breasts bunch, released them awkwardly. *He's playing with me.* Her chin was trembling and she measured the distance to the door.

Something was odd about the room. No sharp edges. No glass. No sheets on the cot. No clothes. It was like the violent ward, a lush-plush rubber room. And on three large easels were several rough drawings on yellowed paper. She recognized it as a storyboard for a movie. They all crudely portrayed a naked girl atop the large H of the HOLLYWOOD sign.

"They're over seventy years old," the writer was saying. He was looking past her to the door. "Murnau was blocking out the final scene for his very strange film. It was about The End of Days, the Advent of which is being celebrated right now up at the house. All around us and everywhere. The vampire has always been a part of me. And I a part of him."

She felt the tension crawling up her spine, felt a twitch in her cheek.

"How long have you been in here?" she asked in a quavering voice.

"About a thousand years. Is this Friday?" His smile was

unnerving and institutional. "Sit down," he commanded. She lowered herself cross-legged on the wooden deck. "Let me see you." His eyes were on her face as he slid back across the tub away from her. "Let me see you without your clothes. I won't hurt you. To hurt you would be my own death."

Oh my God. Her face reddened. *Why was I born with skin like a barometer?*

He had flicked an unseen switch activating a light hidden in the Jacuzzi. The water suddenly turned a deep warm red. He was moving slowly but there was something dangerous and coiled and explosive about him.

Her voice wavered. "I don't think that's such a good idea. I have a boyfriend up at the house and he's probably wondering where I am right now."

"I've lived forever and I understand all things. He's disappointed you because he's so insensitive. You thought he was something but he wasn't and it's not the first time. No man's ever appreciated you, your love has never been returned. You've always been hurt but still you know in your heart you're helplessly romantic. You've never lost hope and no one else knows how much it's cost you."

He was lighting another candle. "Paula, do you remember the lake? Do you remember his dark hands on your breasts while you stared across the water and wondered where your sister was?"

She was stunned.

"I know all about you. You've always felt different. No one's ever understood you and you've wished you could die sometimes. You've dreamed of finding out who you really are because all you've ever been sure of is that no one can see the real you."

She felt a tightness in her throat. She'd seen it in the wards: *Crazy people, sometimes they can see right inside you. They talk and it shouldn't make sense but it does and you've got to stop them, get them out of your head or they'll sweep you right—*

"How did you get started? Writing, I mean."

No, that was stupid. I don't want him to think I'm shallow.

He was saying, "Have you always felt you had a destiny, Paula? Have you always known you were unique?"

She was feeling dizzy. *I've always felt I would do something remarkable if just given the chance. But it's a line, it's probably true of most of the women in the world and I bet he's used it a thousand times.* "I haven't read any of your books. Stop it. Stop talking to me."

He was lighting another candle and she saw that his hand was trembling. She knew even as he said it that he couldn't stop. "You don't have to read them to know the story. Of all the millions yours alone is the appointment. You've always known the fear, the nameless groundless fear that didn't have a face."

I have known. Depression. Anxiety. Like I was living the wrong life, that mine should be more exciting and special. Stop it. Stop doing this to me. Why are you—

"You've *always* been waiting. Until now."

"Waiting for what . . ." Her voice numb.

I do know: the dizzying moment. When I'd take an awful leap so daring that I'd never be able to take it back because I would be transformed. And scared all the time that when it came I wouldn't recognize it, or if I did, that I wouldn't be equal to it.

"Paula, I know who you are." His voice hoarse; his eyes wild. "I thought it was Eva, at first. And I was wrong. And then I thought she was betraying me, and I was wrong. I didn't recognize her, but I know now what she is. The White Witch."

He took the amulet dripping from his neck and handed it to Paula.

"You must give this to Eva. Please tell her that Stephen is sorry for the pain he's caused her."

She took it numbly, bewildered—but he was already

speaking, breathing high and excited in his chest.

"Your whole life has led you inexorably to this moment in time. You've felt like a terrified stranger in the world, but now everything that's been so meaningless is going to make sense. It's been a long sleep. But now you're going to wake up."

Her mind was racing. *I'm too emotional to deal with this. Everything is strange, there's no reference to the familiar. This isn't happening to me. There's nothing to hold on to. I can stop it. I can stop it now before it's too late. I'm afraid.*

She was surprised at the alacrity with which she stood up lightheaded, her heart thudding once or twice to catch up with her thin and racing blood to send it rushing in her ears. *It's not too late.* Her clothes were rustling as they fell around her knees. *For the first time in my life I'm doing something really extraordinary. Finally, something is happening to me.*

She was slipping into the pool. The water was hot and violent under the surface. She could hardly stand. The current rushed and swirled in a strong vortex that pulled and swept her, alternately pushing and sucking. She tried to look as if she were not struggling. She felt her skin reddening and hoped she would not look like a lobster. The warm flow flushed rapidly between her legs as her stomach vibrated with the sharp jets of foam. She felt sweat forming instantly under her nose and lips as her eye makeup turned greasy and began to run.

She was melting, smelting down into her elemental chemicals. Her sweaty scalp tickled with the hair that fell in the hot mist to cling in tight ringlets to her forehead. Perspective was so different in the tub. Now she, too, was blurred and burning. It was a more intimate communion than she had imagined as the same invasive water that flooded under his arms and between his legs swirled and hugged her wetly, churning them together.

The water was pulling her closer. Her knuckles were

white as they gripped the edge of the tub. He slid toward her, his body shimmering in the froth. Her legs spread absently in the undertow as she was lifted by the water from the bottom of the pool, the muscles in her straining arms beginning to ache and cramp. Her breath, too, was trapped high in her chest and she couldn't move it. *Dizzy. I'm going into hyperventilation.*

He was rising up out of the tub on slender arms, pulling her along with him. She imagined she saw herself from behind, short legs straining and fleshy buttocks dimpled with cellulite, the pale elastic stretch marks she had massaged all summer with cocoa butter. *Why am I—* Her knees weakened with confused emotion.

Her scalp felt the brush of his lips and suddenly his fragile nakedness was against her, trembling with aching need as if he had a chill. His hands were almost timid. *My mind is separating from my body.* The child inside her was grateful and moved deeper into his encompassing closeness.

His arms were around her neck, his soft stomach against her breasts. Her mind was thrashing and clutching for balance. He was lowering her onto the carpet. Shame began to singe her cheeks.

Stephen Albright was offering his beseeching eyes for refuge. His small feet had hooked around the arches of her own as if they were stirrups. He began desperately to kiss her neck and her shoulders and her arms. *Larry.* There were dark fingers between her legs exploring with furious curiosity her hooded secrets. She experienced an unexpected warm weakness of letdown, moist involuntary confession of flesh. *I don't understand. He's not physically my type at all.* But her body was sensitive as a safecracker's abraded fingertips.

She began to cry. His taking possession was clumsy and tremulous. It was as if he had curled weakly into her and started to wither, his breath frightened pants in her ear.

Oh, no. She pressed his trembling body close to her breast in a reflex that was maternal; his shivering shoulders seemed to relax, and she gradually sensed him growing inside her. He rested there in his unexpected fullness, his lips kissing her with trepidation. His soft breath was warm in her nose.

He's home. He's lost inside me. He arched his neck to kiss her forehead and there was released in her a rush of malice for Larry. The conflict gave bitter edge to her own excitement. *It's not supposed to be this way.*

Now she felt that creative energy coursing through her. He was rolling her pleadingly onto her back, moving deftly under her leg so that she was on her side, her fleshy buttock against his soft stomach as he ran himself in and out slickly along her leg in a gently fulfilling coming and going. His febrile surging and receding was becoming confident and regular as the rhythm of waves. She closed her eyes to become part of it, knowing her face was betraying her desire.

The writer was growing stronger within her womb. *For the first time in my life, I am not ashamed of my breasts.* He varied his rhythms, and each change was a new inflection of sensation with its own pleasant dynamics. She was receiving redly pulsing responses to the signals of her own contractions; and all the time his eyes never left her face as if terrified of breaking the connection and falling off the edge of the world.

Who are you?

She did not know if the question was hers or his. When the wantonness rippled over her she tried to turn her head away, but the gravity of his eyes was too strong and she was like a moon swung out centrifugally yet unable to escape its magnetism. She saw something in his gray eyes. *Is this it? Am I going to understand?*

She tried to scream but stumbled on little cries of pleasure high in her own lungs. Her searching fingers clutched at the hypotrophic ridges of scar on his back as her excitement quivered and flushed around him.

He threw back his head and pain convulsed his face as a scream tore his throat. It happened for her at the same time. She heard her own cries as she felt them both dissolving into light.

She huddled drained and exhausted against him. The beating of his heart relaxed her and she felt a strange deep sleep coming on. The sleep was alive with visions.

24

Phil DeMarco

PAULA SAW HERSELF IN A PLACE OF FLICKERING OR-
ange shadows. It was the main room of Lugosi's mansion.
Paula was naked and there were black unlighted candles at
the four points of the funeral bier on which she lay drowsily as if drugged. Loy Bang and Eeka and Eva LaPorte stood
over her, their hands positioning her gently. Paula's slug-
gish mind took inventory of all her physical flaws. She felt
exposed and vulnerable but the hands, Eva's especially,
were calming as they tenderly spread and arranged her
hair in a red corona over her head. Then Loy Bang motioned for the electric lights to be extinguished. The room
was dark until Eeka lighted the soft candles.

Paula sensed the black girl with green cat's eyes gesturing or communicating to Albright's guests to come forward. She felt their stammering approach, sensed their
feet shuffling around her, was warmed by their breath.
There were shy hands on her body, timorously exploring
her stomach and legs. A plump and bespectacled matron
moaned with startling abandon and brushed her long hair

over Paula's eyes and breasts. Paula saw the fan club queen's face lumpy and foreshortened above her, nostrils cavernous as if seen through a fish-eye lens. It seemed to signal a relaxing of general inhibitions as if creating a new entity out of the gathered. She felt their press and murmurings as their hands on her flesh became bolder and more insistent. She felt the palms on her breasts, the fingers running along her thighs, the faces filling even her closed eyes.

It was all almost suffocating and unendurable when the wall flickered to life under the blaze of a movie projector. Paula was aware of a new dynamic suddenly in the room. There was a coldness. Hands entwining the fingers of other hands. Soft cheeks inclined onto shoulders. All heads turned in unison and Paula herself strained to see. It was a scratchy black-and-white silent film and its young starlet looked very much like Paula herself.

It was night and she was atop the H on the great HOLLYWOOD sign. She was on the bed—no, a gynecological table, her feet bowed in the stirrups. Over her was a dark and faceless figure, but she knew instinctively it was the vampire. The wind whipped The Bloodletter's robes as he turned her head to look at Hollywood spread below them.

It was the town below revealed as earthbound eyes could not behold it. It was the fantastical place, a dreamscape she'd never been able to imagine. In the alleys off Sunset she saw the dead walking and the crawling things scrabbling up from the broken and blasted tombs of Forest Lawn. Bright-eyed children skittered naked trailing haunted laughter into doorways of abandoned homes and storefronts. The corpses streamed from the theaters and the dead ate the living in the streets. The Villa del Monica flashed hell light from its isinglass windows boiling with furnace flames, burning away the earth until she could see underground to the peeled skulls of the dead.

No.

Pale shadows of damned souls were drawn skyward in an updraft from cracked hell below.

Hollywood!

Then Paula felt her stomach swelling and pulsing. And the film had changed, though she was still on the gynecological table. The vampire's face was now hidden behind a filthy surgical mask. On a table were different gleaming invasive tools, all hooks and scalpel edges. Below the sheet she was horribly exposed, her bent knees clamped in black iron stirrups. A sponge stick, dilating her. She strained with arched back against a metallic intrusion. *A curette in the gloved fingers—*

Then the film broke. There were grumblings, and then DeMarco was mounting a small dais and the projector lamp threw his stocky shadow against the wall. He held up a squirming black bat and inspected it closely before declaring with mock jubilation, "Congratulations, Paula—it's a boy!"

The discarded bat fluttered spiderlike upward, and then his smile was oily and there was sweat above his upper lip as he calmed the unrest with fingers like pig sausages.

"Jesus," he was saying, loosening his collar, "I love this town."

He cleared his throat and his smile was weak and nervous.

"It is The End of Days, as you all know. The key to the city is *yours*. Tonight you will rise. On a more personal note, it looks to be another great year for Venus DeMarco Slim and Fitness Salons!"

Deftly dismounting the dais with the projector's lamp following him like a white pin spotlight, he positioned himself by the great casket, which was propped now against the wall. Joey Tipp and a black-leathered Bike Bitch were removing the heavy lid from the coffin.

"And who made this all possible?" DeMarco asked rhetorically.

He made a flourish with his hand as he announced grandly. "I give you—

"The vampire!"

Albright's eyes fluttered open in a face on which the shadows traced the underlying skull. The candles made his gray flesh cling to his bones. A dark stain was spreading across his loins as she watched, and each face in the room burned eyes an elliptical yellow.

Albright raised an emaciated arm in the moldy grave clothes and uncoiled an accusing finger. On command, the covey of undead parted with a sibilant gasp. Paula's heart was pinging like a thrown rod in the Toyota, but the obedient gazes were focusing past her to an indeterminate point in the far corner of the room.

She saw it. It was a quivering naked form that receded against the wall in terror. It was bleeding and pathetic in its abject panic. In its center she recognized Larry's eyes. At the same time, she felt a disturbing arousal.

Then the Rodeo Drive matrons, the bikers and punks, the porn queens and ancient fan club queens, were hissing and arching their backs like cats. Eva's face had become that of a Siamese. Paula felt dizzy with paralyzing revulsion, and the stabbing guilt at her own craven impulse to escape. Around her the claws were bared, the teeth exposed in slavering gums as all descended on the writhing Larry, ripping and savaging with guttural sounds until she saw his briefly revealed face. What was left—a hash of gore out of which one dead and lidless eye gazed at her beseechingly . . .

Paula started awake with a cry in her throat.

My God. She was still on the floor by the hot tub in Albright's mad room.

She had fallen asleep in someone's arms. That had never happened to her before. *Albright's arms.* But she had felt so complete and so safe. And now?

I'm alone. He left me here on the floor.

She felt abandoned and betrayed. Used. The night was blue in the frame of doorway. In her ears, the humming of the hot tub's hidden compressor.

The door was open.

Didn't even wake me or say good-bye. The sonofabitch.

Tears started to her eyes. She groped on the floor for her clothes, struggled to dress herself. *What's wrong? What did I do? Where did you go?* She lurched anxiously to her feet, shoes in hand, to stand just outside the door in confusion.

The night was not empty. The fleeting carbonated laughter from the house, a wind chime tinkling of distant voices that chilled her. A rustle of dry leaves. Clumsy steps. She cowered against the woody vines of a convenient bougainvillea. *Someone moving.*

She slipped backward, down the mossy lip of concrete with a splash. The rank green water of a pond. The water was cold and her lips began to tremble. *Did he hear me?* She started to sob, waiting for the ripples to subside. It seemed as if something was with her in the water. A clammy shadow, dark fingers tentative on her ankle, then grasping and holding tightly.

She lurched out, grappling at soil and grass. Panting and checking her ankle. Her heart stopped. It was a black mummified hand, torn at the roots. *No. Moss.* She shook it off, sliding to her knees, which were dissolving underneath her.

A figure was framed in the doorway of the cabana, his back to her. A throat was cleared, and in her mind's eye she saw the guttural shifting of phlegm. She recognized the stolid silhouette and the white suit that almost glowed in the moonlight.

"Stephen," it said with alarm.

"*Stephen!*"

DeMarco whirled, and she saw yellow lines of fear on the contorted face. When he saw her, his mouth opened in shock. He lurched out, looking helplessly one way, then the other, tossing the cigarette to the ground.

"Here," she said. "Help me."

He lifted her, his hands gripping her shoulders and hurting them. He was in her face, frightened and angry. "What happened—what did you do? *Where is he!*" He released her and spun on his heel, frantically searching the darkness.

"I didn't mean to—"

"You let him out," he called back to her in frustration. "You did it, little sister. You let him out!"

He paused, inhaling once. But not deeply enough, almost gasping, then turning to her. "Your friend got sick up at the house. I wanted to let you know. So I came out here, I couldn't find you, and then I saw the door—"

"Larry? What's happened?" Fear and guilt scrabbled over each other.

"Fuck Larry. You kids come out here and eat my food and drink my booze and wreck the house. Everybody takes advantage of me. Steal my shit, drive off in the cars . . ."

He was trying to calm himself down; he had the Gelucil in his hand. "He's all right, he was in the first floor bathroom with one of the girls when she started to scream. He was throwing up. You were nowhere to be found so I had to have someone take him to your motel—"

The next instant he was hardly aware of her in his distractedness, his mind working furiously.

"Follow me, goddamnit. I'm getting you out of here. And if I never see you again, it'll be too soon. You don't know what you've started."

He was hurrying toward the house and she tried to follow, clutching her shoes in wet fingers, her soaking dress clinging to her with night chill, after DeMarco's white sports coat stretching up and down across his shoulders as he walked toward the lights of the house. He threw a frightened glance back at her once. He started to speak but the words strangled in his throat disgustedly.

25

Anemone

WHEN DEMARCO STEPPED OUT OF HIS PORSCHE, HE still seemed swaggering and superior, but the demeanor was crumbling. Eva noted that he'd been drinking. She'd waited until two in the morning in the Cadillac on Harold Way, watching the headlights of approaching cars in her rearview mirror, until the beams of DeMarco's sports car had widened in the frosty glaze of her windshield as it pulled in behind her. His eyes were frightened and she saw why: it wasn't Stephen Albright who was with him.

A shock.

Paula.

Her patient was a dream vision expelled by the unconscious, trembling and still dripping with primal fluid. The clumps of moss on her shoulder and streaking her hair were like uncleaned afterbirth. The wet dress clung to her. DeMarco had put a towel on his bucket seat to protect it.

"Eva." Paula's face was bewildered. Her dead eyes had come alive with fear and betrayal and then relief.

"Eva!"

Eva thought: and *you*.

She was really not such a child. The fleshy face was dappled with freckles. The chest sagged in resignation, one strap slipping wetly down the arm to reveal a soggy foam shoulder pad. The dress was torn and ruined, the filmy material clinging like a second skin so that Eva could see the form of the legs, the shadow of pubic hair. The shoeless feet were ragged and bloody.

Paula was sobbing convulsively. Her face was red and bruised from crying. Eva's heart was racing. She felt the contracting knuckles of her fingers tighten clawlike within her black gloves and she put her hand briefly, but consolingly, on her shoulder while she spoke sharply to the agent.

"Where is Stephen? What's happened now?"

Paula's eyes were dazed; Eva saw her expression peripherally. *She's going to act helpless. She's going to make me her caretaker.*

"Just all hell is breaking loose," DeMarco said rapidly. "I lost track of this person, she was at the house tonight. I had Stephen all safe under lock and key and she got in somehow and when I found her he wasn't there anymore. I found his pills. He hasn't been taking them."

"Eva," Paula interrupted, "it was *horrible*."

You? And Stephen? You were with him? Eva's voice was flat and clinical like a mask she'd pulled over her emotions. "Paula, what happened."

The girl was obviously afraid of DeMarco and wanted Eva to protect her. Then the girl's cold nose was in Eva's hair and her clinging wet dress against her arm.

"It was Albright. We had a *sexual encounter*."

She squeezed her weepy eyes shut with shame and tears were pressed out of their corners. "And, Eva—he wanted you to have this. And to tell you he's real sorry—for the pain he caused you."

Eva was dazed and numb for a moment as she held the chain in her hand. Something was taunting her. *Stephen, you had her. You shared the nectar of experience with her . . .*

DeMarco was suddenly garrulous. "Eva?"

Paula was hugging her obliviously. Eva felt the stinging pain and her ears were ringing. She was flooded with a sudden contempt for the writer. *Her? Paula?*

"I thought you were dead," Paula said, struggling for composure.

Control. Eva measured her words. "You're all right now."

"I'm not!" It was a cry from Paula's throat and she began to sob again. Eva patted her shoulders tentatively but resisted putting her arms around her; the big girl had to stand shivering against her.

DeMarco was uncomprehending. "You two know each other? I don't get this, it's all going too fast for me—" He looked helpless, stammering. "I've got to get back to the house and look for him. I can make some calls and get some help. We gotta find him, first."

"Do you have any idea where he might have gone?"

"Where's a guy like him gonna go? No, this has never happened, I don't know what's happening—"

Eva's voice was level. "Do you think he might come here?"

"Huh? I don't know. He might. If he could get a ride."

"Did he know I would be here?"

"I was gonna wait till I woke him up. He was s'posed to be doped. There's Green Eyes and the Rolls—I can't remember if it was in the garage when I left."

"I'd better wait here. Take Paula back to—"

Now the girl and DeMarco were suddenly allies in their astonishment. Paula's mouth had fallen open. *Eva, don't leave me.* DeMarco found his voice first. "Hold on. There's a little containment problem here. I'd feel better if this thing was under wraps until we resolve this. I don't wanna draw any more people into this than I got to." He looked uncomfortable even about talking in front of the girl.

Paula was moaning. "Eva, I don't know who he thought I was. He knew my name but he thought I was some-one—"

Thanata. It was her all the time.

"Shut up," she snapped, surprising herself.

DeMarco's oblivious voice was whiny. "Am I responsible? I mean, Eva, could he be dangerous? Who wants to think that? About a guy who's been like a son to you. Or a little brother. You don't want to see him hurt, you hope he'll snap out or something and it's a bad dream. You hope you're wrong, or that you can handle it from your end."

He was leaning a little unsteadily against his car and almost lost his footing.

"DeMarco," Eva said, "do you have a key to the apartment? She can stay here with me."

"I don't know if it's safe. What if he shows up—"

"If he does, I can handle him."

Come to me, Stephen. I dare you.

It was all over Paula's head. DeMarco's eyes were dull, but he reached into his coat pocket, swore as he tried to remove the key from the Porsche insignia ring with his big fingers. "Goddamn. Here, you try it."

Eva took off one glove and quickly removed the key.

"I'm outta here," DeMarco said. "But if he shows up, you call me. Understand? And no one else, a deal?"

Eva wanted the agent instantly away and out of her sight. She needed to extract a promise, first. "And if you find him, you'll call or bring him here."

DeMarco nodded, both their eyes wary at the uneasy alliance. As the Porsche drove off up the street Eva and Paula looked at each other, then Eva turned and her heels clicked up the walk. *Apartment B.* The door was scarred, almost hidden between two overgrown rosebushes, the twisted and thorny branches also obscuring the windows reinforced with security bars.

Unlocking the door, she stepped inside ahead of the round-shouldered Paula. The odor was strange, close and musty like a sickroom. The girl exclaimed, "This is Stephen's apartment?"

The disappointed voice sounded whiny to Eva. Irritating. She felt in the dark for the switch, found it, but nothing happened. *The power is off.*

She didn't like the way Paula was looking at her, needy and clingy, and she tried to ignore her as she studied the shadowy walls and meager furnishings. There was a Gothic candelabra on the coffee table. She fished the cigarette lighter out of her purse.

"Close the door," Eva said brusquely.

Paula wondered, *Am I being too sensitive? She can hardly bear to look at me.*

"You'll want to wash that off," the other woman said in a hoarse whisper. *What did he see in you?*

Why am I afraid? Paula asked herself. The psychiatrist was smaller, almost slight. But Eva was the type of woman who had always intimidated her: self-possessed and svelte, with a severe and confident mouth that brooked no nonsense. Paula had never dared look at them together in the same frame of mirror.

Eva was looking dimly around the dark room illuminated only by the flickering shadows of the wax candles. Boxes and trunks. *He was getting ready to move.* Eva felt an inflating breath of wonder in her chest as she tried to slow the beating of her heart.

The room frightened her. It wasn't the room of a millionaire bestselling author. It was a different kind of room, a closed-off place haunted by a disturbed personality and evoking its own reality. An old sofa and coffee table, but no other furniture. The kind of room where someone sat and stared, not answering the phone and maybe cowering in the corner, listening to internal voices and defining nightmare faces in the whorls of plaster while waiting for nightfall. *Lugosi's old apartment,* Eva noted. *He died here.*

There were piles of books and magazines: *The Wizard of Oz. Famous Monsters of Filmland. Terrors of the Screen. Fangoria. Cinefantastique.* Videocassettes were stacked against the wall and in disarray on the floor. *Abbott and Costello Meet Frankenstein. The Three Stooges. The Creature from the Black Lagoon. I Married a Monster from Outer Space. The Mummy's Curse. Beauty and the Beast. I Walked with a Zombie. Cat People. The Bowery Boys in Spooks Go Wild* . . . Hundreds of them with the titles meticulously recorded on the boxes.

Paula was taking out her contacts because her eyes hurt; now, she was blind.

"You better clean up," Eva said. "Your knees are bleeding."

Paula groped along the walls obediently toward where she hoped the bathroom would be found; Eva felt a pang of guilt and followed her with the candles, which she set on the dirty sink while she ran hot water on a blue washcloth. Paula put her foot up on the toilet and pulled the dress to expose her knee, still shivering.

Eva started to work but felt faint. It was the sight of blood, Paula's blood, on her hands. There was a sudden intimacy that surprised Eva and of which the girl seemed unaware. Eva found herself transfixed by the tiny red crescent moons that slipped to form around her cuticles, the crimson wetness on the whorls of her fingertips. She suppressed it. *No. I know who I am. I know what I'm not. Paula is suffering. Stephen is suffering. They are my primary responsibilities and I have to be* . . .

"You better get in the shower," she said abruptly. Paula seemed startled but timidly began peeling soggy clothes off

her dimpled flesh. Eva knew her voice had been harsh and
added more mildly, "The warm water will help you relax."
The psychiatrist watched the girl's heavy movements behind the diffuse glass when the girl stepped into the mil-
dewed stall.

Why? Because it is entrancing.

The spattering of water on the tiles softened and modu-
lated with each shadowy movement of the girl, the smoky
flesh shifting and changing with suggestion behind the
blurry surface. *Don't let me feel what I'm feeling.* Eva's arms
prickled and she felt the needles on her own breasts, the
water massaging and quickening the blood. She was reminded, strangely, of pajama parties as a girl.

"The water feels good," Paula said.

The darting eyes of candlelight seemed to impose whispering. Eva did not answer. There was the mirror above
the toilet. Eva looked in it and saw Albright's face and
caught her breath.

His faces.

The studio portraits were taped to the glass in profusion
until they overlapped. There seemed to be a hundred studies in black and white. Perhaps for book jackets? She could
see why they would have been rejected; he was nearly nude
in most of them, his privates scrupulously concealed. Each
was a little drama, a vignette of angst. The boyish bodies
were tensed, the muscles flexed and oiled. The composi-
tion of shadows was painstaking and artistic. Many were
shot from below to make his head and the chest with its
almond-shaped inverted nipples appear impressive and
powerful. Each was a statement of pain.

Many were spattered with dark blood. *I know. This is
where. He did it in the bathroom.*

She pictured the writer locking the door and huddling
there in a corner with the pistol. No, he must have been
standing before the mirror. Nude. The look of expectancy

on his face as he positioned the muzzle of the gun against his naked breastbone. The flash which he perhaps never even heard as the bullet cracked brightly and twinkling through bone and cage and soft yielding tissue to splatter red Rorschach against the wall.

Twisting, falling, regarding the blood pattern with fading sight and finding it beautiful.

The darts of water ceased. Paula's hair was wet, clinging to clarify the round lines of her skull. The shower door clicked open and Paula took the towel Eva numbly offered, turned her back as she rubbed herself dry.

"Thank you, Eva." The psychiatrist seemed to turn away. *What's wrong with her?* Paula wondered. *Or is it me?* She followed Eva into the front room, the soft black towel wrapped around her. She started to shiver uncontrollably.

"Rest for a minute," Eva said. There had been a worn green comforter across the back of the sofa and she wrapped Paula in it. *She might be in shock when what's happened catches up with her.* "You're hyperventilating." Eva didn't know why she said that. *She's not. But my suggestion will make her do it. If I tell her to be afraid, she will be afraid.* Paula had begun to gasp, and Eva felt ashamed. She set the candelabra on the coffee table and tried to soothe her.

Paula huddled shivering against her. Her white flesh seemed to pour from the line of her chin down her neck and shoulders like spilled milk onto the folds of the comforter. Both were stricken by the intimacy, and for a moment Paula stopped breathing.

"Relax," Eva said soothingly. "No one's going to hurt you. I'm with you."

The realization: *I'm trembling, too.*

I don't understand what I'm feeling. "You're going to go to sleep and everything will be fine," Eva said. She felt the girl relax responsively. In a few moments, Paula's eyes were clouding with drowsiness. *The depressive's reaction to stress.*

The dark was still, the strange room quiet. Paula's chin fell and her breath stirred through her mouth.

The scene was suddenly familiar to Eva. *The study parties at Brown, the exhausted dawns after we'd stay up all night around empty coffee cups and textbooks, the floor thick with scrawled notes. Then, sometimes, in that six-in-the-morning ener-vation, all the giggling and hugging and marijuana had awak-ened something in our stomachs. The impulses didn't disturb us that much. I never acted on them, none of us did.*

Under the girl's closed eyelids her bloodless and rather heavy lips parted and Eva saw the teeth underneath.

She looked away, but something had coursed in her stomach. She'd looked away because she'd seen the teeth and felt her own tongue alive in her mouth. The tongue wanted to push against the teeth and past them, to explore the girl's pink palate.

The forms of the imagination.

The blanket fell open and the candle revealed Paula's breast. Eva saw the hummingbird. She thought she felt on her sensitive upper lip the faint wash of the iridescent em-erald wings.

Then Eva saw her own thin tremulous fingers raised, saw the red nails and the Gucci watch on her wrist. She exhaled heavily, desperately, as she rested the hand lightly on the bosom.

It was warm. She closed her eyes and her lungs seemed swollen. She bent slowly and the rustle of her clothing was the only sound in the room.

She rested her lips against the breast, not moving.

I don't believe this, I don't— She felt her heart pounding, the race of blood that made her contorted joints ache as she sat there frozen over the girl.

It was one of those carried-away moments she'd had years and years ago during her brief free-love phase, expe-rienced after a party or in a locked jetliner restroom or in the backseat of a car, her mind suddenly arching across the tortured sequence of logic to sudden realization she had wound up in some incredible posture with someone else's body. *What am I doing?*

It seemed she had been a hundred years on the couch. Her own tongue darted in her mouth, frightened of itself. Finally venturing the quarter inch beyond her own teeth.

I want to. Maybe I've always wanted. Her lips parted and her tongue tasted the cool air. She gently probed the soft pink bed of the nipple in the rosy aureole of breast.

God.

God . . .

Her own small teeth had parted, fastening lightly on the nipple she caressed with her quick tongue.

I am burning.

She moistened a finger and ran a long red nail exploring along the line of stomach to the slumbering woman's cleft beneath the soft streak of carroty pubic hair, felt the incredible softness of the labia. *I've never touched another woman.* The smoothness, the beauty, was all invitation like the willowy closure of the sea anemone. Eva's finger was a small fish, the inviting strands curling infinitesimally at the slightest touch and then tightening around the mysteries. Her lips were crawling up the breast, over the ridge of bone, to the soft diaphragm hollow of the throat.

This is how it happens, just this simple. "All passions require victims."

She felt it then, so easy to pinch the tiniest fold of flesh between her tiniest teeth, just a stinging pinch. *And I'm in.* The tiniest sprint of blood oozed onto her lips. *She's so exhausted. If I'm gentle she won't even wake up.*

The warmth spread between her lips. Paula moaned.

I am drawing on her throat. I am swallowing her blood.

In that moment Eva saw it all unfold, felt the heart underneath her lips and the pounding and rushing of arteries. *For him. He wants me to.*

But what do I want? She squeezed her mind shut, tore out the frazzled electric jack of logic and plugged it quickly into her amplified senses. She let her lips wander back down the throat to the heaving breast, leaving a track of blood. As she arced her neck her small ankle nudged the coffee table and the candles wobbled and flickered. Eva started and the nipple popped ruddy from her mouth, a thread of saliva snapping and falling across the smooth breast. At the same time she saw it in the mirror.

What is it?

There was the lambent form of the girl, round flesh pink under the rough blanket and the black petals of the towel. The shadows that covered her began to sharpen. Something crouched over her. It was some obscene thing, all arched elbows and knees, bent like a spider. The face, the sucked cheeks, the eyes glazed in their hollows, the mouth open and dark with hunger.

Me.

Eva saw her own face, and her eyes were the eyes of the dead cat. And Paula was the trophy of her prowess. *"Sure, The Bloodletter would love to make Paula a vampire. But any vampire that bites her will die and he can't find one dumb enough. It's one rare vampire that'll do that."*

Her stomach nearly heaved.

Eva LaPorte, look what he's done to you. Look at your face and see what you've become.

She saw the amulet, then. She must have put it on the coffee table. Impulsively, she put it around her neck. Her hand closed on the talisman, and she realized how desperate she was for any semblance of protection. She felt ridiculous, but did not take it off as she rose carefully.

Looked around the shadowy four walls as if she were see-

ing them for the first time. The posters tacked there. *Th*
Corpse Grinders. The Thirsty Dead.

A manila envelope on the coffee table, almost hidde
under a copy of *Bloodletter, Book Six: The Revenant;* from it
unsealed end, the corners of a sheaf of glossy photograph:
She took a look and at first thought they were bizarre pir
ups of the girls in that punk club where she had first me
the writer, girls painted with blood dots and coroner'
seams.

No. These girls were dead. *In situ.* There was a stomach
impossibly sunken and concave. Across the stomach was a
stream of seminal fluid like egg white through which ant
tracked in a neat row. Then, an upper torso. *This is wha*
DeMarco meant. What he saw in Stephen's apartment. The face
was goggle-eyed, the lips blue and out-turned expulsively
above the burn marks on the neck, like the mouth of a
carp from which the hook had been ripped.

The picture is swallowing me. There was no left breast, only
the hollow depression hemmed by splintered ribs, the
starved mouths of major arteries. *The heart missing.*

She fought her nausea as she shoved the pictures back
into the envelope. She picked up the candelabra and stood
weakly. *What am I looking for?*

She walked into the kitchen. Pages of illegible notes,
scrawled in a childish hand, were scattered across the sink.
The *i*'s were tiny daggers, the other characters like spiders.
She looked in the refrigerator. Empty. She absently pulled
open the door of the vegetable crisper.

The tissue was a bruised gray-blue fringed with a sick-
ened white where it swam among dust-like hovering motes
in the preservative of the jar. The aortal smile. The gaping
mouths of the torn ventricles. Veined, like a scrotal sack.

Her gorge rose in her stomach.

She recalled the books, something The Bloodletter had
said to Caligula.

"As with most moments of intense insight, the vision of truth fades . . . Souvenirs help prolong the experience and triumph. The victim has been reduced to a trophy of the moment when the private ritual reached its climax . . ."

She slammed the crisper shut. For a moment it had looked like something else. A fetus.

Her mind was suddenly swamped by another overpowering image: the smell of ether. The institutional-green wall. The doctor breathing through his nose. Dully aware of the scraping, knowing it was a small instrument, though it felt like a tractor discing her insides. *There.* The sound dully metallic, something slopped horribly into a pail. She had told Todd, "It's wrong. I can't." "Yes you can," he had said intensely glancing around the college library to see if they were being overheard.

Punishment from God, the scar tissue residue on the inside of my uterus.

She heard the voice in her blood. The Bloodletter? Or Albright? They were interchangeable now. *Trying to draw me in, seduce me one more time.*

She felt a fury. *Fuck you, you monster. You used me. You twisted sonofabitch. You don't get me. You won't get her, Stephen Albright.*

She was rousing Paula, tucking the blanket tighter around her pale shoulders, and feeling a stab of remorse as she saw the purple welt on her neck. *I'm so sorry*—but there was not even time for that. She had to interrupt the story as Albright had scripted it. She was glancing both ways out the door before she hustled the incredulous Paula up the walk and into the Cadillac. She didn't turn on the lights until she was safely down the street headed toward Rogerton and Edgerwood.

26

DeathMaster 2000

DAN SMILED TO HIMSELF, EXPLORING TONY'S CONDO
with a flashlight. His large hands throbbed on his wrists; he
could feel the hair curling tighter on his knuckles. Time
had slowed down. His skin was so sensitive. The world was
washed in something magical. The breeze through the
window made him feel he was wearing women's silk panties, but all over.

He was thinking of Eva LaPorte's clothes. He had
opened the closet door and just mashed his face into them,
intoxicated by the aroma as if they were crushed gardenias,
inhaling the lush vestigial perfume and woman scent and
Fem Fem and Arrid Extra Dry. Crush them in your fingers
as if they were grapes and smear them on your face. Then
he was biting the silky material, tearing and rending the
blouses and camisoles with his teeth, gnashing and ripping
until they were in shreds around his feet.

He padded around naked. Nice place her ex had. Gaff-
ers and Sattler oven. Litton Generation Two microwave,
the kind that really did a number on his mother's cock-

atoo, the tangerine bird screeching and ballooning up and then exploding with a squawk into tomato paste that dripped and sizzled down the thick window. The carpet was plush and sensuous. Nice stuff, really, tasteful but not ostentatious.

He looked into the mirror now and smeared Eva's lipstick into red gashes around his mouth. It made his nicotine-stained teeth look more frightening. He regarded with disgust Eva's choice of powder eye shadow—Lavender Silk Trio.

He had brought his own. Real makeup. "Man's makeup," he said out loud. The thick Tru-Cov that made those crow's-feet vanish, and Rosatint, powerful industrial-strength cosmetics used by morticians to cover knife wounds and plug bullet holes, strong enough to make the dead look alive. *And the alive look dead.* He almost frightened himself, a corpse-man with a clown's face grimacing in the mirror.

Dan had never seen the vampire so pissed.

Can we be sure, this time? Dan had wondered.

"Stephen went all the way with this One."

From his Tupperware tote bag, a premium from a long-ago party, he took the thing. The DeathMaster 2000. Really, it was a modified Skil Power Tool, a Professional Duty Cordless ⅜-inch Drill/Screwdriver. Variable speed, reversing for easy withdrawal from bone and cartilage. 0–750 rpm, no load speeds, removable battery pack that fully recharged in less than an hour. He liked the heft of it: only 7.5 pounds. He had modified it by wrapping black friction tape around the grip and inserting the modified bit. He called it a Screwpel—combination screw and scalpel. A surgeon's Michigan blue-steel scalpel with flat edge honed and temper-curved so that it cleaned as it drove.

He flicked the switch and the implement buzzed in his hand, surged and sent shivers up to his elbow. The blade was flickering, spinning, almost invisible like a dragonfly's wings.

He stood on the toilet and unscrewed the globe from the overhead fixture, placed it carefully in the sink. He took the green cellophane and wrapped it around the hot bulb, *ouch!*, fastened it to the bulb neck with a rubber band. An eerie green light was cast over his face. He liked the effect.

He turned on the shower. Hot, door open, let the steam come out, fill the bathroom. And he stood on the toilet again. Bathroom door closed. Waiting. He knew he could wait forever that way, in the glow. Wait until she would open the bathroom door and stand there silhouetted.

Eva, you let us down. The Bloodletter knows everything.

He didn't hear but sensed the car. Her arrival with the other girl. Sensing someone had been in the condo. *Has the ex returned home unexpectedly?* Not likely. "You wait here," she'd be saying to the plump one. An icicle forming from her heart to her diaphragm, trying to sound calm, but that old involuntary system you can't control curling and tightening. Then, the hiss of the shower. The pipes groaning, shuddering, then still.

He turned off the water.

As soon as she had come through the door, Eva had headed for the phone in the master bedroom. It was time for police. It was time to turn herself in and try and salvage the life she'd built over the years if there was anything left of it. Get help. Get help for Paula. Only for Paula?

She knew that she, too, needed therapy. She needed to tell someone the whole truth. Someone who could help her recover—

She noticed the closet door was open and could not recall leaving it that way. *Stephen?* How would he know to find her here? Then she began to tremble.

I'm in your blood, Eva. I know where you are and what you think.

She slipped off her shoes and followed the dim glow from the hall toward the sound of dripping water. Following the plush carpet up the dark hall to the crevice of light beneath the bathroom door. Stopping, listening.

"Stephen?"

Then she relaxed. It wasn't like someone had scrawled in blood on the walls. She'd probably left the closet door open herself. And left the light on in the bathroom and not shut off the shower completely. She'd been beside herself when she left.

That was the whole problem—Eva was beside herself. She stood there undecided and waited for an impulse one way or the other. Took a deep breath and searched for her center like a long-lost friend.

On the other side of the door, Diver Dan, the Master Blaster, a Hefty Eight-Balled Hunk of Steamin' Junk listening to the gurgling of water down the drain, waited. He knew she was gonna do it. Open the door. *These career types can never admit when they're afraid. Mother was the same way.*

The mist rising out the open door, curling out at Eva, her eyes trying to adjust, *can't be true Oh Yes.* Swallowing back once at the horror caught there freezing her brain.

I'm a sight, Dan thought. The green light washing hellishly down, the thing dripping there in the corner in some impossible posture with one bent leg in the toilet bowl, the other braced against the wall.

The DeathMaster lashed out once, a tongue of blue steel.

She stared speechless at her extended arm. It seemed to change. The flesh parted, seemed to open slowly as blood crept out to puddle thickly and drip to the floor.

He gripped her.

She saw the fingers tight around her wrist, then she was pulled into the steam. Her face was being pummeled. She'd fallen, clawing at the carpet. Lips bruised, jaw sagging as she was dragged ankles first into the bathroom. He was tearing at her clothes, the ripping and pulling, the snap of buttons, the rough jerking of her skirt past her knees, ripped from her ankles. *Goddamn I'm good.*

Let her be stunned there for a minute, his other hand taking a nylon cord from the top of the flush box and tossing it over the exposed hot water pipe running across the top of the old thirties-style shower stall.

He saw the excitement parting her numbness. He stood between her and the door, his heavy breasts jiggling, busily twisting another length of rope in his hands, concentrating on the knot. The starved hollows of her buttocks were deepened in the arctic coldness of porcelain and white linoleum.

He was raising her to her feet. *Can you catch me off balance? Try it—* She lunged at the door, clawing at the knob, lacquered nails snapping in succession. But one hand covered hers and the other covered her mouth. She was slammed into the wall of the shower, and then the cord was around her neck and stretched tightly, pinching off the cry. He heard the vertebrae of her neck pop like knuckles as she was hoisted off the floor.

In the medicine cabinet mirror they both saw the surprise swelling on her reddening face, smoothing the crow's-feet. *Her hair's a disaster.* Her hands clawed and fluttered spastically. *I like that.*

"Just hang in there," he said. "I'll be back." He flicked the switch on the DeathMaster and it buzzed like a rattlesnake before her face. "Don't start without me, you hear?" He opened the door so he could keep one eye on her from the other room.

He watched his own feet plodding down the hall. He was

whistling and thinking of Eva—*she'll dress out at 120–130 pounds.*

The girl was in the front room. *You? Thanata?* Standing there, terrified at the noises from the bathroom, half of her wanting to run and investigate and the other half wanting to run and haul ass. But the whistling had thrown her. *Who could be whistling in the hall if there was a—* Leaving her transfixed there like a mouse in front of a cobra. *Confused by this fat clown nude before her with fright-wig hair and some sort of power tool, maybe he's a plumber—*

"You must be Paula," he said. "And I'm the guy that dug up your grandma and fucked her face." That really stunned her, and that hesitation was all he needed. Grabbing her shoulder, crumpling her like a chain-whipped puppy, boobies bouncing, hog-tying her there on the floor in a neat package of pink flesh just the size to fit in the trunk of his DeathMobile 88 parked in the alley *if I take out the spare tire—*

Back up the hall. No need to whistle now, everything under control. He wished he could do the plump one right in the house, but The Bloodletter always wanted to meet them first, make a production out of it.

From the far end of the hall he could see the skinny one in the bathroom, still thrashing with the last milligram of adrenalized death terror, kicking with her feet at the rope where it was tied securely around the shower faucet. He slowed his steps, savoring the agony, and a bit entranced at her ocher nipples jiggling in a frenzy, nice flat stomach sucking in and sucking out trying to draw breath.

Then the most amazing thing happened. She was kicking at the rope, no way it would have become untied, and then the faucet handle, he saw it hanging there crooked, realized what she was up to, then lurched and started to run toward her. And then it actually came off, the Satco chromium and plastic shower faucet, right off the pipe, and he was running, and the rope was slipping off, then whipping out as she crashed to the floor, he was almost to the door, but she shoved it with her head in the same motion as she fell, her hands wriggling free. The click of the lock was like a hermetic seal on his intuition that this wasn't going to go as smooth as he thought.

He tried the knob. Goddamn. "I don't suppose," he said plaintively, "you'd believe me if I said I wouldn't hurt you if you just let me in?"

No answer. He pictured her getting the rope off her neck, the purple burns, a big white fury filling his heated brain like a drive-in screen, a rage to cut her head off and watch her spinal column whip like a severed pneumatic hose. He rammed it with his shoulder; waves of pain exploded; he'd always had delicate bones. Heavy, oak. Weird. Who lived here? Was he paranoid or something?

He lost it, then. He was screaming, the noise tearing his lungs, ripping up his chest. "I'M GOING TO EAT YOUR FUCKING WHOREFLESH!," and then the words were lost in splutter and drool and even tears as he kicked at the door, the big sobs heaving his shoulders.

Pictured her there on the floor, her head to one side, probably seeing out of at least one eye now as the vessels dilated to admit the flow of blood from her nearly expended heart, bleeding from the chunk the DeathMaster had taken out of her arm as a Howdy-Do. "I'M GOING TO BURN YOU TO THE BONE, BITCH!" Pictured her rousing herself with new terror, squatting there wobbly, her hair ragged before her face and the floor slick underneath her with steam and blood and sweat. He knew he needed one good idea, and it came.

He ran out the patio and into the backyard, the night air cold on his skin, one big goose bump, his flesh giggling, eyes full of fear now too. *The Bloodletter will be so mad.* Run-

ning and lurching up onto a planter box, prying open the
little bathroom window, sticking his head in, lungs heaving.

She was there all right. Unconscious. *Shock?* And then he
saw, blood on her temple. She'd banged her head on
the sink when she fell. Barely did the panic number on the
door and then the old eyes just rolled up as maybe a minor
skull fracture kicked in, her body just flopping back against
the wall. In fact she was right under the window, mouth
open and tongue lolling out, he could see the part in her
hair now matted with blood.

He reached his arm in, fingers outstretched. If he could
just grab a hank of that hair, pull her up far enough to get
a good choke hold . . . but his fingers groped futilely, the
top of her hair a good twelve inches out of reach.

He fired up the DeathMaster then, he could just get his
arm and his head into the window, the DeathMaster in his
fist, blade whirring as he aimed it right down at the top of
her skull. And he saw into the next minute, saw the bit
auguring down right through the part in her hair right
into the skull, felt the satisfying crunch of bone, little curls
of skull flying out with a dentist drill's whine, fine as shav-
ings from a pencil sharpener, and then the sexual give as it
punched through to the soft brain, whirling and slicing
and dicing like a Vegematic and turning it to fucking mani-
cotti, the eyes whirling in her head, the whole head jumping and shivering, maybe biting her tongue in two—

But it wouldn't reach. *Won't reach.* He kicked himself in
the ass. He'd considered making the Screwpel bit just an
inch longer, but he'd worried it would break off between
ribs or get hung up in the goddamn pelvic intricacies;
women were built like fucking Chinese puzzles.

That was it. *No use.* He smiled with admiration at the unconscious woman just out of his reach, hawked a big green one up from the bottom of his hate and his lungs and spat on the top of her coiffed head, watched the spit sizzle and fry there as if to mock him, too.

"I'll see you later, bitch!"

27

Algernon W. Sherwood

EVA FELT HER BODY RETURNING FROM THE DEAD. There was warm sunlight on her face. She was under the H under the H O L L Y W O O D sign, the sun broiling her skin and the freeway traffic passing below. But no, the rushing noise was not cars, but her own splitting head. She was *not* under the H—the warmth was caked blood and the sun was coming through Tony's bathroom window.

She tried to do some damage assessment. The bloody and lacerated arm in her lap looked very bad, but the strange cut was so clean as to be almost surgical. It had stopped bleeding. Then she moved her neck experimentally and heard and felt the grating. It was painful and she had limited range of movement. She'd felt the same way once before in her life—when she'd survived a car wreck. At least, she was intact. She would live. Her voice was a ragged whisper when she tried to speak—

She looked down at her left leg, the one that had been exposed to the sunlight through the window, in new horror. Large water blisters had formed and seemed to pulse under her stricken eyes. She writhed away from the light and huddled terrified in the corner.

What's happening to me?

She pulled herself up onto the sink and forced her red-dened eyes to look in the mirror. She felt instantly light-headed, and her reflection was clotted with paisley dots of fear that made her reflection murky. She slid instantly back down to the floor and collapsed, as frightened of hal-lucinatory psychosis as by the other possibility—

I am infected. Something is raging through me.

In the feverish instant of the glance in the mirror it had seemed she had seen underneath her own skin.

I am fading. Eva is disappearing.

Only the amulet seemed to have definition and reality, and now it seemed to be irritating her skin.

She'd assumed the living dead just woke up and found themselves antiseptically transformed. But what of the *living* living dead? It was one thing to be changed in a twin-kling, and quite another to watch your own flesh and mind betray and abandon you to something else . . .

She was paralyzed by helplessness, the impending loss of self from the inside out.

How much time do I have? She was thinking of her . . . *condition.*

I need to go to a doctor, she thought. I need to have my blood cleansed. I need to be monitored by specialists. I need a virus identified and an antidote or antitoxin or anti-biotic . . .

An anticlimactic? Eva, don't fight. Go gentle into that good night . . . That thang that thang . . .

She tried not to hear the voice in her blood. What had Albright's novels claimed?

The death of the infector alone can reverse the malign influence over mind and body as the victim slips into un-death. There is no other reprieve . . .

She moaned, reconstructing herself by sheer effort of will, splicing her severed nerves back into her voluntary system. It was an agonizing ordeal to crawl over the blood-smeared linoleum to the door. Then the terror as she remembered.

He may still be here, waiting just outside.

Paula.

She found her legs and steeled herself to open the door. She was imagining Paula on the floor like one of those girls in the photos: filleted and turned inside out.

She explored stealthily, the breath caught in her chest. Nothing. Gone. *He took her. Why? Maybe she's not dead. Not yet.*

Maybe the agent's found him. DeMarco's number. She retrieved the scrap of paper from her purse as she struggled into pants and a blouse that was torn, ripped; but she didn't care.

DeMarco's voice. "Where the *hell* have you been? Where did you go? You got no idea what I've been through—"

"What time is it?"

"Three in the afternoon, I waited for forty-five minutes and kept calling, but—"

"Paula Kightlinger is gone. She's been taken. Have you been in touch with Albright—"

"Yeah, yeah, don't worry. He's safe. I even talked to him on the phone."

Albright is safe? What about Paula?

"Where is he right now?"

"Huh? He's safe. Talking goofy, but he's safe. He showed up at the location outside of Palm Desert where they'd been filming. He's been there all night—Green Eyes dropped him off. They've got him there under watch where he won't hurt himself."

"What is he saying? What kind of things?"

There was that stammer. He had apparently recovered

enough from the previous evening to be once more patronizing and in control.

"Sweetheart, I think I made a mountain out of a molehill, maybe even got hysterical. I talked to the cops. They got an all-points out on Strachan. They say they doubt if he'll let himself be taken alive. About a forty-sixty chance. I can work with that."

Eva felt the blood simmering in her veins. It began to dawn in her: Sure. The asshole. The cops would probably take care of Strachan, and with him dead there'd be no one to implicate his client. Then for sure it would all blow over, maybe his fiction machine would be stabilized, the imperiled production salvaged.

"Our lawyer's here. He says even if they catch Strachan alive and he says Stephen brainwashed him in the hospital, who's gonna believe him? He promises me that Stephen's mental condition is his own best defense, anyway. Hell, he think's he's The Bloodletter right now."

"Does he still want to talk to me? What does he say?"

"Crazy things."

"Like what? *Exactly?*"

"Well, he's The Bloodletter and he's now in control of all things. Caligula is going to bring Thanata to him and that's why he went out to the desert."

"Why the desert?"

"The symbolical significance, he said. It's the Ripening of Days and he's The Bloodletter and they're gonna do Thanata together right there on the old movie set where Murnau and Lugosi failed before him. Impossible, huh? He's out of his mind. He wants you and me to come out there and says no more talking on the phone. See what I mean?"

"Did you know Strachan was here?"

"Strachan?"

"Diver Fucking Dan, that's who! Remember him, and he took the girl—"

"Took her? Where?"

"I think he's taking her to wherever Stephen is because Stephen thinks she's Thanata. That's why Stephen couldn't kill her himself when he was with her last night. He wanted me to do it. And when that failed, he sent Strachan."

"How did he know where to find you both?"

Because he is in my blood? Because he knows my every thought all the time?

"Eva. Let's cool off—"

"It's too late for that kind of cosmetic job. It's gone too far. I've seen what's in Stephen's apartment."

"Oh? And what was that?"

She knew he'd clean the place out, if he hadn't already.

"Paula is my patient. She's been kidnapped by a psychotic and I think he's delivering her to Stephen Albright."

She knew he was chewing it over. What if Strachan killed Paula? One less incriminating loose end to be tied up. "Let's think," he said slowly. "What's the worst that could happen at this point?"

She collected herself, wondering what there was inside DeMarco that she could appeal to. She had an inspiration. "The worst that could happen? Strachan delivers Paula to Stephen and disembowels her right on your set. Right on your front porch."

"How can you be so sure?" DeMarco said with equal parts defense and alarm. "He's safe, no way he could get in touch with Strachan if he wanted to."

"Maybe the arrangement is Strachan is to kill her *unless* he hears from Stephen."

Now the panic was there on the other end for sure. *If*

something happened at the site, attendant publicity investors financing points shares stock distributors . . .

He whistled low. "We're moving too fast on this. Give me some time to think—"

"There isn't time. I don't care what happened between me and Stephen or what you do. I'll blow this whole goddamn thing wide open, and a lot of it's going to stick on you and Albright no matter what. I'll see to it."

"Is that a threat? You're threatening?"

"Tell me about this place where Stephen is."

"Way the hell out. The site's been shut down for two months while we film interiors in Burbank. I got a guy out there I really trust, been with me a long time."

"He's the only one there?"

"Who else do I need? Just somebody to watch the gate and protect the property."

He paused before speaking reluctantly. "I guess I gotta call the cops. My lawyer says I gotta tell them everything or I'll be an accessory before the fact. No matter what Stephen says."

"What does Stephen say?"

"He's paranoid. He says not to call the cops or Thanata will die. But I gotta call the cops. Don't I?"

"Maybe I could talk to Stephen by phone." *If I can appeal to the Albright part of his personality, if he's not entirely . . .*

"I tried to talk to him a half hour ago. Begged him. Bello says, no dice. Bello's my man out there. I'm gonna tell Bello to call the sheriff out there, he knows him. Tell him to send just a couple detectives out there. Real low-key. Cover our ass. Maybe get together and send some of my own people, too. People I trust."

He's paranoid of authority figures. Cops and doctors. She had the sudden vision of a SWAT team standoff, one of those hostage situations where one of those detectives with a bullhorn and only a Saturday psychology seminar under his belt tried to cajole and threaten a psychotic to cooperate, really hoping to draw him to a window where a rifleman could get a bead.

Eva interrupted. "We can't tell any police and we can't use anyone else. We don't know what kind of arrangement he has to rendezvous with Strachan. If Stephen panics, we don't know what'll happen."

She felt his mind working, trying to figure angles. She didn't let him finish. "I'm going out there. You're going with me. You're taking me there."

He snorted. "Alone? Eva, you're out of your fucking mind. I'm fifty-three years old." His strained voice was incredulous. She smiled bitterly.

"I'm coming over to your offices right now," she said, "and we'll start out—"

"Hell, no! No, not *here*. While we're talking right now I've got a vice president of a studio on the other side of this wall. And don't think I'm not shitting bullets, dear. You can't be seen here. You can't be seen at all, can you? You're a missing person."

He made a derisive snuffling noise. "I'm thinking, thinking. Keep your shirt on."

She could hear the wheels turning; finally he spoke.

"I know a place more discreet. It's midway between us. Alger Sherwood's place on Observatory. You know him? Doesn't make any difference, he hosts my 'Chiller Theater.' Not only senile, he's in my pocket, goes way back with Stephen. But he doesn't know anything about this. I'll tie things up at this end maybe coupla hours—"

"We don't have time!"

"I know, I know, all right, you go right to his place now, you're closer. I'm forty-five minutes away, traffic at four o'clock, give me an hour or so. I'll call him to expect you and I'll cut myself loose here."

"That's too long, we need to go immediately."

"You think so? I've got to find a gun . . ."

"Why? Why don't you wash your car, too? You don't want to find them in time, do you?"

He was angry. "There's gotta be police. Bello's discreet and he knows the sheriff. Just two detectives, plainclothes. To help him keep a lid on things just in case— Sorry, but you're insisting I go out into the desert looking for a fucking freako. You're a piece of work. Fine, let him kill us, too. Or go without me. Find them your own self. I'm adamant on that."

"Get started," she said in frustration.

"Wait—hold on," he was saying.

She paused. He seemed bemused. "Don't you want Sherwood's address? See what happens when you run around like a crazy person?" His voice was contemptuous as he gave her the directions, muttering under his breath so she could hear it. "Fucking women . . . Writers should just stay the hell away from them . . . That's twenty-five years of experience talking. I'll see you later."

Eva's empty stomach weakened with all the dips as she drove slowly on winding Observatory Street, a street of beautiful 1920s Mediterranean-style houses huddled together as if afraid of falling down the steep hillside below Griffith Park. The blood had already soaked through the bandage she had applied to the arm that now pulsed with only a dull ache thanks to Demerol. As she got out of the car her throbbing head swam, and she had to hold on to the door until the dizziness passed.

Her eyes had seemed dilated in the bathroom mirror as she had bandaged her wound. Mild concussion. Got to keep going, don't think about it, mind over pain.

Algernon W. Sherwood, she thought she'd heard, was the world's preeminent horror film fan and collector. He had looked wretched recently on the commercials for his "Chiller Theater."

He greeted her amiably with a cane at the door, his eyes curious. "My. What happened to you?" He was looking at her arm, her temple.

"Nothing, really. I had a minor car accident."

"Looks fresh. On the way over?"

She shrugged and he respected it; then he was leading her down back steps to a basement workroom where the walls were frantic with framed stills, lobby cards, and huge movie posters. His bony buttocks were lost in his sagging pants as she numbly followed his stiff progress through the maze of pressbooks and memorabilia from movie scenes.

"I told Philip to just come on down here when he arrives. He seemed rather stressed, but he's a high-pressure person, anyway."

He picked a cigarette out of a crumpled pack and lit up despite the NO SMOKING signs at intervals on the wall. His throat swelled as he sucked in the smoke and she saw the pink lips of a tracheotomy scar just above his breastbone seem to pucker and give her an obscene raspberry. "He's happiest in a state of panic. This morning I thought I had given him a myocardial infarction, my own employer, imagine—"

He pulled absently at the crotch inseam of his baggy pants, which had unaccountably ridden up.

"This morning?" she asked.

He caught his breath. He tried to laugh, but a dry, sucking rack of cough choked him momentarily. "Would you like something? Coffee? No? He called me twice today, I feel inflated with self-importance. Especially after not hearing from him personally for six months." Sherwood turned, started to open a desk drawer, and she observed the fuzz around the horseshoe-shaped scars on the rear quadrants of his skull. Tumors. *He must be full of them.* She saw him as an X-ray, transparent and insubstantial except for the black clots of disease battening on him from the inside like giant leeches.

"He heard from one of his lackeys that Stephen had sent me something in the mail last week and got very excited. Told me that he would come over and pick it up today, personally. Not to let it out of my sight."

He was breathing painfully, pausing for rest. She tried to make her voice sound casual. "Yes, he told me. That's why we were to meet here. Do you have it, now? I should read it."

"Read it?" He looked at her suspiciously. "How? It's a videocassette. There was no note, I think Stephen was just testing me."

She decided to gamble. Besides, she saw that the old man was eager to tell someone. "What's your opinion of it?"

"That's an interesting question. It purports to be some fragments from *Der Vampyre Magnus,* Murnau's lost classic. A little rarer than a papyrus from the Dead Sea scrolls. I know Stephen's been searching for it since his college days, since he researched Murnau. He felt a special kinship with him."

"Yes," she said a little too boldly. "I'm Stephen's psychiatrist. Murnau has an elemental hold on his imagination."

"His psychiatrist? Well, I'm glad to hear he's in psychotherapy. But I might have suspected it. So was Murnau. Lugosi tried AA."

She concealed her confusion. "Yes, it's interesting. His special identification with them."

He nodded. "All of them obsessed with the Bloodletter legend. Stephen believed Murnau brought him back, and then, after he died, Lugosi wanted to revive him. Remake Murnau's film. I guess the story of Cesare and the vampire is sort of an analog to any artist who becomes overwhelmed by a creature of his own imagination.''

She lit his cigarette and he inhaled deeply. "Stephen believes that Peg Entwistle committed suicide to render the film incomplete because she actually was a reincarnation of Thanata and wanted to prevent it coming to the screen. Or perhaps The Bloodletter had to destroy her before she destroyed him in some other way, regardless of her importance to the film.''

Eva's throat was tightening, bringing a spasm to her back.

Sherwood continued. "The legend of The Bloodletter and Thanata is older than Murnau. It's from the Middle Ages. You've read Stephen's books? You know that the vampire was brought back by a hapless magician who sold his soul, made a pact with Bloodletter's spirit. In researching Murnau's life for *A Soul on Film*, Stephen uncovered—so he says—the German director's private papers of his own research on the Bloodletter theme. Which were apparently extensive; Murnau was as obsessive as Stephen.''

And? He gathered his breath to continue.

"The vampire's rebirth throughout the eons has been dependent on a magician, or artist if you will, who recovers him from his limbo of damnation to cut a deal with him at the cost of his soul. Only two things can return him to that limbo. Thanata, the female nemesis who will bring about his destruction, or the death of the magician whose imagination supports him. Obviously, the vampire would have a vested interest in the death of Thanata and the continued good health of his nexus in this world, his magician.''

She tried to keep her voice even. "Murnau. Lugosi. Stephen Albright. They were all like Cesare, if the legend's to be believed.''

"Bloodletter's windows into this world. And before them, how many anonymous scribes and bards and tellers

of ghost tales at campfires? 'The vampire must be sung'
. . . and sung, and sung, and sung.''

"You've whetted my curiosity, Mr. Sherwood. Let's take
a look at it, now.''

He raised his grizzled eyebrows quizzically.

"Oh? Phillip was rather adamant that I not show it to
anyone. He said it could embarrass Stephen, might even
incur some legal liability for him. That it could conceivably
have some evidentiary importance in the near future and
could damage him irreparably—''

"You know Phil. Anyone but me, I'm sure. I may be
charged in the immediate future with preparing psychiatric testimony on Stephen for a superior court hearing in
which his sanity will be a crucial issue. The sooner I see this
evidence, the sooner I can formulate my evaluation and
help him.''

"Evidence? I don't see how . . . Tell Phillip that if there's
anything I can do, well, I'd like to help, certainly.'' He was
already taking a padded envelope from the desk drawer.
His narrow back was to her as he turned down the sound
on the television in a wall niche opposite two chairs. She
moved an ashtray so she could sit down.

He slipped the cassette into the player and pulled a chair
close to her, flicked off the overhead bulb. The cracked
and crumbling death masks on the low ceiling beam took
on personality, the vacant eyes flickering with shadow in
the spattering light of the television. "There is some uncomfortable stuff in this,'' he said with a tremulous eagerness. The tattered images burst brightly, burning to life on
the tube.

A black eye appeared on the screen, lit with a penlight.
*No. A vagina between two dimpled knees. Elliptical, like a cat's
iris.*

The camera entered into the uterus and was lost for a
moment in blackness. A desert at night was revealed, and

in the foreground, a single lonely structure. Eva started in her chair. Unmistakably, it was the Villa del Monica Motel.

Occasional palmetto and yucca shot out the vacant windows like pikes through its eyes. Cactus had sprung from cracks in the pavement. In the background two giant pillars rose out of the desert floor. A crowd of mesmerized dead had gathered. Eva squinted. She recognized the Hollywood Boulevard street people who ate out of trash cans, and the teenagers with white faces. Their skin was the tinted blue-gray of pickled calf's tongue, mottled with corruption.

Some faces were uncannily familiar, considering the film was supposed to have been shot seventy years ago. *My imagination.* The film stock was poor, but she could almost imagine she saw DeMarco among them. The camera was slowly ascending, the figures shrinking.

"What a shot!" Sherwood whispered reverently, touching her arm tentatively, once.

The camera closed again, quickly, holding her captive.

A charred cross erected in the shattered interior of—a church? No, a hospital room—no, motel room. Through the denuded timbers that shot starkly from the broken walls the night sky glistened hungrily. Towering against the moon was a giant H cockeyed and tilted as if one leg had sunk crippled into the earth.

The camera receded slowly to reveal a strained body stretched on the roughly splintered post, hands upstretched and bleeding over his head, impaled by a single spike.

"That would be Cesare. Looks rather like Stephen, no?"

It certainly did, uncannily so. Down to the cunning little hummingbird on its silver chain around his neck. The face was haggard with pain beneath a crown of twisted celluloid. He looked imploringly upward in a parody of Christ's passion. The camera rolled backward on an unseen track to reveal a secondary cause of the distortion of his features: a nude young girl was bent intently at his knees and fellating him.

Enter the vampire. He seemed both larger and more sexual than life.

Shot from below, the shadows dramatized the dark features. Eva felt an involuntary arousal, an unexpected reflex to the brutish desire in the hypnotic eyes. He was startlingly powerful and seductive in his charisma, and strangely familiar. She could not take her eyes from his face. The long black hair flowed over his shoulders. The sensual lips were livid. Next to him the other two figures looked like the corpses, the living dead.

"Doesn't he, too, resemble Stephen? Look in those eyes."

It was true. Maybe Stephen had seen this fragment of film as a youth and begun to mold his personality toward this platonic image until the basic structure of his own face responded, until he had re-created himself around it.

A superimposed sound of drums began on the soundtrack, the pounding crawling from the vibrating floor and up her legs, which ached from exhaustion.

He was lifting the girl to her feet, and for the first time Eva saw the hummingbird on her left breast. Her face was familiar, too. Eva saw the hairless and budlike pubis. The three faces seemed to float now as if the plane of existence on which they enacted their dance was some deep eternal remove of the mind.

The crucified Cesare was speaking, and in his vulnerability and sensitivity, Eva saw Stephen again. She could not make out his tortured words, but she knew he was trying to intercede for the girl who was Thanata. The hot klieg light burned white spots into the harsh aluminum whiteness of his forehead.

The Bloodletter seemed sadistically fascinated by his en-

treaties, and his smile, which was more of a leer, brought
back the nightmare with Albright in the motel room when
she'd seen his other personality emerge. The camera
closed on both faces in a two-shot and the effect for Eva was
almost hallucinatory, as if she were seeing the two faces of
Albright confronting each other in reality. Then the vampire kissed the Cesare figure full on his dry mouth, his face
seeming to cover the other man's until his lips were
smeared with blood.

The girl looked a little like Paula, Eva realized—the
same type. The Bloodletter had raised her to his side, and
for Eva it was as if she was herself being raised; it was an
effort not to stand as she felt the wind whip her hair, rush
coolly between her thighs. He was enfolding the girl inside
his robe and they were flying up in the night, to the top-
most pillar of the vast H.

The hunchback was waiting there. A subtitle identified
him—*Caligula!* He was self-consciously trying to cover his
almost lipless rotting gums. His skin was spoiled and burst
like overripe fruit.

Sherwood looked away, coughing in his handkerchief.

Abruptly, the camerawork had become amateurish, like
an outtake, or unedited footage. The lights seemed to
brighten and tilt, glaring. The soundtrack choked. A
shadow appeared in the corner of the screen, someone's
head, then disappeared.

The figures were atop the rusted steel platform high
over the desert, but the backdrop of night was too obviously phony—a movie set. The girl was on a gynecological
table, her feet bowed in the stirrups—no, it was merely a
bed.

The wind that whipped Bloodletter's robes was from the
blades of a wind machine. Curtains hung in an invisible
window rippled in the air surreally. Green curtains. The
covers of the bed billowed and swirled off. The bed from

the Villa del Monica. It was as if the H on the Hollywood hillside had erupted from the ground like a great tree and swept up in its branches the room of the motel, carrying it into the night sky.

Baron Bloodletter, standing in the furious blast, let his robe fall in a languorous gesture. The wind flailed it away and he stood there naked—almost. He wore around his stomach a heavy black strap with a dangling attachment, his legs trembling. Something conical, black and shiny as onyx. Spotlights played frenziedly on his spiderlike form scrabbling atop the pinnacle while studio lightning flashed in the background. He slowly mounted the girl, who screamed silently against his attack. Another splice, or a merciful break in the film.

When the picture returned, Caligula was next to the vampire and eagerly removing his own sackcloth raiment at his master's command. His naked torso was soft and un-healthy, the fleshy hairless breasts with collapsed nipples almost feminine. He was bending over the girl to smirch her face with his pulpy mouth. Eva looked away. She knew what was happening, felt it in the convulsion of the mus-cles of her back. The Bloodletter could not kill Thanata, so his evil familiar would do it.

When she finally glanced up, there was something in Caligula's hand. At some moments it looked like a knife in the flashes of light; at others, a film-cutter's heavy black shears. He was raising his flabby arms, concave chest glis-tening with sweat, while the vampire directed his motions with detachment and apparent satisfaction. The blade flashed furiously, ripping up the cleft between her legs. In her mind Eva heard the slashing sound of the penetration, a sound like sex, only crisper and drier.

It was happening. She felt she was inside Thanata along with the hand. She tried to withdraw, to squeeze her mind shut and sealed like a sandwich bag. She was feeling the blood bubbling in the girl's lungs and then there was the soft crunching sound of a rotten apple being repeatedly squashed underfoot.

Black jets spurted across Bloodletter's face as the camera recorded unrelentingly the hunchback's insensate slashings until he collapsed on top of her. A long thread of spittle hung from the misshapen mouth.

Inside her head, Eva was drowning and clawing to the surface through the thick gurgling in the woman's throat as the blood ran down the vampire's muscular chest.

The Bloodletter posed heroically and triumphantly against the night sky, lit dramatically from below like a medieval gargoyle. Then he rolled the girl's body off the table-bed and off the edge of the world, a rag doll with arms flailing through the night as stars and desert slashed past, her hair a flaming corona behind her.

Her eye.

Up, through her eye to where The Bloodletter stood panting on the ledge high above. He held her heart in his smeared hand. No, it was a fetus. A squalling baby with the wizened face of a demon.

The girl's body, again. The dead face looking wonderingly at Eva with her own sequined eyes, cold and pale as Paula's. Then the picture dissolved to buzzing static.

I am here, Eva thought.

I am in Hollywood, she reminded herself. *In an old house on Observatory.* Sherwood was spitting thickly into a handkerchief as he turned off his set. He did not turn on the light. Her hands were shaking. She hadn't eaten anything for twelve hours. *I'm not sure I could eat.*

Sherwood was sitting beside her, again. A wave of pain crossed his face and seemed to ripple across his shirt as if a great worm inside was changing position. He tried to shrug, his shoulder hackles pointed suddenly as if he were being raised on two pikes.

"I believe," he said sententiously, "what we're really watching in this film is the unraveling of an artist's mind. The final deterioration."

"Murnau's," she whispered.

His face was puzzled.

"No," he said. *"Albright's."*

28

Stevie

DEMARCO'S CADILLAC SEVILLE SPED ALONG THE
darkening desert highway with Eva hunched intently over
the wheel. The tailpipe clattered, roared, then receded.
The shifting sands seemed to lap across the blacktop at the
tires as if to swallow and swarm them. Grainy drifts shifting
in the wind. Night was falling, first in the deepening shadows of the mountains so strangely stereoptic in the clear
air, then in purple billows of shadow that spread like blood
around the rock and cactus.

DeMarco snored on the seat beside her, his eyes hidden
behind his Ray-Ban designer sunglasses. He had nodded
off a quarter hour before, chin sagging, chest gulping air.
His head rolled onto her shoulder and, irritated, she
pushed him to the other side, but not too roughly. She
didn't want him to wake. Not yet.

Not all bad, she thought. Not at all bad, that rich corpu-
lence. The silence of the desert was quickening, and she
could see quite clearly in the dark. She was feeling incandescent, a neon tube of liquid fire. She felt like hot wax

that could melt over DeMarco. A perverse tenderness welled up and she saw him as a dying flower to be preserved, pressed between her own pages. Thoughts were coming into her mind of doing things to him in his helplessness. The more she tried to stanch them, the more unspeakable they became. She saw his eyes falling back into his head, his teeth rising through the lips as the skin tightened the pure strong lines of his skull. He seemed pared down, and even beautiful, that way.

The left front radial hit a chuckhole and snapped Eva out of her reverie. *Christ, what's happening to me?* She felt a new desperation.

There is no such thing as vampires, she said to herself. Stephen Albright is insane, and insanity is as infectious as mental health. He has gone crazy, and his gift and his curse is that he has always had a very seductive way of taking people with him. But, Eva, the time has come for you to pull out.

But she reflexively fondled the amulet around her neck and tried to recall the encounter on Observatory when DeMarco had arrived at Sherwood's to pick her up.

"I'm exhausted," he had pleaded when he'd shown up at the door. "Running around like a crazy man, and I've been awake for twenty-four hours—"

"Get in the car."

He was amazing, really; with everything that was happening he had stared at her breasts when he noticed the top button of her blouse was missing. She'd caught him; that was when he'd put the sunglasses on, those reflecting ones that assholes wore; but that was fine, she didn't want to look at his eyes anyway.

"I know you don't like me, Eva," he had almost whined. "But I'm really not such a bad guy. I'm a victim in this thing, too. You know, since I took Stephen under my wing my life hasn't been the same. It hasn't been my own. I've been midwife and father confessor and doctor and agent. I've felt at times as if I was a character in his story, that he was running my life. That's the difference between the public perception and the reality of my position, so don't judge me.''

She tried not to listen, irritated beyond words, her head pulsing with pain. ''I know I'm a joke to a lot of people,'' he said. ''To everyone, maybe. But let me tell you a story not many people know. About a kid who grew up in Hollywood in the shadow of an alcoholic father who was a clown, whom anyone at the Derby with money for a shot could wind up for a laugh. But he wasn't a clown to his kid. Who loved him, who wanted him to be something, wanted someday to be something for both of them. Who swore at his funeral that someday nobody would laugh at the name Phillip DeMarco. Which wasn't his real name anyway . . . But you're not listening, are you?''

She hadn't answered.

''And when my son was born—yeah, I was married— and that little boy had scoliosis, and I knew he'd never walk straight, I busted my hump for the best doctors, and I swore that even if he never walked tall, at least he'd never have to be ashamed of his old man.''

He might have sensed her slight weakening, his voice mock-humble.

''And did they correct the curvature of his spine?''

''Yeah, they did,'' he said softly. ''Don't see him much now, in Great Neck with his mother—divorced eight years. She was younger than me. I kick myself in the ass. I paid for jeet kune-do lessons for her. Why not? Self-defense, right? We lived off of Melrose at the time. And she runs off with the Chink instructor. I send the checks to Wing Chun because that's what she calls herself. It means Beautiful Springtime. Goddamn.'' He mimicked a female voice. '' 'Phil, I'm a brown belt.' The only belt the Chink cared

about was the one holding her pants on. If you think it's
been a bed of roses for me . . ." His voice had trailed off,
muttering. It had been difficult to restrain a smile, some
relief from the unremitting tension.

DeMarco: he had accepted with equanimity that Sherwood had showed her the film Albright had sent. A deteri-
orating mind.
   No, not Murnau's. Albright's.
Sherwood had leaned closer to her. "I thought it was a
joke at first. That he was trying to test me. I don't think this
is footage from Murnau's *Magnus*. I don't think it's the res-
toration of an old film at all. I think it's a new film."
He had scratched nervously at a patch of eczema on his
elbow. "There was a period preceding Stephen's last suicide attempt when he directed several of the Thanata
screen tests himself. They were extravagant and self-indul-
gent; he threw himself into them obsessively. I understand
they were strange things—I believe this is one of them.
That it is Stephen Albright in the film as both Cesare *and*
the vampire."
   "The eyes of the vampire were Stephen's, and there
were similarities, but—"
   "Imagine Stephen with prosthesis and putty. Imagine
The Bloodletter without the dramatic lighting and the
shadows, the makeup which subtly transformed his face."
   It did seem possible. "But the film looks so old," she had
said.
   "Perhaps the stock is old. Stephen has always loved old
films better than new; it could be an Albright touch. Why
he might have sent it to me at this point, I don't know.
There are little ironic statements in it which hint at its personal symbolism for Stephen—the film editor's shears instead of a knife. Cesare as a Christ figure with a crown of
celluloid rather than thorns. It may be a message in a bot-

tle. A cry for help from a desperate personality that could not articulate it any other way.''

Or, Eva thought, a confession of murder. Albright is Cesare. Albright is the vampire. Two personalities locked in struggle within one body. No wonder DeMarco had wanted to confiscate the film. Just like he probably cleared the incriminating evidence out of Albright's apartment. She was sure that was what he'd had to do that was so vital that afternoon.

Night was falling, just as it had become dusky in the brain of Steven Lloyd Leach.

That was Albright's real name, Sherwood had said as they waited for DeMarco's arrival. ''Few people knew that. He was 'Stevie' to his family and hated it. He covered his tracks well. He sent me his first horror story when he was about fifteen. Terrible. I was active as an agent, then. I wanted to be honest with him but he was the kind of person . . . so pathetic . . . you couldn't bear to hurt his feelings. He stuttered, too. But the stuff was so off-center, he could have used a psychiatrist back then. Sick stuff.''

He had nodded with appreciation as Eva lit another cigarette for him.

''When he was older he started coming around on Saturday afternoons. Shy kid, poking around and asking questions. Never had a girlfriend so far as I knew. Any friends. A feeb, not very talented. But sincere, so desperately wanting to write himself out of his crummy existence . . .

''He eventually sold a few stories now and then—but who would have thought? I didn't see him for a few years, I guess he went to Europe later, the student thing. Next thing I knew he'd written a bestseller—and then another. And I'd let the horror fiction find of the decade slip through my agent's fingers. I saw him once and asked him, 'How'd you do it?' He says, 'Simple. I sold my soul.'

''Maybe that's why I don't brag about this. Albright, he

called himself. That was the name of the hero in that first
story he'd written at fifteen. And now I work for Phillip
DeMarco instead of the other way around . . ."

She was turning onto Desert Springs Road. She switched
on the Cadillac's headlights and pushed DeMarco from
where he had come to recline against her shoulder once
more. "Huh? Oh, yeah." He cleared his throat, straightened.

And why had the girls died? Because they threatened
him. Sexually and emotionally. Bloodletter, the big bad
strong one, had to take care of weak little Stevie. He was
the psychological liaison between the writer and the impressionable psychopath he'd conned into sharing his
delusions in Eisenhower Psychiatric.

"Is this it?" she asked.

DeMarco took off the Ray-Bans and squinted into the
dark where it seemed as if desert and night sky joined in
one seamless illimitable expanse. "Close. Watch, it's coming up on the right."

It was a dirt road; she would have missed it. She put the
Seville into neutral and DeMarco climbed out apprehen-
sively, searching his pocket for the key ring. He unlocked
the padlocked gate in the barbed-wire fence, walked
quickly back to the car. "It's five miles up here. Easy on the
car, this road is bad and I just had an alignment."

She shook her head, sighing with resignation out of the
side of her face he could not see. Brittle sage scraped like a
wire brush against the undercarriage of the rocking Cadillac. She felt the car strike some small desert animal. When
she looked in the mirror, puddled tissue curled pinkly
around black bristling hair, a head melded indistinguisha-
bly into an obliterating tire print.

"Did you bring a gun?" she asked.

He smiled wryly.

"Doesn't seem like such a bad idea now that we're out here, does it?" He exhaled through his nose, opened the glove box. "It's a .32 automatic, kind of small, but all I could come up with in a pinch." He released the safety and checked the clip. "Loaded. I learned to shoot in the Reserves. I was a drill instructor. You wouldn't have thought that, would you?"

I wouldn't have been surprised at all. And that was the last time the smile played on her lips.

Because they had left all that was familiar far behind; the night and desert were swallowing them. It had been over an hour since she'd seen any sign of human life or habitation. She tried to think of Paula out here, alone with a maniac. *Two maniacs.* What must the last twelve hours have been like for her? If she was dead already, perhaps it was better. The fear was a taste in her mouth. She tried to swallow it, send it back where it came from, but suddenly her arms were so weak it was hard to keep the bucking car on the road. *I'm a terrified woman again, panicked and wobbly. I wish none of this had happened, wish DeMarco had never called that day, wish I had my life back and Paula hers. It's my fault. I wish this night was already over.*

And I thought I was bored and wished something would happen to me. I wish Albright had never seen me because then he wouldn't have put me in his story and I wouldn't be here—

"Hey, now. See that? Stop. We're here."

She looked through the windshield and waited for the cloud of dust that had followed them for a quarter hour to catch up with the car, then float past so that she could see. There was no mistaking. *We're here.*

29

Villa del Monica

FROM THE ROAD'S DEAD END WHERE IT VANISHED IN the desert they saw it against the sky. The light revealed where it loomed then disappeared. A vast rusted metal H rotted in a clearing, corroded and stained by bird droppings, anomalous as a spaceship settled in the desert.

"This is where we've been shooting. The same site used by Murnau in the twenties, and Lugosi ten years later. Because Stephen wanted it that way. What Stephen wants, Stephen gets . . ."

He paused with his mouth open. Half-hidden in a hasty camouflage of scrub was a dusty and apparently abandoned '67 Chevy Impala with its trunk sprung. The personalized license plate

PAPER BACK

"The all-points," DeMarco said in a dead voice. "That's Strachan's car."

She didn't want to see his slight tremor, the tentative

quality as he started to open his door then paused to look at her from a face queasy in the dash lights.

"I'm going to turn off the headlights," she said.

He nodded numbly, seemingly waiting to follow her lead. The lights were extinguished and the desert vanished into blackness. Their eyes gradually adjusted.

DeMarco hadn't moved in his seat. "What are you waiting for?"

"I'm looking for Bello, my security man," he said. "He was supposed to meet me right here where the road ends. And where's the sheriff cars?"

"Are you sure your man got through on the phone?"

He seemed stuck to the seat. "He promised he was gonna call right away. They shoulda been here. Right here."

She searched the darkness. "Well, they're not."

Not a good sign. Not a good sign at all.

"Did you bring flashlights?"

DeMarco seemed dazed. "Huh? I did, sure, under the seat on your side."

She got out of the safety of the car and closed the door quietly behind her. DeMarco got out, crept around the back of the car to stand behind her squinting into the darkness. "Don't turn on the light yet," she said. "He's probably seen the car, but he doesn't have to see us if he's out there. And we should be quiet."

"Strachan?"

Strachan. Albright. The Bloodletter. I don't know.

She didn't bother to answer, started to walk slowly toward the set.

The moonlight was bright. On the horizon a hazy corona of pink rose softly. Blood on the moon. She turned to check on DeMarco's progress, his feet in their Italian shoes stumbling in the dark. It would have been ridiculous if she hadn't been terrified, and when she turned again it was as

if in the second of glancing away she had come so much
closer. The jagged teeth against the night were not mountains, but broken walls. It looked to be an old mission. It
was the remains of a motel built in the style of a mission. A
sign.

VILLA DEL MONICA.

Collapsed adobe crumbled in a moraine of rubble in
which desert life skittered, ticked, and slithered into crevices. She saw the supporting beams propped in the sand. It
was a false front. Abandoned movie set. The façade stood
with the Spanish windows and door gaping open upon the
stars.

She walked under the archway. The courtyard was awash
with moonlight. At her feet, something black and cylindri-
cal. A film canister. The skeletal remains of a black klieg
light next to a rotting automobile tire. The wind blew over
the walls and rippled her hair, touched her skin.

"Jesus, Mary and Joseph," DeMarco hissed under his
breath behind her. He was crossing himself. *Maybe you
should have brought some garlic, too.* But she followed his nodding glance to the H, his flashlight beam now playing on it,
a ghost of light that grew weaker the higher it climbed
until it was a faint smudge at the top. She saw it, too.

A lone figure atop the H. *Paula.* She was tied there, arrayed now in a gown of some sort, a diaphanous material
that flowed in the wind high up; it looked like she was
bound and gagged, something in her mouth. She seemed
still, but perhaps she didn't dare move because it might
make her plummet to the cactus below. Perhaps it
wouldn't matter, perhaps they were looking at her dead
body anyway—*but perhaps it wasn't too late.*

"I don't believe it," DeMarco was saying in something
like awe. "He thinks it's a fucking movie."

"What?" Eva asked.

"There, on top of the H. That's like the new ending for the picture. Thanata and the vampire and Caligula up over the lights of Hollywood."

The line between art and reality has blurred beyond all recognition for Stephen Albright, Eva thought. He was recasting all their realities to conform to psychotic fantasy.

"Where would he be if he was here? Albright."

DeMarco turned his head, snapping off the light. "My man said he had him locked up over there."

"Where?"

"The motel set. Some of the rooms are really rooms. They doubled as barracks for Murnau's crew in the twenties. Too dilapidated now; we used our trailers because of the air conditioning—" He saw the impatience on her face. "Bello had fixed some of them up and he was sleeping in one. There should be a door that says two-fourteen. He said he had Albright fixed up in there."

Two-fourteen. There was a lump of cold concrete in her stomach.

"How did Strachan get her up there?" she whispered.

"There's a ladder up the back. Jesus, he must be one strong sonofabitch."

"Go to her. Now."

"Alone?" He was incredulous. "But you think he's out there. Strachan."

She felt contempt even as she understood his terror. She tried to calm him. "You've got the gun. You keep it."

"And what are you gonna do?"

"I'm going to look for Albright. I think if I can talk to him I might be able to bring him back to earth for a while. Maybe nobody has to get hurt any more than he is."

DeMarco nodded numbly, lost-looking, watching her walk away toward the motel set. She felt herself growing smaller while her fear grew larger as his frightened face

receded behind her; not looking back, afraid of his beseeching eyes and that he would lose what little nerve he
had left.

Two-fourteen. The door was half open. *Open. Strachan let
him out?*

She placed a foot on the rotting step, into the room. She
flicked on the small flashlight. Rotting boards. Night visible through slitlike cracks in the walls. She stepped inside.
The air was humid and close despite the open door.

A noise. It was like a cat; *no*. A soft whimpering. A shud-
der tripped across her shoulders as she pulled the door
shut behind her. She tried to sharpen her city-bred ears, to
distinguish between the night sounds and the noise she
had thought she'd heard, the keening. A child's sobs. The
sound harrowed her bones.

Another door. She snapped off the light after checking the
floor for broken boards, followed the memorized steps toward the opening into the next moldy room.

The noise is in the room. She tried to still her pounding
heart where it threatened to bruise her ribs. She flicked on
the light in the direction—

God God God Jesus Mary and Joseph—

Something to say, to put in her mind that was flooding
with the rushing noise again; the sound of her own fear
like a wind through her stomach. It was there near the corner. Then it stirred, and the pale and guilty face snapped
upward. The lips were rimed with blood and she realized
the tongue had been lapping at the neck of what she now
recognized as a corpse, a male corpse with a twisted face
and a strange star-shaped hole in the center of the forehead.

Stephen Albright smiled faintly. He wore a dark suit, but
it was filthy, and his white shirt was torn underneath the
gold key to the city askew around his neck. His

pale face was like a heated blade in the yellow light of the flash, eyes terrified above the stark bones. He began to sob. "I didn't do this, Eva. I didn't kill this . . . person."

He stopped crying then, looking up at her. She knew he couldn't see her face, must have been blinded, but stared right back at the light burning into his eyes.

"Eva," he said brightly. "Eva, I've done something very horrible. I've done something bad." His hands hung limp over his knees, the tremulous lips relaxing into a pathetic but sly smile. "Eva, will you kill me? You can, Eva. Yes you can. You're the White Witch, I see that now. I mean, it's only like an abortion, isn't it?"

Her legs were shaking; his smile was unsettling and incongruous as he stood weakly.

"Don't be afraid of me. They captured me and brought me here. I've been infected, Eva. I didn't have the amulet. I gave it to you. And now I don't have much time. He's going to own me completely."

He pulled down his shirt collar, but she could not be sure that she saw wounds in the shadows.

"You're the strong one, Eva. Stronger than I am. You even resisted The Bloodletter, more than I can do. It's the only way now, Eva."

He stood uncertainly, stepping farther back into the corner almost unconsciously.

"I think you've known it for a while. There's no other way out for me. Or for you. Or her. Do you have a pistol? I think it will work if you blow my head off. My *whole* head."

Eva felt shocked and nauseated, but found her voice.

"Paula. I've got to know, Stephen. Please tell me if she's still alive."

He was nodding his head exaggeratedly, but the words that trembled from his lips were not in agreement. "I think so. No . . . I don't know. I was humiliated. I couldn't do anything for her. To stop it. The Bloodletter wanted us all to be here. Together. I'm so sorry. But you can stop him. By stopping me."

He smilingly pointed to the center of his forehead with a trembling finger. That was where he wanted the bullet. Then his eyes widened and then he began to laugh. A laugh that chilled her.

There was a breath on her neck. Then a smell. It was vaguely familiar, ammoniac body sweat. And then a whistling. She felt the stream of air from the piercing sound in her ear and started to turn, but the hand was over her mouth, a rough hand crushing her lips against her teeth and contorting her face. She dropped the flashlight.

She couldn't tell up from down, felt herself lifted and then slammed onto the splintering floor, flopped on her stomach, her arms pinned back behind her deftly as if there were four hands she was struggling with, then the bite of the nylon cord as her wrists were bound painfully over the small of her back.

The writer, she noticed, was gone. The hand lifting her then, testing the tension of the knots, dropping her back to the floor on her face. The pain as the amulet was ripped from her throat, as she gasped for breath.

She felt the boards sag as he sat beside her, couldn't see the face when she tried to turn her head, only the impression of the mammoth shadow. In the meaty hand the amulet was held aloft.

"Guess you won't be needing this," the voice said casually.

The shadow shifted heavy weight.

"Eva." He was panting. "I told you I'd be back. Where'd that fruity little genius go, now?" He put the chain and medallion in his pants pocket, studying her face almost tenderly. "Eva, I've got to get inside your head. What are you thinking right about now?

She was thinking of Stephen Albright. I should have found him and killed him before all this, she thought with a hopeless resignation. *There were so many things I should have done differently.*

"The Bloodletter is certainly very disappointed in you. First he counts on you to help Stephen continue with his work and instead you try to have sex with him, you horny little whore cunt. You mess everything up. You're such a pain in the ass that he began to seriously wonder whether Stephen wasn't wrong, whether *you* weren't Thanata."

Yellow teeth, grinning. *We should never have left the car,* she was thinking. *We shouldn't have separated.* DeMarco had the gun. But now he was probably dead, too, because of her; and Paula might already be dead; *and I'm going to die, too. Make it quick, goddamn you. Do it!*

"The Bloodletter wants you done real slow, Eva. It might take hours, it might take days. It might take weeks. I'm your main squeeze now, Eva. You're on a slow boat to hell."

What a wasted life I've had, she was thinking.

Even before all this, with Tony. She hadn't loved him. What if he'd known that all along, and perhaps knowing that, he never tried to learn to love her? What a useless wasted life. A few books, and now alone out in the desert in an abandoned movie set and about to be a corpse.

"Just do it, you psychotic fuck. You impotent, necrophilic, disgusting shit," she spluttered, tried to generate enough spit in her mouth to fire into his face, hoping he would lose it and break her neck in his rage, mercifully.

He was making a clucking noise with his tongue. "Such temper. And here I am wanting to make love to you in the worst way. In fact, I will. In the worst way. I'm going to ride you like a horse. I'm going to work your bones, woman. And you won't have a thing to say about it because you're going to be dead."

He was struggling to his feet. "And when I'm through, I'm going to freeze-dry your brains and make coffee. Your tombstone's gonna be a Proctor-Silex."

He was leaving. *Don't go. Do it now.*

There was a whirring, a dentist's drill. No. Something in his hand, the whirring blade flashing. She saw his face then in the light from the door, wished she hadn't.

The whirring stopped. "Living better electrically." He winked and was gone.

She was breathing heavily, felt the shock creeping up from her legs. The taste in her mouth, the blood from her nose, maybe broken. Listening to the night sounds. She wished she were dead already, that she could kill herself and deprive the sadistic motherfucker of the pleasure . . .

She listened, tried to still the breaths raggedly sawing her lungs so she could hear. She had lost all perception of time; in her terror it was hard to tell a second from a minute and an agonized minute from an hour.

Something distant. The clatter of a diesel car engine. Headlights burst brightly in her irises, flashed across the wall; and then the sound of brakes; car door opening. *Maybe the police. Thank you, Jesus.* And then the terror.

Maybe it's Steven's Big Brother the Vampire. Maybe I'll finally meet him. *Maybe he's come to pick up Stephen, to take him back to his word processor so he can write the chapter about the death of Eva and Paula and Thanata—*

The heavy steps, the flashlight in her eyes, the silhouette in the doorway, the tapered body and the tousled mane of white hair.

DeMarco.

She felt some dam of emotion burst inside her, and he was running into the room, kneeling beside her, the flashlight on the floor as he struggled to untie her hands.

"Help me, quick," she said between sobs, and as soon as she was free she found herself cowering against his man-warmth, not particular at all at the moment, felt his awkward hands around her. Then he saw the body.

"Aw, sweet Christ. Christ. That's Bello."

When he turned to her his forehead was shiny with sweat. "Who did all this? Strachan—?"

Eva ignored his stammering questions. "Paula," she said. "She's dead?"

He straightened, looking in her eyes. Then he couldn't look in her eyes.

"I guess I lost my nerve, this all seemed so suicidal. I ran back to the car, not even thinking, and then I was headed down the road when I thought of you here, thought of what might be happening to you and wondering if I would ever be able to live with myself if I didn't at least try . . ."

She nodded; she understood. Even an hour ago, she wouldn't have. But now she did; wasn't sure it still wasn't the best idea for both of them.

His neck stiffened suddenly, his head alert.

"Did you hear that?" She started to speak but he shushed her imperiously to silence, his finger to his lip.

He finally said, "I heard something. I think he's here."

"Outside?"

His eyes were darting, found her face. "Trust DeMarco on this one."

"Strachan?"

"No."

He had risen to peek out the vacant window, one hand gesturing for her to be still. He had taken the automatic pistol out of his waistband as he lowered himself cautiously to his knees. "Jesus," he said. "My heart's beating like a jackhammer."

She crawled quietly across the floor, crawled beside him to peer into the dark.

"Is it Albright." It was hardly a question, flat words; she felt drained even of terror now.

"No, it wasn't Stephen, I'm sure of that."

What?

He looked into her face and his eyes were more than frightened, his voice terrified.

"The Bloodletter. *The Bloodletter!*"

He stood then, startling her. She was afraid he was going to bolt like a rabbit and leave her again. He was pacing quietly, his eyes darting out the window, moonlight on his face with its quivering lips.

"What makes you think it was him?"

His face was twitching nervously as he tried to compose his thoughts.

"Think about it. I know Stephen. I know how he thinks. Follow this for a minute. Work with me, Eva."

His back was to her, the words coming in a rush. "Someone contacts you to help Stephen, to help him keep writing and under control. Stephen's paranoid and figures out what's goin' on, so he tries to kill you. Only the vampire interrupts him and taps you for some blood. Kills two birds with one stone. Makes you think Stephen's some kinda multiple personality, plus he infects you. With me?"

She nodded numbly, amused in the back of her mind by his fingers tapping at his capped teeth.

"The vampire figures, Hell, I can use her, she'll come in handy manipulating a guy like Albright. Pussy's his weakness. *Capice?*" Go on, her eyes told him desperately.

"Now, process of elimination. Who fits the bill? Who else but Stephen could have met Strachan at Eisenhower and got inside his skin enough to recruit him?"

"No one but Stephen."

"Now that's where we part company. Somebody else had access to Strachan at Eisenhower. Somebody who went there often to visit Stephen. Let me ask you this: what if it was the same person that suggested to me that I contact you?"

"Yes," she said slowly. "I think I know what you mean. I'd never thought . . ."

He was nodding his head quickly, kneeling in front of her to hold her hands tightly, focusing her eyes in his face. "You know who I mean."

She nodded again comprehendingly. He spoke fiercely. "No one suggested to me to contact you. Therefore . . ."

He stood, his back to her, fingers in his mouth, lost in thought; and when his hand fell she saw the teeth there, the partial plate. "Eva, it's the only thing that makes sense. I must be The Bloodletter."

When he turned his eyes were amused. An elliptical yellow. "It must be me, Eva. And it wasn't my dad who worked with Lugosi and knew Murnau, but me. It was me set Stephen up and used you. There were no other doctors. No calls to the cops. I put those disgusting things in Stephen's apartment. Me that's in your blood. It was me all the time."

For the first time, she was aware of the soft pattering of rain on the boards over her head. *The reign of blood.*

The rushing sound of terror was pouring into her ears and just beyond the walls was a wailing of voices cowering together, but the sound was from her own head. The Bloodletter had decided the time was ripe to reveal himself. The dust was rolling up heavily before her eyes. She watched paralyzed and withering. DeMarco seemed to crawl upward along the wall like a lizard. Her head was vibrating on her neck, tiny denials and rejections from her sanity. *No no no.* There was a noise from DeMarco like a sucking of breath, and it loomed over her; the electric-blue starlight casting a stark chiaroscuro like a scene from a silent film.

There was a slow growl and she saw him then, the sensual liver-colored mouth stretched wide around the icy teeth, the cold gelatinous threads of saliva stretched to snapping between the lips, trembling in the long catlike hiss.

Her scream plunged up to her throat and then down to her legs as she reeled, running, colliding with something soft but resisting, insensible to the pain as she tripped, smashed to the floor, groping to pull herself up. A hand helped her. Diver Dan.

"Son-of-a-bitch!" he was saying with awe and admiration. The eyes of the one who had been Phil DeMarco were burning with unearthly fury. Strachan was saying, "He's out there, I saw him—"

"You didn't touch him?" The threatening voice was resonant as if from the bottom of a well. The book jackets hadn't done him justice. No earthly artist could. It was as if with a blink he had released her from a spell and she could see him in his reality.

"—I didn't touch him, I left the girl over there—"

There was a mastery and brutal charisma to the lines of his sensual face, the deep and dark eyes. Terrified as Eva was, part of her even now wanted him to touch her. He was striding out the door, DeMarco for a moment, and then something else, shifting like thoughts, so tall the head seemed to brush the ceiling; the flowing hair dark in the moonlight and the cruel features ruddy in the interstices of shadow through the split roof.

Then the rough psychotic hands of the other one, the panting breath as she was lifted, dragged along and down a dark corridor of warped boards. Strachan's feet were clumsy and crashing, but The Bloodletter's passage was noiseless and unerring as if the dark were his element. She was being taken with them into another room.

Paula. She was nude, shivering on a crude mattress of tick. Eva's mind was racing back over the lies, the deceptions, the way she'd been seduced. *You're going into the desert with me,* she had insisted. *You're taking me there . . .* The perfect victim, racing to her own murder and dragging her murderer with her, making sure he was there.

She was thrown to the floor, the bone in her neck cracking excruciatingly again, curling reflexively into a protective fetal position. Her face was opposite Paula's on the other side of a room. There was a gag in Paula's mouth, but her eyes were alive, wide and terrified, reaching out to her. It was too painful, her terror, and Eva looked away, stung by conscience then as if she had abandoned her patient in some way in her final moments. She forced herself to look back and meet the girl's horrified gaze across the foul floor.

Strachan had taken a squatting position between them, chortling, his back to Eva. She saw through his thin T-shirt, saw he was wearing a black brassiere underneath. She could see only Paula's face and her shivering legs on either side of Strachan, who began to rock back and forth with delight in time to the on and off flicking of the power tool in his hand, the blade whirring wickedly and stopping, whirring and stopping, an angry buzzing that filled her head.

"Not yet," The Bloodletter said softly, the warm dark voice of nightmare from her most private precincts of fear. Only now she was in the nightmare and there was no waking up because it was real.

The Bloodletter stepped nude out of the shadows and Eva was shocked and repulsed by the two heads of his swollen member. He exhaled once with anticipation, and the breath was hot. Then he was mounting Paula; Eva felt vomit rising in her nose and throat. The vampire's face burned, gleamed brightly. The Bloodletter threw his head back to the moon as if bristling over a kill before a pride of hungry females.

Eva concentrated on Paula's terrified face, the helpless ravaged eyes. Eva held her eyes and they were lost in one another. *It won't last forever. Look in my eyes. Hold your eyes on mine and you won't feel alone and even when you're dead you won't be alone because I'll be there with you.*

She thought the vampire's lunges quickened, saw the muscles in his buttocks tense fiercely as his orgasm fled into Paula, who shivered almost convulsively in the horror at the violation of flesh and soul—

The vicious head turned on the thickly muscled neck.

Strachan, startled, had flicked off the blade. A shadow in the doorway. It was a shadow of a person, the shadow of Stephen Albright. Shattered, pale and flickering like something empty and insubstantial, he stood there, wavered in the doorway. Eva could see in the wash of moonlight the cold blue of the automatic pistol he held under his chin. DeMarco must have dropped it. His eyes were bright, almost fevered as he met Eva's.

And Paula's, too.

Such a look of rage swept The Bloodletter's face as he disengaged himself slowly and stood, his stomach rising and falling rapidly, bloodied; his pulsing and lubricant organ gnarled and shiny. He stood there, but when the vampire spoke it was with DeMarco's voice, unctuous and charming.

"Stephen, are we sure we want to do that? Lower the gun. We'll talk about this."

Albright advanced one timorous step into the room, the hand with the gun shaking under his chin; the pistol shaking and barrel trembling until he jammed it against the soft skin with its two-days' growth of shadow to steady it.

"Stop," Strachan was muttering, his eyes frightened. "Stop."

"Stephen," the voice of DeMarco was saying soothingly, "I have the most wonderful idea for a sequel—"

Strachan was shaking, bewildered, a child, his head shifting from Albright to The Bloodletter, confused by the fear in the naked vampire's eyes. "Stop. Please, stop." Albright took a step closer, the vampire retreating before him with hands held out in a suggestion of truce or placation.

Eva held Paula's eyes, but Paula was transfixed by the image of Albright where he stood. *No.* The gun muzzle pressed against the carotid artery.

"SSSSTTTTTOP!" It was a ragged hoarse bellow, a trombone smear of terror, and Strachan had lurched up, bra askew underneath the shirt, shoulder hunched at Albright; and then there was the flash and the explosion that sent drifting dust and silt from the cracked ceiling. Albright had flown backward, just the impression of his vacant face with the sudden cowlick of hair splayed up from the top of his scalp; and Strachan still had ahold of him, grappling and crashing with the suddenly limp weight into the brittle wall with a splintering and shattering of wood. They were a heap on the floor, a confusion of limbs.

DeMarco had not moved. It was DeMarco, and then it was The Bloodletter, the image flickering from one to another, DeMarco's terrorized face and The Bloodletter's unearthly rage, back and forth faster and faster like the sputtering of a strobe, and then the faces were transposed one over the other and then it was Albright's face, too.

The mouth opened in an airless scream and there was a glow like a burning blue gas inside the mouth, behind the eyes; DeMarco The Bloodletter Albright all confused, and then the face empurpled and engorged as the flesh convulsed; the thing writhed with a shriek so ear-splitting Eva thought the seams of the earth were coming apart.

Paula. *But Paula was not there.* She had risen, there was an impression, a smear of pink flesh in the shadows, scrabbling across the floor. She had a splintered board in her hand. She plunged it deeply into The Bloodletter's center and a jet of blood covered her face.

Eva squeezed her eyes shut from the horror, tried to

turn her head away; but there was no escaping the scream rising across the desert like a thousand tongues of fire. Flames like blue methane were licking out of the vampire's eye sockets, horrible acridity filling the room. The Bloodletter whirled in horror and desperate fury. Smashed through the wall and into the night, dancing spastically in the flames. Redly alight and scorching with flailing arms, the unearthly wail from inexhaustible bellows of lungs a scream from hell.

Then the fire was flickering, consuming itself smaller and smaller as if they were seeing it through a camera aperture that was gradually closing, leaving only an angry red ember which, too, was swallowed by the desert night.

Eva turned, then, the wail still a hollow echo in her deafened ears. She saw Albright, his eyes open, the horrible red grin below his chin, his life gushed out onto his shirt front.

Strachan was rising, rousing his stunned self, and then the hate came back into his shapeless features. And a half-smile as he saw what Eva now had in her hand. The Death-Master 2000. He was finally going to get to see it work up close.

He raised his hand, not to protest, but to straighten his brassiere; but it never got there because the whirling dragonfly in Eva's hand had plunged into his eye, auguring and swirling in a moist flurry of blood and bone chip that curled out to cover his smiling stupefied face.

30

Kate

THE SUN WAS SHINING IN EVA'S FACE AS SHE DROVE down Santa Monica Boulevard. It felt good. The death of the vampire had freed her from the curse, and sometimes it seemed her skin lapped gratefully at the light of day she had always taken for granted. A cloud seemed to have been lifted from all of Los Angeles. The police task force on cult activity claimed credit for disorganizing and disbanding such unsavory underground groups as the Morgue Rats, but Eva knew the real reason they had vanished: jilted by their Redeemer.

It had been six months but she was still in the neck brace. X-rays had revealed that George Strachan had inflicted on her what her surgeon had described as a well-digger's fracture—a pernicious sort of whiplash where the spur of a vertebra is broken and causes the muscles to spasm. It had required surgery. Other than soreness she was experiencing no aftereffects. Businesswise, Eva's practice was once more thriving. Her regular receptionist had never returned, but Tisha had stayed and proven herself invaluable.

The bureaucratic aftermath of the night in the desert hadn't been as grueling as she'd feared. Albright had been suicidal for years and merely finally succeeded. As for DeMarco, there was no corpse to explain. Nothing at all. Thankfully, no one was looking to her for answers about him. He had apparently never really been popular, and the police inquiry into his disappearance was surprisingly short-lived. The official verdict was that he had probably met his fate at the hands of George Strachan. Detectives had even dug up the desert around the set, cursorily. Eva supposed that whatever was left of Phillip DeMarco resided again in the vampire limbo Stephen Albright had so compellingly described in thirteen books.

Through her sunglasses she noticed the high concrete-colored walls of weed-grown Hollywood Memorial Park Cemetery, where Stephen Albright had been interred in the niche across from Valentino. The writer had purchased it with a prescience not so strange, perhaps, considering his history of suicide attempts.

He would have loved the funeral. The viewing was at Pierce Brothers, just like Lugosi's. The candles, the speakers amplifying the soundtrack theme of *Bloodletter—The Movie,* which would never be completed. The disenchantment of scandal-weary studio stockholders had resulted in a corporate coup d'état by more conservative elements, amidst a flurry of golden parachutes. Many said the moment of the vampire had inexplicably passed and pop culture was on to the next fad.

The vampire fans had kept a raucous all-night vigil on the steps, which included a black mass, two séances, and one epileptic seizure. Several young women had fainted in the line as they approached the casket. The local high priest of a satanic church eulogized sympathetically.

"Albright perceived this life as a shadow. Art transmutes transient material into ultimate forms. It is a sort of death, sealing the moment. But Hollywood did not know who he was. This town is a paradigm of the generalized attempt to disguise the falsity of life. It is a mask of human nature. A few recognized him. A cult grew around him. They wanted his secret and they hated him when he would not share it."

An alert student of film would note on local television the next day that the exact words had been used to eulogize Murnau sixty years earlier.

The cortege to Hollywood Memorial Park. The popping of flashbulbs, police lines, yellow cordons of ribbon. Frenzied clutching for souvenir flowers, young women led away by uniformed officers. A twenty-four-hour security guard at the mausoleum until the vault could be sealed.

Then the legal wrangling had started. Mrs. Alma Ray Leach had sued the estate when probate revealed she had been excluded from her son "Stevie" 's will, which left everything instead to Algernon W. Sherwood, who was now comatose and on life-support systems in a San Fernando Valley hospital's oncology ward.

Eva turned the BMW up Gower, crossing Hollywood Boulevard, then east and north to the old Alto Nido Apartments, where she put two quarters in the meter and locked the doors. She walked quickly into the lobby, announced herself on the intercom, and waited for the security door to unlock.

Kate met her at the door with a smile. That was Paula's name now—a new name to symbolize a fresh start. Kate invited her in to the spot she had cleared for her on the frayed settee.

"Coffee? I can't drink it, myself. You know why."

She smiled.

Someone was playing the piano downstairs. The notes were coldly haunting. Paperback books were piled on the makeshift shelves along the wall.

Eva tried to visit her every week. They both enjoyed the meetings. Kate eased her girth into the wicker chair, propped her feet up onto the coffee table, wincing, then smiling at a pang as life stirred. Her stomach was distended full and round as the moon. Amniocentesis had confirmed it: a boy.

"It looks like you're coming along fine," Eva said. "You're blossoming—in every way."

Kate smiled proudly, the dappled freckles deepening. The contacts had started to bother her, an unexpected side effect of the pregnancy, and she had taken to wearing large horn-rims.

"It's almost my third trimester."

Looking in her smiling eyes, Eva felt a sudden attraction, like a bubble in her blood; not a voice, just the faintest whisper; then it was gone. She would call Elliot tonight. He was a Beverly Hills surgeon whom she had met at the UCLA seminar where she had read her paper "Endometriosis: Emotional Side Effects and the Surgical Solution." Her own surgery three months ago had cleared up her gynecological problems. She had delayed it so long, probably, because she was afraid of being put under, the helplessness and out-of-control feeling of someone else holding her life in their hands. *His* hands. That was before she had met Elliot.

But maybe she would not call him. She liked the direction her life was taking. She might avoid relationships for a while longer. It was all right to be alone. There was her practice, her writing; there was Kate.

". . . I'm doing so much better," the young woman was saying. "I actually went out of the apartment by myself today. All the way to the post office. And it was okay, I didn't feel like someone was watching me or following me or going to jump out at me—maybe because I really am never alone anymore." She placed her fingers on her stomach.

It was an awkward moment. Eva tried to smile. Who is the father? *That boy . . . Larry? Or Stephen Albright? Or—*

But that possibility was too horrible, too nauseating to consider; she felt herself blanch, concentrated on the maintenance of her smile.

"I've been doing some writing of my own, Eva. I do a little more every day."

"That's great. You'll let me read it?"

Kate nodded. "I was hoping you would say that."

Eva talked to her for a while and then glanced at her watch. She had an appointment. It was with the twelve-year-old daughter of the head of a major studio; the girl could not stop changing her clothes.

"Eva?" She paused at the door.

"Yes?"

Kate was biting her lower lip.

"When I went to the post office today? A letter." Her lip was white and bloodless, the words stuck.

"I don't know how he found me. He's done some articles for *Rolling Stone*. He's thinking of doing a book about Stephen. He says there might be a TV movie in it and he wants to interview me. I'll never talk to him, of course. But he says he's already started research, and if he can't get cooperation he'll just fictionalize the whole thing and make a novel. You know . . ."

She was fumbling for a manila envelope under the beige cushion of the settee. "He even sent me an outline, it's here, look—"

Eva felt the skin of her face pinching as she studied the

typescript, tried to hold the thin watermarked paper in her fingers without betraying the tremor that was starting at her knees.

The Man Who Talked to Vampires: The Stephen Albright Story.

And her eyes froze there, her vision swam. In her brain was no thought, just a single sound, the sound of water dripping as from a great height onto a still pool on a concrete floor. "There is a monster in each of us . . ." The gimmick, the writer said in his synopsis, was that Albright's vampire would be an actual character in the story. That was how he would trace the writer's obsession in a way visual and imaginative, plus possibly managing to obviate legally the inconvenient restrictions in the author's will by just changing the names.

She was aware of Kate's voice, the undercurrent of fear she was struggling with.

Eva composed a smile, softened her eyes. "That's crazy, isn't it? Well, it certainly is a free society, and people can write anything they want. That's the wonderful and the not-so-wonderful thing about a free society, huh?"

Kate nodded uncertainly.

"You know what's really bothering me? I'm sure it's stupid. You don't think there's a chance . . . do you . . . like I could have a vampire baby or something?"

Tears were in her eyes. Eva, because of her own experience, had not been able to counsel the girl with much conviction to get an abortion. Then, there was the girl's Catholicism. More than that, though, Kate needed so desperately to be needed, to have something return love to her. Someone of her own.

Eva folded the page, placed her hand on Kate's round shoulder and the girl seemed to collapse then, hugging her.

"Paula . . . *Kate*. Don't you worry, because your life is going to be very full and I promise you'll be safe all the

time. You just have to worry about staying healthy and
treating yourself and your baby right. Promise?"

Kate looked up at her, blue eyes moist and bright, and
smiled through a sob, hugging Eva once more.

"If it makes you feel any better, you just call me if you
have any more communication with this writer person or if
he bothers you. In fact, I'll keep this upsetting stuff and
you just don't worry about it."

Eva had the envelope, subtly tucking it under her arm,
still smiling. "Do you have his address, this man—?"

"It's on the envelope, I think."

"Be good and be happy. I'll stop by in a few days."

She kissed Kate, turned and was out the door. The sun
was out but now it was too bright and hurt her eyes until
she was behind the tinted windshield and underneath her
dark glasses.

That dirty-white van with *Skee Zoyd* painted in psyche-
delic colors on its side was parked in the alley as Eva pulled
up to her practice. A cat slipped out of the vehicle's opening door. The musicians in Tisha's band were a cadaverous
crew underneath their long hair and dark glasses. Apparently they had brought by the teething Kareem for a visit
with his mother.

Eva had removed her coat and was behind her desk
when the toddler came through the door and crawled up
into her lap. The wall thermostat was set too low, and Eva
shivered. She held the child, who in his innocence seemed
not to sense her preoccupation.

*And if I talk with you, Mr. Writer, what will I say? "This vam-
pire must not be sung"? Or will you already be impressed that this
story seems to come replete with a ready-made agent who's perhaps
already mysteriously introduced himself? Prodding and encouraging, and promising you the world? Someone who wants to promote
your career and asks in return only—*

"Long-distance for you—on one," her receptionist

called from the other room. The stale, cold coffee in the cup on Eva's desk rippled.

"Yes?" She had picked up the phone with her free hand and noticed at the same time that one of the fish in the aquarium had died; it floated at the top, a small and lifeless sliver. Eva closed her eyes against her headache. She had felt her womb contract in a body memory at the recollection of her recurrent nightmare: she was in a casket and The Bloodletter was standing over her with a large stake. But the stake was engorged with pulsing veins and he was driving it not into her heart, but between her legs and up her uterus—

Eva opened her eyes because Kareem was screaming. She was horrified to see that the fingers of her left hand were pinching the child, who had wrenched out of her lap and run to the arms of his mother, who now stood in the doorway. Eva began to stammer an apology in her confusion. "I'm so sorry, I don't know what—"

She realized no apology was necessary at the same time she became aware there was only a hollow silence from the phone she held in her hand.

Tisha was smiling.